Praise from both sides
        of the Atlantic for

# BOMBER

EVENTS RELATING TO THE
LAST FLIGHT OF AN R.A.F.

# BOMBER

OVER GERMANY ON THE NIGHT
OF JUNE 31, 1943

## By Len Deighton

A SIGNET BOOK

NEW AMERICAN LIBRARY

Although I have attempted to make its background as real as possible, this is entirely a work of fiction. As far as I know there were no Lancaster bombers named *Creaking Door, The Volkswagen* or *Joe for King*. There was no R.A.F. airfield named Warley Fen and no Luftwaffe base called Kroonsdijk. There was no Altgarten and there were no real people like those I have described. There was never a thirty-first day of June in 1943 or any other year.

L.D.

*Ritual:* A system of religious or magical ceremonies or procedures frequently with special forms of words or a special (and secret) vocabulary, and usually associated with important occasions or actions.

> Dr. J. Dever,
> *Dictionary of Psychology*
> (Penguin Books)

Between February 1965 and July 31st, 1968, the American bombing missions in Vietnam numbered 107,700. The tonnage of bombs and rockets totalled 2,581,876.

> *Keisinger's Continuous Archives*

The attitude of the gallant Six Hundred which so aroused Lord Tennyson's admiration arose from the fact that the least disposition to ask the reason why was discouraged by tricing the would-be inquirer to the triangle and flogging him into insensibility.

> F. J. P. Veale,
> *Advance to Barbarism*
> (Mitre Press, 1968)

# 1

It was a bomber's sky: dry air, wind enough to clear the smoke, cloud broken enough to recognize a few stars. The bedroom was so dark that it took Ruth Lambert a moment or so to see her husband standing at the window. "Are you all right, Sam?"

"Praying to Mother Moon."

She laughed sleepily. "What are you talking about?"

"Do you think I don't need all the witchcraft I can get?"

"Oh, Sam. How can you say that when you ..." She stopped.

He supplied the words: "Have come back safe from forty-five raids?"

She nodded. He was right. She'd been afraid to say it because she did believe in witchcraft or something very like it. In an isolated house in the small hours of morning with the wind chasing the clouds across the bright moon it was difficult not to fall prey to primitive fears.

She switched on the bedside light and he shielded his eyes with his hand. Sam Lambert was a tall man of twenty-six. The necessity of wearing his tight-collared uniform had resulted in his suntan ending in a sharp line around his neck. His muscular body was pale by comparison. He ran his fingers across his untidy black hair and scratched the corner of his nose where a small scar disappeared into the wrinkles of his smile. Ruth liked him to smile but lately he seldom did.

He buttoned the yellow silk pajamas that had cost Ruth a small fortune in Bond Street. She'd given them to him on the first night of their honeymoon, three months ago; he'd smiled then. This was the first time he'd worn them.

9

As the only married couple among Cohen's guests, Ruth and Sam Lambert had been given the King Charles bedroom with tapestry and paneling so magnificent that Sam found himself speaking in whispers. "What a boring weekend for you, darling: bombs, bombing and bombers."

"I like to listen. I'm in the R.A.F. too, remember. Anyway, we had to come. He's one of your crew, sort of family."

"Yes, you've got half a dozen brand-new relatives."

"I like your crew." She said it tentatively, for just a few trips ago her husband had flown back with his navigator dead. They had never mentioned his name since. "Has the rain stopped?" she asked.

Lambert nodded. Somewhere overhead an airplane crawled across the cloud trying to glimpse the ground through a gap. On a cross-country exercise, thought Lambert; they'd probably predicted a little light cirrus. It was their favorite prediction.

Ruth said, "Cohen is the one that was sick the first time?"

"Not really sick, he was ..." He waved his hand.

"I didn't mean sick," said Ruth. "Shall I leave the light on?"

"I'm coming back to bed. What time is it?"

"No," said Ruth. "Only if you want to. Five-thirty, Monday morning."

"Next weekend we'll go up to London and see *Gone with the Wind* or something."

"Promise?"

"Promise. The thunderstorm has passed right over. It will be good flying weather tomorrow."

Ruth shivered.

"I had a letter from my dad," he said.

"I recognized the writing."

"Can I spare another five pounds."

"He'll drink it."

"Of course."

"But you'll send it?"

"I can't just abandon the poor old bugger."

There were cows too, standing very still, asleep standing up, he supposed; he knew nothing about the country. He'd hardly ever seen it until he started flying seven years ago. There was so much open country. Acres and acres young Cohen's family had here, and a trout stream, and this old house like something from a ghost story with its creaking stairs, cold bedrooms and ancient door latches that never closed properly. He reached out and ran his fingers across the tapestry; they'd never allow you to do that in the V. and A. Museum.

Some of the windowpanes were discolored and bubbly and the trees seen through them were crippled and grotesque. At night the countryside was strange and monochromatic like an old photograph. To the east, over the sea beyond Holland and Germany, the sky was lightening enough to silhouette the trees and skyline. Eight-tenths cloud, just an edge of moonlight on a rim of cumulus. You could sail a whole damned Group in over that lot, and from the ground it would be impossible to catch a glimpse of them. He turned away from the window. On the other hand they'd have you on their bloody radar.

He walked across the cold stone floor and looked down at his wife in the massive bed. Her black hair made marble of the white pillow and with her eyes tightly closed she was like some fairy princess waiting to be awoken with a magic kiss. He pulled the curtains of the ancient four-poster bed aside and it creaked as he eased his body down between the sheets. She made a sleepy mumbling sound and pulled his chilly body close.

"He was just tense," said Lambert. "Cohen's a bloody nice kid, a wizard damned navigator too."

"I love you," Ruth mumbled.

"Everyone gets tense," explained Lambert.

His wife pulled the pillow under his head and moved to give him more room. His eyes were closed but she knew he was not sleepy. Many times at night they'd been awake together like this.

When they married, in March, it had rained when they arrived at the church, but as they came onto the steps the sun came out. She'd worn a pale-blue silk dress. Two other girls had married in it since then.

Her face pressed close to him and she could hear his heart beating. It was a calming, confident sound and soon she dropped off to sleep.

The one-time grandeur of the Cohens' country house was defaced by wartime shortages of labor and material. In the breakfast room there was a damp patch on the wall and the carpet had been turned so that the worn part was under the sideboard. The small, leaded windows and the clumsy blackout fittings made the room gloomy even on a bright summer's morning like this one.

Each of the airmen guests was already coming to terms

with the return to duty and all in their different ways
sensed that the day would end in combat. Lambert had
smelled the change in the weather, and he chose a chair
that gave him a glimpse of the sky.

The Lamberts were not the first down to breakfast.
Flight Lieutenant Sweet had been up for hours. He told
them that he had taken one of the horses out. "Mind you,
all I did was sit upon the poor creature while it walked
around the meadow." He had in fact done exactly that,
but such was his self-deprecating tone that he was able to
suggest that he was a horseman of great skill.

Sweet chose to sit in the Windsor hoopback armchair
that was at the head of the table. He was a short,
fair-haired man of twenty-two, four years younger than
Lambert. Like many of the air crew, he was short and
stocky. Ruddy-complexioned, his pink skin went even
pinker in the sun, and when he smiled he looked like a
happy bouncing baby. Some women found this irresistible.
It was easy to see why he had been regarded as "officer
material" from the day he joined up. He had a clear, high
voice, energy, enthusiasm and an unquestioning readiness
to flatter and defer to the voice of authority.

"And an ambition to get to grips with the Hun, sir."

"Good show, Sweet."

"Goodness, sir, I can't be any other way. That sort of
thing is bred into a chap at any decent public school."

"Good show, Sweet."

Temporarily Sweet had been appointed commander of
B Flight's aircraft, one of which Lambert piloted. He was
anxious to be popular: he knew everyone's nickname and
remembered their birthplace. It was his great pleasure to
greet people in their home-town accent. In spite of all his
efforts some people hated him. Sweet couldn't understand
why.

This month the squadron had been transferred to pathfinder duties. It meant that every crew must do a double
tour of ops. Double thirty was sixty, and sixty trips over
Germany, with the average five percent casualty rate, was
mathematically three times impossible to survive. Lambert
and Sweet had already completed one tour and this was
their second. Actuarily they were long since dead.

Sweet was telling a story when Flight Sergeant Digby
came into the room. Digby was a thirty-two-year-old
Australian bomb aimer. He was elderly by combat air
crew standards and his balding head and weathered face
singled him out from the others. As did his readiness to

puncture the dignity of any officer. He listened to Flight
Lieutenant Sweet. Sweet was the only officer among the
guests.

"A fellow drives into a service station," said Sweet. His
eyes crinkled into a smile and the others paid attention,
for he was good at telling funny stories. Sweet knocked an
edge of ash into the remains of his breakfast. "The driver
has only got coupons for half a gallon. He says, 'A good
show Monty's boys are putting on, eh?' 'Who?' says the
bloke in the service station, very puzzled. 'General Mont-
gomery and the Eighth Army.' 'What army?' 'The Eighth
Army. It's given old Rommel's panzers a nasty shock.'
'Rommel? Who's Rommel?' 'O.K.,' says the bloke in the
car, putting away his coupons. 'Never mind all that crap.
Fill her up with petrol and give me two hundred Players
cigarettes and two bottles of whisky.'"

It was unfortunate that Sweet had cast the driver as an
Australian for Digby was rather sensitive about his accent.
Appreciative of the smiles, Sweet repeated the punch line
in his normal voice: "Fill her up with petrol and give me
two hundred cigarettes." He laughed and blew a perfect
smoke ring.

"That's a funny accent you're using now," said Digby.

"The King's English," acknowledged Sweet.

"I hope he is," said Digby. "With a ripe pommy accent
like his he'd have a terrible time back where I come
from."

Sweet smiled. Under the special circumstances of being
fellow guests in Cohen's father's house he had to put up
with a familiarity that he would never tolerate on the
squadron.

"It's just a matter of education," said Sweet, referring
as much to Digby's behavior as to his accent.

"That's right," agreed Digby, sitting down opposite him.
Digby's tie had trapped one point of his collar so that it
stood up under his jawline. "Seriously, though, I really
admire the way you fellows speak. You can all make
Daily Routine Orders sound like Shakespeare. Now, you
must have been to a good school, Flight Lieutenant Sweet.
Is that an Eton tie you're wearing?"

Sweet smiled and fingered his black air force tie. "Harrods actually."

"Jesus," said Digby in mock amazement. "I didn't know
you'd studied at Harrods, sport. What did you take, modern lingerie?"

Sweet saw Digby's attitude as a challenge to his charm.

He gave him a very warm smile; he was confident that he could make the man like him. Everyone knew that Digby's record as bomb aimer was second to none.

Young Sergeant Cohen played the anxious host, constantly going to the sideboard for more coffee and pressing all his guests to second helpings of pancakes and honey.

Sergeant Battersby was the last down to breakfast. He was a tall boy of eighteen with frizzy yellow hair, thin arms and legs and a very pale complexion. His eyes scanned the room apologetically and his soft full mouth quivered as he decided not to say how sorry he was to be late. He had less reason than anyone to be delayed. His chin seldom needed shaving and most mornings he merely surveyed it to be sure that the pimples of adolescence had finally gone. They had. His frizzy hair paid little heed to combing and his boots and buttons were always done the night before.

Batters was the only member of Lambert's crew who was younger and less experienced than Cohen. And Batters was the only member of Lambert's crew who would have contemplated flying under another captain. Not that he believed that there was any other captain anywhere in the R.A.F. who could compare with Lambert, but Battersby was his flight engineer. An engineer was a pilot's technical adviser and assistant. He helped operate the controls on takeoffs and landings; he had to keep a constant watch on the fuel, oil and coolant systems, especially the fuel change-overs. As well as this he was expected to know every nut and bolt of the airplane and be prepared "to carry out practicable emergency repairs during flight," of anything from a hydraulic gun turret to a camera and from the bombsight to the oxygen system. It was a terrifying responsibility for a shy eighteen-year-old.

Until recently Lambert had flown fifteen bombing raids with an engineer named Micky Murphy, who now flew as part of Flight Lieutenant Sweet's crew. Some people said that Sweet should never have taken the oxlike Irishman away from Lambert after so many trips together. One of the ground crew sergeants said it was unlucky, some of Sweet's fellow officers said it was bad manners and Digby said it was part of Sweet's plan to arse-crawl his way to become Marshal of the Royal Air Force.

Each day Batters hung round the ground crew of his airplane watching and asking endless questions in his thin high voice. While this added to his knowledge, it did nothing for his popularity. He watched Lambert all the time and hoped for nothing more than the curt word of praise that came after each flight. Batters was an untypical flight engineer. Most of them were more like Micky Murphy, practical men with calloused hands and an instinct for mechanical malfunction. They came from factories and garages, they were apprentices or lathe operators or young clerks with their own motorcycle that they could reassemble blindfolded. Battersby would never have their instinct. He'd been a secondary school boy with one afternoon a week in the metalwork class. Of course Batters could run rings round most of the squadron's engineers at written exams and luckily the R.A.F. set high store by paper work. His father taught physics and chemistry at a school in Lancashire.

I marked your last physics paper while on firewatching. The headmaster was on duty with me. He'd given the sixth form the same sample paper but he told me that yours was undoubtedly the best. This, I need hardly say, made your father rather proud of you. I am confident, however, that this will not tempt you to slacken your efforts. Always remember that after the war you will be competing for your place at university with fellows who have been wise enough to contribute to the war in a manner that furthers their academic qualifications.

This week's sample entrance paper should prove a simple matter. Perhaps I should warn you that the second part of question four does not refer solely to sodium. It requires an answer in depth and its apparent simplicity is intended solely to trap the unwary.

Mrs. Cohen came into the breakfast room from the kitchen just as Battersby was helping himself to one pancake and a drip of honey. She was a thin white-haired woman who smiled easily. She pushed half a dozen more upon his plate. Battersby had that sort of effect upon mothers. She asked in quiet careful English if anyone else would like more pancakes. In her hand there was a tall pile of fresh ones.

"They're delicious, Mrs. Cohen," said Ruth Lambert. "Did you make them?"

"It's a Viennese recipe, Ruth. I shall write it for you." They all looked toward Mrs. Cohen and she cast her eyes down nervously. They reminded her of the clear-eyed young storm troopers she had seen smashing the shop

fronts in Munich. She had always thought of the British as
a pale, pimply, stunted race, with bad teeth and ugly
faces, but these airmen too were British. Her Simon was
indistinguishable from them. They laughed nervously at
the same jokes no matter how often repeated. They spoke
too quickly for her, and had their own vocabulary. Emmy
Cohen was a little afraid of these handsome boys who set
fire to the towns she'd known when a girl. She wondered
what went on in their cold hearts, and wondered if her
son belonged to them now, more than he did to her.

Mrs. Cohen looked at Lambert's wife. Her WAAF
corporal's uniform was too severe to suit her but she
looked trim and businesslike. At Warley Fen she was in
charge of the inflatable rafts that bombers carried in case
they were forced down into the sea. Nineteen, twenty at
the most. Her wrists and ankles still with a trace of
schoolgirl plumpness. She was clever, thought Mrs. Cohen,
for without saying much she was a part of their banter
and games. They all envied Lambert his beautiful, child-
like wife, and yet to conceal their envy they teased her
and criticized her and corrected the few mistakes she
made about their planes and their squadron and their war.
Mrs. Cohen coveted her skill. Lambert seldom joined in
the chatter and yet his wife would constantly glance
toward him, as though seeking approval or praise. Cheerful little Digby and pale-faced Battersby sometimes gave
Lambert the same sort of quizzical look. So, noticed
Mrs. Cohen, did her son Simon.

It was eight-fifteen when a tall girl in WAAF officer's
uniform stepped through the terrace doors like a character
in a drawing-room play. She must have known that the
sunlight behind her made a halo round her blond hair, for
she stood there for a few moments looking round at the
blue-uniformed men.

"Good God," she said in mock amazement. "Someone
has opened a tin of airmen."

"Hello, Nora," said young Cohen. She was the daughter
of their next-door neighbor, if that's what you call people
who own a mansion almost a mile along the lane.

"I can only stay a millisecond but I must thank you for
sending that divine basket of fruit." The elder Cohens had
sent the fruit but Nora Ashton's eyes were on their son.
She hadn't seen him since he'd gained his shiny new
navigator's wing.

"It's good to see you, Nora," he said.

"Nora visits her mother almost every weekend," said Mrs. Cohen.

"Once a month," said Nora. "I'm at High Wycombe now, Bomber Command H.Q."

"You must fiddle the petrol for that old banger of yours."

"Of course I do, my pet."

He smiled. He was no longer a shy thin student but a strong handsome man. She touched the stripes on his arm. "Sergeant Cohen, navigator," she said and exchanged a glance with Ruth. It was all right: this WAAF corporal clearly had her own man.

Nora pecked a kiss and Simon Cohen briefly took her hand. Then she was gone almost as quickly as she arrived. Mrs. Cohen saw her to the door and looked closely at her face when she waved good-bye. "Simon is looking fine, Mrs. Cohen."

"I suppose you are surrounded with sergeants like him at your headquarters place."

"No, I'm not," said Nora. They seldom saw a sergeant at Bomber Command H.Q.; they only wiped them off the blackboard by the hundred after each attack.

After they had finished eating Cohen passed cigars around. Digby, Sweet and Lambert took one but Batters said his father believed that smoking caused serious harm to the health. Sweet produced a fine ivory-handled penknife and insisted upon using its special attachment to cut the cigars.

Ruth Lambert got up from the table first. She wanted to make sure their bedroom was left neat and tidy, no hairpins on the floor or face powder spilled on the dressing table.

She looked back at her husband. He was a heavy man and yet he could move lightly and with speed enough to grab a fly in midair. His was a battered face and wrinkled too, especially round the mouth and eyes. His eyes were brown and deep-set, with dark patches under them. Once she had written that his eyes were "smoldering."

"Then mind you don't get burned, my girl."

"Oh, Mother, you'll both love him."

"Pity he can't get a commission. Do him more good than that medal."

"A commission isn't important, Father."

"Wait until you're living in a postwar N.C.O.s' Married Quarters. You'll soon change your tune."

He felt her looking at him. He looked up suddenly and

winked. His eyes revealed more than he would ever speak. This morning, for instance, she had watched him while Flight Lieutenant Sweet was theorizing about engines, and had known that it was all nonsense by the amused shine in Sam's eyes. Sam, I love you so much: calm, thoughtful and brave. She glanced at the other airmen around the table. It's strange but the others seem to envy me.

Mrs. Cohen also hastened away, to pack her son's case. Left to themselves, the boys stretched their feet out. They were puffing stylishly at the large cigars, and clichés were exchanged across the table. They could talk more freely when a chap's mother wasn't there.

"We'll be on tonight," predicted Sweet. "I feel it in my corns." He laughed. "We'll put a little salt on Hitler's tail again, eh?"

"Is that what we are doing?" asked Lambert.

"Certainly it is," said Sweet. "Bombing the factories, destroying his means of production." Sweet's voice rose a little higher as he became exasperated by Lambert's patronizing smile.

Cohen spoke for the first time. "If we are going to talk about bombing, let's be as scientific as possible. The target map of Berlin is just a map of Berlin with the aiming point right in the city center. We are fooling only ourselves if we pretend we are bombing anything other than city centers."

"What's wrong with that?" said Flight Lieutenant Sweet.

"Simply that there are no factories in city centers," said Lambert. "The center of most German towns contains old buildings: lots of timber construction, narrow streets and alleys inaccessible to fire engines. Around that is the dormitory ring: middle-class brick apartments mostly. Only the third portion, the outer ring, is factories and workers' housing."

"You seem very well informed, Flight Sergeant Lambert," said Sweet.

"I'm interested in what happens to people," said Lambert. "I come from a long line of humans myself."

"I'm glad you pointed that out," said Sweet.

Cohen said, "One has only to look at our air photos to know what we do to a town."

"That's war," said Battersby tentatively. "My brother said there's no difference between bankrupting a foreign factory in peacetime and bombing it in wartime. Capitalism is competition and the ultimate form of that is war."

Cohen gave a little gasp of laughter, but corrected it to a cough when Battersby did not smile.

Lambert smiled and rephrased the notion. "War is a continuation of capitalism by other means, eh, Batters?"

"Yes, sir, exactly," said Battersby in his thin childish voice. "Capitalism depends upon consumption of manufactured goods and war is the most efficient manner of consumption yet devised. Furthermore, it's a test of each country's industrial system. I mean, look at the way we are developing our airplanes, radios, engines and all sorts of secret inventions."

"What about man for man?" said Digby.

"Surely after the great victories of the Red Army you don't still subscribe to the superman ethic, Mr. Digby," said Battersby. "Evils may exist within our social systems but the workingman who fights the war is pretty much the same the world over."

They were all surprised to hear Battersby converse at length, let alone argue.

"Are you a Red, Battersby?" said Flight Lieutenant Sweet.

"No, sir," said Battersby, biting his lip nervously. "I'm just saying what my brother told me."

"He should be shot," said Sweet.

"He was, sir," said Battersby. "At Dunkirk."

Sweet's rubicund face went bright red with embarrassment. He stubbed his cigar into a half-eaten pancake and, getting to his feet, said, "Perhaps we'd best get cracking. Just in case there's something on tonight."

Digby and Battersby also went upstairs to pack. Lambert was silent, sipping at his coffee and watching the cigar smoke drifting toward the oak ceiling.

Cohen poured coffee for himself and Lambert. The two of them sat at the table in silence until Cohen said, "You don't believe in war?"

"Believe in it?" said Lambert. "You make it sound like a rumor."

"I think about the bombing a lot," admitted Cohen.

"I hope you do," said Lambert. "I hope you worry yourself sick about it."

On the squadron Lambert usually spoke only of technical matters and like most of the old-timers he would smile without committing himself when politics or religion was discussed. Today was different.

"What do you believe then?"

"I believe that everyone is corruptible and I'm always

afraid that I might become corrupt. I believe that all societies are a plot to corrupt the individual."

"That's anarchy," said young Cohen, "and you are never an anarchist by any measure. After all, Skipper, society has a right to demand a citizen's loyalty."

"Loyalty? You mean using another man's morality instead of your own. That's just a convenient way of putting your conscience into cold storage."

"Yes," reflected Cohen doubtfully. "The S.S. motto is 'My honor is my loyalty.' "

"Well, there you are."

"But what about family loyalty?"

"That's almost as bad: it's giving your nephew the prize for playing the piano when the little boy down the street plays better."

"Is that so terrible?" asked Cohen.

"I'm the little boy down the street. I wouldn't have even got as far as grammar school unless a few people had let a prize or two go out of the family."

"What you are really saying," said young Cohen, trying to make it a question rather than a verdict, "is that you don't like bombing cities."

"That is what I'm saying," said Lambert and the young navigator was too shocked to think of a reply. Lambert drained his cup. "That's good coffee."

Hastily Cohen reached for the pot to pour more for him. He wanted to demonstrate his continuing admiration and regard for his pilot. "Coffee isn't rationed," said young Cohen.

"Then fill her up, and give me two hundred Players."

The roses on the table were now fully open. Lambert reached out to them but as he touched one it disintegrated and the pale pink petals fell and covered the back of his hand like huge blisters.

"Men are disturbed by any lack of order." The voice by his shoulder made Lambert start, for old Mr. Cohen had entered the room without either of them hearing him. He was a tall man with a handsome face, marred only by a lopsided mouth and yellow teeth. He spoke the careful style of English that only a foreigner could perfect. However, a nasal drone accompanied his flat voice, which gave no emphasis to any word nor acknowledged the end of a sentence.

"You and I might be able to see the virtue of chaos," he continued, "but dictators gain power by offering pattern, ranks, common purpose and men in formations. Men want order, they strive for it. Even the world's artists are asked only to impose meaning and symmetry upon the chaos of nature. You and I, Sergeant Lambert, may know that muddle and inefficiency are man's only hope of freedom but we will not easily convert our fellowmen."

"You are mocking me, Mr. Cohen."

"Not me, Sergeant. I have seen men line up to dig their own graves and turn to face the firing squad with a proud precision. I am not mocking you."

"The British are not easy to regiment, Father."

"So they keep telling me, my son, but I wonder. In this war they have gained the same sense of national identity and purpose that the Nazis gave the Germans. The British are so proud of their conversion that they will almost forgo their class system. I see the clear eyes and firm footfalls of the self-righteous and that is a good start on the road to totalitarian power. History is being quoted and patriotic songs revived. Believe me, the British are proud of themselves."

There was a commotion outside as Digby stumbled down the stairs with his suitcase, but Mr. Cohen did not pause.

"Someday, in the not so far distant future, when the trade unions are being particularly tedious, students are being unusually destructive and the pound is buying less and less, then a Führer will appear and tell the British that they are a powerful nation. 'Britain Awake' will be his slogan and some carefully chosen racial minority will be his scapegoats. Then you will see if the British are easy to regiment."

Sergeant Cohen smiled at Lambert. "For goodness' sake don't argue with him or we'll be here all day." He got to his feet.

"I wouldn't mind that at all," said Lambert. The old man bowed courteously. As the two airmen went into the hall old Mr. Cohen followed Lambert closely, as if to separate him from his son. Lambert turned to the old man and waited for him to speak but he didn't do so until his son had left.

"All fathers become old fools, Lambert," he said and stopped. Lambert looked at him, trying to draw the words from him as one does with a man who stutters. The words again came in a rush: "You'll look after the boy, won't you?"

For a moment Lambert said nothing. Sweet came down the stairs. He took the old man's arm and said airily,

"Don't worry about that, sir," but Cohen had selected only Lambert for his plea.

Lambert said, "It's not my job to look after your son, sir."

Young Cohen was still within earshot on the balcony above them. Digby saw him and felt like tugging the back of Lambert's tunic in warning.

Lambert knew they were all listening but he didn't lower his voice. He said, "It simply doesn't work like that. A crew all need each other. Any one of them can endanger the aircraft. Your son is the most skillful navigator I've flown with, probably the best in the squadron. He's the brains of the airplane; he looks after us."

There was silence for a moment, then Mr. Cohen said, "He certainly should be good; he's cost me a fortune to educate." The old man nodded to himself. "Look after my boy, Mr. Lambert."

"I promise." Lambert nodded to the old man and hurried upstairs, cursing himself for saying it. How the hell could he protect anyone? He was always amazed to get back safely himself. He passed young Cohen, who was coming downstairs with a large case.

When he was alone with his son the old man said, "You hear that? Your Captain Lambert says you're the best."

Mrs. Cohen appeared from nowhere and brushed her son's coarse blue uniform distastefully.

"His captain says he's the best. Best on the squadron, he said."

Mrs. Cohen ignored her husband. She pulled a piece of cotton from her son's sleeve. "I see that Mr. Sweet, the officer, is wearing gold cufflinks. Why don't you take yours with you? They look so nice."

"Not in the Sergeants' Mess, Mother."

"How old is Captain Lambert?" she said.

"He's not a captain, Mother, he's a flight sergeant. That's one rank above mine. We call him captain because he's the senior man on our aircraft."

His mother nodded, trying to understand and remember.

"Twenty-six or twenty-seven."

"He looks much older," said Mrs. Cohen, looking at her son. "He looks forty, an old man."

"Do you want him to fly with a child?" said Mr. Cohen.

"This Mr. Sweet can help to make you an officer, Simon."

"Oh, Mother, you've been talking about me."

"Would it be so bad, Simon?" said Mr. Cohen.

"It would mean changing to another crew."

"Why?"

"They don't like officers flying under N.C.O. captains. Anyway, it would make Lambert's job more difficult, having me sitting behind him with shiny little officer's badges. And we wouldn't be together in the Sergeants' Mess. And perhaps I'd have to go away to a training school."

"Quite a speech," said Mr. Cohen. "The most I've heard you say all weekend."

"I'm sorry, Father."

"It doesn't matter. But if Mr. Lambert is such a fine fellow, why is he not an officer? You tell me he has more experience, medals, and does the same job as your friend Mr. Sweet."

"Surely you know the English by now, Father. Lambert has a London accent. He's never been to an expensive school. The English believe that only gentlemen can be leaders."

"And this is the way they fight a war?"

"Yes. Lambert is the best, most experienced pilot on the squadron."

Mrs. Cohen said, "If you became an officer perhaps you could fly with Mr. Sweet."

"I'd rather fly with Lambert," he replied, trying to keep his voice amiable.

She said, "You mustn't be angry, Simon. We're not trying to make you stop flying."

"That's right. Just thinking of you earning more cash," his father joked.

"I keep telling both of you I'm just not ambitious. I'm never going to be an officer and I'm never going to be a philosophy professor like Uncle Carol. Nor a scientist like Dad. I'm not sure I could even run the farm. This job I'm doing in the air force ..."

Cohen raised a finger to interrupt. "There is a common mistake made by historians: to review the past as a series of errors leading to the perfect condition that is the present time. It's a common mistake in life too, especially in one of our closed societies like a school or a prison camp. It's easy then to forget that the outside world and future time exist. Now in the middle of 1943 your Messrs Sweets and Lamberts seem to have attained the highest pinnacle of prestige and achievement. But it's all glamour and tinsel. When the war is over, being the finest bomber

crew that ever flew across Germany won't get any of you
so much as a free dog license."

"You've got the wrong idea, Dad. I don't like being in
the air force. It's dangerous and uncomfortable, and a lot
of the people I work with are pretty nasty fellows." The
old man looked up quizzically. "But if nasty fellows can
destroy the fascists I'll put up with it. I know how to do
my job theoretically at any rate so don't worry about me.
You've both got to understand that this is my life now.
The whole of my life and I've got to live it in my own
way. Without gold cufflinks or your talking to anyone
about commissions or pocket money even. And most of
all, no more parcels."

Mrs. Cohen nodded. "I understand, Simon, I always
overdo things. I've embarrassed you with your captain,
have I?"

"No, no, no, it's fine. It's been a wonderful weekend
and wizard food."

"Wizard," repeated Mrs. Cohen, making a mental note
of the superlative. She reached for her handbag but after
a warning glance from her husband did not open it.

"Have a good journey, Cosy," said his father.

"My nickname is Kosher. Kosher Cohen they call me."

"So what's wrong with that?" asked his father. Kosher
smiled but did not answer. The old man nodded and
patted his son on the arm. They were closer than ever
before.

"Nora Ashton always asks about you," said Mrs. Cohen. "She's a fine girl."

The hall clock struck nine. "I must go. They are waiting. There's probably too much moon but we might
fly tonight."

"Over Germany?"

"There's not time to go far on these short summer
nights. Probably we'll be dropping mines into the North
Sea. All the boys like that; it's a milk run but it counts as
a full operation."

Digby heard the last bit of that. "That's right, Mrs.
Cohen. These gardening trips go off as quiet as a Sunday
in Adelaide."

"Phone me in the morning, Simon."

## ❧ 2 ❧

"ONE thing about these short summer nights," an elderly Wing Commander said. "We can usually short-list the target files and have them in the old man's hands the moment he makes the decision."

Nora Ashton, the young WAAF officer, smiled at him briefly and then went back to checking the target files. Each one had been started on orders from the Targets Selection Committee at Air Ministry. She identified each file by its code name: Whitebait was Berlin and Trout was Cologne. The code names were the idea of the Senior Staff Officer, who was a keen angler. Recently he had taken up collecting butterflies and moths but the C. in C. said that code names like Broad-bordered Bee Hawk would be inconvenient. Inside each target file there were population figures, industrial descriptions, photos and intelligence about searchlights and guns. The files varied a great deal: some files were as fat as phone directories and packed with reports from resistance workers and secret agents, while many contained little that didn't appear in a prewar city guide. Others were contradictory or out of date, and some were so thin that they scarcely existed at all. In each file there was a record of Bomber Command's previous attacks.

"The Ruhr tonight," said the elderly Wing Commander. "I'll bet you my morning tea break: Essen or Cologne."

"What, on my wages?" said the WAAF officer. "When you buy three or four sticky buns?"

He shrugged. "You would have lost."

Quickly she picked up a newspaper and turned to the astrology section. Under Aries it said: "Someone dear to you will make a journey. Financial affairs promising." She folded it and pushed it into the drawer.

She said, "Someday I'll take you up on one of your bets. Anyway, look at the moon chart. After the casualties we've had on recent light nights they might decide a full moon is too dangerous."

"Too dangerous for some ops," said the Wing Commander, "but the Ruhr looks messy on radar screens. Moonlight gives a visual identification of the target. If the met. man predicts some cloud cover they'll go, and the Ruhr's the only logical target."

The girl looked up and nodded agreement. It was 0905 hours; another hour and a half before morning tea break.

She said, "What was the weather like when you came in, sir?"

"Quite delightful, a perfect summer's day—not a cloud in the sky."

"I do hope so," said the WAAF officer. "Last night I had to get out of bed and close the window. The rain came down in torrents." She had planned to have her hair done that afternoon: rain would ruin it.

"My garden needed the rain."

"So did the met. people: they'd been forecasting it every day for a week."

Neither of them raised their eyes to the met. map on the wall, where was written the finest weather prediction that money and daring could provide. Each hour it was amended according to reports from weather stations, airplanes and ships at sea.

There was certainly no indication of prevailing weather conditions from inside this underground Operations Room, known to its inmates as "the hole." The air was clean and at constant temperature and the bright lights shone unchanging night and day. Here arrived the strategic requirements from Churchill's Cabinet War Room and from Air Ministry. From here went the orders that sent four or five thousand airmen into a three-dimensional night battle over Germany.

Every square foot of wall space was crammed with information. At desks around it sat the top brass of Bomber Command, an awe-inspiring array of rank. An army officer sat near a hot line to the C. in C. Home Forces and a naval captain clutched an armful of Enemy Shipping reports. Two American officers had small change spread across a desk top while a WAAF officer explained for the third time that thirty of these big coins made half a crown. "Then what makes a whole crown?"

"Nothing makes a whole crown," said his colleague.
"It's like saying what makes a bit. Two bits may be a
quarter but you can't have a bit."

"I think I've got it," said the first American doubtfully.

At this moment the S.A.S.O. (Senior Air Staff Officer)
and the Group Captain i/c Operations began to give the
C. in C. a summary of the previous night's bombing of
Germany. All eyes were on the thirty-foot-wide blackboard upon which the previous night's objectives and orders were chalked in yellow and results added in red.

Even as they spoke a sergeant climbed the ladder and
altered the Failed to Return tally from 26 to 25. "What's
that make it?" asked the C. in C.

"Four point five percent."

"Not bad; I was expecting worse."

"What are we going to get tonight?" the met. man was
asked.

"Here are the predicted positions of the fronts for
midnight. Well-broken cloud all along the northwest coast
but clear from Hamburg northward. Residual thundercloud with thunderstorms near the cold front."

"The Ruhr?" The elderly Wing Commander heard the
C. in C.'s question to the met. man and nodded significantly.

The met. man shuffled his notes. "At present thunderstorms are moving across the Rhine with this cold front
but they will clear by this afternoon. Midnight: thin layer
of medium cloud somewhere between 1,000 to 20,000 feet
but it will probably have gone by 0100 hours. There's a
chance of a little stratocumulus at 2,000 to 3,000 feet.
Expected visibility moderate."

"What about northern France?"

"Fine; moderate visibility. Well-broken layer cloud in
northwest."

"And the weather over U.K. for the aircraft's return?"

"Fine. A little stratocumulus at 2,000 or 3,000 feet.
Excellent visibility."

The C. in C. walked slowly across the highly polished
floor to look at the quarter-inch map of northern Europe
that almost covered one wall. Each of the target towns
was marked by a color-coded reference on a flat pin. He
looked back toward the moon chart, then moved nearer to
peer at the Ruhr. The short routes were marked with
colored tapes and his eyes scanned them, calculating the
flying times and fuel loads that each target would demand.

As the C. in C. followed the routes a knot of staff

officers moved with him, murmuring discreetly like Harley Street specialists about to collaborate on an expensive job of surgery. Always their glances went back to the met. wall. As the moment of decision arrived the officers ceased to talk. The only sounds were the air-conditioning and the clock. Suddenly the voices began again; the decision had been taken.

"Target files, Harry," a young Group Captain called to the elderly Wing Commander, for, although it was a high rank on the Squadrons, in this place a Wingco was a dogsbody. Nora Ashton pushed it toward him. Once again they had guessed the target to within a few files.

"Krefeld as primary, Bremen as weather alternative," said the C. in C. "H hour will be 0130 hours. No gardening tonight."

In the center of the room were large drafting tables. On one was a map showing enemy radar and night fighter units. Another displayed overlapping photographs mounted together to make a mosaic of the whole Ruhr. The C. in C. walked across to one and tipped it flat. The Krefeld target file was open and large-scale maps, target maps, plans, diagrams and vertical photos were arranged around it.

"What's our availability?"

"We've much better deliveries from the factories this month. We are showing 783 heavy bombers, 148 mediums. The strength of the training units is unchanged."

"Well, I'll use 650 heavies and 100 mediums. This target will give them all a chance."

"Very good, sir." The Staff Officer put a form headed "C. in C.'s Daily Allotment of Targets" on the table, and arranged the most recent reconnaissance photos of the target.

"Krefeld then, with 750 aircraft. I'm going to increase the proportion of high explosive to incendiary bombs slightly. I know that the H.E. raises dust at the beginning but we need the blast damage in order to expose the interiors and have something to set alight. Let's have twenty-five minutes' pause before the second wave goes in. That increases the risk from night fighters but gives us a chance of killing his firemen and policemen and air raid people. I'll give that second wave mostly H.E.; one-third of the aircraft will carry one bomb fused for long delay to keep them worried."

While he was talking, the C. in C. filled in the Daily Allotment of Targets form.

"Put some Mosquitoes over Berlin to make the sirens go and some leaflets on to Ostend. I want the Berlin route and the Ostend route near enough to our mainstream route to confuse them." The C. in C. passed the written order to the Controller. He got up slowly and left the Operations Room.

As he stepped out into the daylight the sentry gave a smart salute. Bomber Command H.Q. was hidden in thickly wooded countryside but the sky seen through the beech trees was clear and blue.

The center of the depression had moved across northern England and out into sea area Dogger. It was a young, vigorous depression and pulled the cold front eastward after it, leaving England to enjoy a period of anticyclonic weather. There would be no rain.

Even before the C. in C. was through the door the S.A.S.O. was on the phone to the first of the Group Commanders.

"It's Krefeld tonight, old boy. Weather alternative Bremen. Our met. chaps seem sure the weather will clear but we'll have the usual met. conference call. I want to leave it as late as possible today. Naturally you'll plan for sky marking just in case. . . ."

The Operations Room clocks showed that it was 0955 hours. Double British Summer Time. In Germany the clocks—set to Central European Summer Time—showed the same.

# 3

"AREN'T you glad we no longer live in Krefeld?" Anna-Luisa asked.

"You said there would be lions and tigers, and wild animals," the little boy said accusingly.

"There are lions and tigers, and yesterday I saw an elephant in the woods near Frau Richter's farm."

"You're always saying that," the little boy said with a chuckle. "You just make those stories up."

"If you've finished your egg you ought to get along to school. It's nearly nine o'clock."

She took a handkerchief and wiped a trace of egg from his lips. Hansl hurried to get his schoolbooks. "Take your raincoat, Hansl," she called. "I'm sure it will rain."

Anna-Luisa made sure his coat was buttoned and his collar straight. She checked the schoolbooks in his case and ran a comb through his short hair. When all was approved she gave him a little salute. "All is in order, Herr Leutnant. Say good-bye to Pappi."

The little boy saluted gravely. Anna-Luisa reached for a second egg and placed it carefully in the simmering water. "Breakfast, Herr Bach," she called.

Neither the little boy nor his father, for whom she was preparing breakfast, belonged to Anna-Luisa. She was a member of the R.A.D.w.J., a uniformed labor force of mothers' helpers and social workers. A little over a year ago she had gone to work for Frau Bach in Krefeld, twelve kilometers away in the Ruhr district. She had liked the job, adored the child, and Frau Bach had been a not unreasonable employer. Within a month of her starting work Frau Bach had been killed in an air raid. Herr Bach and his elder son, Peter, an infantry private just eighteen years old, had been flown back from the Russian Front.

The authorities had a simple solution. They wanted to evacuate little Hansl to a Hitler Youth camp in the Protectorate of Czechoslovakia, but Herr Bach preferred that Anna-Luisa should stay with the boy. He wanted someplace that he could think of as home, although the cost of renting an apartment just for one ten-year-old made terrible demands upon his Oberleutnant's pay.

Herr Bach's cousin suggested that they should move into this apartment in the town of Altgarten not far from the Netherlands border. It had been the home of Gerd's father but had been unoccupied since the old man's death almost two years before. Gerd had loaded Bach's salvaged furniture into his grocer's van and brought it here from Krefeld. That was a year ago, and since then August Bach, Luftwaffe Oberleutnant and Commanding Officer of radar station Ermine, had learned to call it home. Now that he was stationed on the Netherlands coast he was able to see his small son every two or three weeks. Last Christmas his grown-up son, Peter, had also come home on leave. It was a happy time.

"Breakfast is ready, Herr Bach," called Anna-Luisa.

"Did you hear the thunder?" asked Bach.

"I made Hansl take his raincoat."

"It's just a summer storm," said Bach. "If it does rain it will soon be over."

"I hope so," said Anna-Luisa. "You've such a long journey."

When August Bach sat down to breakfast she noticed that he was wearing his best uniform. She approved of his uniform, for although he was forty-six years old he was tall and slim and his graying hair served only to emphasize the tan on his face. At his throat the Pour le Mérite medal glittered.

"The milk is sour. The thunder must have caused it," said the girl.

"It doesn't matter."

"This is the last of the real coffee you brought. Do you know, Herr Bach, I am so used to ersatz coffee that the real beans you bring from Holland keep me awake at night."

"Where is an egg for you, Anna-Luisa?"

"There were only two, Herr Bach. The hens are not laying, and they cost six Reichsmarks each. There is a terrible shortage this month."

"Have this one. The Luftwaffe live well in Holland.

Only last week Willi, my Stabsfeldwebel, laid his hands on some cream." He passed the egg to her.

"You'll never believe me, Herr Bach, but I don't remember the taste of cream."

"I believe you," said August Bach. "I'll speak to him when I get back and see if he can't find some for me next month when I come."

"Did you notice, Herr Bach, little Hansl has picked up this terrible local accent?"

"Like my cousin Gerd's," said August, smiling.

August Bach watched the girl eating his boiled egg. She looked up and smiled. What did an accent matter? She was very beautiful, especially when she smiled. Without her he would have no home and, unless you counted the occasional printed postcard from a Hitler Youth camp in the Protectorate, no young son either. Nowadays the children were being evacuated farther and farther away. Bombed-out children from Cologne had gone to Bulgaria and Hungary.

"Herr Bach," said Anna-Luisa. "Is it true that many R.A.D. w.J. girls are going to work on flak sites? There is a rumor that they will even be manning the guns."

Bach had always feared that someday Anna-Luisa would decide that looking after little Hansl was not a great enough contribution to the war effort. Worse still, he feared that the R.A.D. bureau would decide that for her, but here in the country the pace of things was slower. There was no R.A.D. bureau in Altgarten, no S.A., and even the Party H.Q. was closed on market day.

"Are you unhappy, Anna-Luisa?" he asked. "Are you thinking of leaving us?"

"I would never leave you, Herr Bach," she said. "Never. I will look after Hansl all the rest of my life."

"Now, now, Anna-Luisa, you mustn't make promises like that."

"I will, Herr Bach. I will. I love Hansl as though he was my own child."

"Then why do you ask me about the R.A.D. girls going to the gun sites?" asked August.

She got to her feet and began to clear the breakfast table. "Have you finished your coffee?"

"Yes."

"I'm sorry, but there is now only the ersatz."

"Answer me, Anna-Luisa."

"Herr Bach," she said. She was standing at the sink now with her face turned away from him. He waited for her to

continue. She was attractive in her neat white blouse and
brown skirt, with her blond hair drawn back into a severe
knot. Why had he not noticed before her long slim legs
and strong young arms? Undressed, she would look . . . He
killed the thought immediately. She was only a child,
perhaps a year or so older than his infantryman son. Her
service in the R.A.D. was a patriotic duty. It was his job
to look after her, not lust after her.

"Are there"—she paused—"any R.A.D. girls working at
your radar site?"

August Bach didn't laugh, although the thought of girls
in that desolate spot on the Dutch coast made him realize
how little she understood the rigors of his life there.

"There are no girls, Anna-Luisa. I only wish there
were," he joked. And he looked up at her, still smiling, to
discover her face racked with tears. He took his handkerchief to dry her eyes. "Anna-Luisa, whatever is the matter?"

"Be careful of the washing-up water on your fine uniform," she said, raising her face to him, and the next
moment he found that he was kissing her. She was sobbing
as though she would never stop. It was difficult to understand what she was saying, but August Bach suddenly
found that everything made sense to him. "I love you,
Herr Bach," she said. He smoothed her blond hair and
made little clicking noises with his lips in the hope that it
would stop her crying.

"I love you," she said again. "Whatever shall we do?"

"You can stop calling me Herr Bach for one thing," he
said.

"What will people say?" she said.

"Does it matter?"

"This is a little country town, Herr August . . ."

"Just August."

"August . . . people gossip here. There is no telling what
stories will go round." He had his arms round her and felt
her sobbing gently. He patted her shoulder awkwardly and
paternally.

It was a damnable situation. Almost the whole town
knew August's cousin—Gerd Böll the grocer—and
through him half the town knew August. Often strangers
would talk to him in the street as though they were lifelong
friends. "We must take things slowly," said August. Anna-
Luisa nodded.

"Oh, for God's sake," he said, "do you think they're not
gossiping about us already?"

"They are," said Anna-Luisa, "but it does not matter. I love you." He held her more tightly and less paternally.

"And I love you," said August and he realized that he did. All these months of spending his leaves in the same house with this young girl. No wonder neighbors talked. To her he must have seemed unnatural or inhuman. He looked at her; she was a simple girl and for her perhaps he was a frightening figure. He asked himself to what extent he had been hurrying back here to see the child and to what extent because it was his home, a home that Anna-Luisa had created, a place where his favorite foods were placed before him and his favorite records near the gramophone. August realized that all these months he had been hurrying back to Anna-Luisa. "I love you, Anna-Luisa," he said. "I want you to marry me." She raised her reddened eyes to him. Her hair had fallen forward. She was remarkably beautiful even in this disarray. Even more beautiful, perhaps.

"There are my parents, Herr Bach. You will have to visit them or at least write."

"I will do that today," he said. He stroked her head again and took her hand. It was a slim hand reddened by hard work, scrubbing floors and washing Hansl's clothes and August's shirts.

"Damn, damn, damn," said August Bach under his breath, and then began to undress her, still declaiming loudly about how foolish they were. He unpinned the R.A.D. swastika brooch from her blouse and set it aside carefully.

"How old are you?" he asked suddenly.

"Twenty-two," said Anna-Luisa.

"Well, there you are," said August. "It's stupid, absolutely stupid," but he did not undress her more slowly. The nearby church clock struck nine and a horse and cart clattered past the house. It made their intimacy more conspiratorial to hear the town going about its business just a few yards away.

"I love you, Herr Bach," said Anna-Luisa.

"August," insisted August.

"You'll write?"

"Every day," swore August.

"And to my father?"

"This afternoon."

"I love you, Herr August," said Anna-Luisa. "I love both of you. We shall make a perfect family. You just see.

I will buy new fabric for the front-room curtains, and
Hansl needs new shoes."

He pulled the pins from her hair and it tumbled down
over her face. He had never seen her with her hair loose.
It had always been rolled tight at the nape of her neck in
a style suitable for her uniformed appearance. She laughed
and kissed him again. By now they were in the bedroom
and the big brass bed creaked loudly as she climbed onto
it. August leaned across the bed to her, but she moved
aside and giggled at outwitting him. For a moment, a
terrible moment, August thought that she was just teasing
him. It was the sort of thing that a young girl might do to
an ardent lover of forty-six. But no sooner had the
thought entered his mind than she undressed herself. Still
standing on the bed, she threw her starched white uniform
blouse across the room and stepped out of her brown
skirt. Her underwear vanished as if by magic and there
she was, naked, spinning round before his startled gaze.
She pulled back the bedclothes and slid under them. Only
her tousled flaxen hair and bright blue eyes were visible as
she pulled the eiderdown up to her nose. It was the yellow
silk eiderdown, which his wife had been so proud of, Bach
remembered. They had saved so long to buy it.

He unbuttoned his uniform jacket and pull it across the
back of a chair.

"Don't come to bed with your medal on, Herr August.
It hurts," she called.

He pulled the black-and-white ribbon of the Pour le
Mérite over his head.

"Show me." He threw the beribboned medal to her. He
continued to undress while she looked at it.

She put the ribbon over her head and admired herself in
the mirror, stiffening her naked body like a soldier on
parade. The blue and gold of the medal matched her eyes
and hair.

"It's the Pour le Mérite, isn't it?" she asked.

"That's very clever of you."

"I asked someone about the cross you wore at your
throat. What did you do?"

"I shot down eleven English airplanes in the first war."

"You must have been only a boy."

"I was seventeen when I shot down the first one."

She opened her arms to him and he climbed onto the
bed with her.

"You know," she told him in a whisper, "I have seen
this room a thousand times from every place. I have even

crawled under the bed to sweep and clean but I never thought I would see the room from this viewpoint." Her skin was soft and warm and contrasted with the cold stiffly starched sheets under his touch.

"In future you will see it from this viewpoint as often as you wish," he said with a smile.

"I shall always wish it so," said Anna-Luisa seriously. She touched his face with her fingertips and he caught the harsh smell of kitchen soap as it mingled with her cologne.

"It's a gloomy room," said August. The wallpaper was dark and the oak wardrobe huge and ancient. They were both reflected in its mirror. Their eyes met. A streak of lightning came through the lowered blind and lit them momentarily like a flashbulb. There was a growl of thunder. Anna-Luisa blushed and looked away. Hung here and there were old family photographs; unwanted in the sitting room, but difficult to throw away. On the washstand a basin and jug glinted in the rosy light coming through the pink blind. A potted plant silhouetted against it shivered in the draft from the window. Anna-Luisa touched the Pour le Mérite medal. She grinned. "It looks better on me," she said.

"It does," he agreed, and reached out for her.

"And the red ribbon?"

"For the East Front," he said. "The *Eisbeinorden.*" The cold feet medal.

"That must have been terrible."

"It was." His voice was muffled as he kissed her ear.

"Herr August," she whispered as they began to make love. "Shall I always sleep in this bed now?"

"Yes," said August. Close to, he noticed that her hair was almost white and under its fringe her eyes were reddened by sobbing, and the tip of her nose was too. She smiled at him again. The light faded and there was the chilly gust of air that precedes a storm. Without hurry August made love to her as the thunderclouds darkened the gloomy room.

Afterward she clutched him very tightly and made his arm wet with her silent tears. He reached for his cheroots and lit one. He wanted to tell her everything he had ever done and show her everything he had ever seen. There was so little time before he must go.

"Will you be kind to me, Herr August?"

He kissed the side of her nose. "Kindness in a man is a

quality few women admire," he said. "Especially very young, very beautiful women."

"I shall always admire you, Herr August. Tell me about the medal."

We were all victims of these symbols and trinkets, totems and taboos, thought August Bach. Why should the girl be attracted by the blue-enameled cross? What could it mean to her?

"The airplanes were different then. Biplanes: fragile little affairs of sticks and fabric." Why was he using those old clichés? They were tough little planes and agile too. Not like today's sophisticated metal machines so full of fuel pipes, radio gear and delicate equipment that even a heavy bump on takeoff made something malfunction.

"They were painted with strange patterns of mauve and pink and gray. I can remember them." It wasn't true. He could no longer remember the difference between a Halberstadt and an Albatros. It was the smell that he remembered, the fuel and the dope, shrill smells that caught the back of the throat. He remembered too the sound of the Mercedes motor firing and the roar of it echoing against the side of the hangar.

"I remember the day I shot down my first Englishman. It was a beautiful day, not a cloud in the sky." Or was he telling it correctly? Surely that was the day he got the telegram about his mother dying. It was pouring with rain the day he shot down his first Englishman.

"Were you afraid?" asked Anna-Luisa.

"I was afraid that someone would think I might be afraid," he said. It was a conventional answer. The true answer was that at eighteen he didn't have enough intelligence to be afraid with.

"Did you see the Englishman?"

He tried to remember. "It was a two-seater. I saw the pilot's white silk scarf floating out of the cockpit. I came out of the sun."

"Were you proud?"

"I'd killed two men, Anna-Luisa. It's a terrible thing." He wondered what sort of men they were or might have become. The British should never have sent men out in those B.E.-2s, not over the lines anyway. After he landed and claimed his first victory his Staffel commander said, "A B.E.-2, I suppose." This one had already been shot up but he fought like the devil. On the third pass the gunner ran out of ammunition. He waved and pointed to his gun. A white-faced fellow with a moustache, no youngster. The pilot seemed unable to open the throttle. He looked over his shoulder to see how close the attack was coming. They stood no chance. He went out to the crash, to salvage the roundel markings as a trophy, but there was blood all over the canvas upon which they were painted. Both British fliers were dead. The sentry told him that one of the medical orderlies had kept an Englishman's scarf. He'll sell it for five marks, said the sentry. Bach had declined.

"I want to walk with you, Herr August. Can we go shopping together?"

"And we will lunch together at the Stube," he answered.

"It will be wonderful, August." She stroked his head.

"We will walk everywhere, Anna-Luisa. Everyone shall see us arm in arm."

"I love you, August. I shall always love you."

The room lit up bright pink.

"One thousand," said Anna-Luisa. "Two thousand ..." When he puffed at his cheroot he found it had gone out. He reached for his matches and relit it carefully, then he held up the match and Anna-Luisa blew it out but still counted on. When the thunder came she pronounced the storm to be four kilometers away. There was still no sound of rain.

"Did you know how to tell how far away a storm is?" she asked.

"You can never be sure," said August.

# 4

THE huge layer of cold air that was approaching Altgarten moved eastward across Europe at twenty miles per hour. As it moved, the cold front's sharp edge chiseled under the unstable humid summer air and levered it skyward to form thunderclouds. There was thunder too and lightning and in places rain. Eighty miles northwest of Altgarten the rain fell upon the IJsselmeer, the great inland sea that opened the heart of Holland to the northern storms. At first the rain was light and constant, dropping from the low nimbostratus cloud like black columns that propped up the sky. Then came the rain from the cumulonimbus, falling ten miles, right through the nimbostratus, and crashing in great sheets upon the rough waters of the IJsselmeer. The wind had veered to the north and sudden gusts of it pushed the rain horizontal. It deluged the little lakes near Utrecht. Hundreds of ducks, herons and other water birds sheltered miserably along the water's edge and under wooden piers from which even the anglers had departed. At Kroonsdijk the rain beat upon the farm-style buildings and the duck pond and hammered the flat cobbled and asphalt causeways, so that fine spray rebounded like tall white grass.

In building number 31 the rain awoke Oberleutnant Baron Victor von Löwenherz when even the thunder had failed. He looked at the clock; it was ten o'clock Central European Summer Time and the barometer had fallen dramatically. He reset the barometer, for when the pressure started to rise and the wind steadied and backed he would know that the cold front and its line squalls had nearly passed. Löwenherz took a close interest in the weather, for he was a pilot and Kroonsdijk was a Luftwaffe night fighter airfield.

The military installations had been designed to look like
Dutch farm buildings. The big roofs that sloped almost to
the ground and the timber exteriors disguised concrete
blockhouses. The shutters, painted with gay peasant de-
signs, were made of six-millimeter steel. Instead of a
rectangular fire hydrant tank, there was an oval pond, and
upon it the Luftwaffe had installed ducks to complete the
illusion. Grazing near the runways were herds of pantomime cows made from lath and plaster. The subject of
jokes and derision, they were enough to deceive the air
cameras.

Outside the window, motor vehicles and beyond them
twin-engined fighter airplanes were parked under the
trees. Nothing had been left to chance. This site had been
selected, surveyed and decided upon, the architect's plans
had been completed and all was ready, three years before
Holland was invaded. Now Kroonsdijk had become a key
factor in the air defense of Germany. It lay upon the
direct route from the bomber airfields in eastern England
to the heart of industrial Germany, as a tollgate on a dark
busy road.

It was not surprising that Oberleutnant Baron Victor
von Löwenherz had many times been photographed for
the Nazi magazines *Der Adler* and *Signal,* for he was the
personification of National Socialist propaganda—although they often chose to omit his title, for the new
Nazi state had created its own aristocracy. Tall, slim and
elegant, he had blond hair, which by this time of year the
sun had turned almost white. His face had the sharp-edged
bony look that sculptors invent and his teeth were white
and even.

He jumped out of bed and did his physical exercises—
twenty pushups, eight hundred paces on the spot, knees
high, stretching, knees bending and arms flinging—
watched with deadpan interest by the young bulldog that
was lying in its usual spot under the writing table.
Löwenherz's room was small and rather dark, for windows were kept as small as possible to reduce the danger
from blast and shrapnel. In one corner was an iron bedstead with gray blankets, which he now carefully remade,
folding each corner neatly and expertly as he had done
every morning since he joined the army as an officer cadet
in 1937.

For well over three hundred years the Löwenherz
family had supplied soldiers to Prussia. A Heinrich
Löwenherz had served under the mighty Wallenstein and

shared his grim defeat by Gustavus Adolphus at Lützen in 1632. But Heinrich's son had become a senior officer in the Kriegskommissariat of the Great Elector and had lived to see the Swedes driven from the battlefield of Fehrbellin some forty-three years later.

There was a painting of Heinrich on the staircase of the house in Grawiec: a pale-faced man with the Löwenherz nose and dark, broody eyes. His beard and moustache are trimmed in the Spanish style and he is wearing the broad lace collar and red sash even upon his breastplate and leather fighting clothes. As a child, Victor had been frightened to go past it down the stairs, especially after dark when there were only flickering candles to light the hall and the howl of wolves came from the hills above the village.

In the First World War Baron Hans-Georg von Löwenherz—Victor's father—had lost an arm at Langemarck, Ypres, serving with the Prussian Guards, and had gone on to become a staff operations officer. After the war he had taken command of one of the secret instruction schools that the Reichswehr formed to replace the Military Academy forbidden by the peace treaty.

It was natural that Victor should go into the army and although he had never been truly happy as a cadet he could look back upon it with pride and pleasure. Tucked into the corner of a silver-framed portrait of his mother there was a fading snapshot taken in Austria—as it then was called—at the time of the Anschluss. Five smiling cavalry officers, their caps bearing the commemorative Brandenburg dragoon eagle of which they had been so proud. The following day, in Linz, they had caught a glimpse of the Führer himself. A month later Löwenherz had been transferred from the army to the Luftwaffe and was a part of the intensive air crew training program that followed the Munich agreement.

He looked again at those boys who had been his close comrades through the agonies of cadet school. They'd teased him mercilessly when they heard of his application to become a flier, but they'd come to the railway station at four-thirty in the morning to bid him good-bye. He looked at their childish faces; the amateur photo was creased and faded. One was buried in Narvik, another had been crippled in an amphitheater near Sparta, the third was an Oberst on Manstein's staff at Army Group Don. The fourth was commanding a Bewährungskompagnie (a suicide unit for enemies of the regime) near Kharkov.

The group in the small ivory frame was his class at the Neu Bieburg A/B Flying School, with an Old Bücker biplane in the background. Only half of those recruits finally got their wings.

Twenty-five men sepia-toned and defaced by youthful signatures: pupils and instructors at Schleissheim Fighter Pilot School. He was blinking in the strong sunlight. He'd just completed two hundred flying hours when that photo was taken. It had seemed a lot at the time. Scowling in the front row was his present commanding officer, who, like most of the instructors there, had just returned from fighting in the Spanish Civil War. To Löwenherz he had seemed a remote and glamorous figure with his four victories over Loyalist Spanish planes. Now, he supposed, the new replacements on his Staffel saw himself as a similarly forbidding figure: distant and cold and expert. Löwenherz hoped so.

He stopped looking at the photos and pulled on his silk dressing gown before going to the end of the officers' billets for a shower. He scrubbed himself energetically under the cold water and dried himself thoroughly. He had a catlike grace of movement that fitted his fastidiousness with food and his concern for clean personal linen. When he returned to his room he spent forty minutes ironing the shirts and underclothes that he had washed and left to dry the previous night.

When Löwenherz finished he put away the electric iron and dressed carefully. He inspected his gleaming high boots and fixed the Iron Cross and the German Cross Order to the pocket of his newly laundered tunic. He briefly checked his appearance in the mirror: the white tunic was immaculate and he slanted the white-topped cap rakishly. The bulldog came out from under the table and prepared for the walk through the woodland to the Officers' Mess.

"It's wet outside, Bubi," he warned, but, like his master, the dog enjoyed walking through the fragrant grass. The rain had ceased and sunlight shone upon the wet grass. The dog sniffed each patch of it and ran across the road and cocked its leg at the slit-trench bomb shelters. Löwenherz used to scold Bubi for doing that, but since the shelters had never been used from the day they were dug he had ceased to care if the dog fouled them.

As Löwenherz stepped out from his quarters four Dutch civilians arrived carrying mops and brooms. Behind them cycled Feldwebel Blessing, the civilian staff overseer.

The Feldwebel dismounted from his bicycle when he saw
Löwenherz and saluted him with precision. Blessing was
a young, overweight Bavarian with heavy features and
small piercing eyes.

"Good morning, Feldwebel Blessing," said Löwenherz.
"There's rust in the water supply again. The same trouble
as last March, I suspect."

"It will be investigated, Herr Oberleutnant."

"Excellent, Blessing, I am confident that it will." Although he was unpopular, Blessing's efficiency was a by-
word and his civilians kept the billets clean and shining. A
few generals like Blessing in the O.K.W. and perhaps we
shouldn't be on the defensive in the East, nor preparing
Italy for an Allied invasion, thought Löwenherz. Blessing cycled energetically away toward the main barracks
with Bubi barking at his rear wheel. Löwenherz walked
toward the Officers' Mess and soon the dog returned,
racing after him, splashing through the puddles.

Along the perimeter fence sat hundreds of sea birds
driven inland by the summer storm. Bubi chased them
along the fence, barking and jumping high into the air.
Lazily the wet white blobs stretched their wings and cir-
cuited briefly before settling back into place.

As he neared the Officers' Mess, Löwenherz recognized one of his pilots walking toward him through the
sun-spotted woodland. The boy would probably have
avoided a meeting with his Staffelkapitän if he had been
looking where he was going.

Christian Himmel was a twenty-two-year-old Unteroffizier. His basic pay was one hundred marks per month plus
another forty marks in Wehrsold (war pay) and seventy-
five marks Fliegerzulage (flying pay). This, even allowing
for income tax and contributions to Nazi funds and winter
relief, still left him with more comforts than he had known
in civil life and just double what his father earned as a
gardener. He was a muscular boy with short untidy hair
that he inexpertly trimmed himself. His face was round
and his serious mouth full-lipped. "Angel Face" he had
been called at the camp where he had done his labor
service, and the lack of wrinkles in his clear skin did make
him look like one of those carved cherubs that crowd
together around the altars and pulpits of the baroque
churches near his Bavarian home town.

Himmel was shy, although no one at Kroonsdijk had
less reason to be daunted by Oberleutnant von Löwenherz than he had. In July 1940, during the Kanalkampf

(as the Luftwaffe named the early period of the Battle of Britain), the circumstances had been very different. Löwenherz was a young ensign newly posted to a Messerschmitt 109 squadron where Himmel was a very experienced pilot, with a Polish Lós bomber and two Spitfires to his credit and a novel reputation. It was said that Himmel had shot down more enemy aircraft than he claimed, and on at least three occasions he had been more than generous in allowing kills to be credited to others.

Löwenherz's first two kills—a Hurricane and a Defiant —had a considerable number of Himmel's bullets in them, as Löwenherz was the first to admit. But Löwenherz had been Himmel's wingman, and, as Himmel said, a good wingman should share credit for every victory. A wingman flew two hundred yards on the beam of his leader and covered him from stern or quarter attack. The leader navigated, led the attack and made the decisions. Himmel had done that well. Himmel was also a skilled mechanic. His concern for the aircraft on the Staffel amounted almost to hypochondria, an obsession that was his excuse for being shy, silent and alone. When he spoke with his ground crew men he tried to confine the conversation solely to technical matters. Sometimes Löwenherz could almost believe that Himmel ticked and whined and roared, and made better contact with his machines than with his fellowmen.

"Good morning, Himmel."

"Good morning, Herr Oberleutnant," said the boy. There was a gust of wind and Himmel, clad in black mechanic's overalls, shivered.

"Plugs still oiling up, Christian?"

"They fitted new rings but that was just a waste of labor, Herr Oberleutnant. There's only a very slight improvement."

The dog made playful rushes at the Unteroffizier's boots. Himmel pretended to punch Bubi's head and the dog growled and made fearsome open-fanged passes at his fast-moving hands.

"Kugel won't be able to do it today. The Major has had trouble with his supercharger capsule. He's given strict instructions that his plane must be ready this evening."

"Then Kugel will be busy," said Himmel.

"Very, very busy." Löwenherz smiled, picturing the potbellied old mechanic facing the Gruppenkommandeur's wrath.

Löwenherz said, "I'll tell him to do a run up when you

land tonight. If you're still getting a drop in revolutions I'll tell him he must fit a new engine. How's that, Christian?"

"Thank you, Herr Oberleutnant."

"Are you going to breakfast?"

"I'm not hungry. I will have coffee when it's sent out to the dispersal. Shall I take Bubi with me?"

Löwenherz passed Bubi's collar and lead to Himmel. Bubi barked happily. Löwenherz watched the young N.C.O. and the dog move out of sight through the trees. Himmel was running and the dog chased him until Himmel's black overalls merged into the patches of shade.

The temperature had dropped slightly in spite of the sunshine and Löwenherz noticed that the gusts of wind were coming from the direction of the H.Q. buildings to the northwest. The cold front had moved well past Kroonsdijk now, and the great cold air mass was steadying. When he reached the Officers' Mess he looked at the barometer; it had risen. Everything pointed to a few days of fine summer weather.

Löwenherz was a methodical man. He deposited his peaked cap on the cloakroom counter and picked up a copy of the *Berliner Börsen-Zeitung* that was set aside for him. He looked up the prices of his Daimler-Benz, Zeiss Ikon and Siemens shares. He believed in good solid companies. He'd bought a few shares of Sachs Engineering because it was owned by the father of his radar operator and, although they had done wonders until a year ago, they had now begun to stick a little. He thought he might sell. He looked at the back page for the annual reports but there was nothing of interest. Neither was the war news of any great importance. The war was at a time of hiatus. He didn't want to fold the paper and stuff it into his pocket for it would make bulges in his newly pressed uniform jacket. So he rolled it carefully and took it with him. There were no new notices on the board. Glancing at his reflection as he passed, he smoothed his hair and opened the door of the dining hall.

The Mess Hall was a large sunlit room with long refectory tables and a high ceiling. At the far end there was a patriotic mural covering the entire wall. Firm-jawed soldiers and radiant girls in peasant costume and flaxen plaits marched with flags under a canopy of bomber formations. There were posters that reminded crews of the dangers of careless conversation in public places. Another depicted a gull in flight: "Pilots, he too is your enemy!" A photo of a birdstrike-damaged plane was also shown. A cartoon pilot said, "If you are lost, climb to safety height. Don't descend through cloud—it's dangerous."

Over the serving hatch there were listed the civilian rations side by side with the more generous Wehrmacht issue of the same items. "Remember . . ." it was headed.

There were two officers of his Staffel sitting over a pot of coffee. Löwenherz joined them. Some of the tables were set for the brunch-style meal that the night fighter crews had at midday after sleeping late. It was still only 10 A.M. and as yet these three fliers were the only ones up and about.

"Can I join the *Kaffeeklatsch?*" said Löwenherz.

"The whole points system should be revised," said Leutnant Kokke, a young Berliner. He was a swarthy man with long black hair, full moustache and a beard trimmed just close enough to fit under his oxygen mask. Löwenherz noted his grubby gray shirt and unpolished boots. Kokke was noted for his devastating sarcasm and polished flying skill, but he was invariably the untidiest officer on the unit. Löwenherz decided that he must speak to Kokke about this on a more suitable occasion.

Kokke went on, "On the Eastern Front any fool can shoot down a dozen a day. One hundred victories, two hundred victories, what's it matter? Any day now they'll have a fellow there with three hundred victories."

"While we struggle and sweat to see who will be the first man to get thirty," complained Beer, a sad little Leutnant from Regensburg who before the war had been a racing car driver. His face was lined with worry and his wavy hair surmounted a very tall forehead. He too was trying to grow a moustache but after nearly three weeks its growth was less than luxuriant. He fingered it for a moment before laying aside his copy of the *Völkische Beobachter*, and sipped at the bitter coffee.

A mess waiter put a plate of chopped raw yellow turnip on the table along with a fresh pot of coffee. The Luftwaffe medical authorities said it would improve night vision. Few air crew ate it, fewer still believed in it, but Löwenherz bit into a piece now to set a good example. Then he reached for a tin of vitamin tablets and took two.

"Do you think the tablets improve night vision, Herr Oberleutnant?" asked Beer.

"Night adaption," corrected Löwenherz.

"Yes," said Beer.

"There's a whole world of difference," said Löwenherz.

"And you think the vitamin A tablets improve night adaption?" asked Beer.

"It's on orders," said Löwenherz. "Two each morning before breakfast and two immediately before flying."

"They should revise the points system," said Kokke. "At present a pilot has to destroy, say, thirteen four-engined bombers at three points each and a twin-motor escort at two points in order to get a Knight's Cross. At night! My God, we should get a Knight's Cross just for finding one. And now with this wet weather our radar aerials will be all to hell."

Beer nodded agreement. It was all Kokke needed to expound further. "Why, on the Eastern Front you can knock down a couple of antique American Airacobras and a couple of LaG3s every morning before breakfast and get yourself a sheet metal tie in a week or two. Isn't that right, Herr Oberleutnant?"

"Are you two still talking about Knight's Crosses?" said Löwenherz. It was no surprise, though; that's what everyone in the Gruppe spent their spare time talking about; perhaps the whole damn Luftwaffe did. "Knocking down Ivans is not so easy," said Löwenherz. "I've never seen a LaG3, but its newest variant is the La5FN. It's got fuel injection, a 1,650-h.p. motor, and the exhaust gases—carbon dioxide and nitrogen—are passed into the fuel tanks as a precaution against incendiary bullet hits. It's got two cannons with supplementary rockets. A Red pilot defected with a new one last month; I flew it at Rechlin Testing Center. It's a good plane."

"How fast?" asked Kokke.

"I got nearly 400 m.p.h. out of it at 15,000 feet."

"That's fast," said Beer.

"But what can it do at higher altitudes?" asked Kokke.

"It doesn't matter what it can do higher," explained Löwenherz. "It's a low-altitude air war in the East. If the Ivans are ground strafing, or bombing at low level, then we've got to come down and fight them."

"I suppose so," agreed Kokke.

"What's more," said Löwenherz, "our technical people say its air-cooled motor will be simpler to service in bad winter conditions than the liquid-cooled ones are. The report also said that the air frame will take more punishment."

"We could do with a few of those La5s to replace these

crappy old wrecks that we have to nurse through the air," said Kokke.

"There's nothing wrong with the Richards," said Beer. "Last year I was flying 110s. That really is an obsolete design."

"Nothing wrong with the Richards?" scoffed Kokke. "Where did you read that, the *Völkische Beobachter* in 1937?" He tapped off criticisms on the fingertips of his stubby pianist's hands. "Designed as a dive bomber; we're using it as a night fighter. Four years out of date. Poor pilot visibility. Very high landing speed. So, land a dive bomber with poor visibility at night with a high landing speed and you've got a handful of airplane."

"I like having a handful of airplane," said Löwenherz. "Anyway, next year we'll have the Heinkel 219."

He was inclined to agree with Kokke about the Ju88R, especially in respect to the landing speed, but the last thing he was prepared to do was to destroy the confidence his air crews had in their equipment.

"With all respect, Herr Oberleutnant," said Kokke, "next year might be too late."

"By next year we shall all be on the East Front," said Beer. He helped himself to bread and cherry jam. A wasp was buzzing round the table and Beer shooed it away nervously.

"You're a miserable bastard," said Kokke. "When shall I ever hear you say a cheerful word?"

"Well, I don't say defeatist things like you do," said Beer. He smiled thinly as he said it, but there was more than a trace of accusation in his voice.

"What did I say?" Kokke reached for Löwenherz's *Börsen-Zeitung* and swatted the wasp with a loud crack.

"The war in the East was like a traveling circus and a traveling zoo battling in a wilderness to decide which should put on a show."

"Are you sure you didn't just make that up?" asked Kokke.

"Oh, shut up," said Beer angrily.

"More coffee, Herr Oberleutnant?"

"Thank you, Kokke," said Löwenherz. He watched the bearded man handling the coffee cups. Those were a musician's hands. Kokke had wanted to be a professional pianist until the war had interrupted his studies. By now a career of the sort he'd once hoped for was impossible. He had only to touch the mess piano to know how much skill had slipped away from him. Kokke poured coffee for

Löwenherz and grinned at him provocatively. Some people said the young Berliner was an agent provocateur in the pay of the Gestapo. Löwenherz suspected that to be a story Kokke himself had circulated to provide an excuse for constant criticism of the regime and its methods and equipment.

"Here's to our Knight's Crosses," toasted Löwenherz with coffee.

"I'll not drink to yours," said Kokke, smiling. "If the bloody thing isn't on its way by now, it must be because they've decided to stop awarding them."

Löwenherz bowed gratefully at the compliment. He had gained more than enough victories for the coveted Knight's Cross to be at his neck. His seniority and experience deserved a promotion but the Führer's birthday, a traditional date for promotions to be announced, had come and gone.

The pilots drank their coffee in silence and Löwenherz held his napkin carefully in his free hand lest a drip of coffee fall upon his gleaming white summer jacket. Somehow Löwenherz always had the answer and the technical data to back it up. It was amazing how he found time to handle the office routine and paper work that fell to him as Staffel leader, as well as reading and remembering all the intelligence reports, doing the same blind flying minimum that he had ordered for his Staffel, consistently winning the clay pigeon stakes as well as maintaining a string of girl friends from Brussels to Wilhelmshaven.

Finally it was little Beer who spoke. "The Knight's Cross is always conferrred by Hermann Göring in person?"

"A visit to Karinhall." Löwenherz nodded. "And the cauliflower for the Knight's Cross means an audience with the Führer."

"With the knives and forks they give you a two-bedroom apartment at Berchtesgaden," said Kokke mischievously.

"It's all right for you two to talk of oak leaves and swords," said Beer. "You, Herr Oberleutnant, have twenty-eight confirmed victories, and Kokke has twelve, but as yet I have none and might never get one."

"Cheer up," said Kokke. "We all have the Iron Cross on our pocket."

"That makes it even worse," said Beer. "How do I explain that mine was awarded for doing twenty flights without ever catching sight of a *Tommi?*"

"Perhaps you'll get a chance tonight if the weather clears," said Löwenherz.

Beer pinched his face and refused to be cheered up. "Each night the controller sends up his most successful crews first. They get first crack at the Englishmen while the rest of us spend all day practicing instrument flying and all night playing chess."

"It's necessary for the defense of the homeland that the best crews are put into battle as soon as the first radar contact is made," said Löwenherz.

"Beer thinks the war has been arranged solely for his sport," said Kokke.

"You must remember that these bombers are tearing the hearts out of our cities," said Löwenherz. "Ask Kokke if he prefers the best crews to go up first when it's his town of Berlin that's being bombed, or ask poor old Oberfeldwebel Krugelheim, my chief mechanic, whose wife was killed in Stuttgart last April."

Kokke added, "Or Leutnant Klimke, my radar man, whose wife and three children were killed in a bombing raid on Duisburg last Christmas, one day before he went on leave."

"All I want to do," protested Beer, "is to help shoot the murdering bastards out of the sky."

"Don't be downhearted," said Löwenherz. "You will soon have your opportunity." He finished his coffee and wiped his mouth carefully with his napkin. He stood up and after nodding a good day to them he eyed Beer's black leather zipper jacket, breeches and high boots.

"You're not thinking of flying in those boots, Leutnant Beer."

"No, sir," said Beer.

"Good. There is a regulation about it. The Luftwaffe medical service has informed High Command that foot injuries are very difficult to attend to if the injured crewman is wearing close-fitting high boots."

"I read your memo, sir."

"Excellent; then that's clear. Good morning, gentlemen." He looked at his newspaper with the remains of the wasp spattered across the headline in ugly brown stains. He didn't pick it up.

They both nodded good-bye to him.

"*Kaffeeklatsch*," said Beer. "Patronizing bastard."

"May I quote you?" said Kokke.

"It's all right for a *Krautjunker* like him," said Beer.

"Son of a baron, enormous estates in East Prussia well out of the reach of the R.A.F. . . ."

"That's why he's worried about those Russian airplanes," said Kokke. "You know, the mechanics across on Staffel number three have got a nice fiddle going. When the long-range Aunty Jus fly in with spares, the crews bring tins of caviar from Odessa to swap for bottles of Dutch schnapps. They say that that tall Oberfeldwebel with the motorcycle is making a fortune out of it. The other day the mechanics opened a tin of caviar out there on the dispersal apron. They were sitting around in the sun eating it, when Löwenherz walks up. The Oberfeldwebel gives him a big salute and spreads a great heap of caviar on a biscuit and offers it to him. 'Beluga caviar, sir,' he says. Löwenherz looks down his nose at it and says, 'Never mind what kind of caviar it is, Oberfeldwebel. Have you washed your hands?' "

Kokke laughed heartily at his own story but Beer didn't. "Prussian bastard," said Beer. "And that damned white jacket he wears as though this was a peacetime training school. Did you notice him looking at your dirty shirt? I bet there'll be another reminder about officers' appearance circulated next week."

"Screw him," said Kokke.

"He's always wiping his mouth and fingers," said Beer. "He makes me feel like I'm suffering from some sort of contagious disease."

"You are," said Kokke. "It's called poverty."

"Well, you know what I mean. And I hate men who wear cologne. He's obsessed with cleanliness; he's always in that shower whenever I want to use it."

"Which isn't often," said Kokke. "Well, that's probably because he's terrified of getting a dose of clap from all those girls he runs around with."

"One of these days, Kokke, you're going to get yourself arrested saying things like that."

"Yes; well, I can always count on you to help. Fancy telling Löwenherz that stuff about the East Front."

"A man should be prepared to live with the statements he makes," said Beer.

"You know, Beer, sometimes I think you would have made a bloody wonderful pope."

As Löwenherz reached the foyer of the mess half a dozen air crew officers were arriving for their noon meal. He nodded curtly to each of them and collected his peaked cap from the orderly in the cloakroom. In the foyer there were soft leather chairs and low tables with copies of *Luftwelt, Signal* and *Der Adler* scattered on it. Sitting nervously on the edge of his armchair was Blessing, the man in charge of civilian labor. Sitting next to him, leaning well back and reading the *Deutsche Zeitung,* there was an elderly man in civilian clothes. Blessing tapped the other man on the knee. He lowered his paper and looked up. Blessing nodded toward Löwenherz. The man was too old to be local civilian labor, and his clothes were a little too good and of German cut. My God, thought Löwenherz, it must be a relative of some recent air crew casualty. The man reached for a soft hat and leather briefcase, got to his feet and approached Löwenherz, with a sad smile.

"Oberleutnant Victor von Löwenherz?" said the man. The suit he was wearing was of prewar quality but had been darned carefully at the corner of the pocket. There were three pens in his waistcoat and under it he was wearing a gray home-knitted sweater. The man's eyes stared calmly at him through gold-rimmed spectacles. His eyes were moist, as old men's eyes become, but they were as active and alert as they had ever been. His face was heavily lined and had the mauve tints that afflict the skin of heavy drinkers. His stiff white collar was of an ancient style and the knot of his tie was secured by a gold pin. A doctor or lawyer most people would have guessed him to be, and rightly. Blessing saluted carefully while the man extended a hand to Löwenherz. It was while they were shaking hands that the man said "Heil Hitler" in a disinterested voice that he also used for commenting on the weather. He smiled bleakly and introduced himself. "Feldwebel Doktor Hans Starkhof of AST Nederlands, Group IIIL."

The man's eyes flickered shortsightedly behind his spectacles and yet Löwenherz wondered whether this myopia —like his hesitations and eyebrows raised in surprise— was a ruse feigned for his own purposes. The man watched for Löwenherz's reactions to his low rank and the manner of its coupling to his doctorate, and to the Nazi greeting with his soft civilian handshake. He watched too for the reaction to the word AST—the Abwehr, or Military Intelligence, office: the technique of surprise was one that Starkhof had perfected many years ago as a criminal lawyer in Hamburg. There was always work for a criminal lawyer in Hamburg and a surprise immediately upon meeting could often help a case to a quick conclusion. From Löwenherz came no reaction, but Starkhof still had a card to play.

"Perhaps I should introduce ..." He half turned toward Blessing.

"Feldwebel Blessing I already know," said Löwenherz coldly.

"Ah yes, precisely, which is why I should tell you that Blessing is employed by R.S.H.A. and has a SIPO rank of Untersturmführer."

"May I see your identity papers?" asked Löwenherz.

"Alas, we carry none except a Wehrpass, but you may phone my office if you are worried."

"I am not worried," said Löwenherz.

"Excellent." He gestured toward the entrance. "We'll talk as we walk," he suggested. "You'll perhaps feel more comfortable in the open air." He put on his trilby hat and stepped out into the sunshine. The three men walked down the long gravel drive, their shadows sharply drawn on the path by the warm sun. When he realized that Löwenherz had no intention of speaking first, the man said, "There has been a theft of some documents, Herr Oberleutnant." He paused but still nothing came from Löwenherz. "Some secret documents," he added. "We are in no doubt about the identity of the thief."

"I am sure," said Löwenherz, "that you have not come here to boast to me of your success."

"Precisely," said the man in civilian clothes. "We should value your frankness and aid."

"You will in any case be treated to the former," said Löwenherz. "As to the latter, until you are more forthcoming who knows what it might entail?"

"Dear comrade Löwenherz," said Starkhof. "You must be patient with an old man. Secret documents have been stolen and they must be recovered."

"This is the Medical Center, Herr Doktor," interrupted Blessing.

"They were stolen from this building," Starkhof explained to Löwenherz. "We know the thief but lack the ..."

"*Corpus delicti,*" supplied Löwenherz.

"Precisely," said Starkhof. He turned to his colleague. "The *corpus delicti*, Blessing, that's what you must find."

They stood on the road between the farmlike headquarters buildings. Everywhere was quiet, for the true working day of this night fighter station had not yet begun. A lorry

rattled noisily through the main gate, loaded with oil
drums. Outside the Pay Section a line of men had formed
and assumed the relaxed attitudes with which servicemen
accept inevitable delay. From the Medical Center two
orderlies were bringing chairs and piling them together in
the sunshine, while from inside came the sound of buckets
and mops and tuneless singing.

Starkhof said, "The thief first misappropriated the
documents. It was later that he stole them."

"If that means that someone hid them behind a cupboard and went back for them later, why not say so more
clearly?"

Eagerly Blessing said, "The papers were secreted behind
a cupboard and the thief did return later. How did you
know that?"

"Deduction," said Löwenherz. "And I'll tell you another deduction too."

"If you . . ."

"Comrade Untersturmführer Blessing." The old man
interrupted them. He raised a finger at Blessing. "My
witness, I believe." He smiled; Blessing nodded.

The old man said, "My dear Löwenherz. We should
both be most interested in your deduction."

Löwenherz said, "You knew where the documents
were, and yet did not retrieve them. Then you hoped to
catch the thief taking them to some other place . . ."

"Or other party." Starkhof nodded. "Excellent, Oberleutnant."

"You do not have the documents, therefore you did not
catch the thief in . . ." Löwenherz paused.

"You were about to say *flagrante delicto*, my good
friend. Do say it." In a quick aside to Blessing the old
man added, "Red-handed, my dear Blessing." Blessing
smiled.

It was difficult to be sure whether the man was trying
to make a fool of Löwenherz or of Blessing. When
Löwenherz walked forward again the others kept by his
side.

Löwenherz said, "Since Blessing pointed out the Medical Center to you, I deduce that you have not seen it
before. So it was"—Löwenherz feigned difficulty with
the S.S. rank and pronounced it in a precise and ponder-
ous manner—"Untersturmführer Blessing who set a trap
for the thief but was outwitted."

"*Sunt lacrimae rerum,*" said the man to Blessing. "Tears

are a part of life, as I said to Blessing at the time."
Blessing scowled.

"Is it someone on my Staffel?" said Löwenherz.

"There you go again," said Starkhof. "Straight to the
heart of the problem. Yes, it's someone on your Staffel."

"Unteroffizier Himmel," supplied Blessing.

"Young Himmel," said Löwenherz. "Why, that's impossible. I'd stake my life on Himmel."

"Is that your considered opinion, Herr Oberleutnant?"
asked Blessing weightily. They walked in silence for a
moment, then Starkhof said, "Of course not; the Herr
Oberleutnant was speaking merely as a comrade in arms.
Such sentiments nobly become front line soldiers."

"Would you stake your life on this thief Himmel?"
persisted Blessing.

"My dear Blessing," said Starkhof. "The Oberleutnant
often does exactly that. For isn't Himmel one of his most
experienced pilots and thus essential to the safety of the
whole Staffel?"

"Young Himmel is a fine pilot, hard-working and loyal," said Löwenherz.

Blessing said, "You went to breakfast at a few minutes
to ten?"

Löwenherz said, "I spoke with you." He said it quickly
and defensively, and was angry at himself.

"And you gave Himmel your dog?"

"Himmel took my dog to the dispersal."

"Did Himmel often walk your dog?" asked Blessing.
He smiled at Löwenherz and filled the simple question
with complex innuendo.

"The dog chooses carefully the people with whom it
will walk," said Löwenherz.

"Himmel was one of the chosen people?" said Blessing.

"You seem better provided with malice than with evidence," said Löwenherz. "Perhaps it's merely that Himmel is easier to apprehend than the real thief, who seems
to have eluded you so effortlessly when the crime was
committed."

"Dear comrade Löwenherz," said Starkhof wearily.
"You are not the judge in this case and, even if you were,
it is not Blessing who would be on trial. We have asked
your assistance merely to recover the documents which we
believe—with excellent reason—Himmel stole from the
Medical Center."

"How can I help?"

"Thank you, Herr Oberleutnant. That is what I was hoping that you would say."

"Earlier," added Blessing.

"Blessing," sighed the older man, "there are times when I believe that making witnesses hostile is your sole creative endeavor." He turned again to Löwenherz. "Last night Unteroffizier Himmel had this document in his bedside locker. This morning when Blessing arrived at his billet to arrest him he was not there. Neither was the document. The only person he met this morning was you. . . ."

"What do you suspect Himmel did?"

"There are many possibilities: he might have learned it by heart and then destroyed it; he might have buried it so that he could return to retrieve it; or he might have handed it to an accomplice."

"You don't seriously think Himmel is a spy?"

Starkhof shrugged.

Löwenherz said, "How did he gain access to this document?"

"By accident, we think. He was due for a routine medical check on the fourteenth of the month. Eighteen N.C.O.s attended the medical section that morning. Himmel was tenth; when he saw the Medical Officer to have his card signed, the document was on the desk."

"Sounds circumstantial," said Löwenherz.

"I don't think so," said Blessing.

"I rather agree with Löwenherz," said Starkhof. "The way the evidence is at present it would be difficult to put a very good case."

"Impossible to put a case at all unless you mean against Blessing for incompetence."

"That's rather severe, Herr Oberleutnant," said Starkhof. "But I must say, Blessing, you will come out of this looking rather foolish, and your chiefs are probably expecting you to prove that a young SIPO officer can run circles around an antique Abwehr Feldwebel like me."

Blessing said, "I will take that chance."

"There's the Medical Officer too," said Starkhof reflectively. "He was undoubtedly negligent. Secret papers should go into the safe." He noted Löwenherz's face. "Never mind; as long as the culprit is caught and the papers recovered there will perhaps be no need to bring any of Himmel's colleagues or superior officers into this. You hear me, Herr Oberleutnant?"

"I do."

"Splendid. Young Blessing and I searched along the

perimeter this morning—in the hedge, in the ditch—and then retraced our steps on the far side of the fence. Nothing there, I'm afraid. I'm glad to see you're concerned about the fate of the doctor. A charming man, I thought, something of an aristocrat, one might almost think." He smiled. "If it wasn't for that unfortunate Austrian accent."

"Where are you taking me?"

"Taking you? My goodness, we're not taking you anywhere, Oberleutnant. You have your duties for the Third Reich just as we do, but if you can spare us a moment, the Kommandeur was kind enough to take an interest in our problem."

Löwenherz looked carefully into the man's wrinkled face. Starkhof stared back coolly with an amused contempt for all the world. On the estates in Prussia Löwenherz had seen the same easygoing manner among the senior farmhands and foresters. It was the quality one looked for when employing or promoting such men. Some policemen had it and so did high court judges. It came from dealing with many people and being able to predict their reactions well in advance. It came from the certainty that no one would ever disobey the suggestions that made orders unnecessary.

They walked into the Operations Building, Blessing in the lead. The Kommandeur must have seen them through the window for he stepped out to greet them. He was dressed in boots, breeches and gray uniform shirt. At his throat dangled the coveted Knight's Cross. "My good Untersturmführer Blessing," he said, "and Herr Doktor Starkhof."

"Heil Hitler," said Blessing.

"Heil Hitler," said the Kommandeur.

"Heil Hitler," said Starkhof, doffing his hat cheerfully to the Kommandeur.

Major Peter Redenbacher put on his jacket and buttoned it. He was thirty-three years old: elderly by fighter pilot standards. He commanded Löwenherz's Staffel of ten aircraft plus two other Staffeln that shared Kroonsdijk. He was an impressive man in spite of his battle-scarred appearance. His shortness of stature and some false teeth were common among those who had grown up in the blockaded Germany of the First World War. His powerful arms were an inheritance from his furnace worker father in Essen, and his clear blue eyes and full-lipped mouth from his hard-working *Mutti*. The thick muscular legs were developed in his teens by sixty-eight-kilometer week-end cycle rides to a D.L.V. gliding club. Most weekends he had come no nearer to a flight than hauling the winch, positioning the club's sole glider or helping to build a second one. The small scar visible under his closely cropped blond hair dated from a heavy landing at Was-serkuppe, on the bare high plateau of the Rhön. That year he had won a minor prize in the National Gliding Championships. The permanently arched little finger of his left hand had come under a Communist boot after holding a Nazi standard aloft in Essen in 1927. The sustained hatred that made him a killer was born in March 1923, when he saw a French officer of the occupying army strike his father and uncle for not removing their hats as a military funeral passed. The cold confident gaze dated from 1934, when he was one of twenty chosen from four thousand applicants to go to the Deutsche Verkehrsflieger-schule at Brunswick. This airline pilots' school was a secret training center for the Nazi air force. When the Luftwaffe was officially born in 1935 Peter Redenbacher was stunting a Bücker Jungmann biplane above the heads of Hitler, Göring, the foreign press and a deliriously happy German crowd. His forearm was scarred badly because there was no doctor in the Spanish village of San Antonio when a Republican Rata shot his He51 down in flames there in November 1936. He landed by parachute in the village. The Russian pilot did a low pass over the rooftops and waved to Redenbacher from the open cock-pit: a big smile and an ancient leather flying helmet, and low enough to see that the pilot was a woman. No one would believe him, until in January 1937 a high-ranking Russian woman was shot down near Madrid.

It was at the Schleissheim Fighter Pilot School near Munich that a pupil turned without power on takeoff, thus writing off an old He50 biplane that would have floated unharmed to the ground hands off. It was the worst crash of all. The pupil died and Redenbacher spent six weeks in hospital. Although he would never admit it, even to his wife, still to this day in cold weather the base of his spine ached like the very devil.

His four victories in Spain, fourteen on the East Front and thirty-two French, R.A.F. and U.S. airplanes downed had brought him a Knight's Cross with oak leaves and made him something of a celebrity. He had been shot down over the sea by an American P-47 the previous May, and had spent four miserable hours bobbing from wavetop to wavetop perched on a one-man dinghy. He was too old to take that sort of punishment without suffering aftereffects. A medical board had detected his symptoms in spite of Redenbacher's denials. He had been advised that a staff job was to be his. Meanwhile he flew every sortie possible.

When he went to spend the rest of his life flying a desk he'd asked that Löwenherz should take over as Gruppenkommandeur. He had been one of his pupils at the fighter school, and one of his best. Redenbacher was glad to have a young aristocrat like him in his Gruppe because, for Redenbacher, National Socialism meant the end of classes and social groupings. During all the wars of the last century only a hundred or so German N.C.O.s had been made officers. In this war, under National Socialism, thousands and thousands of rankers had so far been commissioned. There were, at that moment, twelve Nazi generals who had come from the ranks. It made Redenbacher very proud to be a member of the Wehrmacht. It had become a simple matter of being a good Nazi.

Redenbacher looked at the men across the room. The young SIPO officer was a good Nazi. There was no other explanation. Only a dedicated young officer would be happy to do his duty as a lowly Feldwebel engaged on menial tasks. The old Abwehr man was a more doubtful case. Why had he never been promoted to officer rank? That shrewd old swine, like too many men in today's Germany, guessed Redenbacher, survived by evading conflict. Major Redenbacher walked round his desk, but he did not sit down behind it, neither did he invite the others to sit. There were in any case only two chairs. The white-painted office was bare and austere: only a framed portrait of the Führer, one of Reichsmarschall Göring, and a small photo of Redenbacher and his wife framed by Nazi banners on their wedding day.

The Major's tabletop was clear and efficient. A gleaming piston top from the wrecked Heinkel biplane stood near the blotter. It would have made a fine ashtray for anyone who dared to smoke here. Instead it was a paperweight but there were no papers awaiting attention; the trays were empty, inkwells full and sharpened pencils placed to hand. The Major picked one up and tapped the tabletop reflectively. He raised his eyes to Löwenherz. "What do you make of Himmel, Victor?"

Löwenherz came correctly to attention, his white-topped cap clutched tight under his arm. "He has six

years' service, sir. Service record excellent." Löwenherz
related Himmel's service record. It was easy to remember,
for so much of it was the same as his own.

"But is he loyal, Victor? Is he a true National Socialist?"

"Yes, Herr Major."

Blessing came to a noisy attention. "With respect, Herr
Major, loyalty is something best left to my department."

"I'm sure my Oberleutnant had a reason for testifying
to Unteroffizier Himmel's loyalty," said Redenbacher. He
nodded to Löwenherz.

"Himmel was one of the pilots assigned to the Führer's
Kurier flight in March 1941 for three months. All personnel were cleared for security by Kommandostab R.F.-S.S."

For a moment there was a complete silence.

"Why the devil didn't you say so, man?" said Starkhof
angrily. Redenbacher admired the way in which Löwenherz had caused the old man to lose his careful temper.

"No one asked me, Herr Doktor."

"That was over two years ago," said Blessing.

"If his clearance had been changed recently, I would
have been informed," said Redenbacher.

"Even our Kommandostab security people are not infal-
lible," said Blessing, taking folded papers from his pocket.
"Let me read you a part of a letter written by Himmel. . . ." There was a knock at the door. "Come in," said
Redenbacher.

Leutnant Kokke entered. He was the Gruppe Technical
Officer in addition to his other duties. In his hand he was
carrying neatly drawn training schedules for the coming
twelve-week period.

"I'm sorry, sir," said Kokke. "I will come back." He ran
a hand through his black untidy hair.

"Come in, Kokke," said Redenbacher. Kokke was an
excellent example of the new order. From the melting pot
into which National Socialism had poured the old Germany had come men like himself and Kokke. In the old days
they would have had no chance to become professional
officers. Kokke pretended that he would sooner be a
musician, but this cut no ice with Redenbacher, who
recognized him as a man born to be a pilot as few men
were. He still had much to learn—there was no shortcut
to experience—but Kokke might be a great flier of tomorrow's Reich. Even now—Staffelkapitäns excepted—he
was one of the best pilots on the Gruppe. He had top
grades in navigation, instrument flying and engine: theory

and practical. He reminded Redenbacher of the oil-stained old pilots home fresh from the first war, with their medals, tall stories, hard drinking and acid *Galgenhumor*.

Many people thought that Redenbacher was too soft on Kokke, but this was because he knew that Löwenherz kept a tight rein on him. He looked at them now: young Löwenherz in his white jacket, standing primly with his cap under his arm like a fashion plate, and Kokke, relaxed and smiling, with his shirt bulging under his short air force jacket and bread crumbs on his tie.

"Do you know what brings these officers here today, Kokke?" asked Redenbacher.

"No, Herr Major. Is it something in connection with the ablutions?"

"No," said Redenbacher. "The man you have in the past known as Feldwebel Blessing, overseer of the local foreign labor, is an officer of the Sicherheitspolizei."

*"Ach so!"* said the satanic Kokke with a smile. "Congratulations, Blessing." He said it as though Blessing too should be surprised at his new status.

Blessing clicked his heels.

"Unteroffizier Himmel has stolen some documents," said Major Redenbacher. "At least it is alleged so. He spoke with the Herr Oberleutnant here shortly before breakfast. You were seated by the window. Kokke. Perhaps you saw Himmel this morning."

"He spoke with Herr Oberleutnant Löwenherz."

"I have just said so, but did he meet anyone else?"

"Didn't he meet Blessing?"

"No. I was waiting to arrest him at his barracks," said Blessing.

"But didn't I see you tiptoeing through the woods, Blessing? I would have sworn it was you. Your ears, if you don't mind my saying so, and a huge fat arse very reminiscent of yours came past the mess window just about ten o'clock. I turned to my friend Beer and said, 'Tell me if my eyes deceive me, Beer, but doesn't that look very like the big protruding ears and great arse of our friend Feldwebel Blessing who cleans the ablutions?' At the time of course I had no way of knowing that Blessing was an officer."

When Kokke stopped speaking Major Redenbacher said nothing; he flicked open the training schedules that Kokke had drawn neatly in colored inks. This inquiry was distasteful to him. They all waited for him to comment. The gossip on the Staffel said that Redenbacher had not been

truly well since his ditching last May. Some said that he
would soon be posted to a less active unit. In which case,
thought Kokke, that humorless stuffed shirt Löwenherz
would probably take over the Gruppe. Ah well, he was a
fine pilot, bloody efficient and fair-minded, so it could be
worse. He'd never replace Redenbacher in Kokke's eyes
though. The Major was a tough, barnstorming veteran
who would break every rule in the book for his men.
What was more, unlike Löwenherz, Redenbacher had a
sense of humor. Redenbacher still said nothing.

The old Abwehr man said, "If you did speak to Himmel, you may as well tell me, Blessing."

Blessing was indignant. "You are not taking this
clown's words seriously?"

Kokke said, "Don't you remember, Blessing, the dog
tried to bite you?"

"If you saw Himmel with the dog, say so," said the old
man severely to Blessing.

"Of course he saw them," said Kokke. "Look at his
boots, look for yourself." Even Major Redenbacher
looked away from the schedules and stared down at Blessing's grass-wet boots.

"That's where the Oberleutnant's dog peed on his boots.
You know how that dog pees everywhere, and Blessing
was mistaken for a tree by the careless beast."

Blessing knew that he was being provoked by Kokke
but he kept his temper and even managed a ghost of a
smile. It was important that Redenbacher should not think
him vindictive or precipitate.

Starkhof took off his spectacles in a gesture which had
once been a part of his courtroom technique. "Did Himmel have a parcel? It was foolscap size with a brown
cover."

"It's difficult to remember," admitted Kokke. "As I
said, there was so much activity."

"Thank you, Leutnant Kokke," said Starkhof.

"Blessing," said Redenbacher, "what evidence do you
have against Unteroffizier Himmel?"

Blessing was still holding Himmel's letter. He said, "This
is a letter from Himmel to his father dated May 27,
1943." He skimmed through it mumbling, " 'Weekend . . .
well and happy . . . thanks for the homemade bread . . .'
Ah, here we are!" Having found the place, Blessing's voice
changed to one of stern officialdom. " 'Do not be alarmed
when the English terror bombers get through because that
too is part of the Führer's plan. Grandmama and Cousin

Paul had to die and our cities must be laid waste as part of a great strategic scheme that my poor brain cannot guess at. It's the very measure of the genius of our highest commanders that they can allow the *Amis* and *Tommis* to drop bombs on us while they lose the war. What fools the Russians must be to think that they are winning the war merely because they are advancing on all fronts. What simpletons the British were to fall into the trap of destroying the Afrika Korps and capturing the whole of North Africa when all the time our beloved Führer had planned it thus. Trust the Führer, he is full of surprises.' "

Blessing looked up triumphantly.

"Well?" he said. The words had brought a terrible silence upon the group.

"Well what, Blessing?" said Kokke. "Wasn't it a noble letter?"

"The traitorous swine," said Blessing. "The sarcasm stands out a mile."

"What sarcasm?" said Kokke. "Did you detect sarcasm?" he asked Starkhof.

"Styles of writing can be deceptive," fielded the old man.

"Perhaps you'd better point out which passages seem preposterous and quite beyond your belief, Blessing," said Kokke.

Blessing looked again at the letter. No one spoke. Aircraft were doing circuits and bumps. One approached down the funnel, slid on to runway 25 and, at the very moment of landing, gunned the throttle and climbed away into the circuit again. The sudden noise of the motors being opened up to full power shook the windowpanes. Three more did it before Major Redenbacher said, "I think you'd better tell me what other evidence you have against Himmel."

Blessing came to attention again. "The stolen document was in his bedside locker last night and the previous night."

"How do you know that?"

"My staff reported it."

"I see," said Redenbacher. "How many of your civilian staff work for the Sicherheitspolizei?"

"Respectfully, Herr Major, I could not say."

"But they have keys to bedside lockers?"

"Yes, Herr Major."

"My quarters are cleaned by your local civilians, Blessing. Do they have a key for my bedside table?" Blessing did not answer. Redenbacher said, "What about this Operational H.Q. Do your staff examine my files and desk here in this office?"

"Not regularly, Herr Major."

"Only when you instruct them to do so, eh, Blessing?"

"With respect, Herr Major, we must confine the conversation to the arrest of the spy Himmel. I request permission to take him to the Wehrmacht Prison in The Hague where a case against him will be prepared."

" 'Be prepared'?" echoed Redenbacher indignantly. "This is Nazi Germany, 1943, Blessing, not some damned little South American republic. We work by the rule of law, not by the odds and ends of guesswork that you assemble when you've slept too late on the morning you should have made your arrest. My soldiers are entitled to freedom and bread and the rule of law. If you want to deprive my combat station at front line readiness of one of its most skilled pilots, you must provide the proper work from your side."

"With respect, Herr Major, fighting Communist spies and traitors is also front line work. It is your duty to let me take Himmel to prison, where he belongs."

"I don't need you to remind me of my duty, Blessing," said Redenbacher. "As for fighting Communists, I was doing that in the streets of Essen when you were still wetting your bed."

"You are refusing to let the prisoner be taken away?" said Blessing.

"No, no, no," interrupted Starkhof. "The Herr Major has made his position very clear, Blessing. And a very reasonable position it is too, if I may say so." He nodded at Major Redenbacher and smiled. "He feels that you are going off at half cock and wants to prevent you from making a fool of yourself. He's advising you to procure more evidence, prepare your case more thoroughly, and I agree with him. At this moment I really couldn't support you, Blessing. I think you'd better release this fellow Himmel, on the Kommandeur's assurance that he's kept confined to the base."

Starkhof had judged his timing nicely. His previous silence enabled him to sound like an arbitrator (although he would have said "like a judge").

It took Blessing a few seconds' silence to realize that he had been outmaneuvered by the wily old Abwehr man.

"Heil Hitler," Blessing called loudly, stamping into the salute.

"Heil Hitler," replied everyone in the room, but Kokke's voice was shriller and louder than the others. Blessing left before the old man, who took his time shaking the hand of each of the airmen. As he got to the door he turned and smiled to them. "You young gentlemen have had your fun with Blessing, and it might well result in Himmel's dossier becoming my sole responsibility. If it does, gentlemen, then when I return we must talk more seriously than we have today. We will start afresh. And you must be careful of what you tell me, for as we lawyers say, *'Decipi quam fallere est tutius.'* " He smiled again. "Herr Oberleutnant Löwenherz will translate." He closed the door.

"It's safer to be deceived than to deceive," translated Löwenherz.

"What a character!" said Kokke.

"He's an Abwehr man," said Löwenherz. "There's no love lost between them and the SIPO."

Redenbacher said, "Victor, do you think that he precipitated the arrest of young Himmel just to take over control of this case by those very means?"

"Yes, sir, I do," said Löwenherz. "I realize now that my conversation with him on the way here was largely dedicated to making me antagonistic to Blessing."

"The old fox," said Redenbacher. "If I thought he was deliberately sabotaging the work of the Sicherheitspolizei I'd report him."

"I wouldn't help those bastards get their hands on my worst enemy," muttered Kokke.

# 5

THERE were many inhabitants of Altgarten who could
remember it a half century ago. By that time the cramped
little houses built for the men who made the railway had
become slums and although each doorstep had gleamed
white and the curtains in each window were clean and
pressed, few people then would have wished to walk
through the town after dark. There was not enough work
at the gasworks to help Altgarten's poor and the unemployed stood on street corners and waited for their wives
to return from scrubbing and washing and cooking in
other persons' homes. Nor did the land provide for the
desperate. In those days a wet spring would inevitably
mean a hungry winter.

Now in 1943 the Burgomaster could look across a
thriving town where never a hand was idle, although many
of its menfolk were in far parts of the world. He saw
them in the corridors of the Rathaus, for the servicemen
came here to have their leave documents endorsed and
signed. Young Tornow had just come home on leave. He
was now a Kapitänleutnant. He looked elegant in his
dark-blue naval uniform with gold braid rings on his cuff
and the snappy white-topped summer cap that U-boat
captains favored. Tornow's father owned the Altgarten
printing works and had servants, a fine house and a fast
Mercedes car.

"Hello, Tornow," said the Burgomaster, passing him on
his way to lunch at Frenzel's. "This is fine weather for you
sailors, eh?"

Hans Tornow had grown used to such remarks. He had
long since given up explaining that he was an accountant
in the Paymaster's Department at Hamburg, a grim old
building with tiny windows and inadequate lights. As for

66

the ocean, he hated those occasions when he had to take cash to ships anchored in the Elbe, for even the slightest swell made him a little queasy. "Yes, Herr Bürgermeister, it's sailors' weather," said Tornow.

All Altgarten envied those citizens who had chosen that weekend to begin their holiday, for the weather promised to be superb. In spite of the thunder the black clouds had passed and it was sunny. No rain had fallen upon the town for over three weeks. The air was crisp and dry. For the last week the humidity readings had not risen above forty-five percent and had gone as low as thirty. The old center of Altgarten was principally of wooden construction and its timber was dry and contracted.

Winds up to fifteen miles an hour fan the flames of a large fire but a faster-moving wind can make even a small fire into a disaster. This day the wind came in gusts from the potato fields and orchards and the strongest gusts measured eighteen miles an hour. As a fire hazard the town of Altgarten had few equals.

The buildings in Dorfstrasse were parched and dusty and the once-red swastika flags that rippled in the wind had faded to a light pink in the sunlight. Many of the vehicles moving along the busy roads were horse drawn and the horses hurried as they neared the end of the journey. From Frenzel's a considerate drayman brought water for the two gray cart horses that had delivered the beer, and watched them as they drank greedily.

Fire fascinates men and fire services never run short of recruits. Johannes Ilfa had always wanted to be a fireman. It was an ambition interrupted at the age of twelve by a short-lived desire to enter the priesthood. In 1935, aged eighteen, Johannes had entered the Altgarten fire service as a trainee. A hard-working and intelligent son of a Bierkeller owner, he had risen in rank until in 1942 he had been selected for attachment to the Cologne brigade and had been on duty there during the night of May 30, 1942, when the town was attacked by almost one thousand R.A.F. bombers. In this and other attacks Johannes had seen terrible sights. In fact he had offered comfort and last rites to more people than had any priest in Altgarten. In one raid the previous winter a shell splinter had punctured his lung. For one month he was in hospital and then he was posted back to Altgarten. In smoke it pained him to breathe even now but he never mentioned this.

For Ilfa, membership in any Nazi organization was out of the question. He could still only see the Nazis as the coarse Bavarian toughs who frequented his father's bar and staged fights in order to get away without paying their bill. If he must be a part of their war, then the fire service provided him with a way of fighting only the evils of it.

He was a battle-scarred veteran of twenty-six, a dark-eyed man with short hair which he kept carefully brushed and a large moustache of which he was quite proud. His teeth were even and white and so much water had kept his hands white too and lately his rank had enabled them to become soft like those of a girl. But his body was hard and his physical condition was excellent except for his lung. Over short distances his energy was exceptional and he had won many a bet to race younger firemen to the top of the practice tower with the hook ladders.

He was a Gruppenführer, the senior man on the finest and newest engine in Altgarten. He sat beside the driver and directed his seven-man crew as they extricated pedestrians from under buses, pulled the electrocuted off live cables, sawed free young children trapped in railings and dealt with chimney fires and hayrick blazes.

Today the fire station was cool and quiet and the sun glinted on the polished brass hose fittings and on the engines. Respirators, gloves and steel helmets were lined up neatly. Under each hung the metal disks with the letters that enable messengers, hosemen, attack troopers and water troopers to be recognized in the smoke and heat of a fire.

So far there had been no alarm. Johannes Ilfa was lecturing the full eighteen-man complement of the Altgarten fire brigade upon the various types of R.A.F. bombs. On the classroom table there were dummy examples of the small phosphorous canister, the 30-pound phosphorus bomb, the 250-pound liquid fire bomb (benzol and rubber) and the hexagonal 4-pound incendiary stick bombs.

"The 30-pound phosphorus bomb is 810 millimeters long. You'll recognize it by its dark-red color and a broad light-red band around the body," read Johannes Ilfa aloud from an instruction book. He smiled. "Unless of course it goes off."

Some of the firemen laughed a short quiet nervous laugh. "Pieces of flaming phosphorus will fly thirty meters or more and will keep floating down for fifteen seconds, so don't run toward it too quickly. If you get the smallest piece of flaming phosphorus anywhere upon your clothing you must immediately remove that clothing and douse it thoroughly in water. Then scrape it all off, otherwise it will ignite again as soon as it comes out of the water."

A fireman asked a question. "How do you do that in the middle of an air raid?"

"I don't write these handbooks, I just read them." He paused "Just don't get any of the damned stuff on you." He rubbed his moustache nervously. He'd seen phosphorus bombs and they horrified him.

Some of the students wrote in their notebooks. Any one of them was liable to be assigned to one of the fire services in the Ruhr, in which case he would need to know what the war was like.

"That's the end of the lecture," said Johannes Ilfa, looking at his wristwatch. The senior fireman called the class to attention and when Ilfa had gone he dismissed them for lunch. Seven of the men lived sufficiently near to eat at home and they hurried to the cycle shed to collect their bikes.

The fire station was at the unfashionable end of Mönchensstrasse. Two young Waffen S.S. soldiers cycled past it on their way to the shops of Dorfstrasse. The Scheske twins were just eighteen and until last month they had never been more than five miles from their native town of Insterburg on the Pregel in a distant part of East Prussia. Here in the extreme west of the homeland, so near to Paris and Brussels and Amsterdam, about which they had read in their schoolbooks not long ago, there was so much to see. Even this cycle ride into Altgarten to fetch some razor blades for the guard commander held promise enough for both boys to be carrying their new Exacta cameras.

They were shy lads and did not respond to the teasing their Slavic name drew from the race-conscious S.S. men stationed at the Wald Hotel camp. Everything about the new Nazi Germany was an adventure. Together they had been the mainstay of the Hitler Jugend choir back home and at party celebrations they were invariably chosen to augment the S.A. men's choir. Alas, at their camp in Altgarten there was no choir. Mausi had suggested that they find out if there was a choir at the Liebefrau church, but luckily Hannes was in time to prevent him making a complete fool of himself by suggesting such a thing in front of other S.S. men.

So now they sang lustily as they cycled through the

town. It was the chorus that often ended the party meetings back home.

> "When the S.S. and the S.A.
>   March up in formation. Taratata!
> Firm is the stride.
> Firm is the pace,
> Left two three four, everyone wants to join
> And so one marches today through every little
>   town
> And every German girl dreams of this today
> Because the black S.S. and the brown S.A.
> Have what pleases everyone today
>   And it's the most beautiful thing in the world."

They finished it in polished harmony. "We'd better hurry," said Hannes, "or we'll miss lunch."

"What must we buy?"

"The commandant's medicine from the druggist, razor blades for the guard commander, a smoking cure for the fat fellow in the cookhouse and I want some color film."

"If we missed lunch we could take some photos of the old marketplace where the vegetable stalls are."

"Good idea; let's miss lunch."

An elderly Saxon TENO engineer named Ueberall—Fuchs to his friends because of his red hair, now turning gray—had also decided to miss lunch. He waited as the two cyclists passed him before crossing the road. "Nazis," he muttered under his breath as he heard the song they sang. He'd heard it as the prelude to many a brawl in which he invariably found his friends ranged against the singers. That was when Fuchs had worked as a diesel fitter for a boat company on the Elbe. As a young man he'd been a keen trade unionist and even now he worried that old documents would be found and bring him under police scrutiny.

Fuchs was a huge man with giant's hands and a square jaw, but his shrill Saxon voice did not belong to such a man. He, more than anyone else in the pioneer battalion, disliked military life. The previous year some skilled engine fitters had been released to factory work but Ueberall's application had been turned down. Now he looked forward only to his card-playing evenings, for it was the nearest thing to being a civilian that he'd managed to find in the army. He liked his two friends very much: Gerd Böll had been a college professor and Oberzugführer

Bodo Reuter never had occasion to remind him that he was also his senior officer.

Fuchs Ueberall often missed lunch, and almost always it was in order to play skat. All three men wondered sometimes what they had in common besides a similarity of age and outlook, a lack of family responsibility and an easily renewed faith that they would win the next game. But, as Gerd said one day, wasn't that enough to have in common?

# 6

WHEN choosing a site for an airfield it doesn't matter that the ground is not flat, for it can easily be leveled. The deciding factor is drainage. The inhabitants of Little Warley had always known that the potato fields to the east of the village drained into Witch Fen. The land between there and the line of ash trees at The Warrens is hard, fertile and as black as coal. It's subsoil is firm enough to take the weight of a bombing plane. So it was no surprise when, as war began, Air Ministry teams surveyed the place and pronounced it suitable for a Bomber Command airfield. After that came earth-moving machinery, concrete mixers and asphalt pourers. A tarmac cross was drawn across Warley's countryside and around it went a road complete with a circular pan for each airplane. Men dug sewers and drains, laid water pipes and strung power lines. Telex and phone cables crossed the fields. Corrugated-iron Nissen huts appeared as if by magic, huddled together like wrinkled gray elephants sheltering from the cold East Anglican winds. There were hangars too: black cathedrals higher than the church steeple and wider than the graveyard. Finally out of the clouds came the sound of an airplane and ten minutes later Warley Fen was truly an airfield.

The boxlike control tower stood alone, commanding a view as far as Witch Fen. Behind it dozens of buildings provided the complex necessities of service life from A to Z. Armory, Butchery, Cinema, Dental Surgery, Equipment Store, Flying Control, Gunnery Range, Hairdresser, Instrument Section, Jail, Kitchens, Link Trainer Room, Meteorological Section, Navigators' Briefing Room, Operations Block, Photographic Section, Quarters for Married Officers, Radar Building, Sick Quarters, Teleprinter Section, Uniform Store, Vehicle Repair Yard, Water Tower, X-Ray Department, Y.M.C.A. Hut, and a zebra-striped Aerodrome Control Post. Later there were also added a large vegetable garden and extensive pigpens.

A sign was painted—R.A.F. STATION WARLEY FEN—and erected at the entrance. The wooden shed there was painted red and white and adorned with a notice: ALL VISITORS MUST REPORT HERE. In no time at all it seemed as though the village had always known the bustle of one thousand and eighty-three noisy airmen: bicycles were stacked outside The Bell every evening and Mrs. Jenkins had had to write NO CIGARETTES on her window in white-wash in order to save a few smokes for her regulars. There were girl airmen too, to the villagers' dismay. They flaunted painted lips and waved hair and worked as hard as the men. Sometimes they were heard to swear as hard as the men too. They set an awesome example to the village girls. Some said the whole aerodrome was a "black Satan's nest" and hurried past it after dark, especially if the roar of aircraft was rattling the village window panes like a thousand furies.

Dispersed all round the aerodrome were the squadron's bombers sitting on their tarmac circles. The six-foot-high fence that surrounded the airfield was little more than a boundary mark, for human logic had torn great holes in it where it had blocked the paths that led from the dispersals to The Bell. Even the armed sentries who stood all night at the main gate would, their duty finished, wander off through gaps in the fence to save themselves a hundred extra yards' walk along the perimeter track. It was through one of these gaps that the Bedford lorry bumped and caused them all to lose their balance. Digby and Battersby hit their heads against the metal uprights. "Hold on!" shouted Flight Lieutenant Sweet from his seat in the cab.

"Now he tells us," said Digby as the lorry pulled up in front of B Flight offices. The tail flap crashed open and Sweet took Mrs. Lambert by the waist and floated her down in a movement that would have done credit to the Sadlers Wells ballet company. Still holding her by the waist, Sweet gave her a decorous kiss. *"Droit du seigneur,* Lambert," he called. "The driver will take you to the Ops Block, Mrs. Lambert; it looks like there's something on for us. It's a good thing that I decided to look in here first."

The Lancaster bombers were alive with airmen. Engine

mechanics, riggers, electricians, instrument fitters and radio mechanics swarmed all over the great four-motor aircraft. The newcomers automatically looked across to the north corner of the airfield. There a group of hillocks looked like prehistoric burial mounds with a concrete entrance to each. It was all surrounded with blast walls and laced with pulleys and tackle. Inside that was the bomb store. Around it were queues of bomb trains. Armorers bent low over fuses and fins, and patted the bombs into place on the trolleys. There were general-purpose bombs and high-capacity bombs and target indicators and canisters packed with ninety shiny 4-pound incendiaries. No one was painting "Hello Hitler" on them; that was something the press photographers did. For armorers there was nothing humorous about a bomb.

"Looks like we're on the battle order, chaps," said Sweet. "There's a bit of luck. I'll enjoy putting some H.E. amongst the square heads."

"Bombs or mines?" said Digby.

"Can't see," said Cohen.

The flight offices were a complex of tin huts, which rattled as one by one the engines were tested up to full revs. The sergeant clerk saluted as Sweet entered the shabby little room marked B Flight Office. Eric, the airman clerk, stopped typing and stood up at attention. It was a dismal place. There were two filing boxes, two tables and two chairs. In the corner there was a sink with chipped railway cups and a brown metal teapot upside down to drain. A notice board on the wall was crammed with ancient announcements and memos. The blackboard was marked to show the serviceability of B Flight's Lancasters. Above it Sweet had had the lettering bod write "B Flight Bombs Best" in Saxon lettering. There was a dirty smudge under it where another opinion on the subject had been clumsily erased.

"Good morning, Percy, good morning, Eric," said Sweet. "Are we on?"

"Yes, sir; maximum effort," said the Sergeant.

"I hear you're making a book on the squadron cricket match on Saturday, Eric. Put me down for five bob."

"On us, sir?" said Eric.

"You cheeky sod," said Sweet. "Aren't I the best batsman in the Group?"

"That's it, sir." Sweet smiled appreciatively and patted Eric's shoulder.

Sweet picked up a tin of pennies and shook it. A

hand-lettered label said "Village Children's Xmas Party."
Last year and the one before that, the clerk Eric Sedge
and L.A.C. Gilbert, the squadron artist, had arranged it,
but this year Sweet had put the full force of his persuasive
personality behind it. Smilingly he demanded contributions
from all ranks and insisted that any raffles or sweepstakes
held among the lads of B Flight must pay ten percent
"tax" to the Christmas party.

"How much more since Friday, Eric?" Sweet rattled the
tin again.

"A few pennies, sir."

"Get the names in the book?"

"I don't put down less than sixpence."

"Get them all in the book, Eric. It's only fair. Then at
Christmas we'll see which section has contributed most."

"Yes, sir."

"And put the teapot on, Eric." Sweet walked through
the door marked "B Flight Commander." It was very hot
inside and a wasp was buzzing hysterically. Sweet hit the
wasp with a rolled-up copy of *Picture Post* and then
opened the window. He scooped up the wasp and put it
outside. He leaned out far enough to see Lambert talking
to his wife. Sweet inhaled the perfume of freshly cut grass
and looked long enough at two airmen on fatigue duty for
them to go back to work. Sweet sat down at his desk.
Over it a poster with the slogan "Bread is a munition of
war—don't waste it" had a Johnny Walker label obscuring
the first word. The office was equipped from many sources.
There were pub ashtrays, a cinema seat, a Victorian
wardrobe containing Sweet's working uniform and some
spare flying kit. There were also a small stove with a
homemade chimney, a threadbare piece of antique carpet
and a suitcase full of gramophone records (including a
course spoken in German). Through the window were the
Lancasters he commanded, standing on the skyline like a
frieze.

Sweet's own plane was *S for Sugar*, although by now
he had persuaded almost everyone on the Squadron to call
it *S Sweet*. It was the newest airplane on B Flight. Its
Perspex was bright and clear and its interior shiny bright.
It had one bomb painted on its nose.

Lambert's airplane—*O Orange*—on the other hand, was
an ancient machine, with line after line of yellow bombs,
totaling sixty-two. From outside it looked the same as the
other bombers, covered for the most part in black mat
paint with dull green and brown on the upper surfaces.

But if you went inside and looked at the bright alloy formers in its nose and wondered why the port side of the interior had dulled and tarnished while the starboard interior was gleaming fresh silver metal, you might guess that it had not escaped unharmed from its sixty-two trips. She had been back to Servicing Flight for major surgery. She'd had a new tail section, the port flaps were new, and the nose and port wing had several riveted plates where flak had holed her. Bomb doors were the most vulnerable part and this plane had used up eight of those.

When Lambert's crew had first got her, fifteen trips ago, they had looked with silent awe upon the battle-scarred machine until Micky Murphy, the flight engineer, said, "A creaking door hangs the longest." Digby christened her *Creaking Door*. The machine seemed to revel in the name and although she flew like a bird, the tail section did creak a little, especially over the target. Or so swore Flight Sergeant Digby.

If one hadn't known what a cynical unimaginative type Digby was, it would be easy to accuse him of sentimentality about *Creaking Door*. It had cost him many pints of beer to hear its life story from Flight Sergeant Worthington. For bombers belonged to the ground crew; air crew only borrowed them.

*Creaking Door* was one of the very first Lancasters ever built. The factory was producing a disastrous two-motor airplane and as an emergency measure the designers asked if they could try putting two extra motors on it. The Air Ministry experts said no, the factory ignored them and begged, borrowed and stole bits and pieces in order to try it anyway.

"That's how the best bombing plane of the war was designed. What a typical pommy fiasco."

"I told my father that it was a fine example of British engineering genius," said Battersby.

"An accident, sport. But she's a beaut, a real vintage beaut."

"What remarkable luck," said Binty Jones, the mid-upper gunner, looking up from his comic book. "We'll sell her to one of those museum places when we have finished with the clapped-out old wreck."

"Money, that's all you dills think about," said Digby. "I'm talking about art. I'm talking about history. Yes, planes like this will be in museums when the war is over, preserved as a masterpiece of twentieth-century taste and culture and beauty."

"We all will," said Lambert.

"I should have known better than trying to talk serious-ly to you mob," said Digby.

Next in line along the dispersal was *L Love*, which was having a new name and symbol painted to surmount the fifteen yellow bombs on its nose: *Joe for King* was now its name. Sergeant Tommy Carter flew *Joe for King*. He was a handsome red-haired orphan from Newcastle. After the orphanage he'd become a messenger boy and then a Newcastle policeman until his Inspector found him read-ing *Das Kapital*.

"What the devil are you doing with that damned rub-bish, Constable Carter?"

"It's for my evening classes, sir. I've got *Mein Kampf* here in my other pocket."

"Don't bring that poison into my police station, Con-stable. Do you understand?"

"I do, Inspector."

Two months later he joined the R.A.F. He had a huge ginger moustache that had originated as a disguise for a scarred lip. He'd encouraged it into the slightly clownish handlebar shape that was fashionable among many air crew. Tommy Carter thought the R.A.F. was the most marvelous thing that had happened to him, and *Joe for King*, he said, was the finest Lancaster ever manufactured. The machine was fifteen trips old; Tommy's crew had done eight of those with the exception of Collins. He was their bomb aimer. Only survivor of a crash landing in February, he'd completed twenty-nine trips. Tonight would be his last before going for a rest.

The next Lancaster bomber was *Z Zebra*. It was almost out of sight behind the ash trees of The Warrens, where even in daylight wild rabbits ran across the tarmac pans. Under the shades of *Zebra*'s wingtips, in the damp-smelling black soil, there were now puffball mushrooms for frying and in the autumn delicious blewits in fairy rings and red fly agaric that men said could kill.

*The Volkswagen*, they called *Z Zebra*. Its skipper was Pilot Officer Cornelius Fleming; newly commissioned, with three hundred fifty flying hours at training schools, he was a soft-spoken introvert from York, an ex-student of medicine. He had done his elementary flying training in Alberta. Canada's bright lights and informality were a startling change after blacked-out wartime Britain, and the ease with which he'd got lost flying over the prairie had been a fearful lesson in its dimensions. Three times a week he wrote to Tracy Rybakowski, a girl in Edmonton. After the war he was going back there to marry her and make his fortune, but so far he'd not told his parents. His brief time in medical school had now faded so far into his memories that he couldn't believe that less than two years ago his ambition was to be only a doctor.

It came as no surprise to Fleming and his crew to find that as newcomers they'd been assigned to one of the shabbiest aircraft on the flight. When they'd first climbed into it the interior was littered with old newspapers and oily rags and the Elsan lavatory had not been properly emptied. There was a faint but pervasive smell of sweat, excrement and rotting meat. Fleming had conscripted his whole crew for the cleaning job. Now the plane smelled of fresh oil, metal polish and disinfectant. As Fleming had remarked, now it smelled "as clean as a hospital," but he'd regretted the comparison as soon as he'd made it. Naming the plane *The Volkswagen* had been part of Fleming's desire to give the dirty old *Z Zebra* a new image.

Fleming's bomb aimer and rear gunner were also officers. All three of them were standing around Fleming's Austin Seven watching one of the electricians fix into it a length of Air Ministry wiring. The car was undergoing a major overhaul at the expense of His Majesty. The three officers had come to B Flight, with the rest of *Zebra*'s crew, six weeks ago, but so far they had not flown on an operation. They spent most of their time together and felt estranged from everyone else, for, as Fleming had remarked to Sweet, most of the other fliers of B Flight—including four of Fleming's own crew—shared the Sergeants' Mess with their ground crew counterparts. It sounded like a provincial workingman's club. "Think yourself lucky not to be a member of it," Sweet had said, smiling. "The only conversation is speculation, intoxication and fornication. Wait until you go to a Sergeants' Mess dance; then you'll get an insight into the great unwashed."

Sweet, however, had no time for anything more than passing affability and they seldom saw him. They drifted around B Flight aimlessly. Faith, Hope and Charity, the sergeants called them. They were creedless bishops, lost in a chapter of rough-tongued Jesuits. They knew that the first three operations by a new crew risked five times the normal casualty rate. They exchanged the litany of technical gen and letters from home and awaited their baptism. It would come tonight.

A mile or more away across the airfield, Sweet could

see the nearest of the other Flight's aircraft, and to the right of it, beyond the bump, the control tower. On its roof a Meteorology WAAF officer was reading the instruments in the louvered box. At the sound end of the runway there was the Aerodrome Control Post, and behind that the steeple of the thirteenth-century church in Little Warley village. He had a good view from here. He looked back to where the lorry that had brought them back from their weekend was turning round before going back along the main road past the village and entering the main gate empty, with Form 658 correctly signed just as Sweet had fiddled it with the Transport Officer. Near the gap in the fence Flight Sergeant Lambert was saying good-bye to his wife, who was getting a lift to the Safety Equipment Section, where she worked.

"Be a good chap, Eric," said Sweet. "Tell Lambert that I want a word with him. And on second thoughts I think the Bedford had better go back to the M.T. section straightaway. Can't be too careful."

"I'll tell the driver," said Eric.

"And apologize to Mrs. Lambert. She'll have to walk. I really am sorry, tell her." When the airman left, Sweet closely examined his face in a wall mirror. He wondered why his skin went red and mottled in the sun instead of bronzed and handsome.

"Take my bike, Ruth," said Lambert.

"I can't ride a bicycle, Sam. Not in this uniform skirt. I'll walk."

"You'll be all right?"

"It's only a mile. It will do me good."

"Mr. Sweet would like a word with you, Chiefie," said the clerk.

Lambert kissed his wife good-bye. "You'll know where we are going tonight before I shall."

"Look after yourself, Sam."

"I love you, Ruth. I'll pop in and see you before we go." As he walked back to the Flight Office airmen were forming a line to await the arrival of the NAAFI van with morning tea and cakes. Lambert looked at his watch; it was ten to eleven.

Inside the Flight Office, Flight Lieutenant Sweet was finishing a story as Lambert entered. " ' ... stop doing that, Sergeant,' she says, 'I hold the King's commission.' " The two clerks and Sweet laughed.

He was still smiling as he turned to Lambert. "Well, the

flap's on, Sambo. Looks like everyone else around here has stolen a march on us. You'd better get your crew together and get your N.F.T. done as early as possible. Captains and navigators at 3:30 this afternoon, main briefing at 5 P.M."

"Can I change out of best blue into working uniform?"

"That would mean you all going back to the Sergeants' Mess, and by the time you shower, shave, shampoo and scrounge some coffee it'll be lunchtime." Sweet smiled knowingly. "No, get cracking right away. Borrow parachutes and helmets from Tommy Carter's bods or Mr. Fleming's crew."

"Any buzz on the target?"

"Even if I did have, I'd not be able to tell the chaps." He moved some papers on his desk. "Oh, and by the by, there's a bit of a crew reshuffle. From tomorrow, young Cohen will be navigator S Sweet. Digby will be with me too. My chaps—Billy and Speke—will be coming to you. You're damned lucky to get them, Sambo; they're damned good blokes."

"Transfer?" said Lambert in amazement.

"I know it's damned rotten for you, Sambo. It's just the sort of thing we all hate happening when chaps are crewed up and happy, but Cohen is a raw kid; I'm going to have to nurse him a little." Sweet found a packet of cigarettes locked in a desk drawer. He rarely smoked but now was an exception. He offered them; Lambert declined. Sweet exhaled the smoke urgently. "Look, I know what you are thinking, Sambo, but this is the last thing I wanted, I can tell you." He found a packet of peppermints in the drawer and offered one of those to Lambert but he shook his head.

"Your navigator stinks, and that bomb aimer Speke is what's keeping you at the bottom of the photo ladder," said Lambert. "I don't want to fly with them. You took Micky Murphy, my engineer, last month, after we'd had fifteen trips together. Isn't that enough for you?"

"Ah! So that's it," said Sweet. "It's just because you think it's a bad swap. Had it been Grimm, that duff wireless operator of yours, you wouldn't have minded. Well, I don't run my flights like that, my friend."

"Of course I would have minded. Jimmy Grimm is one of my crew. I don't want any of them shuffled around like nuts and bolts. They rely on me to look after them. All of them."

Sweet put his cigarette down and came round his desk.

He put a consolatory arm around Lambert's shoulder. "Now, now, Sambo, you're upset. Don't say something you might regret. I hate unpleasantness, any sort of unpleasantness. You know that."

Yes, thought Lambert, providing you can get your own way without it.

"Look, old chap," said Sweet. "The new arrangement won't take effect until tomorrow. It's not my idea, you have my word on that. Some bloody wonder in Ops Block. Take it easy. We may all have gone for a Burton by tomorrow, eh?" Sweet smiled in an effort to cheer Lambert up, but failed to do so.

"If that's all, sir, I'll get started."

"Good show, Sambo." He squeezed Lambert's arm affectionately. "Look, about this damned business, tomorrow I'll get the C.O. in a corner of the Officers' Mess and threaten that you and me will do a low-level attack on Air Ministry if he doesn't let you keep your crew intact."

"I want to speak to him myself," said Lambert.

"You've no idea what a blimp he is. Old buffers like him are a menace to all of us. It's no good you even asking for an interview; you'll just have to trust me. If I can't squeeze it out of the old man when he's got a couple of nips inside him after dinner, there's no chance of you doing it in the cold light of dawn in the squadron office." Sweet laughed reflectively, then he asked, "You've not reconsidered the cricket team? We're playing Besteridge at the weekend. They've got a strong side."

"I'm committed next weekend, sir," said Lambert.

"Pity. It might have made all the difference to the old man's attitude."

Lambert said nothing. Sweet said, "Think it over, Sambo; a couple of cricket victories—especially intercommand victories—could put you well in with the old man. And with me." He smiled to show he was joking. "Not that I won't do all I can for you anyway; you know that."

There was a knock at the door. It was Flight Sergeant Micky Murphy, the engineer who had recently been transferred from Lambert's to Sweet's crew. He was a huge Irishman with a white complexion, a square protruding jaw and a gap-toothed smile that he used between sentence as regularly as he breathed. He glanced at Lambert and smiled.

"Well," said Sweet. "Did you find the trouble with the undercarriage?"

"That we didn't find," said Murphy. "We've bled her

out and she's as nice as ninepence, but we found no fault
unless it was the micro-switch playing false."

"It wasn't the switch," said Sweet.

"Did you try the lever a few times?" asked Murphy.

But Sweet threw the questioning back at his engineer.
"Are you sure you switched the indicators over to their
reserve, Paddy?"

"First thing I did, sir."

"Call me Skipper, for God's sake, Paddy," Sweet insisted. "It's that hydraulic fluid; I told you I wanted only
Intava 675."

"At this time of year it can make no difference," said
Murphy. "I still think there was nothing wrong. All the
undercarts stick sometimes. Lowering the lever a couple
of times will often do the trick. No need for the emergency compressed air. It's a big job once the compressed air
is in the system."

"I'll decide when there's a need to use the compressed
air, thank you, Chiefie. How soon will she be ready?"

"She's still on the jacks and the boys will be wanting to
work the undercarriage a few more times to be on the
safe side; it's a fine test for the whole system. After that
we reinflate the emergency air bottle, top up the reservoir,
sign the 700 and off we go." Flight Sergeant Murphy
smiled nervously.

"For God's sake stop grinning, Paddy," said Sweet. "S
Sweet has got a date over Hunland tonight and I don't
intend to miss it, so get mobile. And this time don't mix
the hydraulic fluids when you top up."

Murphy was about to explain what the handbook said
about hydraulic fluids but finally nodded.

"These engineers just want to blind us with science,"
said Sweet to Lambert after the man had left.

"Yes, sir," said Lambert unenthusiastically.

"That's the spirit, Sambo; all any of us want is to make
B Flight the best damned bomb delivery service in East
Anglia, eh?"

Lambert didn't answer. Sweet gave Lambert an encouraging smile, for he didn't want him to feel annoyed about
losing men of his crew. It was Sweet's especial pride that
he was one of the most democratic officers on the camp.
He might also say *the* most democratic. It had become a
standard joke now that at the Sergeants' Mess dances
Sweet would turn up wearing a sergeant's uniform. Sometimes he could be persuaded to sing "Tea for Two" close
to the microphone. The sergeants appreciated an officer

who knew how to be one of the boys. It would need only one miserable bastard like Lambert to spoil the whole atmosphere.

Eric the clerk looked round the door. "Will you be wanting transport to the Officers' Mess for lunch, sir?"

"Affirmative," said Sweet. It was only a quarter of a mile by the shortcut, but the path was always muddy. Last week he'd felt a perfect fool when some ass in the mess had pointed to his shoes and said, "Been running B Flight through the assault course, Sweetie? Nothing like it for working up an appetite."

Even Munro, the Squadron Commander, had joined in the laughter. Good thing the Group Captain hadn't been there at the time. The Groupie was a real old Sandhurst blimp: fussy as hell about officers' appearance; no flying gear in the mess, not even roll-neck sweaters, and him leading the officers in to meals like some old dowager duchess, saying, "I'm employed to kill Huns," as though he'd actually seen one through a gunsight. Still, the buzz was that Munro was getting a station of his own. They might decide to give a flight lieutenant his scraper ring and a chance at the job.

"Righto, Sambo my lad, off you go on a night flying test." And then, "Oh, by the by, Lambert."

Lambert turned.

"The armorers have removed a panel from your rear turret. You authorize that?"

"I did."

Lambert's attitude made Sweet think that perhaps a higher authority had ordered it. He trod warily. "What's the idea?"

"To see better."

"Than through clear polished Perspex?"

"You opened this window just now to see what I was doing."

Sweet smiled.

Lambert said, "Anyway, the Perspex was badly marked, the sergeant armorer was about to change it. I decided it was worth a go."

Again Sweet smiled. "It's just a matter of good manners, Flight. As your Flight Commander it would be nice to be informed."

"Written memo. On your desk last Thursday. It came back signed, so we went ahead."

"Yes, quite. I meant keep me informed how it works out. A good idea of yours, Lambert."

"Sergeant Gordon's idea, sir. If it works he deserves the credit."

"O.K., Lambert. Off you go, and don't forget the Christmas Party tin on your way out, laddie."

Lambert, who was four years older and six inches taller than Sweet, saluted and left.

When Corporal Ruth Lambert had walked a little way along the road she overtook the Bedford lorry that Sweet had sent away. It was waiting for her.

"Jump in, Mrs. Lambert," said the driver.

"Thanks," said Ruth.

"Bloody officers," said the driver.

As the lorry passed near to where *Creaking Door* was parked, one of its engines started. Four birds, frightened by the noise, flew out of the hedge in front of the lorry. The driver braked in time for the birds to climb steeply into the sky.

"Crows," said the driver. "Where I come from they say, 'One for sorrow, two for mirth, three for a wedding, four for a birth.' " He glanced at Ruth and grinned. " 'Four for a birth,' " he repeated.

"Three of those were rooks," said Ruth.

"Oh well," said the driver, "I don't believe any of that stuff anyway."

Other motors started, until the noise was shattering. Flight Sergeant Worthington waited for Lambert. They walked without speaking to the airplane. Flight Sergeant Worthington had been in the R.A.F. twenty-eight years. His overalls were pressed and starched, and his tie was highly polished and he could climb inside a greasy engine and emerge without a hair out of place. He regarded all airmen who had joined the R.A.F. after war began as nothing better than amateurs. "Which war, laddie?" The way in which air crews were automatically given sergeant's rank and membership of the mess he saw as a terrible heresy. Some evenings when the weather was bad he'd sit in the bar, with pints of beer arriving automatically at his elbow, while he told his fellowmen of his peacetime Odyssey to this Ithaca. He'd tell of Bloody April 1917, the rigors of the Khyber Pass, the boredom of Habbaniya and the cruelties of Uxbridge depot. Whether or not he noticed that the young air crew were the most dedicated part of his audience and kept the beer pots coming was not certain, but lately his tirades were more jocular than venomous.

Lambert had joined the Regular R.A.F. in 1938. In Worthington's eyes he was one of the few "real airmen" on the base.

It was January 1936 when Lambert became a part-time airman. He'd had great difficulty in getting six whole weeks off from his job in the garage, but the new manager thought it would be rather smart to boast of a qualified pilot on the staff and let him go, without pay of course. Lambert went to an airfield in Scotland and was the first of the Volunteer Reserve sergeants to be trained under the new scheme. At the end of his course he had soloed and from then on every weekend, wet or fine, was devoted to training. He flew Hawker Harts and sometimes, as a special treat, a Fury. To be nearer the airplanes he got a job as an aero-engine fitter at the flying club that shared the field with the R.A.F. reservists. Now and again the club would let him air-test a light plane, or even instruct.

"Take him up for a spot of dual, a few flick rolls and a loop. No spins and for the Lord's sake don't let the silly little bastard try a landing."

"Thanks, I'd like to do that."

"There's no one else here, Lambert, and I can't leave the office."

In 1938 the R.A.F. offered any V.R. pilot with more than two hundred fifty flying hours a chance of six weeks with a Regular R.A.F. squadron. Lambert volunteered immediately and after six weeks flying Hurricanes he joined the regular air force. He was disappointed to be assigned to twins, especially when war broke out and his old V.R. squadron was given Hurricanes. However, twin-motor aircraft proved to be a new sort of complication and he liked the challenge. When after a tour on Wellingtons and a D.F.M. he first got his hands on a Stirling, his envy of fighter pilots disappeared, never to return. The four-motor planes made him happy and if he had to be in the R.A.F. in order to get hold of one of them, then he would put up with it.

Worthington put his spectacles on and studied the snag book before looking at *Creaking Door* to compare it with the initials of the men who cared for it. For Worthington also felt possessive about these airplanes. As he saw it, the Air Ministry had wisely put this airplane into his good keeping. Without regarding the bomber as his own personal property, he was a little disquieted when Lambert—and

Lambert's amateur crew—took it away overnight and subjected it to indignities and aerobatics and corkscrewing. Sometimes they brought it back damaged by chunks of enemy metal.

Worthington ushered Lambert through its entrance. Like a lecherous medico with a young girl, Worthington stroked and caressed each grip and bulkhead as they passed through the airplane. Her walkways and handholds gleamed like fine silver where so many other men had done the same. It was dark and confined in the slim belly, no wider anywhere than the smallest of today's motorcars. They had to crouch as they moved forward, but Worthington continued to speak. His voice was resonant and to punctuate his words he tapped with his knuckles and the metal sang a note of anxiety and affection like a nervous patient under the scrutiny of a specialist.

"She's a game old bitch, Sam," said Worthington, "but she's not getting any younger." He allowed Lambert to fit himself into the narrow pilot's seat and took a quick glance out of the window to be sure that his fitters were hard at work on the starboard inner engine.

"That starboard generator was giving us half a volt this morning on the run-up. We found a wiring fault but I'm still suspicious of the genny. It's reading high. Your engineer is going to watch the readings on the air test." Worthington allowed himself a smile. "I've given the poor kid a good drilling about it because the accumulators will explode if he lets a big overcharge build up: oxygen and hydrogen, see?"

"Yes, I had heard, Worthy." Lambert touched the control column and rested his feet upon the rudder bar.

"Yes, well, one of these days you'll be glad I'm a bit of an old woman." He discovered a mark on the Perspex and cleaned it with his newly laundered white handkerchief.

"Is that the only thing, the genny?"

"Apart from that, she's bang on. The squadron average oil consumption is 13.2 pints an hour. All of *Creaking Door*'s motors are better than that: 11.5, 12.8, 10.5, 12.4. A good bus. In fact, a bloody good bus."

Worthington gave Lambert the snag book.

"N.F.T. right away, Chief. Could you ask the Sergeants' Mess to save seven lunches?"

"Meat pie," said Worthington, "or what they call a meat pie. Horrible stuff. Does Mr. Sweet know what the target is?"

"If he does, he's not saying. With a full moon perhaps we'll be gardening."

Worthington shook his head. "Bombs, lots of high capacity, incendiaries galore; it's a town. Target indicators too. We are on number two tanks: six hundred and fifty gallons of juice, at a gallon a mile. Plus ten percent for stooging around . . . Three hundred miles away?"

"We can't go far on these short summer nights," said Lambert, still avoiding the unavoidable.

"The Ruhr," said Worthington.

"Happy Valley," said Lambert dolefully. "That will cheer the boys up."

"If that bloody genny plays up, bring her back. Don't try to press on, O.K.?"

"O.K.," said Lambers. He wondered if Worthington said things like that to give him an alibi for survival, for he wasn't the sort of man to libel *Door*'s machinery gratuitously.

"Spam," prounounced Worthington. "That's what gives that meat pie a funny taste."

They both looked across to *Joe for King*.

Lambert said, "It's funny, chief, the way they paint the number of raids the *machine* does. None of the bomb scores on our airplaines coincides with the number of raids the crew has done; it's just the number of raids the machine has done. It's as though the plane goes to bomb Germany of its own predatory volition, as though it takes us along just for the ride."

Worthington decided that it was a little flutter of nervousness. "Old planes are lucky planes, Sam."

"Sometimes I think it's just the machines of Germany fighting the machines of Britain."

Worthington looked at Lambert's dark-rimmed eyes. "You're not on the booze, are you, son?" he asked quietly. Lambert shook his head.

"Sleeping all right?"

"I wake up a lot," Lambert admitted. "I have a funny dream about a kid's birthday party. He's there with this cake and on it there's half a dozen candles. When he goes to blow them out his head melts like wax. Funny dream, eh? I mean, considering I've got no kids."

"Seen the quack?"

"He thinks the air force is divided into officers and malingerers. Can you imagine me reporting sick with a dream?"

"Yes, he's no help with my bunions either. Still, perhaps you won't dream it again now you've told someone."

"It's that bloody mess food," said Lambert, laughing, and wondered how Worthington knew that he'd never spoken of his dream before.

"You don't want to think about it all too much." Worthington changed the subject. "Not playing in the cricket match, Sam? I'd like to see some of those slow bowls again."

"I'm taking the missus up to London."

Worthington self-consciously dabbed a finger of spittle at a corner of Perspex that the cleaning rag had missed. "They'll keep on at you, Sam. I've seen it happen before. Why don't you play a couple of games, get the bastards off your back?"

"I ask myself that every day, Chiefie."

Worthington finished his tiny cleaning task and looked at Lambert. "It's the sensible thing, son. You can't fight the Luftwaffe and the R.A.F. too. It's the sensible way, the comfortable way, the logical way."

"That must be the reason then," said Lambert. Worthington looked at his friend. He'd had too much: too much combat, lost too many pals, took too much responsibility for his crew. Lambert had had it, Worthington decided. He'd seen them go like this before. He shook his head sadly and changed the subject. "Great God, look at all this stuff."

All round Warley Fen airfield the squadron's Lancasters were being bombed up. Girl tractor drivers backed the bomb trains under the open bomb doors. The dark green bombs came in all shapes and sizes, although most were 500-pound general purpose or 500-pound medium capacity bombs: heavy steel cases with relatively small explosive charges inside them. They were the most widely used, and most notoriously ineffective, bombs the R.A.F. dropped. For every ten successfully delivered by Bomber Command six failed to explode.

When the war began Bomber Command's missiles were small and its instruction books advised using a 40-pound G.P. against a house (only if occupied by troops, of course). For a fuel plant a 250-pound G.P. was recommended. The ineffectiveness of the old bombs and the new style of war demanded simpler weapons. Huge 8,-000-pound canisters—little more than steel dustbins—without nose or tail fin were crammed full of explosive and named high capacity bombs. They were designed for use against housing and just one of them could destroy a street.

Curiously shaped containers were packed with ninety 4-pound sticks of magnesium, each of which would burn with spluttering white flame and ignite almost anything it touched.

Because they were acting as a pathfinder squadron there were marker bombs too. They exploded with pretty colors: red, yellow and green, each color denoting the authority and experience of the crew that dropped it. Few markers were prettier to see than the "Pink Pansies": 4,000-pound medium capacity bomb cases stuffed full of benzol, rubber and phosphorus that ignited on impact with a great pink flash of fire easily spotted for miles.

Pretty and not so pretty bombs were winched slowly up into the bombers' black bellies. Calculations had determined their positions in the bay and the fuse-setting control link had been adjusted so that a touch of the bomb aimer's button could release the great weight without upsetting the airplane's center of gravity. The bombs' fins had been straightened and their casings washed so that no patch of mud would spoil their balance as they dropped through the air.

The armorers worked carefully, remembering perhaps the accident at Scampton the previous March, when a 4,000-pound bomb—a cookie—fell out of a bomber during bombing up. It had exploded. The blast of it had completely destroyed six Lancasters and badly damaged five.

The first victim of the Krefeld raid died at 1249 hours Double British Summer Time at B Flight, but it wasn't due to carelessness. Tommy Carter's airplane was the one involved. The carriers had been lowered from its bomb bay and the bombs winched up into it.

Its bombing up had been completed and Aircraftwoman Jenkins had driven the bomb train clear of the aircraft's belly. Aircraftman Grigson, an electrician, was sitting just inside the rear gun turret, from where he could see B Flight Office and was far enough away from the aircraft's door to be able to spring into life checking the wiring if an N.C.O. should enter the airplane. It was a well chosen place to hide while smoking a forbidden cigarette.

Aircraftman McDonald, armorer, had been fitting fuses all the morning and now he was crouched under the bomb bay checking each bomb container. He noticed that one jaw had two shiny cuts in it and guessed that they had been made by shrapnel during a previous operation. He grasped the metal jaw and tugged it. A part of it broke off in his hand. "Christ," said McDonald as the 1,000-pound medium capacity bomb wrenched itself free and fell upon him. The bomb did not explode but as it hit the tarmac the ground shook. Inside the bomber Aircraftman Grigson, halfway through his cigarette, knew immediately what had happened. He scrambled out and ran to the tractor and moved the remaining bombs away from the aircraft. He then disconnected the loaded bomb trolley and returned on the tractor to report to the sergeant armorer, who was the only person at Warley who ran toward the mishap. Grigson quite forgot the cigarette in his mouth and when the sergeant saw him smoking he screamed with a terrible rage and put him on a charge. He was sentenced to extra fire picket for seven days.

No one felt the vibration more than L.A.C. Henry Gilbert, a forty-three-year-old rigger from Lewes. A Sunday painter before the war, he had made a reputation as an artist at Warley Fen airfield. His ladder was on the hard-standing at the nose when the bomb tumbled onto McDonald less than four yards away. The ladder shook and L.A.C. Gilbert paused in mid brush stroke. He had completed his fine portrait of Joseph Stalin wearing a crown and was halfway through writing "Joe for King" under it. Later, much later, he continued work, but the last part of the lettering was very shaky.

Everyone on B Flight was now looking fearfully at *Joe for King*.

"Holy Mother of God," said Micky Murphy, who had been retracting the undercarriage of Sweet's Lancaster for the fourth time when he felt the ground tremble. Together with two fitters and Battersby, he was full-length in a pool of oil waiting for the bang "... and in my bloody best bloody blue."

"*L Love,*" said Worthington to Lambert when they stopped running and looked back.

"You dropped your false teeth, Bert?" shouted *Door*'s electrician to his pal, who was helping him to set up snares along the rabbit warrens behind B Flight. They had dropped into a ditch.

"My oath. Someone will be put on the pegs for that," predicted Digby, looking across the airfield to where *Joe for King* was parked.

"Mind your toes," muttered Corporal Hancock, armorer, who was winching an identical bomb into *The*

*Volkswagen.* He stopped work and crouched low on the tarmac. Fleming and the other two officers of his crew, who had been watching Corporal Hancock's work, didn't flinch. They looked at each other but said nothing.

It took forty-five minutes to fit a new jaw in *Joe for King.* By that time the bomb, the inside of the starboard bomb door and the tarmac had been hosed down by the duty crew. The ambulance had come and gone and so had Groupie, the adjutant and the squadron medical officer. Two firemen in new white asbestos suits had spent thirty minutes wearing looks of bleak disappointment. McDonald's mangled remains had been put into the storage shed at the back of the Medical Section—sometimes called the mortuary—and a sergeant clerk in the orderly room had sent a priority telegram informing McDonald's father in Dundee.

Two sergeant armorers winched another bomb into the bomb bay. The one that had fallen was taken to the far side of the airfield to await the Bomb Disposal Team. Within an hour of the accident the airplane was pronounced bombed up and fully operational, but Tommy Carter, ex-police constable from Newcastle, who was flying her that night, complained that it was a bad omen.

## 7

ALTGARTEN was a small country town with nearly five thousand inhabitants. Five hundred of them had moved there since the regular bombing of the Ruhr district—the so-called Battle of the Ruhr—had begun in March.

In the Middle Ages a great monastery had marked this crossroads where the trade in Flemish cloth met German iron. A fine stone bridge had once been needed to cross the stream that trickled along Mauerstrasse, the eastern boundary of the town. Altgarten never grew large, for a bigger trade route passed south of here, connecting Cologne to the important seaport of Bruges and its Venetian ships. Altgarten remained a spot on the map where travelers changed horses and gulped beer hurriedly in order to reach the Dutch border or Cologne before dark. The monastery fell into ruins, and its orchards—the fame of which had spread as far as Amsterdam—became a wilderness and were gobbled up by the town. Eventually, of the medieval buildings only the Liebefrau church remained, and fruit and vegetable farms covered the flat surrounding country and row upon row of greenhouses trapped the sunshine. There were silk factories too, and now that they were making harness in the sheds behind Frau Kersten's farm, parachute manufacture provided work for nearly two hundred townspeople, mostly women.

The town center, around Liebefrau church, was a cobbled triangle of seventeenth-century houses. When the military convoys passed through, the policemen had to divert them to Bismarckstrasse and past the railway station, for the heavy lorries would never have been able to negotiate the narrow cobbled streets of the old town. The war had brought great change to Altgarten, or at least it seemed like great change to the people who lived there,

for few of them had witnessed the rest of Europe turning
from butterfly into earthworm.

Of course the flowers and fruit on the farms had given
place to vegetables, but that had happened long before the
war. The disused factory near the brewery had become a
cage for Russian prisoners of war while they worked on
widening the main road, but at the rate the Russians
worked they would be there for years. They were a dirty
lot, always hungry, and they seemed to spend most of
their time hanging around the town watching the gutters
anxiously for cigarette butts. Lately they'd brought from
door to door madonnas carved from old crates. Catholic
residents exchanged potatoes, cigarettes and bread for
them.

The hospital had expanded enormously since the air
raids upon the Ruhr had increased. There was an annex
and a training center for Red Cross "Samariter" (as they
called the young trainees who did the three-week emergency nursing course). Adjacent to these buildings there was
a big hutted camp where amputee casualties from the
Eastern Front came for convalescence and learned how to
use their new false limbs. These establishments dominated
the town. Some afternoons Dorfstrasse was so crowded
with medical staff and convalescent soldiers that local
people felt out of place there.

Where Winkel's was once a sea of blossom there was
now a Technische Nothilfe camp, full of specialist troops
ready to send heavy rescue and repair convoys to bombed
towns in the Ruhr. Lately the TENOs had been building a
railway siding there for their heavy equipment. It was
heavy work and each night they drank a lot of Frenzel's
thin wartime beer.

The housing estate on the north side of town, intended
as rehousing for the slums around the gasworks, was now
occupied by doctors, and TENO engineer officers, which
did nothing to endear the visitors to the locals. Not that
everyone complained about the influx of personnel. Herr
Frenzel, who owned the best restaurant in Altgarten, never
complained. The downstairs bar was always full of TENO
engineers and was sometimes a little rowdy, but the restaurant upstairs was chic. It commanded a view across
Liebefrauplatz of the church itself and the seventeenth-
century houses beyond it. This was the very heart of
Altgarten and these buildings, from this viewpoint, were
its proudest asset.

The Liebefrau was one of the hall-style churches that

you get only in the north. The tracery windows were extra large to let in the sparse northern light, and the roof was extra steep to shed the winter snow. Its slim buttresses ran down like anchor chains stretched tight by a stiff tide and behind it the white houses were like chalk cliffs against which it was moored.

By lunchtime the cold front and its dense dark low cloud had passed eastward over Altgarten without causing rain. Now the whiter clouds moved gently, shrinking in the subsiding air to reveal blue sky beyond and permit golden pools of sunlight to hurry through Liebefrauplatz, finger the ancient church walls and transform the gloomy interior with its glowing stained glass pictures. In front of the church a crowd was gathered at a highly publicized fund-raising drive. Anyone contributing two marks to Winter Help was invited to hammer a nail into a wooden map of Britain. Since the Burgomaster had driven home the first nail that morning, many of the town's most influential people had joined in the witchcraft. The map was studded with a pox of nail heads that concentrated around London, for only the tallest could reach Scotland. A Hitler Jugend Fanfare Band was playing, helping with the Winter Help collection. The boys played loudly and expertly and the music was audible inside Frenzel's in spite of the rattle of dishes and the chatter.

FRENZEL'S STUBE was spelled out in carved wooden letters across the doorway. The upper stories were ocher-colored plaster and carved black beams built upon a brick first floor. The ancient house was bent and bowed like an illustration from a book of fairy stories and the interior was dark even on a sunny day like this. There were other, more luxurious restaurants in the old town, but none had Frenzel's chef or was able to get meat as good as Frenzel's served. Whether he obtained the meat on the black market was a matter of constant speculation. Meanwhile Frenzel's Stube was patronized by Altgarten's most important citizens and none of them asked questions. There was good wine in Frenzel's cellar and champagne and old brandy too. For those with money to pay there were Bayonne ham and pâté Strasbourg studded with truffles. For without Britain and the U.S.A., and with the mark pegged artificially high, Germany had become the best customer for Europe's homegrown luxuries.

Müller, who owned the parachute factory, came to Frenzel's almost every night. Nazi Party officials held banquets here. The commanding officer of the TENO engineers was a regular and so was the electricity station chief. So also was Frau Kersten, who ran the vegetable farm. Tonight, however, was to be special. The Burgomaster was sitting near the window with Herr Frenzel himself, planning every detail for the Burgomaster's fifty-third birthday dinner.

Walter Ryessman, the Burgomaster, was six feet two inches tall, a white-haired ex-cavalry officer with a dueling scar on his forehead. He had joined the Nazi Party in 1928, when dignified upper-class members were in short supply. The Burgomaster was still an ardent Nazi but also a German of the old school. He was a calm dignified man to whom honor meant telling the truth, fighting to the death and ruthlessly rejecting all non-Aryan influence. Over half of Altgarten's population had grown up in Catholic homes but the Burgomaster's political creed did not extend to anti-Catholic persecution. The crucifixes in the Volkschule had, of course, been removed and destroyed and there was no longer any religious instruction, but no policemen had ever been posted at the church to record the names of worshipers. As Herr Ryessman had boasted at a Party gathering in Dortmund, "No non-Jewish citizen who is prepared to march forward with National Socialism to victory and honor need fear injustice from me."

But the Burgomaster's greatest and most popular triumph was a bureaucratic one. Just five months previously he had, by string pulling, form filling and judicious bargaining, saved the bells of the Liebefrau church from being melted down for armaments. The response from all sides had surprised him. In one moment he had managed to find favor with Catholics, traditionalists, historians and colleagues. Oddly enough, Herr Berger—senior full-time S.S. officer in Altgarten—had been one of the first people to congratulate him.

"Not a large affair," the Burgomaster explained. "Eighteen persons, most of them of my family."

"I understand," said Frenzel. "I will personally supervise the Herr Bürgermeister's food and wine and service."

"A Burgundy. The same one as last year."

"I have it written down," said Herr Frenzel.

"Who's that with Herr Bach?"

The Burgomaster had respect for August Bach. Not only had Bach had a distinguished career in the First World War but he was a man of good family and a serving officer of the Luftwaffe, a true German, honorable and silent. Furthermore, his cousin, Gerd Böll—although a frivolous and unconventional fellow—was one of the town's most prosperous tradesmen. Mind you, if Bach had paid a little more attention to practical politics he could have done far better for himself than Oberleutnant's rank. A man with the "Blue Max"—the highest decoration of the first war—at his throat should be a general. What couldn't the Burgomaster have done if he'd had that medal.

"His housekeeper," said Frenzel without looking up, for he had already surveyed his restaurant and amended his knowledge of his fellow citizens.

"He's lunching with her?" asked the Burgomaster.

"Yes," said Frenzel.

"How long since his wife was killed?"

"Thirteen months," said Frenzel, who had already calculated it.

"She's a very beautiful girl," said the Burgomaster.

"A beautiful girl," agreed Frenzel. "Her father is from Breslau: a high-ranking official of the Propaganda Ministry."

"Indeed," said the Burgomaster. He fingered the Party badge in his lapel.

August Bach was seeing an Anna-Luisa that he had only suspected might exist. She laughed readily and was delighted with everything he said and did.

"I'm glad to see that Herr Frenzel's sausages also burst out of their skins," she said and giggled. She wasn't used to drinking two large glasses of wine at midday. "They are full of bread," she explained, solemnly stabbing the *Mettwurst*.

"No," said August. "It's a secret ray the British have. A man in London flicks a switch and every sausage skin in the Ruhr splits from end to end. The great *Wurstwerfer* is the British secret weapon."

She searched his face, for she had not yet got used to the idea that this man was capable of teasing her, then she laughed at his silliness and her own happiness. It was a nice laugh.

"*Kirschtorte*," said August. "Frau Frenzel makes it herself."

"Yes," said Anna-Luisa, gazing into his eyes without hearing him.

She was still laughing as they came out of Frenzel's through the barroom. At the bar there were several peo-

ple they knew. A group of TENO engineers waved to
Anna-Luisa and she blew them a kiss.

"They are friends of little Hansl's," she explained. "Last
week they took him for a ride on the heavy crane. He
loved it. Everyone likes your little son, August."

They had walked only a few paces along the street
when they heard a voice calling August's name. Across the
road there was a gray van with the name GERHARD BOLL
painted on its side. Gerd himself was driving. He got out
and came across the road.

Gerd Böll had been a widower for four years. He was
a cheerful little man, with long arms and large powerful
hands which combined to make him look like a laughing
bald gorilla. This resemblance Gerd did nothing to disguise, and after a few glasses of the schnapps which he
distilled in the garage behind his grocer's shop he would
swing around lampposts and frighten people picking their
way carefully through the blackout. At least he used to
frighten passers-by in this way but by now too many local
inhabitants had grown used to it, Gerd Böll's practical
jokes were often of a more complex nature that befitted a
man who had once been a doctor of engineering at
Leipzig University. Gerd Böll had two grocer's shops in
Altgarten and a relative managed another one in Krefeld.
Each evening he reported with his van to the air raid
defense office at the Rathaus. For putting his van at the
disposal of the Luftschutz he was eligible for sixty liters of
petrol per month. After particularly heavy air raids upon
the Ruhr cities Gerd took his van to the bombed areas to
help. Sometimes at the bar he would tell hair-raising
stories of the death and damage he had seen and the
TENO engineers would add tales of their own.

"August," he called. "I've been looking for you. I
stopped by at the house hoping for some of that real
coffee."

"What is it? We are shopping this morning."

"It can wait," said Gerd. "I didn't know you were with
Anna-Luisa."

"We are going to be married, Herr Böll," she said.

August's cousin looked so surprised that both Anna-
Luisa and August laughed. "Is it so awful?" Anna-Luisa
asked him.

"It's wonderful news," said Gerd Böll.

"It looks like it," August said.

"I'm sorry," said Gerd.

"Herr Oberleutnant," called a rough voice from the

roadway. Parked against the curb there was a Kübelwagen, the military version of the Volkswagen. Its
camouflage was hidden under ancient mud and its equally
dirty windshield was folded flat upon the hood. There
were dents in its side and four rusting bullet holes ran in a
line above the rear wheel. The car bore S.S. registration
plates and the rear seat was piled high with kit. In the
front sat an unmistakably Russian driver and alongside
him a Waffen S.S. officer in a very battered leather coat
and dust goggles. The officer threw Bach a perfunctory
military salute. "There is an S.S. unit here?" He looked at
Anna-Luisa appreciatively.

"The Wald Hotel," said August.

"Which way?"

Gerd said, "Go to the end of this road and then turn
right following the old walls. The Wald Hotel is where the
trees begin. You'll see the black-and-white sentry boxes."

"Thank you," said the officer.

"It's no trouble," said Gerd.

"Heil Hitler," said the officer. He glanced at Anna-
Luisa again and without waiting for Gerd to return his
salute he gave the driver his instruction in a language
unknown to the others. They watched the car pull away
with a roar. It steered round the horses and carts that
moved slowly past the Liebefrau church, their metal
wheels rattling on the cobblestones like drum rolls. They
stared after it for a few minutes.

"What was it you wanted?" August asked Gerd.

"It can wait until your next leave."

"I'll be back here in two weeks," said August.

"That's fine," said Gerd. All three looked at each other
in silence, wishing to break away and yet not knowing
how.

"I go back to my unit in an hour," said August. "But
first we must buy a ring, and then I will write to Anna-
Luisa's parents."

"I mustn't delay you," said Gerd, but he didn't take his
leave.

"There's something wrong, Gerd."

Gerd took August's hand and gripped it warmly. "Enjoy
yourself, August, and you too, Anna-Luisa. There is little
happiness in the war for anyone."

They walked slowly across Liebefrauplatz. "He's usually
such a cheerful man," said August. Gerd drove past them
and waved again.

"He's a funny man," agreed Anna-Luisa. "Everyone says that he's the jolliest man in Altgarten."

"He's not jolly today," said August Bach. "He's in a very strange mood."

"Anyway it didn't rain," said Anna-Luisa, anxious to make him smile again.

"That's true," said August, smiling down upon her and hugging her arm secretly. "Although they say the farms need some rain. The countryside is very dry."

# 8

THE River Ouse bisects pathfinder country. To the north of the river, acres of the ancient forest lands darken the road with shadow, but suddenly through a gap in the trees the far horizon is glimpsed across the dead-flat peaty land that slopes down toward the southwest. Rain draining off the airfields could make the sleepy, almost motionless Ouse into a torrent that overflooded its banks and filled the shady lanes with deep mud even in high summer. For there were many airfields, or, put another way, just one airfield, and over it the winged monsters slid, as once went the pterodactyls that are still found fossilized in the nearby chalk quarries.

The day was half gone. The machines were ready and the Daily Inspection Forms initialed. The drone of circulating bombers had not ceased since early morning. *Creaking Door* got the green light from control and Lambert's right hand pushed the throttles gently forward as he had a thousand times. He kept the port ones slightly ahead to correct the swing. Behind his shoulder he felt young Battersby leaning against him to let him know he was there. He brought the tail up quickly. There was that exhilarating feeling on the back of the seat pushing hard against the spine as five thousand pounds of airplane teetered on tiptoe before relinquishing the last touch of spinning tires on runway. Battersby took the throttles, sliding his hand under the pilot's as before him Micky Murphy had done for fifteen N.F.T.s and the fifteen operations that followed them. Now Lambert needed both hands to haul back upon the control column and force the dark nose up through the horizon. Lambert gave the rudder bar an extra touch, for Battersby hadn't kept the port throttles quite far enough ahead.

Cohen was calling out the air speeds from his indicator beside the navigation desk: 95, 100, 105, and the suddenly *Creaking Door* was airborne. Battersby had seen the rudder bar movement and corrected the throttles precisely.

"Climbing power," chanted Lambert.

"Climbing power," Battersby answered.

"Wheels up."

"Wheels up."

There was only sky. The horizon had dropped out of sight like a spent hoop.

"Flaps up."

"Flaps up." Battersby closed the flaps and there was a grinding sound as they slid back into the wings.

"Cruising power." Battersby didn't move the throttles with the considerate slowness that an airline check captain would approve. He altered their position with an abrupt indifference that slowed the forward speed with a jerk and changed the roar to a lower tone.

The nose dropped a trifle. The Lancaster assumed its flying stance.

"Just one round the garden," said Lambert. It was a way of telling Cohen that he wouldn't need fixes or navigation for the short trip.

There was a click as a microphone was switched on. "It's meat pie," said Digby from the front turret. He should have been behind Lambert on takeoff but he preferred to be in front and Lambert didn't mind. "But late lunches will probably have potato cheese."

"Skipper," said Binty Jones from the top turret, "is that glycol on the port inner?"

Lambert looked out. He was fond of his airplane. Seen through this aged Perspex, the world was not bright and new but ancient and yellowed like parchment. Polished a thousand times, the windows had become a delicate optical system that edged the landscape with halos and made of the sun a bundle of gold wire. He looked at the engine covers, battered by riggers' feet and chunks of ice; there was around each panel screw a white calligraphic cross-hatching of screwdriver scratches. From the exhaust dampers came a blue featherlike jet of flame. Its heat had baked the oil spill upon the cowlings. Like antique enamelware the dark brown stains shone with a patina of deep reds and rich greens. Above the exhaust pipes upon the mat paint of the engine cover there was one shiny patch. It was catching the bright afternoon sunlight and

gleaming like a newly minted penny. Battersby also
glanced at it briefly, then turned back to his panel. He
was determined to do his job by the book, better than
Murphy even.

"Fuel pumps of all tanks off," reported Battersby. "No
warning lights."

"A coolant leak can be real big trouble," said Binty,
always a Jeremiah.

"What do you think, engineer?" asked Lambert.

"It's just an oily footmark," said Battersby. "I saw the
rigger do it. I should have had it wiped; I'm sorry." He
didn't turn away from his panel.

Lambert looked at the mark again: it was the shape of
a rubber toe. He tapped Battersby on the arm so that he
looked round. Lambert grinned at him. The white-faced
engineer was relieved not to be reprimanded.

"That generator behaving, Batters?"

"Perfectly, Skipper."

Digby was full-length in the nose watching the sunny
landscape slide under him. He switched on his intercom.
"Skipper, did they tell you what it's going to be tonight?"
As always when Digby was trying to wheedle something
his accent had become more nasal, drawing each word to
its fullest possible extent like soft chewing gum.

"Yes, thanks," said Lambert. He leaned to his right and
bent his head low to watch Digby's reaction.

"Come on, Skipper," said Digby, looking back to him.
"Give us the gen."

"It's Hamburg," volunteered Jimmy Grimm, the wireless operator. "The orderly room WAAF told me. The
blonde job."

"Big deal," said Binty scornfully from the upper turret.
"Who told her, the Groupie last night in bed?"

"Skip," coaxed Digby. "I've got the calculations to do. I
should be told."

"It's a five-tank job: 2,154 gallons," said Lambert.

Squinting into the hot sun coming through the nose
panel, Digby nodded. Lambert continued, "The whole
squadron is bombing the shit out of Adelaide."

They all heard Binty's catcall of joy even without his
intercom. "That's the one, Skipper," said Flash Gordon
from the rear gun turret.

"You pom bastards," said Digby cheerfully.

"Sticky beak," said Lambert. It was one of Digby's
favorite insults.

Jimmy Grimm hunched lower at his table under the

racks of radio equipment and grinned. He was sending the favorite operator's test signal: "Best bent wire best bent wire best bent wire." Who knows who first invented this strange phrase with its jazzlike rhythms, known to R.A.F. operators and Luftwaffe monitoring services alike?

Lambert began a gentle turn. Under the banked wing the green countryside tipped slowly forward like a child's soup plate waiting for a spoon. The Great North Road was black with traffic: long military convoys and civilian lorries lumbered slowly down England's ancient spine.

Lambert looked at the dazzling blurs made by the propellers and superimposed them as he juggled the throttles. Watching the stroboscopic effect enabled him to synchronize the engines. Lambert noticed that Battersby was looking at him. He grinned. Then he ruined the harmony and pointed to the throttles for Battersby to try.

Binty heard the motors go out of synch suddenly and said, "What's the matter with the motors?"

"Nothing," said Lambert. "Battersby is handling the controls."

"Then let me off," said Binty.

"Don't be a fool," said Lambert. "It's better that he should know as much as possible." There was a fearful silence.

Northwest of Huntingdon the countryside changed suddenly. No more weatherboard houses and thatched cottages; now yellow brick dwellings and rusty sheds. Windswept allotments full of caterpillar-nibbed cabbages, shallots, wire fences and old cars propped on wooden blocks until petrol supplies returned. Here the fields were brightly colored: light yellow, gold, green potato fields and bright blue ones full of cabbages.

Round came the flat angular fens and the Ouse, through which had waded Angles, Saxons and Jutes. Danish Vikings too had plundered this land and left their names upon the map. The circle of Bourne airfield came into sight and around it the hovering flies that would be with them tonight.

Godmanchester: unmistakable, two Roman roads like spokes in its central hub.

"Another Lanc ahead," said Digby. It crabbed along, the wind pushing it askew. It was not of their squadron. Nor was it a training flight from Upwood O.T.U. or Woolfox Lodge. Lambert looked at the strange Lancaster. He tried to see it anew, as though he had never seen a Lancaster bomber before. It was a brooding machine;

thirty tons of it. Even counting motors and turrets as one
and excluding nuts, bolts and rivets, there were fifty-five
thousand separate parts. Over three miles of electrical
wiring, generators enough to light a hotel, hydraulics
enough to lift a bridge, radio powerful enough to talk to a
town on the far side of Europe, fuel capacity enough to
take it to such a town, and bomb load enough to destroy
it.

Lambert held his speed. It was just enough to close
distance inch by inch. Is this the view a fighter pilot will
have just before pressing the button that will blow them
all into eternity? Tonight? The prim red, white and blue
roundels on the plane ahead were symbols of Britain. Its
brown and green upper surface was a formalized version of
the land, plowed and verdant, over which it flew. Like
primitive voodoo objects the brightly painted aircraft
defied the enemy, and upon them were painted the little
formalized yellow bombs, or symbols of airplanes destroyed, that showed how powerful was the magic they
could work.

Lambert had seen enough of the other Lanc. He had
got too close for comfort. He moved the control column
and adjusted the throttles and pitch control. *Creaking
Door* lifted like a show jumper, leaving the other plane far
below. That was better. Even a sneeze from a nervous
gunner was enough to send a bomber into violent evasive
aerobatics and like most pilots he feared midair collision
more than flak and night fighters put together.

Stop climbing. Straight and level while he saw where he
was. Six or seven miles away to starboard the countryside
lapped around Cambridge, a ramshackle rash of workers'
dwellings and speculators' suburbia. In its center, lush with
green courts and beflowered backs, the great university, its
spires grinning like dragons' teeth daring the untutored to
seek admittance. Beyond this citadel the countryside
turned green again and there were more airfields. Below
him passed R.A.F. Oakington, Lancasters dotted along its
perimeter. Gentle turn. Warley somewhere off to port lost
to sight among the fenland. He saw the other Lanc turn
that way. This was the flying Lambert liked, in the clear
light on a fine summer's day. This was how he'd fancied it
would be on the day he'd volunteered.

Lambert was flying straight and level now. No compass
needed, for below him, glinting in the sun like a twenty-
mile-long steel needle, was the man-made Bedford River.

"Lambert's compass, I call it." The voice startled Lambert. Kosh Cohen was at his elbow, sitting on Battersby's folding seat and staring out of the window like a day tripper.

Lambert smiled.

"You always come over here, Skip," said Cohen. "Is this where you're going to live after the war?"

"Perhaps," said Lambert. "Your toys O.K.?"

Cohen nodded.

"Let's go and get some lunch," said Lambert and he let the nose dip. Cohen folded back the seat and returned to his dark curtained booth. Since Lambert was flying by visual landmarks there was little for Cohen to do. He had sorted his maps and given the Gee and H2S the routine test. Although it was notoriously prone to technical failures, he was proud of the top-secret radar set that showed him the ground through fog, mist, cloud of darkness like some god bringing wrath to a sinful Babylon. Only "selected crews" had the new equipment.

Lambert's voice came over the intercom asking each crewman if his equipment was in order. Cohen pushed the mask to his mouth to answer yes into the microphone. On his first two operations he had vomited before the aircraft had even crossed the English coast. Apart from the humiliation, it meant that *Creaking Door* had to lose precious height so that he could clean himself up before clamping the oxygen mask back to his face for the rest of the trip. Now he knew the smell of fear, for it lingered in his face mask and was a constant reminder of the dangers of being too imaginative. He sharpened pencils and prepared the elastic strap that held pencils, rulers and protractors from flying loose during violent evasive action. He looked at the topmost map and read to himself the names of Channel ports. He had passed through them on holiday before the war. He switched his microphone on. "Batters," said Cohen on impulse. There was no answer for a moment, then the engineer answered, "Engineer here; who is it?"

"Kosh, Batters. What mob was your brother in at Dunkirk?"

There was no reply for some time. Cohen was debating whether to call again when Battersby answered.

"I made that up, I'm afraid," he said. "My brother is in a reserved occupation, an electricity substation." There was a stunned silence over the crew intercom. Then Battersby said anxiously, "You weren't thinking of telling Mr. Sweet?"

"No," said Cohen. "I wasn't."

Lambert could see Warley Fen straight ahead. The mile-long runways were distinct on the landscape like a black Chinagraph cross scrawled upon a colored map. Lambert took a quick look round to be sure there were no other aircraft in the circuit. High above them he saw a thin streak of a condensation trail in the upper atmosphere. The airplane making it was just a speck.

"Look at him go," said Cohen. Lambert guessed he was standing under the astrodome. He was like a kid on an outing whenever they were in the air.

"It's the met. flight, on his way to look at the weather over our target," said Digby.

They looked up at the dot. "With that sort of altitude," said Lambert, "a man could live forever."

At 32,000 feet the Spitfire had begun to spit a white feathery trail in the thin moist air. The pilot watched the trail in his mirror and put the stick forward. The highly polished Spitfire Mk XI responded with a shallow dive. The altimeter needle moved slowly backward until, as suddenly as it began, the white trail ended. Immediately the pilot corrected his plane into straight and level flight. This was his optimum safety height for today. No enemy could bounce him from above without leaving a telltale trail. Now he need only watch the air below. He checked for the tenth time the notepad and pencils strapped to his knee. He settled back comfortably and ran a finger round his collar; the cockpit was very warm. Few men had seen the world from this height. Few men knew that it was only a layer cake: a rich green English base with a layer of light green ocean on it, then Holland, brownish and flecked with clouds along the coastline. Then the distant horizon, perhaps as far as two hundred miles away, disappearing into white mist like whipped cream. Upon it blue sky was heaped until it could hold no more. To the Ruhr and back would take the Spitfire only ninety-two minutes. He'd have time for a game of tennis before tea.

In the thirteenth century East Anglian wool merchants had brought back from the Low Countries wealth, brickmakers, architects and a taste for fine Dutch houses. There were many houses as well preserved as Warley Manor, with its distinctive curved gables and fine pantiles. Before the war it had been the home of a Conservative Member of Parliament. Art students had regularly come to sketch it. They had sat on the lawn shaded by the ancient elm trees, and had tea and cucumber sandwiches in the Terrace Room. Now it was the Officers' Mess of R.A.F. Station Warley Fen. The Terrace Room was furnished with long polished tables. Between the tables white-jacketed airmen moved carefully, setting the lunch places with white linen napkins and gleaming glassware. Through the folding doors from the anteroom came the cheerful shouts of young commissioned air crew, and a gramophone record of Al Bowlly was playing gently in the background. The sunlight made patterns on the carpet and the glass doors had been opened to let the tobacco smoke escape.

There were sixteen Lancaster bombers at Warley Fen. Each one had a crew of seven. Of these one hundred twelve operational crewmen, eighty-eight were sergeants. (The Sergeants' Mess was a series of corrugated iron huts interjoined.)

The remaining twenty-four fliers were officers; they shared this mess with another forty-eight officers ranging from the Padre to the Dental Officer, plus some WAAF officers, such as Section Officer Maisie Holroyd. She was a plump thirty-eight-year-old woman who had spent eight years running a cheap "meat and two veg" dining room in Exeter. At Warley Fen she was the Catering Officer and even the people who found the present food unappetizing agreed that she did a better job than any of her male predecessors.

The nonoperational officers were mostly middle-aged. They wore medals from the First World War and interwar campaign ribbons from Arabia and India, and a very high percentage had pilot's wings on their tunics. Of the twenty-four operational fliers, thirteen were born in Britain. The others were three Canadians, four Australians, two Rhodesians, and two Americans who still had not transferred to the U.S.A.A.F. Seven officers wore the striped ribbon of the D.F.C., including Flight Lieutenant Sweet of B Flight.

Had he been asked what his talents were, Flight Lieutenant Sweet would not have put flying a bomber anywhere near the top of his list. Nor, which would have surprised his fellow airmen even more, would he have claimed to be a popular leader of men. Sweet felt himself particularly well fitted to be a planner of air strategy. Some of his boyhood ambitions had come to naught, for instance his desire to be six feet tall and his ambition to be head boy. In addition, there was his dream of winning the

hundred-yard sprint and being captain on the Southern
Counties Public School Cricket Eleven, but these were
lesser hopes.

His desire to be a strategist had not diminished with
time as had the desire to be a professional cricketer, nor
had it become unreal like his hopes of being six feet tall.
The war would continue for at least ten more years,
Sweet had decided. There was time enough for this ambition. When we had conquered the Germans the Japs
would be next on the list, and look how long the Chinks
had spent trying to hold them off: since 1931. After that
we'd probably have to put the Russians in their place. It
was going to be a long war and Sweet had decided to
spend the great part of it on the staff side: making
decisions, formulating plans, forging strategy. These were
the things of which wars were made. Naturally a young
ambitious staff officer would have had a dangerous war
behind him and a couple of gongs. These would be his
credentials, his way of making the old-timers listen to
reason. Two tours of bombers, D.F.C. and bar and a job
at High Wycombe: this was Sweet's ambition.

He could handle a bit of schoolboy German and
French. Next he'd learn some Russkie or Jap, or perhaps
even Mandarin. He bought two whiskies and walked
across to the solemn-faced Education Officer, an elderly
schoolteacher who had joined the station only that week.
Education Officers were often called "schoolmasters," and
never more aptly, for this bespectacled pilot officer had,
until ten weeks before, been teaching history and lan-
guages at a secondary school in Harwich.

"How are you finding things, sir?" said Sweet deferentially.

"Splendid," said the Education Officer, wondering why
he should have been sought out by this gay young hero.

"Wizard." Sweet nodded. "That's wizard. My name's
Sweet, Flight Commander B Flight. Look, sir, I would
appreciate your advice. Considering the way the world is
going—the war and everything, you know—I'd like to
hear a broader view than we"—quick look round—"get in
the mess."

The Education Officer looked at Sweet with interest. It
was quite amazing that these boys—in spite of their rank
badges and medals—were only a year or two older than
his sixth form back in Harwich. Younger in a way, for the
war had prevented their minds from expanding in the
normal manner. They thought of nothing but the technical

skills of their job. Most of them failed to realize how
narrow and uncommercial those skills were. After the war
the poor devils would suffer when they started looking for a
job, just as he had, as a young infantry officer, after the
previous war. A brilliant first year at Oxford with its
crowning achievement a commission in a yeomanry regiment. My God, what a fool!

It goes without saying we are all proud of the sacrifices
you have made, Captain, and the decoration you won, but
when there are so many men after so few jobs, it would
be irresponsible and unfair to our shareholders to take
anyone without experience or even a degree.

He had gone out and joined the Peace Pledge Union. "I
remember war, and I will never support or sanction another." And yet here he was supporting another, with
these curious young men. How different they were from
the chaps he soldiered with in 1914. Half these kids hadn't
even got their matriculation exam. He was amazed at the
superficial nature of their conversation: flying, booze-ups
and bints. Even their cynicism was ingenuous. He said,
"I'd be glad to help if I can."

"It's not really for me," said Sweet. "It's for my cousin.
He's a pretty clever chap. No degree, but he could get one
at any time, just like that." Sweet clicked his fingers. "He
was asking me a few questions the other day. He thinks
my advice is worth taking. Can't think why." Sweet
laughed. "He's in the army, he stands a good chance of a
job on staff. They are putting together the real brains now
to start planning the invasion."

"Really," said the Education Officer.

"Yes. This chap will be a brigadier in no time at all.
Anyway this fellow ..."

"Your cousin."

"What?" said Sweet. "Oh yes, my cousin. He's got
German and French pretty well buttoned up and he's
thinking of having a crack at the old Russian or the old
Jap. What do you think would be best? Perhaps Mandarin? I mean, you can't tell the way it might go. What would
you have advised the chap to study?"

"He'd do best to concentrate still on his French and
German. Conversational practice. Vocabulary building,
perhaps working solely with military books." Sweet was
looking rather blank. The E.O. felt that he was expected
to continue. "He should try translating some of the
*Manuscrit de mil huit cent treize* by Baron Fain, who was
secretary of Napoleon's Cabinet. Or there's Danilewski's

*Denkwürdigkeiten aus dem Kriege 1813;* I translated a piece of that once to pass the time away in France. Then for the battle of Waterloo there's the famous *Documents inedits* by the Duc d'Elchingen . . ."

"If I want to read about our victory at the battle of Waterloo," said Sweet, "I don't need any French blighter to tell me about it." He laughed ironically.

"But for your cousin . . ."

"Oh, my cousin doesn't need that sort of thing," said Sweet. "He thinks internationally: Russkie or Jap. Perhaps you don't think internationally."

"I'm afraid I never do," said the Education Officer.

"My cousin always does," said Sweet. "So do I. Look here, sir, I know that in the first war the trenches in France were full of poets and all that, but because chaps beat the mess up once a week, debag some poor blighter and have a little horseplay you mustn't think that they are a lot of shallow-minded muscle men. I mean, these chaps do their bit; some win a gong or two by luck or judgment." Sweet smiled. "But that doesn't mean that when the shouting's over they can't enjoy some good poetry and music and sit down and try and think what the world really means to the common man."

"I don't jump to conclusions," said the Education Officer. "As it is I'm rather proud to be sharing a mess with so many interesting young men."

"Nice of you to say so, sir."

The station commander was standing alone near the cupboard full of squadron silver. Sweet thought he was counting it. The Mess Sergeant thought he was trying to see if the rearmost cups were polished. Actually he was trying to decide if the Command swimming trophy was solid silver or only plated. Sweet turned back to the Education Officer. "There's an operational matter I must speak about with the Station Master."

The Education Officer followed Sweet's gaze. "Oh, certainly," he said. "Don't let me hold up the war." He sniffed burned fat and watery cabbage and decided that he wasn't hungry. He missed his wife's home cooking more than he'd thought he would. What good was he doing here?

"And thanks awfully," said Sweet as he moved among the earnest young drinkers around the bar. The light through the glass doors gave them halos of sunshine. Sweet addressed the Groupie directly. "All alone, sir?

Have I pestered you about my collection for the village children's party?"

"Hello, young Sweet; yes, you had a quid from me last week."

"Of course, sir."

"Your team going to knock spots off those Besteridge chaps on Saturday?"

"I think so, sir. Mind you, Flight Sergeant Lambert is going up to London on a pass. I was rather counting on his slow bowling. Two of their team played for their country before the war, to say nothing of this professional they've got. But Lambert's set on taking his wife up to London. He says he doesn't like playing for the air force."

"Bad show, that, but I'm sure you'll win, Sweet. I'm going to stonewall for you. Anyway, I've got ten bob on us." They both laughed and the Groupie bought Sweet a small beer.

Sweet said, "There's a story, sir, that you scored a century for 3 Group before the war."

"That's true enough. I also played for Fighter Command one year. Before I got this touch of arthritis, or whatever the quack says it is, I was quite a sought-after bat."

"That's what I heard."

"Oh, come along, Sweet, I'm sure I've bored you with the story of my batting at Sandhurst . . . when the umpire tried to catch the ball . . ." and the Groupie was launched into his reminiscences.

Several officers moved aside, for the Group Captain's stories about his cricket powess were familiar to most of the mess. His narrative was laced with monosyllabic four-letter Anglo-Saxon words, which helped the Group Captain to establish a democratic camaraderie with his virile young officers. This, at any rate, was his theory. For this reason the mess still had male waiters and barmen when most others had airwomen doing these jobs. The Groupie finished his anecdote flushed and happy. He said, "If your team win on Saturday the chances are the A.O.C. will invite you for dinner."

"Yes, I'd heard he does that."

"Give you a chance to tell him your theories about staff planning and strategy," the Groupie said, chuckling.

Sweet bowed his head modestly. Groupie said, "But you're a flight commander now, Sweet. You're finding out a thing or two about running a unit, eh?"

"In a small way of business," admitted Sweet modestly.

"But I must say I had no idea of the amount of paper work necessary just to get an airplane into the air."

The Groupie gave a short ironic laugh. "Now you are finding out where the real war is being fought, laddie. Saturation bombing of airfields with Air Ministry bumf, memos, requests and bloody nonsense, each prepared in triplicate and filed under waste paper, what?"

Sweet smiled at the Group Captain to indicate how much he shared his contempt for chairborne warriors. "Especially when all a chap wants to do is get to grips with the damned Huns, sir."

"That's it," exclaimed the Groupie enthusiastically. "I'm employed to kill Huns, and by God, my squadron will kill more Huns of all shapes, colors, sizes and sexes than any other in this man's air force or I'll know the reason why." The Groupie smiled and self-deprecatingly added, "At least, that's what I've told Air Ministry a few times, eh?"

"Yes, sir," said Sweet. "In fact, on this matter of killing Huns there's something you could help with. . . . I say, I'm sorry to talk shop and all that . . ."

"Now then," said the Groupie. "You know my views about those bloody squadrons where they taboo shoptalk in the mess."

"Well, on this business of killing Huns, sir. There's a pilot—a damn good chap, experienced, decorated and all that, a good N.C.O.—but he told me that he thinks our bombing attacks are 'just old-fashioned murder of working-class families.' "

"Confounded fifth columnist!"

"Yes, sir, I knew you'd be annoyed, but that's not all. This war, he says, is just the continuation of capitalism by other means."

"That's Karl Marx he's quoting."

"Yes. It's a misquote of Clausewitz actually, sir."

"It's a bloody disgrace. A chap on my station, you say?"

"Flight Sergeant Lambert, sir. It might be just a touch of the jitters, mind you."

The Groupie's face changed. "Lambert again, eh. Still, he's got a good record, hasn't he? And we've got to remember that Karl Marx is on our side now. Got to hand it to the Russkies, Sweet, they've put up a jolly good show lately. This Stalingrad business could be the turning point of the war."

"I only thought, sir . . . knowing your views on killing Huns."

# BOMBER
113

"You did right, laddie. I'm a Hun-killer, as you well
know; only way to get the war won. I'll be looking into it.
If he's going to lose his nerve for killing Huns it will be
better to put the chap onto something he can manage."
The mess waiter caught the Groupie's eye. He nodded.
"Cleaning out latrines, for instance."

"I thought you'd better know, sir."

"Quite right," said the Groupie. "But then you usually
are, young Sweet, but don't say I said so, what?" They
both smiled.

"Oh, by the way, sir. Perhaps you've heard about this
little experiment I'm doing on one of the rear turrets."

"I heard something about it. What are the details?"

"Well, it came to me one morning when I opened the
window in order to see more clearly. . . ."

In the hall a corporal struck the gong; its soft sound
echoed through the old house. "Come along, gentlemen,
let the prisoners eat a hearty lunch." The Groupie always
said that at lunchtime. In the evenings he said "hearty
dinner."

He turned back to Sweet. "I saw you talking to our new
schoolmaster. Nice chap, isn't he?"

"Indeed he is, sir. A very good type indeed, sir."

"And gives the mess a bit of style having a V.C. here,
what?"

"V.C., sir?"

"The schoolmaster, my boy, Pilot Officer Pearson V.C.
Don't tell me you didn't make a beeline for that purple
ribbon. Everyone does. Nineteen seventeen; killed twelve
Huns with a sword and dozens more with hand grenades,
held a section of Boche trench for two hours until rein-
forcements arrived. Fascinating, what? Seeing an officially
accredited hero in the flesh."

"Yes, sir," said Sweet, trying to remember what he had
said, "but let me tell you about this silly little idea I've had
about the Perspex in rear turrets. . . ."

The Lanc that Lambert followed came in to land on
Warley Fen's main runway. There were no squadron letters or call signs, no bombs painted on its side, no pet
names. There were no guns in the turrets nor gunners to
man them. There was not even an engineer to help with
the fuel changeovers or assist with the controls. It made a
perfect landing and obeyed the tower's instructions with a
care that was unusual. A Hillman car sped out to the
bomber and waited while the pilot checked through the

procedures with the ground crew and the Engineer Leader. The Engineer Officer was Sandy Sanderson, a slim-
hipped Lothario who had bet ten shillings that he'd have
lunch with the ferry pilot. He lost. The pilot, a twenty-
year-old brunette in the uniform of the Air Transport
Auxiliary, declined with a knowing smile. Is it dangerous?
her mother had once asked her. Only after you land,
Mother. As well as flying the four-motor aircraft entirely
alone, she had eaten three cheese sandwiches while doing
so. By missing lunch she would have time to get back to
the storage unit and deliver another aircraft before finishing work for the day.

There were always new modifications on the planes
coming from factories, and this Group, like most of the
others, had special requirements that had to be incorpo-
rated. Wing Commander Munro and Sandy didn't finish
their ground inspection until ten minutes to three.

It was a quarter past three when they hurried up the
steps of the mess. Munro had missed lunch and would
make do with Spam sandwiches and a glass of lemonade.
Not that there was any harm in having a glass of beer at
lunchtime even when they were on Battle Order, but he
felt that he should be marginally more abstemious than his
men. Sandy drank lemonade too.

Munro was a wealthy, desiccated landowner with a
fragile manner and little or no sense of humor. In 1941 he
had been injured in the leg by flak. There were three or
four splinters still hiding somewhere in his ankle. For a
time he had needed a walking stick and even though he
had stopped limping ages ago he had never relinquished
the walking stick. He marched around the aerodrome
brandishing it like a laird striding through the heather. He
was a tall slender man with a lined face and a stubby
moustache. His closely trimmed hair was gray at the
temples and although most of the men flying that night
would be wearing white roll-neck sweaters and stained
battle dress, Munro was never seen on duty in anything
other than his well-tailored barathea with his handmade
shoes polished like patent leather. Like his civilian wor-
steds and tweeds, Munro's uniforms had a patina that only
years of valeting can bestow. The elbows and cuffs were
reinforced with patches of soft brown leather and there
was a special pocket where he kept a box of Swan Vesta
matches. He reached into it and carefully lit his pipe, even
though it seemed to be burning well. Often at meetings
and briefings this gave him a moment's pause in the

conversation. It was, like many of his mannerisms, an old
man's habit. He was thirty-five years old and yet few
people would have guessed him to be younger than forty-
five. This would not have surprised Wing Commander
Munro. He preferred to look forty-five. Munro had been
an officer since 1932, although he had spent a year of
peacetime as a civilian. His wife, Sarah, was running the
whole estate now. It was a beastly war for her: extra
acres under cultivation but many of the staff in the army.
She was looking so much older.

There was a letter waiting for him in the rack. It was
written in bold good-humored handwriting, on a sheet
torn from an accounts book.

Darling,
   How can I thank you for the magnificent handbag?
It arrived on my birthday, which represented a brilliant piece of Munro organization. I don't think I'd
like to see London at the present time. From your
description it sounds like an international madhouse.
I like the way you are always telling me to never
trust strangers and yet you are really absurdly generous with those unregenerate ruffians from the old
squadron whenever you meet them (which usually
means whenever you enter a public house). Perhaps
you should grow a large moustache again at that!
   The beans are going to be magnificent; aren't you
clever? You must be here to taste the first of them.
Those dashed aphids are all over the roses as usual
and they just drink up the spray, belch, and call for
more. The strawberries are doing very well and tomorrow I'm jam-making with cook. I'll send you a
pot of it.
   Now you mustn't worry about us. We both know
that it will take a few years for Peter to build his
strength up to that of other children but he has fresh
air and there is plenty of milk here still. If he went to
Canada who would give him the love that we give
him, and what is more important?
   You remember how short of breath he was when
you were on leave at Christmas? Now he is just as
bad again. It's pitiful to hear him at night and I want
to breathe for him, the darling. He's so good about it
all and Dr. Crawford says that it must be painful for
him sometimes.
   We miss you, darling, but you must worry only

about bringing yourself home to us safe and well. Save your concerns for yourself and your men. Here all is well apart from Peter and for him it's simply time and rest and fresh air. I would not have told you anything of this but you made me promise. I will see you sometime soon. Take care, my darling, do take care. From your untidy slut of a farmhouse wife and dung-spreader-in-chief at 2 A.M. and the accounts not complete.

Love,

SARAH

"That girl and her cheese sandwiches," said Munro.
"Yes, sir?" said Sandy, looking up and suddenly alert.
"Not a bad idea, that."
"Indeed, sir?"
"Eating in the air."
Munro carefully folded the letter and replaced it in the envelope. He took a gold mechanical pencil from his pocket and listed upon its back the things he must do before briefing time.

# 9

IN THE cryptic style of teleprint Meldekopf I—I./Ln. Funkhorch-Regiment West—the radio monitoring and interception department of 12th Fliegerkorps H.Q. received from Palais Luxembourg, Paris (H.Q. of the 3rd Air Fleet), the so-called W.I.M. report. This was the collated result of hostile radio traffic, navigational bomb and radar aids, I.F.F. and jamming devices. Largely, however, it was based upon the brief radio tests made by R.A.F. wireless operators. Radio tests before lunch usually indicated a bomber being readied for a raid that evening. Jimmy Grimm's "best bent wire" signal was just one of the hundreds heard in Paris. The Luftwaffe's No. 1 Fighter Division H.Q. at Deelen was told unusually early to expect a heavy R.A.F. attack that night.

Fernschreiben
+KR        31.6.1943        GEHEIM

MELDEKOPF I
FUNKBEFEHLSSTAND WEST
LUFTFLOTTE 3, HOH.NAFU

GLTD
HVO I. JAGD-DIVISION
FUNKBEFEHLSSTAND MITTE
WIM-MELDUNG
   R.A.F. WITH APPROX 600-700 (AMONG THEM PERHAPS 90 TWO MOTOR) EXPECTED TARGET WEST GERMANY

MELDEKOPF I
BR.B.N.R.3567/43 GEH
GEZ.BOFINGER,LT.

# ♦ 10 ♦

THERE were vehicles that every sentry at the Wald Hotel could recognize. For instance, the commanding officer's Mercedes, the daily mail and ration lorries and the afternoon transport that went to the railway station. For these the ornate hotel gates were folded back well before their arrival. At the approach of an unrecognized vehicle, however, it was customary to challenge it and scrutinize the driver's papers before the gates were opened. The muddy Kübelwagen did not decrease speed when the two S.S. sentries walked to the middle of the road. Mausi Scheske held up his hand but finally stood back behind the sentry box. It was to the credit of the other sentry that he did not jump aside until the last moment, when the front offside fender caught him a glancing blow on the leg. Damage to his kneecap resulted, some weeks later, in the removal of cartilage. The motor stopped after striking and bending a spray of wrought-iron oak leaves. Its fender suffered another dent.

"Officer of the guard!" bawled the man in the front seat of the car, making no attempt to get out nor sparing a glance for the sentry who had been knocked full length upon the gravel. Guard dogs barked and six armed and equipped soldiers stumbled to be first out of the gatekeeper's lodge, which was now used as a guardroom. They were clamping their helmets to head and fixing bayonets and all the time were treated to loud complaints from the officer.

"Open the gates, pick that fool up. Officer of the guard! Why aren't you saluting? Where's that man's pack? Officer of the guard! Move these clowns off the path. You know how long you types will survive on the East Front? Twenty-four hours. Why is that helmet dirty? Where in

118

the name of bloody blue blazes is the officer of this pitiful shambles of a stumbling band of crippled incompetents? Officer of the guard!" He screamed as loud as possible and the starlings in the nearby trees rose into the blue sky in alarm. No less alarmed were the Scheske boys, Mausi and Hannes, who for the first time were seeing a Knight's Cross winner, grimy with the dust of battle, here before their very wide eyes.

"Yes, sir?" said a young officer, still breathless. He'd heard the noise while lying on a bed in the guardroom with his boots off.

Fischer yelled his own particulars like a recruit: "Sturmbannführer Fischer from Panzergrenadier Division 'Leibstandarte Adolf Hitler' on attachment to S.S. Division 'Hitler Jugend,' Beverloo, Belgium." Give these kids and armchair soldiers the whole lot in the teeth, that was the only way to treat them.

"Yes, sir," said the young officer. He took Fischer's travel papers. He'd heard that a new elite S.S. division was being formed. "That's the sort of unit I'd like to be assigned to." Quietly he added, "A man forgets he is a soldier in these backwaters."

"So I notice," said Fischer. He opened his leather overcoat to replace his papers, which the young officer of the guard had not examined. The Knight's Cross tinkled against his top button and he saw the young man's eyes drawn to it. More than anything else the young officer wanted that. A Knight's Cross holder could do no wrong. Headwaiters provided the best tables and hotels their best rooms, queues vanished, girls submitted and even senior officers showed respect. How, he wondered, had this dirty fellow gained his?

He looked at both of the men in the car. Each of them had a P.38 pistol in a leather holster strapped to his waist with a lanyard from its butt. On the V.W.'s dashboard there was a machine pistol in metal clips. There was an oily rag around its bolt and deep into the clumsy wooden stock of the gun the name Fischer had been carefully carved. So had a line of twenty-eight notches.

Fischer removed his peaked cap and wiped its sweaty leather band with a dirty handkerchief. His skull showed pink through the closely cropped hair. On it were the white wormlike scars of childhood bumps and falls and a long furrow that could only have been made by a bullet. He tucked the handkerchief into his sleeve as the English were reputed to do. The young guard commander noted this fine touch of sophistication.

"I want petrol and a new set of plugs." Fischer rubbed his oil-blackened hands together briefly. "We've had trouble with the motor."

"And food, bathroom and bed?"

"The motor first."

"Immediately, Herr Sturmbannführer," said the young officer.

Now the sentries were alert and stiff with anxiety. That's all they needed, thought Fischer, a real soldier here to light a fire under them. The young officer's accent was that of a country boy. Racially pure, outstandingly fit and as ideologically sound as a dull-witted yokel could be. It all fitted Waffen S.S. selection policy but sometimes Fischer wondered if the policy was sound.

"Your kit to your room?" said the boy slowly.

"And put a guard on it. I'm carrying valuables."

"Yes, sir."

"And feed my driver and give him a place to sleep. He hasn't closed his eyes for fifty-six hours."

The young officer looked at the high-cheeked driver. "Are we taking Asiatics into the S.S. now?"

"We have a whole division of them in training—14th S.S. Freiwilligen-Division Galizien. Two hundred and fifty of them have gone to the Junkerschule. By the time you get to the East they'll have Ritterkreuze dangling on their collars and you'll be saluting them."

"Ostvolk?"

"The Reischsführer says they are comrades. You don't object?"

"No, sir," called the young man loudly. Fischer gave a sour smile.

The gates were wide open. Fischer signaled with his finger that the driver should start up.

The young officer said, "Follow the gravel drive. You'll see the old hotel building. I'll phone ahead so that they'll have orderlies to attend to your baggage. And I will phone the kitchen too."

"You're getting the idea, boy," said Fischer as the car rolled forward. He turned to his driver and in careful German said, "Petrol, spark plugs, bath, food, sleep. It's now 1500; the Kübelwagen ready by 2200." He held up his fingers.

"*Frauen?*" said the driver.

"No *Frauen*, you big ape," said Fischer. "This is Germany. Wait until we are across the border."

Half understanding, the Ukrainian smiled so that his narrow eyes almost closed. He nodded his head.

The inhabitants of Altgarten wore the tired faces that years of war, blackout, rationing, overtime and loneliness bring to the people that endure them. The uniforms were coarse and the civilian suits threadbare. The girls' dresses were homemade, although here and there in the crowd one saw fine furs or pearls that had made a journey in a soldier's kitbag.

"What time do you leave?" asked Anna-Luisa. She was giving his shoes an extra polish as she always did before he returned to duty.

"Three o'clock," answered Bach. "A staff car will take me."

"I'm impressed."

"An old friend, on the staff of General Christiansen. He has to go from Dortmund to The Hague several times a month. He often gives me a lift."

"You shouldn't have told me."

"I want to tell you everything," he said. She packed clean laundry into his case, folding and smoothing it with a new-found dedication.

Sometimes Oberst Max Sepp travelled in General Christiansen's Mercedes, complete with imperious horn and flying pennant. Today Bach was disappointed to find him in a Citroën. It was a factory fresh car specially made for the Wehrmacht and newly painted Luftwaffe blue, but it hardly compared with the Mercedes and its throaty roar and silver supercharger pipes. Even Max was less impressive than usual, hunched in a badly creased cape and battered peaked cap. As they stood on the pavement August glanced into the sky. It was a habit he would never lose. Six miles in the sky above him the met. observation Spitfire pilot had seen the whole sweep of the cold front and its attendant hammerhead clouds and black twiglike base. He scribbled upon the notepad attached to his thigh and while his attention was distracted from the controls the airplane lost 500 feet of altitude. This brought it low enough for condensation trails to form, although only for a minute. At 420 m.p.h. that minute meant a thin white scar seven miles long across Krefeld's blue sky.

"One of our fighters," said Max. August didn't reply; he

threw his leather overcoat onto the driver's seat and got in.

Max Sepp was a plump white-haired man in his middle fifties. He was on the staff of the military governor of the Netherlands. He was Controller of Civilian Fuel Supplies, about which, as he freely admitted, he knew little or nothing. Before the war he had been a forestry official.

"This is the life," said August, settling into the back of the car with Max as the driver closed the door and saluted. Anna-Luisa waved and August waved back.

The car moved off. "The best job in the war," said Max. "When I go on leave I feel ashamed at the arduous life they lead on the home front."

The driver had done this same journey a thousand times. From Mönchenstrasse, where Bach lived, he drove across Dorfstrasse, the big main street, and into Richterend, the shortcut round the back of Saint Antonius Hospital. The old building was dwarfed by the new training center behind it, while on their left lines of unpainted huts on the waste ground stretched as far as Sackgasse and the slums behind the gasworks.

"What's that bloody great place?" asked Max. "A concentration camp?"

August Bach looked at his friend a moment and glanced at the back of the driver's head before replying. "No," he said finally, "it's a medical center for amputees. Men from the East Front and civilians from the bombed cities. They learn how to use false limbs there. They take a walk into Dorfstrasse . . ."

"And frighten the kids and look at the empty shops. Lovely."

"Is that what a concentration camp looks like, Max?"

"If either of us knew that, my dear August, we would probably not say."

"Probably wouldn't be sitting here," said August.

"How right you are." Max Sepp smiled grimly. He looked out of the window as the car turned the corner at Frau Kersten's fruit farm and jolted heavily over a badly repaired place in the road.

"An air raid?" asked Max.

"Altgarten's one and only. Last March. An R.A.F. plane jettisoned incendiary bombs across the potato fields and two high explosive bombs. One on the road, one on Frau Kersten's outhouse. She has French prisoners of war working on the farm now. She made them fix up the barn and mend the road."

"They did a better job on the barn than on the road."

"She didn't give them the road to live in."

"Smart woman, Frau Kersten," said Max with a laugh. The car turned northwest onto the road that they would follow to Nieuwkerke and all the way to Arnhem. On the left, Frau Kersten's potato fields stretched away to the flat horizon. Long lines of bent figures were lifting the waxy yellow potatoes that August liked so much. There were children among them, for the schools had given older boys the traditional holiday to help with the crop. As the lines moved forward their forks raised the dry soil so that the breeze carried it in dust clouds across the fields behind them.

"They are fine potatoes," said August.

"Ah, potatoes! How could the Wehrmacht fight without them. Frau Kersten must be doing very nicely out of the war, August. A smart woman. Now that's a direction you might be looking."

"What do you mean, Max?" August couldn't help laughing at the face Max pulled in answer to him.

"What do you *think* I mean, you old rogue," said Max. "You think I believe you spend all your time embracing your binoculars and flirting with those seagulls around that radar station of yours?"

"Just lately the R.A.F. have been keeping me busy."

"Not too busy for that, August."

"I'm in love, Max. I'm going to get married."

"To the R.A.D. girl?"

"Yes."

"We have a lot of R.A.D. girls working in the Military Government. It never works out."

"Whatever do you mean?" said August.

"Marriages with the R.A.D. girl clerks. We have a couple of requests every month. I usually post the girl away. Unless she's pregnant. In that case I post the man."

"You're a coldhearted swine, Max."

"Your girl . . . is she . . . ?"

"Damn you, Max, no. At least . . ."

"There you are, August. Face the truth, old friend. A moment's fun, a convenient relationship." He paused. "For a *time*. Not for a marriage, August."

"I love her, Max."

"See how it goes for a month or two."

"There's a war on, Max. And God knows how old I'll be when it ends! No, this is right for me. And right for her too."

"Cigar?"

"Thank you." August sniffed at it appreciatively.

"The Controller of Civilian Fuel Supplies, Netherlands, is a post that brings a privilege or two."

"All right, she's just a naïve young girl, but I've had enough of complex sophisticated people. If she'll put up with my devious complications, I'll be happy to have her simple soul."

Max smiled and lit the cigar for him. For quite a long time they both looked out of the car windows without speaking. It was odd, thought August: one can know a man for many years, and then suddenly half a dozen sentences reveal how little communication there truly is between the two of you. Perhaps all human relationships are like that. Perhaps the best that he could hope for in a marriage to Anna-Luisa was that disenchantment would come slowly, and the bitter aftermath of disenchantment—the black despairing hatred—never even begin. He looked at Max; how indolent and comfortable he was. He leaned back, his eyes closed, as they sped along the clear main road.

"Our roads," remarked Max. "Could we have imagined such wonderful roads when we were children?"

"Could we have imagined war on two fronts and the need to move armored divisions on interior lines?"

"You're a miserable fellow today. Admit the Führer's roads are wonderful."

"The roads are wonderful, but are roads the thing we most urgently need? I can't help thinking that the great Autobahnen were built across the land in order to convince us that Germany is not a conglomeration of disparate and unfriendly principalities."

"Well, today I bless the fine roads, for we have a detour: Deelen."

"Will it make us late?"

"You won't miss your appointment with the *Tommis*."

"How late?"

"Sixty kilometers to Deelen; Deelen to your radar site can't be more than one hundred and fifty kilometers, even after dropping me off in The Hague."

"How long at Deelen?"

"Stop being so nervous, August. We'll have no local traffic in the border zone, a few convoys between Utrecht and The Hague and then nothing at all in the prohibited coastal zone. When we get to Deelen you'll be fascinated. I'll have to drag you away, you'll see."

The first traffic holdup was on the far side of Geldern.
Teen-age officer cadets, stripped to the waist and gleaming
with sweat, were working like a chain gang to replace a
damaged bridge section in record time.

They were only a couple of kilometers past that when
an oncoming convoy halted them again. August watched
the twelve-ton half-tracks, and the 8.8-cm. flak guns they
trailed, creep past. It was a large battery complete with
fire-control equipment and personnel in full battle order.
Three of the guns were crewed by Flakhelfer. These
Hitler Jugend, some only fifteen years old, were dwarfed
by the seats of the giant tractor. Their steel helmets came
low over their unsmiling faces. They wore brightly colored
badges and shoulder patches and red and white swastika
armbands. At his waist each one had a dagger.

"Hitler Jugend volunteers," said Max.

"Conscripts," said August.

"Kids?"

"That's it." How soon would Hansl be accoutered thus
and fed into the endless war? Max counted the guns as
they rolled past. "Twenty-eight guns," exclaimed Max.
"Fantastic."

"Grossbatterie; under centralized fire control. At first it
was two or three sites combining; now they have up to
forty guns under one control."

"Is that good?"

"At least the flak keeps the R.A.F. up high. Without
flak the *Tommis* would come down on the deck and put
their bombs into our factory chimneys."

"You know, August, my friend, there are quite a few
homeless civilians living in the Ruhr who would prefer
that." He laughed.

A flak officer noticed the dark-blue Citroën with its
Luftwaffe number plates and came across the apologize
for the delay. He was a stern-faced young man, steel
helmet, fair moustache and a nonregulation pair of soft
kid gloves that came into view as he saluted.

"There are road repairs in Geldern," said Max Sepp.
"You won't get these contraptions through the town."

"I know, sir," said the officer, "but we turn off to Wesel
before the road works."

"The road into the Ruhr from Wesel is even worse,"
said Max. "I know this district well."

"Our destination is Ahaus," said the flak officer.

"Why Ahaus?" said Max. "If it was left to me I'd pull
all the flak back into the Ruhr. There you can be sure of a

crack at the terror fliers. You'll be lucky to see any
*Tommis* at Ahaus."

"The policy is still an air defense corridor along the
Netherlands border," said August.

"My lads are eager," said the officer. "They'll be disappointed unless they see action soon."

August replied, " 'No great dependence is to be placed
in the eagerness of young soliders for action. For fighting
has something agreeable in the idea to those who are
strangers to it.' "

The flak officer was puzzled. He pulled at the fastening
of his glove.

"Vegetius," supplied August.

"A Roman military writer of the fourth century," explained Max Sepp.

"As the Herr Oberst wishes," said the officer respectfully. Three huge searchlights trundled past them. He saluted
again and swung aboard one of the slow-moving tractors
to join his young enthusiasts. The Citroën moved forward.

"You shocked the fellow," said Max.

"I didn't mean to," said August.

"Why worry?" said Max. "With that medal at your
throat you can afford to be blasé about heroism. But in
case you should think me an untutored serf, Vegetius was
also the man who said, 'Let him who desires peace
prepare for war!' "

"We all say something we don't mean once in a while,"
said August.

Max laughed, and August wondered if he had not been
too quick to judge his old friend.

There was another quarter of a mile of the traffic jam
before the cause of it was revealed. There a Bedford army
lorry and an Opel car were locked in embrace. A young
N.S.K.K. man was directing the traffic onto the grassy
verge around the debris while three other N.S.K.K. men
were extricating the unconscious driver from under the
lorry's bent steering column. The rear part of the Bedford
had broken through a hedge and from it boxes of fruit
had fallen and split open. Pigs from the orchard were
making the most of their good luck.

"Those bloody British lorries," said Max. "They
shouldn't allow them on the road."

"But after Dunkirk there were so many."

"With right-hand steering. Half of these lorry drivers
are Motor Corps kids. They are taught to drive in three

weeks and then they come on the road and kill anyone
who gets in their way."

The N.S.K.K. boy waved them forward and they
bumped onto the grass. It was well plowed up now and
the Citroën's wheels were spinning for a moment before
getting a grip. Max leaned out of the car as they passed
the traffic man. "Those right-hand drives are death traps,"
he said.

"I don't speak German," said the traffic man. "I am
French." He had the same green and black uniform that
the Germans had but he wore a tricolor badge on his
sleeve and now he tapped it. Max was furious.

"What bloody use are they?" he shouted loud enough
for the boy to hear.

August said, "We're short of manpower, Max. Russia is
drinking our population as fast as we can get them there."

"A Frenchman," said Max angrily.

"They are a logical race. They should make good traffic
police."

"Huh," said Max. "Logical. They put a knife between
your ribs and spend an hour explaining the rational necessity for doing it."

"That sounds like a lot of Germans I know."

"No, a German puts a knife into your ribs and weeps a
sea of regretful tears."

August smiled. "And after the Englishman has wielded
the knife?"

"He says, 'Knife? What knife?' "

August laughed.

From there on, apart from a traffic jam in Cleve and a
long line of traffic crawling through a military police
check at the Waal bridge, they moved fast. August dozed
off until Max nudged him.

"We'll be at Deelen in five minutes or so," said Max.

"Deelen air base or the Divisional Operations Room?"

"Number 1 Fighter Division. They control the whole
damned air battle there: the whole of the Netherlands,
Westphalia, Rhineland-Palatinate, and even parts of Hesse
and Belgium. Been there before?"

"Last year."

"Ah yes, the old sanatorium buildings. Wait till you see
the new bunker. When I first saw it, August, I realized
for the first time that, no matter what the *Amis* and
*Tommis* do, they can never win against organization like
ours. On the control map there is every night fighter,
bomber, flak unit, civil defense unit. It's like magic."

"We need every bit of magic we can get, Max. Last
year the R.A.F. kept flying right through the bad winter
weather. There was no chance for a breathing space. We
must stop these people within the next few weeks or we
can be sure they'll keep bombing us right through next
winter. What's the good of winning a war if our families,
our homes, our cities, museums and culture are bombed to
destruction? We can move our Tiger tank factories deep
underground, but we can't put Speyer cathedral or Cologne underground."

"The experts at O.K.L. say that if we can crack the
morale of the bombers this year, they'll give up bombing
the cities."

"The only way I know of cracking their morale is
shooting them down."

"Well, of course. They say if we could bring their
casualty averages up by just two and a half percent, the
R.A.F. would have to change their tactics."

"Now you understand why I mustn't be back late," said
August. "A short summer night like tonight, the moon
almost full . . . If they come tonight and we don't knock
down a record number of them, we don't deserve to win."

The Luftwaffe Citroën stopped at the first of the
H.Q.'s roadblocks. The Luftwaffe sentries with their sub-
machine guns looked strangely out of place in the candy-
striped sentry boxes. An elderly sentry checked their papers and waved the car on. It had rained heavily here and
the striped box made dazzling reflections on the shiny
road. The bunker itself was in beautiful forest land south
of the airfield. The tall beech trees were dripping onto the
sunlit paths and beyond the woodland patches of heather
were near to flowering.

They got out of the car. There was a smell of resin
from the sun-baked pine trees and also the damp dark
smell of mold. Deelen airfield was only a stone's throw
beyond the trees and from there August caught the sound
of a light aircraft. He waited until it came into view above
the trees. It was a white two-seater biplane climbing steadily and earnestly without showmanship.

"That's what I call an airplane," said August. "If only
flying had stayed like that, instead of giving way to scientists, horsepower, calculating machines and control systems."

"You mustn't complain about that, my good August,"
said Max. "You are a controller, remember."

The white biplane banked and turned neatly. Its fabric

was still wet with rain and its wings flashed in the sunlight. The little plane kept climbing in spirals, like the diagrams in training manuals. Then, just as deliberately, it set course on a reciprocal of its takeoff path and passed over them again. Before they could turn away the puttering of the white trainer was drowned by the roar of a twin-engine Junkers. The great black machine appeared over the leafy oak trees like some new sort of flying beetle. Its stinglike aerial array seemed to quiver as it searched for the other plane. In a moment it had gone.

"What a beauty," said Max. "For the time being, I'll take the calculating machines and horsepower every time."

The bunker was truly gigantic. Its entrance road sloped down to a leveled site several meters below ground level. In spite of this the bunker towered above the surrounding woodland. It was as high as an apartment building and as long as a city block. Its roof was three meters of concrete laced with steel rods and heavy steel girders. Every lesson learned in the first years of war had been embodied in its design.

"It's indestructible," said Max. "It will stand there for hundreds of years after the war is over. Even if you wanted to remove it, it would be impossible."

Max was enjoying August's surprise. "Take no notice of all those windows in the wall," said Max. "That's just to give some light to the office workers. Behind that layer of offices, the concrete internal structure is many meters thick."

The doors were one-centimeter steel, hung on hinges as big as fists. The concrete corridors were noisy with Luft-waffe personnel, many of them young girls. Max Sepp knocked briefly upon an office door and marched into an office crowded with Luftwaffenhelferinnen, uniformed girl communication auxiliaries. Max was on first-name terms with them. He collected a metal document case and gave it to his driver to carry. Max settled down to gossip with one of the girl auxiliaries. From among the young officers who received Max's cigars one elected to show August the "Opera House" itself. He was a dark-eyed young man. He put the cigar away in his desk and reached for his cap. He had grown a blunt black moustache to imitate exactly the one Dolfo Galland, the popular young general of fighters, wore. August guessed he'd smoke his cigar in similar mimicry. With a seeming disregard for convention or discipline, he kept his left hand thrust deep into his jacket pocket in a rakish manner that well suited the night fighter clasp on his chest and German Cross on his top pocket.

The young Leutnant took August upstairs. The outer shell of corridors gave onto the inner chamber at three levels. At the top of the staircase they passed through another identity check by an armed sentry. The Leutnant said to August, "There is a drill on at present—Pheasant Alert—so we must keep very quiet."

As they entered the cool dark Battle Room August shook his head in disbelief. The Leutnant smiled; every visitor was amazed. It had become a showplace for top Nazi V.I.P.s and this was the place to stand for a first glimpse. As August's eyes became accustomed to the gloom he saw that it was indeed like an opera house. Seated rank upon rank in front of them were Helferinnen, each one crisp and neat in her white uniform blouse. He saw only the backs of their heads, as would a person standing at the rear of a steep theater balcony. Far below him, in the orchestra stalls, were rows of high-ranking control officers. Everyone's attention was upon the stage. For hanging where a theater's curtains would hang there was a glass map of northern Europe. The green glass map was fifteen meters wide and its glow provided enough light for August to see the rows of white faces peering at it and the papers on their desks. On the walls beside the map there were weather charts and a complex board that showed the availability of reserve night fighters. The cool air, silent movement and green light conspired to make the atmosphere curiously like that of an aquarium.

Each of the girls in the balcony with them had a spotlight. From the Fresnel lens of each one was beamed a small white T to represent a constantly moving R.A.F. bomber or a green T to represent the fighter hunting it. As the map references came over the girls' headsets they moved the white bombers across Holland and northern Germany in a neat line. Down in the stalls the phones were in constant use and there was a shuffle of papers and movements. The air-conditioning made a loud humming sound and it was cool enough inside this vast concrete bunker to make August shiver even on this warm summer's day. From here phone and teleprinter cables stretched across the land to airfields, watchtowers, radar stations, radio monitors and civil defense headquarters. Even U-boats, and flak ships off the Dutch coast, reported aircraft

movements to this bunker, which the Luftwaffe had christened the Battle Opera House.

Overlapping circles of light had appeared on the map.
Each one was a radar station like August's own. Each one
had two night fighters circling above it waiting to pounce
upon a bomber coming into range of its magic eye. Now
and again one of the T lights was switched off as a bomber
was destroyed.

The young Leutnant had noticed August's Pour le
Mérite and decided that he was worth a fuller explanation than most of the rubberneck visitors that he showed
around. He pointed to the six rows of stalls far below
them.

"It's in the two front rows that the battle decisions are
made. The Major General third from the left is the
Divisional Controller. On each side of him he keeps an
IA—Operations Officer. On the far left is the NAFU or
Chief Signals Officer. Second to the right of the Div.
Controller, the officer with the yellow tabs is the IC or
Intelligence Officer. The old man on his right is the senior
Meteorology man. The second row of officers, the ones
speaking into the phones all the time, are Fighter Control-
lers carrying out the orders. On that same desk there's a
Flak Officer, Radar Controller and Civil Defense Li-
aison."

"Who is the man in the tinted-glass office on the left?"
asked August.

"Radio Intelligence Liaison Officer. He only comes out
to talk with the Divisional Controller. Even then it's in a
whisper." He smiled; he had the cynical attitude to boffins
that operational pilots always have.

The T-shaped lights moved slowly in a straight line
toward Berlin.

"What do you think?" asked the Leutnant.

"It's damned impressive," said August.

"It's not always as calm as this, I'm afraid. On a real
raid things get more hectic. I've seen them shouting at
each other down there."

"And those little white lights don't disappear so quickly," said August.

"Ah," said the Leutnant. "That's the real difference, I'm
afraid." He spoke like a man who knew how big the sky
was on a dark night.

They watched the "air raid" proceed for a few more
minutes. Still the white T lights that represented the bombers kept on their narrow line. The controllers practiced

dealing with the "stream tactics" that the R.A.F. had developed as a way of overwhelming the radar defenses of just one zone instead of presenting single targets piece-meal to several radar sets and accompanying night fighters.

"What about the Mosquito they send in to mark the target? If our planes could get up high enough to knock that down, the stream wouldn't know where to drop their bombs."

"Exactly," said the Leutnant. He swung lightly round on his toes with his arm stiffly akimbo, which gave him a curious effeminate stance. He eyed Bach speculatively and then decided to confide a secret.

"Tonight we have a surprise awaiting them."

"The Ju88s supercharged with nitrous oxide?"

" 'Ha-ha' they call them—laughing gas, you see. You've heard about them, eh?"

"What idiot thought of that code name?"

"And 12.8 guns on railway mountings; we are going to try everything we know tonight. I don't know; some fool in Air Ministry, I suppose."

"If they cooperate by flying over the railway guns," said August doubtfully.

"They always come in from north to south, and always toward the Ruhr because—we think—that's the limit of the electronic range. So we can make a guess at it. We'll be more or less in position."

"Radio intercept predict a big one tonight," said August. He looked at his own radar station on the glass map, its range indicated by a dully lighted circle. It was exactly placed between the R.A.F. bomber airfields of East Anglia and the Ruhr. "I'm at Ermine," said August.

"I know, sir," said the Leutnant. "I don't think you'll have much sleep before morning." Now August could see that the young Leutnant's stiff left arm was artificial.

# 11

LIKE all such depressions, this one had been born when moist air from the Azores met the cold dry air of the Arctic. The resulting muddled air mass moved eastward over Britain until it reached the sea area to the west of Denmark, which was called Heligoland. Here the center of the depression paused. Hinged upon this depression, the cloud-marked cold front, like a thousand-mile-wide door, swung across Europe at twenty miles an hour. The front curved because its southern edge couldn't keep up the pace. That southern end had only reached Bilbao in Spain when the center was darkening the skies of Lyon and the northern sector was deluging the streets of Esbjerg with torrential rain.

In the high pressure region that followed the front the heavy air subsided, warming by compression as it dropped. There was no more than the lightest of breezes, the clouds shrank even as you watched them, and the sun shone.

England had had its thunderstorms during the night and a morning of sunshine, but already a little cumulus had appeared over Wales and parts of the west country. At Kroonsdijk, however, where the cold front had only recently passed, the skies were blue and the sun warmed the wet grass.

Unteroffizier Himmel eased himself into the pilot's seat of his Ju88 parked at the end of the dispersal. The sun had been upon the metal fuselage for several hours and now the seat and controls were hot to touch and the smell of warmed fuel was as powerful as *Glühwein*. It was a luxury to be alone for a moment, and apart from the sounds of the ground crewmen doing their preflight inspection it was as peaceful as a country graveyard. Him-

133

mel looked at the wet grass where an oil patch made a
rainbow pattern of red, yellow and mauve. A sandpiper
landed and bobbed around the brightly colored grass
looking for worms until a mechanic closed the dinghy
stowage hatch forcibly enough to frighten it back into the
air.

The old piece of fuselage that the fire section had set
alight sent a quill of white smoke into the still air. At its
nib, Leutnant Beer in overalls was wielding a fire extinguisher under the command of Horst Knoll, the senior
N.C.O. of the fire section. Horst was a bad-tempered
fellow who hated officers and did his best to make their
lives as uncomfortable as his legitimate duties permitted.

"On to the base of the flame," he was shouting to Beer,
who was reluctantly closing in upon the foul-smelling
wreckage and cursing. Horst Knoll, knowing exactly what
the moving lips were saying, smiled and urged him forward all the more. "Don't be afraid of the smoke, Herr
Leutnant, get much closer and put the jet onto the base of
the flame. Much closer, Herr Leutnant, much, much
closer."

At the far end of the line of mat-black aircraft Major
Redenbacher's airplane poked its snout from the dark
hangar. Most of the spare mechanics were working on it.
Suddenly the peace was shattered by the sound of engines.
A Junkers with Leutnant Kokke at the controls was also
preparing for an air test. Its chocks were pulled aside.
Kokke gave a blip of throttle to start it moving around
the perimeter. It moved away beyond the Alert Hut,
where the air crew spent so much time. Outside it a dozen
air crew—air tests completed—sat sunning themselves.
Most of them were younger than Himmel and few had
been in the Luftwaffe as long as he had, but they'd come
from all manner of units, as their clothing showed. They'd
seen service on war fronts from Finland to Egypt: British
Army bush shirts, Czech flying boots, old Hitler Jugend
shorts and Swedish leather jackets. Some sat shirtless, eyes
closed, in the deck chairs, two played chess and some
sprawled full length on the wet grass arguing about engines
and firepower and girls and promotion and medals.

No matter how much Löwenherz disapproved of their
unsoldierly appearance, it was a standing order of Major
Redenbacher that at their Alert Huts the air crews could
"dress informally, always providing that the regulations
concerning the wearing of identity tags around the neck
are not disobeyed."

Three fliers were standing in the hut doorway. Himmel looked at his watch and guessed that they were listening to the B.B.C., for this was the time that they broadcast the fliers' program. The carefully written technical talks always ended with a list of Luftwaffe personnel newly captured and newly dead.

Suddenly there was a loud thunder of cannon fire and they all swung round to the firing butts. Above it a thin veil of blue smoke showed where Löwenherz's plane was having its guns harmonized by the armorers. Someone made a joke, and then Himmel saw them all laugh and relax. It was the long wait for nightfall that built up the tension. That's why Himmel always left his air test as late as possible.

One of Himmel's ground crew removed the rudder lock and then walked around the airplane to check the ailerons and control surfaces. Himmel slipped his toes under the rudder-bar loops and fastened his seat straps. He ran his hand down his oxygen-lead connection to check it and then moved the control column forward and back and twisted the antlers to be sure that the controls were free of obstruction. Old Krugelheim, the chief mechanic, was getting a little impatient. Under his black overalls he was shirtless and without trousers, but still he sweated as he paced about under the nose of Himmel's machine. He kept looking across to the hangar and Major Redenbacher's aircraft. The cowling had been removed from its port motor and its most intimate parts bared to the oily inquiring hands of the fitters. The black-garbed men stood on a platform, arrayed around the disemboweled motor like witch doctors at a Black Mass. One of them, chanting a line from a textbook, bent low into its entrails and flashed a torch deep inside. His open hand appeared and wordlessly a wrench was put into it.

Krugelheim looked up to where Himmel sat in the cockpit high above him. "The fuel pump," explained Krugelheim.

Himmel hoped sincerely that the black men would work their healing magic soon, for it was 1520 hours already and if his own plane was not in service by nightfall, when the killing began, the Major had a habit of taking the nearest one. Himmel's plane—*Katze Four*—was the nearest.

He slid the cockpit fully open and called down to the chief mechanic, "Have you seen Unteroffizier Pohl?"

"No," said old Krugelheim. "He's probably still talking to the signals officer."

"These aerials are a trial to us," said Christian Himmel. The old man walked under the nose to look closely at the "toasting fork."

"It's the rain," he said. "If they stay dry for a few days they work perfectly. Here comes Pohl now."

Someone in flying overalls, yellow life jacket and parachute harness emerged from the hut, but it wasn't Himmel's radar operator. For a few paces he was obscured by the tail of another Junkers 88, but as he came round it they recognized Löwenherz. On this warm day none of the other fliers were wearing flying overalls. Like Himmel most wore lightweight helmets, shirts, shorts and life jackets. It was just like Löwenherz to be in full flying gear.

"What does the bloody Staffelkapitän want?" said old Krugelheim. As if having a faulty fuel line on Major Redenbacher's machine wasn't enough trouble for one day.

"Cheer up, Kugel," said Himmel. "We'll soon find out." To call the grumpy old Oberfeldwebel "Kugel" was a privilege earned by only the most seasoned of Kroonsdijk's N.C.O.s. Although it meant "bullet," the pot-bellied old chief mechanic was short enough in stature to realize that it also meant "globe." Kugel came close under the cockpit.

"You were in his Staffel during the Kanalkampf, weren't you, young Himmel?"

"He was in mine. I took him on his first operational sortie as my wingman. He was a lively fellow in those days."

"Then the war has sobered him," said the old man.

"It's sobered a lot of us," agreed Himmel.

"Huh," exclaimed the mechanic bitterly.

Himmel smiled at the old Oberfeldwebel. His misanthropy was what kept these airplanes in such good order. The old man too had been a lively youngster once, but there are more casualties of war than the doctor ever sees. Kugel clicked his heels as Löwenherz walked past him without a word and proceeded to inspect and waggle each control surface to be sure they were unlocked and free of obstruction.

Himmel looked down to the hatch as Löwenherz climbed up the metal ladder. The soft inner hatch opened and his head appeared level with the floor of the cockpit behind Himmel's feet. "I'm flying with you instead of Pohl," he said. One of the ground staff passed Löwenherz's briefcase up through the hatch.

Himmel nodded and turned to exchange a pained glance with the chief mechanic below while Löwenherz strapped himself into the radar operator's seat behind him. The backs of their heads almost touched, but between their seats there was a slab of steel armor. The Staffelkapitän carefully made sure that his intercom cable went down his back and was clipped to his overall. It was an inconvenience, but Löwenherz had read of several cases of air crew being strangled by their own radio leads and it was a pet subject for his memos. Himmel hoped that he wouldn't notice that his leads were not correctly positioned.

"All set, Christian?" fussed Kugel. "It's warm today; radiator gills full out while you're taxiing, then fully closed for takeoff. Watch the cooling indicator." Himmel nodded. "Frei!" yelled Kugel.

"Frei!" replied Himmel and pushed the button. The starter motor whined, jerking the blades. A bright blue flame escaped from the exhaust, in spite of the dampers. Then there was an ear-splitting roar. The panel vibrated and the instruments blurred. Himmel throttled back. He started the other motor and waited while the fuel- and oil-pressure needles came alive. The whole plane was rocking on its tires now. He slid the side window closed in spite of the heat, for it was one of Löwenherz's well-known instructions. The instrument panel and the windshield chattered with the pulse of the motors. He pushed the throttles wide open and saw the rev counters flick around to 2,800. Even through his flying helmet the sound was piercing. The ground crew had hands clamped against their ears and their black overalls rippled in the wind. Two of them tugged the chocks away from the wheels.

Himmel took an extra look round the cockpit: flaps up, mags off, undercarriage locked, fuel full, straps fastened, oxygen ready, brakes on. The instruments were color coded: yellow for fuel, brown for oil and blue for air. Each of them read correctly and yet still Himmel worried. All pilots did; this was the moment of worry; once they were airborne the tenseness would ease a little.

Himmel hooked his oxygen mask into the forehead of his helmet and pushed closed the studs of his throat mike. Löwenherz, taller than little Pohl, struggled to notch the seat back. Himmel was about to help but decided that

Löwenherz was not the sort of man who liked being helped.

"Pilot to radar operator," said Himmel self-consciously. "All correct?"

"All correct," said Löwenherz.

In his rear-view mirror Himmel saw Löwenherz fingering the radar controls.

"*Katze Four* to control: request permission to take off." The controller told them to move off. Himmel released the brakes and the airplane rolled forward. Old Kugel waved him away like a swarm of flies.

Control told him to taxi to the far side of the airfield, wait until *Katze Two* was airborne and then move on to the end of the runway. He moved slowly along the perimeter track and past a wrecked Junkers 34. It had been there ever since Himmel could remember and had become a landmark for the aerodrome. Three months before, a salvage gang had removed the motor, only to find that it was an ancient Bristol Jupiter instead of the German power unit they had expected. A typical Luftwaffe balls-up, thought Himmel. So now the disemboweled plane had its rusting motor displayed alongside like a museum exhibit.

Parallel with the fence was the water-filled ditch, bright green now that summer sun had covered the surface with tiny cress plants. The dijk itself was two and a half meters higher than the aerodrome and upon it was the road to Utrecht. Its edges were neatly marked in white paint and its surface cobbled with the large stones that the Dutch call "children's heads." Military convoys buzzed upon it like angry bees and the wooden wheels of local cyclists crawled along with a bone-shaking clatter. Along the dijk road came a company of metal-shod infantry. Himmel noticed the tired sweaty soldiers look his way with envy as they trudged past under the weight of full packs, blankets and rifles. They were singing, "*In der Heimat, in der Heimat, da gibt's ein Wiedersehen.*" In the homeland we'll meet again.

Himmel and Löwenherz watched Kokke's plane as he ran its engines to maximum revs and then roared along the runway climbing steadily toward the east. Then Himmel followed.

It wasn't one of his best takeoffs, but to have Löwenherz sitting calmly behind you waiting to do the routine radar interception test that was really the duty of meek little Unteroffizier Pohl was downright disconcerting.

The land flashed past beneath them. The sun shone down upon Kroonsdijk so that half of each street went black with shadow. Children pointed at them, a dog fled, a horse needed comforting. Gulls went into the air like a handful of white confetti, caught the breeze and in unison swooped back toward earth. The undercarriage thumped into the nacelle. A line of laundry wriggled, cyclists stopped. A silk patch of blue lake was tacked to green countryside by the taut fishing lines of a hundred anglers, hoping to supplement their meager rations. The flat heathland was like purplish brown sandpaper scratched with irregular pale footpaths. The fields and lakes grew smaller as they fell away. An empty road grew busy, reached a fishing village and ended. Boats crammed tight to crowded quays, then there was just the empty blue water of the IJsselmeer. Over it there was a haze of summer heat like smoking fat on a frying pan.

Control called him. *"Katze Four* steer 090 for practice air interceptions. Rendezvous at two thousand meters; grid reference: Heinz Marie Nine."

Himmel pulled a map from his flying boot. "Deelen," supplied Löwenherz before he could unfold it. Himmel spread the map and glanced down at the ninth square of the H and M reference. Of course Löwenherz was right. Himmel smiled; the big plane was flying perfectly. In the mirror he saw Löwenherz look over his shoulder.

"Is this gun loaded?" asked Löwenherz.

"Yes, sir."

"I'll test it while we are over water," announced Löwenherz.

Behind him he heard a burst of firing as he tested the gun. What a good thing the ground crew had loaded it. They often didn't bother, for in the night fighter's war these little machine guns, swiveled round by the radar man, weren't much use. Himmel could smell the sour cordite fumes and tightened the oxygen mask against his face. They were circling Deelen when their airfield control called them to say that Kokke's Junkers had returned to Kroonsdijk with a technical fault. Leeuwarden airfield would supply an aircraft for them to test the airborne radar. They must go to Ameland, an island off the northern coast of the Netherlands.

It was Löwenherz who first saw the plane below them. It was only when you saw another aircraft in the sky that you realized how fast you were moving. It was a white biplane, an Arado 66 with a red warning streamer flying

from its wingtip. It seemed a long time since Löwenherz
had flown his first solo.

"See that, Himmel?" said Löwenherz. "Below to
port?" The little trainer crawled across fields of ripening
rye and dark fir woods.

"He's going well, sir, steadier than I was."

"And steadier than I was too," agreed Löwenherz.
"Come round behind him; perhaps I can pick him up on
the radar."

"He's very low. I think we'll get ground echoes," said
Himmel, but he put the plane's nose down and came
round to creep up behind the pretty machine that was
popping along merrily like a toy.

"I'll put the Kurier dead ahead," said Himmel, using the
code word for enemy aircraft. The little white biplane had
become an enemy bomber, for in what magical rites and
rituals do we not manufacture an enemy from clay or
wax. Or even from wood and fabric. The doll that looks
like your enemy is called by his name. Stick pins into it
and set it alight and believe that those same misfortunes
will befall the ones you hate. Pretending it was dark, the
two men acted out their game, stalking after the white
quarry with all the skill that their years of war had taught
them.

Himmel's head twisted and turned like an anxious sparrow's. Veteran fighter pilots survived by scrutinizing every
sector of the sky regularly and Himmel never rested his
eyes on one thing for more than a moment. Victor
Löwenherz, on the other hand, with some effort of will
power concentrated solely upon working the radar. As far
as he was concerned the plane was under Himmel's control. His father had always boasted that he could ride
better, shoot better and even groom the horses and polish
the equipment better than any man under his command.
Similarly Oberleutnant Löwenherz was proud of his skill
on the radar sets. Of course it was all very simple when
your pilot was steering at the machine ahead for a test. In
the black of night when the pilot relied solely upon his
radar man's guidance it was very different. He adjusted
the controls again but the elevation tube was a mess and
the range tube was almost as bad. It was closing far too
fast. Himmel throttled back and even used some flap, but
the old biplane was so slow that Himmel had to break
away to port and come round behind him again.

In his mirror Himmel saw Löwenherz crouching close
to the three radar screens. He said, "You're right, Him-

mel, the ground echo at this height just wipes out the
elevation blip. We're probably scaring the fellow half to
death."

And scaring me too, thought Himmel. Here we are,
perhaps the two most responsible and experienced pilots
on the Staffel, compiling a blueprint for an air disaster:
low altitude, speed close to stalling and formating on a
strange aircraft. An accident investigation board would
pillory both of us should anything happen.

Himmel rolled the little control wheel to close the flaps.
He pushed the yellow throttle knobs and the engine note
modulated from baritone to tenor. It was a relief to open
up the motors. The Richards were powerful machines but
the heavy radar equipment and clumsy aerial array on the
nose made them only too easy to stall. He made a wide
arc round the little white biplane so that it wouldn't be
thrown around by the propwash. Himmel smiled as they
passed, for the pilot had been so closely concerned with
holding his horizon steady that he noticed the Junkers now
for the first time. He stared in amazement at the huge
black machine and its secret radar aerials. Then the white
biplane dipped as the pupil began looking for his airfield.

The Junkers climbed steeply and continued north, skirt-
ing Leeuwarden to the west and continuing out to sea. To
starboard lay Terschelling, one of the largest islands in the
Frisian chain. The weather was excellent except on the far
northeastern horizon, where ice crystals of cu-nimbus
clouds reached miles into the air and wore the dark skirt
of falling rain. They continued over the Frisian Islands
and out into the North Sea. Flecks of cloud made shadows
on the water below them and sometimes there were shreds
of white stratocumulus large enough to swallow the plane
for a moment.

A few miles out they saw a coastal convoy. Keeping
well clear of the wrecks that littered this coast, but inside
the minefields that protected it, the convoy was making
good progress through the calm sea. The Junkers was low
enough to see the seamen moving on the decks and some
of the old coal burners were making columns of smoke
tall enough to reach them. They were a battered collection: half-painted funnels, rusty winches, dribbling scup-
pers and misplaced hatch covers. Some of the deck cargoes were only half covered and a deck party was working
feverishly on the tarpaulin. Himmel wondered why they
bothered. The grimy condition of the coasters was belied
by the fresh rain that had glossed their decks and given

their hulls the polish of old jackboots. Two freighters had
deck cargoes of honey-colored fresh timber looking good
enough to eat. There were Danes and Dutchmen; ancient
coastal tankers low in the water, and at the front two
French cargo liners making down the coast with machinery and chemicals. They were sailing the routes they had
always sailed, some since before the first war. Strange that
now they should have German naval destroyers, frigates
and U.J. boats fussing around their formations and German aircraft protecting them from the determined attacks
of R.A.F. planes. Stranger still when some of those
R.A.F. planes were manned by Frenchmen, Dutchmen
and Danes. Two U.J. boats—converted trawlers of about
four hundred tons—detached themselves from the convoy
and hurried to the rear. Now the convoy began changing
course, but kept convoy discipline and good formation.
Each wake was scratched crisp and white upon the azure
ocean. It was a beautiful sight, enhanced by the red and
yellow lights that climbed higher than the masts. The light
cruiser was covered in winking lights as though every
seaman aboard was sending a message to the plane, as
indeed he was. Suddenly there was an explosion.

"They're firing at us," yelled Löwenherz, but his voice
was drowned by the fierce bangs of the shells bursting
around them. Now Himmel knew what was under the
tarpaulins: guns. A near miss rocked the airplane and
wrenched the port wing upward. He didn't correct. He let
the airplane skid down in a violent sideslip. Each exploding shell hung a new black smudge in the sky but the old
smoke did not disappear, it slowly turned brown, and the
air around them was blotched with smelly smoke like a
three-dimensional disease. The plane dropped through the
bursting shells until the extra lift of the down-pointing
wing, and the Junkers' lateral stability, flattened it into
straight and level flight just a hundred feet over the
wavetops.

Now they were within range of the flak ship's 3.7-cm.
guns and even the multiple 2-cms. The pom-poms added a
new descant to the bass rhythms of the heavies. Himmel
let down even lower until they were only ten feet above
the water. The sea was a different color close to: a cold
steely gray flecked with dirty spume. Broken timber and
refuse pockmarked its heaving surface, and so did the
splashes of flak shells.

Himmel moved the throttles forward and, with touches
of rudder, danced across the wavetops low enough for

spray to mottle the windshield. The ship's gunners were aiming off skillfully. Their yellow lights spanned the water to make a fairy bridge between airplane and convoy. Soon they were far enough away for the bridge to fall into the water behind them. Himmel reset the trim wheel and pulled the nose up into a gentle climb.

Ahead was Holland. Marking its coastline high in the air there was another "land" of cumulus conjured up by the sea breeze from a cloudless sky. Himmel kept the Junkers' nose up. By the time they reached the coast they would be above those clouds. How beautiful they were: dark gray undersides, golden rims and fluffy white tops with occasional gaps revealing intense blue sky above.

"Are you all right, sir?" asked Himmel.

"I'm fine. Is the aircraft functioning?"

"It took a couple of knocks but the controls are working."

"That was damned remarkable flak, Himmel."

"They get a lot of practice."

"They get trigger happy too," said Löwenherz.

They both laughed too much and the tension was relieved.

"Do you remember that fellow they called Porky?" asked Löwenherz.

"Ostend in May 1941. When Karl Reinhold phoned him at the alert Hut and told him he'd been awarded the Knight's Cross ..."

"... for low-level attacks against friendly shipping," hooted Löwenherz. "Then he phoned me, but luckily you'd warned me that they would play pranks upon the new boys."

"They always did."

"You saved me being made a fool of, Christian."

"You were a good wingman."

"And now I'm your Staffelkapitän. It's funny how things work out."

"You should be the Kommodore," said Christian Himmel.

"For God's sake, Christian, why did you take those documents?"

"Is that why the Herr Oberleutnant came along?" Himmel had moved into the respectful third person.

"Of course it is, Christian."

"It was a matter of honor, Herr Oberleutnant."

"Honor?"

"Those documents shame us all."

"What are you saying? What sort of documents were they?"

"They didn't tell you, eh? Well, perhaps they were ashamed. Even shame is progress." Himmel reached into his flying overalls and pulled out a bulky document with brown paper covers. He passed it over his shoulder to Löwenherz. "Read it first, Herr Oberleutnant. Then you'll see why I have to go through with this."

It was not an impressive-looking dossier. There was a metal clip holding it together and a Luftwaffe eagle rubber-stamped onto the cover. Along the top it said "Luftwaffe High Command: Medical Corps: Secret." It wasn't a printed document. It was a duplicated typescript and in places the words were scarcely legible.

"Go through with what?"

"Please read it, sir."

At first Löwenherz was inclined to return it to Himmel unopened. He feared he was being drawn into a tacit conspiracy. For some time he stared out from the cramped little pulpit and watched the green sea creep past. By the time they crossed the coastline the cumulus fractus was below them, but only by an arm's reach. It stretched before them like a blinding white wasteland of ice and snow. The motors held a bass note like an organ pipe and the plane trembled with its power. Oberleutnant Löwenherz made his decision: he undid the metal clip and began reading the stolen medical report.

The convoy resumed the proper course after its evasive zigzagging. The destroyers and other armed ships hurried up and down, chivvying the merchantmen into line with loudspeakers and signal lamps. At the rear the light cruiser *Held* maintained a dignified straight course like a mother hen. The *Held* had been the 3,500-ton light cruiser *Jan Koppelstok* of the Royal Netherlands Navy until 1940, when she was seized by the Germans and refitted as an antiaircraft ship. In the forecastle battery, hidden by the steel door, a gunner named Franz Pawlak was smoking a cheroot. His loader cleaned the breech of the 10.5-cm. Model 37 with care and affection. They were both wearing the hooded furlined winter clothing that had been designed for the Russian Front. It gave them some protection against the piercing North Sea winds that even in the middle of summer chilled professional sailors to the bone.

The gun crews suffered even more, for many of them

were ex-Luftwaffe personnel, most of whom found it hard to adapt to the rigors of a seaman's life. Obergefreite Franz Pawlak did. He had joined the Luftwaffe during the Battle of Britain, when cinema newsreels showed pilots relaxing in deck chairs between jousting amid puffy white clouds, yelling "Spitfire" and smiling in the sunlight as high-ranking leaders shook their hands firmly and garlanded them with medals. Franz had been washed out of pilot school after a very bumpy solo landing. His marks in navigation theory had precluded his transfer to observer school and by the time he arrived as an officer candidate for the flak service he was confused and demoralized. He flunked, and was now an Obergefreite on a flak ship with precious little chance of becoming anything better. Franz loathed all airplanes with a terrible and sustained hatred. The previous month he and his gun crew had been credited with an R.A.F. Blenheim bomber shot down. The gun barrel wore a white ring to celebrate it. Franz wanted to add another ring only a little less than he wanted to become a civilian again. His K3, a plump butcher's delivery boy from Königsberg, was flushed with the exertion of loading 15-kg. shells onto the awkward, steeply inclined loading tray. He was arguing with Franz. "You can't paint a white ring on the barrel until the destruction of the plane is confirmed. That's the captain's orders."

"You saw it come down," said Franz. "Now am I the best gunner in the whole damn convoy?"

"It may have dived to sea level to avoid the gunfire, Admiral." Both his friends and his enemies called Franz Pawlak "Admiral."

"Get the white paint. We shot it down, I tell you."

"I still say it might have been one of ours."

"What are you talking about, Klaus? Every gun in the convoy was firing," said Franz.

"They didn't start until you did," said Klaus.

"Exactly. When I started, old Glass Nose gave the order."

"I'm still frightened it might have been one of ours. It looked very like a Junkers 88 and it flew south to escape."

"Beaufighter. A Bristol Beaufighter. Anyway, it was an airplane," said Franz. "Airplanes drop bombs and any airplane that comes within range of this contraption gets shot at. Now will you get the white paint?"

"Whatever you say, Admiral. We'll be the only gun on the *Held* with two victory rings, providing the old man doesn't make us paint it out again."

"I'll tell you something, Dikke," said Franz, prodding his friend in the belly. "We're averaging eight and a half knots and if that damned Danish bucket doesn't have any more steering gear trouble we'll be sailing past the Hook of Holland by midnight. That's the place for airplanes; the R.A.F. are over there nearly every night lately." He stroked the barrel of the big gun. "By tomorrow morning, Heini, we might have three rings on our *Würstchen.* Now wouldn't that be something to write to your cousin Sylvia about?"

Klaus Munte looked at his friend and smiled, but if there was anything he hated more than to be called "Fatty" it was to be called Heini. "By tonight the war might be over," said Munte.

"It won't be over for me," said Pawlak.

In this, as in so much of his plausible patter, he was wrong.

What Löwenherz had before him was one of the most bizarre, macabre and horrifying documents produced by a civilized society.

"Freezing Experiments with Human Beings" was a thirty-two-page report drawn up by Dr. Sigmund Rascher of the Luftwaffe Medical Corps, helped by a Professor of Medicine at the University of Kiel. The experiments took place at Dachau concentration camp and consisted of putting naked prisoners into ice water or leaving them out in the snow until they froze to death. Their temperatures were taken from time to time and recorded by the doctors. After death there was an autopsy.

Dr. Sigmund Rascher had moved the Luftwaffe's decompression chamber from Munich to Dachau concentration camp a few kilometers down the road. Two hundred prisoners were put into this chamber and each was depressurized until his body exploded. The report on this series of experiments was sent to the Medical Inspector of the Luftwaffe in the summer of 1942.

The third and final part of the stolen file was a report of Dr. Rascher's "warming experiments." These were even more perverted. Male prisoners were frozen almost to death in ice water and then placed in a bed between two naked women. (The women were prisoners from Ravensbrück concentration camp.) Dr. Rascher noted in great detail the sexual reactions of the half-dead men and to what extent these improved their chance of survival. He

reported in a paper dated February 1943 and marked
"Secret."

It stabbed Löwenherz to the heart of his belief. Of
course he had misgivings; few men didn't. Baron Löwenherz, his father, had not disbelieved the rumors; he called
them symptoms of unrest. The Nazi Party was a bridge to
sanity, a stage between the 1918 breakdown on the home
front and the return to a natural state of things where a
strong German officer corps held Germany's honor in
trust. For the time being the nation was in the hands of
these Bavarians and among them there were some vil-
lainous rascals, but better this sort of revolutionary than
the Bolshevik variety, who was prepared to butcher
families because their hands were clean or their names
patrician. Inventive, creative men are inclined to be ruth-
less, the baron had told him. We must work with these
Nazi *condottieri*, just as Leonardo had to work with
Machiavelli, with Cesare Borgia and with his Count
Sforza; just as three centuries later the Industrial Revolution pushed aside philosophers and humanitarians so that
single-minded despots ruled Europe. They put children up
chimneys and women down mines, they bullied, cheated,
bribed and literally worked their employees to death. They
caused misery and strife but, as we now know, the Industrial Revolution put Europe a century ahead of the rest of
the world.

Now the Nazis are transforming Germany with a similar singleminded ruthlessness. Of course we can't approve
of the sort of things that occur, these camps that people
speak of in whispers, the witch hunts for Jews and Communists, the "gunboat diplomacy" that Hitler used to
annex Austria and then Czechoslovakia. These things are
bad things, but they are all things that Britain did, or
would have done if necessary, to achieve its position as a
world power. If Hitler cheats he cheats for Germany; if
he steals he steals for Germany; if he kills then this he
does for Germany too. If he needs our help then the
officer corps must give it, generously and unstintingly.

All these things that his father had told him Löwenherz explained to Christian Himmel, but Christian remained unconvinced.

"But what would you achieve if you gave these unpleasant documents to the British? Would you like their propaganda people to reveal such things to the world?"

"I? Give them to the British?" said Himmel. "Is that
what they told you?"

"Then what do you want with the papers?"

"It's very simple," said Himmel. "These things are being done in our name, Herr Oberleutnant. Oh, it sounds very grand when you say it's for Germany, but these things are being done on behalf of us aviators. The research will be used to help us survive should we force-land in the ocean or the Arctic. But, Herr Oberleutnant, do you know a flier who wouldn't sooner die than have these disgusting experiments done to prisoners?"

"None," agreed Löwenherz. "But that's because we should ask them the question while they are warm and dry and on the ground, perhaps sitting back in the mess with a cognac in their hand. Ask a flier that question a few moments after he has crashed in the cold sea and perhaps he'll decide differently."

"I won't."

"No. Because you are an idealist, Christian. I remember the time when you spoke of the Nazis as though they were saviors of our land." Exactly, in fact, as the old baron had spoken of them. "Now you're disillusioned," continued Löwenherz. "You're bitter and resentful of your own ingenuous feelings. You're angry because the Nazis have never delivered something they didn't promise."

"Of course I am," said Himmel, "but that doesn't mean I was right then, nor that I am wrong now."

"It means that you should consider matters at greater length and not rush headlong into danger."

"No; with respect, Herr Oberleutnant, no. We have all delayed too long. While the victories arrived on schedule we all put our conscience in pawn to success. It's only now, when the future looks less rosy, that we are beginning to wonder if the 'new order' has been built upon sand."

"But the documents, Himmel. What do you want with them?"

"I made twenty-three photographic copies of the documents. Each copy was sent by normal mail to a Luftwaffe officer. I considered the list for a long time, Herr Oberleutnant. You are number twenty-three; that is your copy. The original has been posted to the Medical Inspectorate of the Luftwaffe in Berlin."

There was silence. A tuft of cloud was decapitated by the black wing. Other larger tufts raced after it. Then Löwenherz said, "It doesn't make it legal because you sent it only to Luftwaffe officers. It was a highly secret document."

"It's hardly less secret now that twenty-three Luftwaffe officers have a copy. But from now on they can't pretend they don't know of these things. They must protest. They must raise their voices. From now on they can never say they have not heard of concentration camps. . . ."

"What do you know of concentration camps, Christian?"

"I know, sir, that at least three airmen at Kroonsdijk have spent time in such places for small political offenses. Even if we have three times the average, that still leaves one man on every Luftwaffe airfield who has been in such a place. How much longer can the whole nation pretend that they don't know what we are doing in Europe, from Bordeaux to Leningrad: prisoners tortured, civilians killed, hostages executed? Now this is something that puts the honor of the Luftwaffe in jeopardy. Reichsmarschall Göring will have received one of these copies. He will understand what must be done." A large cloud fragment swallowed the airplane and disgorged it.

"They will arrest you, Christian," said Löwenherz. "Perhaps as soon as tomorrow."

"Yes," said Himmel. "Tomorrow I shall be arrested. But tomorrow I shall not be agonizing with my conscience, nor shall I be making excuses for the Nazis, nor shall I be fighting so that even more foreign prisoners can be experimented upon in concentration camps by insane doctors wearing the same uniform that I am wearing."

"Stop talking, Himmel. I must have time to think." The cloudtop was higher inland and suddenly the Junkers was totally enveloped in it. Now that it was pressing against the window it was no longer soft, dry, white, sun-tipped and inviting. It was gray, wet, cold and threatening. They could see nothing. The cloud gave a curious unnatural constant light to the cabin, and the two men sat very still, brightly lit and shadowless, like specimens on a microscope slide.

# 12

WHEN August Bach emerged from the gloomy chill of the
air-conditioned Divisional Fighter Control bunker the day
had ripened into one of those mellow summer afternoons
when the air is warm and sweet like soft toffee and
anyone with an ounce of sense is reclining in the grass
smelling the honeysuckle and wild strawberries, half listening to the insects, and watching blues and brimstones
fluttering fast enough to avoid the swallows above them
that glide and wheel and wait and wait.

Both Max and August dozed contentedly, hypnotized
by the sunlit countryside that moved past like a swinging
watch. The dark-blue Luftwaffe Citroën made good
speed down the main road from Arnhem past Utrecht all
the way to the small town of Tempel, where it turned off
north through Leiden, heading toward The Hague, where
General Christiansen, First World War ace fighter pilot,
was now Military Governor of the Netherlands.

They were beyond Leiden before Max awoke from his
reverie. He stirred and lit cigars for both of them.

"You were on the East Front last year, August. Perhaps
now that the sun shines on the great grasslands of the
Ukraine you wish you were back there: birch forests, long
summer evenings, buxom country girls, balalaikas, caviar,
medals arriving with the mail."

"That's what it says in the recruiting pamphlets. All I
remember is endless snow, my eyelashes iced over and on
Christmas morning one of the sentries frozen alive so that
we had to hack his rifle out of his hand with an ax."

"So that's how we all got *aufs Eis geführt*," said
August. It meant "led up the garden." Max looked anxiously at his driver but he seemed not to have heard.

"Were you ever stationed with your son?"

"For a month. Near Lake Ilmen in March of last year. His battalion was pulled out of the line after their casualties had reached sixty percent during the winter offensive. For a month they were on communication assignment not two miles from the airfield where I had my radar installation."

"That was good."

"He is not commissioned yet, so I couldn't take him to our mess. It was in any case only a grain store with a stove and some old chairs."

"You must have had plenty to talk about."

"Staying warm. That's all anyone talks about in a Russian winter. My Luftwaffe unit was still wearing its summer uniforms. Peter's infantry regiment had some overcoats they had taken off Russian backs and some odds and ends of furs and lined boots that Goebbels had persuaded German civilians to part with. Peter bribed his quartermaster to let me have some coats and hats. In return I showed him how three skilled men, under cover of darkness, could steal two dozen loaves from a mobile bakery unit. It makes a man very proud to exchange such knowledge with his son."

"For a month you were together?"

"It was the first day of the spring thaw when they left: March fifteenth. There was a watery sun that noon and for an hour there was the slightest of breaks in the intense cold. I went down to the railhead to say good-bye. His unit had found a piano factory almost intact. When they fired bullets into the lines of pianos there were strange resonant trills and jangling overtones. Hand grenades made a demented musical scream. Peter said it was the best fun he'd had since the attack on Vyasma the previous October."

"Are you frightened for the boy, August?"

"My God, Max, I am."

"Could you not arrange a posting? After all, he has served on the Russian front for ... what? eighteen months?"

"Twenty-one months. He'd never forgive me, Max. How would he feel? How would any of us feel?"

"Not doing our duty, you mean? I'd feel damn good, August. What would you do if you were posted back there? Would you do your utmost to avoid it?"

"Who knows, Max?"

"Seriously, August."

"For God's sake, Max! Do you think I've never thought about it? Do you know what it's like to find yourself wishing your own son would have his leg shot off, just so he will survive?"

"I'm sorry, August."

"Forget it, Max. It's not good to think of these things in advance. In war all things are possible and nothing inevitable."

"Who said that?"

"I said it," said August. "There is but a second of time, a stroke of a pen, a misinterpreted look, a fingered trigger ... between us and a Knight's Cross, a court-martial, sainthood or eternal damnation."

"Do you hear from your son?"

"Every few weeks."

"And he hates the war as you hate it?"

"Max, my friend, I have to tell you he likes it. We have given our world to our children. Can we be surprised that these children are destructive? Every fit, aggressive youngster who tries hard can get himself a bomber or a U-boat or an artillery battery and wreak havoc upon the world that it's taken us old men so long to put together. Nineteen-year-old children creep up on a 20,000-ton merchant ship, press a button, and watch it die, writhing like a wingless fly. They set fire to great cities and turn our society upside down in return for bits of colored ribbon. Where have we failed Max? What manner of children will they breed, and what manner of world will they shape? We ask them to count their victims like headhunters, marking each death with a notch, a painted tally or a new promotion. What will they unleash upon us, Max?"

"Dare I say you are a hypocrite, August, my friend? You pronounce judgment upon the men who fight, you call our heroes murderers, but you do not disdain the respect and admiration due to a fighter-pilot expert. And at your throat you wear your trinket; your tally is well known and gains for you respect from soldier and civilian alike. Oh no, August, you want to eat your cake and throw it into the faces of lesser men like me."

"You don't understand."

"Then explain."

"You are confusing heroism with morality. A man can be brave and yet do dishonorable things. His individual act might be honorable and yet the result dishonorable."

"Give me an example, August."

"The R.A.F. bomber crews. They are brave men, the risks they run are high and yet they kill women and children."

"You go too far, August. They are cowardly monsters. They drop their bombs and take to their heels in the darkness, leaving people to burn."

"So do our U-boat crews who torpedo a merchant ship and steal away in the night, leaving people to drown. Yet both are brave."

"Talk, talk, talk, August. You know as well as I do that we are all victims of circumstance. When the order comes we shall press the trigger, merely because the individual cannot challenge a system. Why try? As you said earlier, whether a man is commanding a U-boat, allocating civilian fuel supplies or even flying an R.A.F. bomber is largely a matter of chance."

"Perhaps you are right, Max. Perhaps I have too much time to think."

He watched the people on the crowded pavements of The Hague. For every happy bemedaled young officer there were a hundred men and women who looked tired and dejected.

"Ah, August, my friend. Why so sad? This was but a friendly fight, such as two old friends might have over a cigar." The car turned into the Plein and the Luftwaffe sentry saluted the car without caring if it was empty or full.

"Go carefully with me, Max. A man in love is fragile."

Max smiled. "But it's a good cigar, eh, August?"

"Magnificent."

"Then take the box. A man in love never knows when he might need a box of cigars." August tried to refuse them but Max closed his hands around August's and pressed the big box of cigars on him. "Major Georg Tuchel will be doing this run for the time being. Phone him here any weekday morning if you want a ride. I have already spoken with him; there'll be no difficulty." Max turned to the driver. "Take the Oberleutnant to radar station Ermine. I'll log you for another two hours and see you in the morning at the usual time."

The driver closed the car door and saluted Oberst Max Sepp. Max stayed on the steps and waved to August as the car departed.

For nearly an hour the driver drove silently, but as they entered the prohibited zone August sensed that he had something to say. He offered him a cigar but he preferred a cigarette. Here near the coast he was driving more slowly. It was a strange, deserted place. Occasionally they passed a farm cart with its heavy-footed Zeeland horses, or a bicycle with homemade wooden tires slapping the cobbles.

When the last village had vanished behind them the narrow concrete road became a sandy track and suddenly the North Sea appeared through the mist. The scrubby grass-topped dunes are twenty or thirty feet high and beyond them is only a table-flat beach of fine sand and then the sea. From it had come the dense white mist that clings like icy steam and reduces visibility to fifty feet. The sentries were wearing their overcoats and they walked stiffly around the radar station, which, like this whole coastline, was a forest of barbed wire and steel stakes.

The bushes and wirelike grass had been bent double by the wind from the sea. In the lee of the dunes the air was still and the white mist scarcely moved, but the bushes were still deformed and bowed. The only creatures happy to be there were the birds, which skimmed low over the bunkers and could breed protected by barbed wire. Even the bird watchers couldn't get near them now and five hundred square miles of northern Europe's coast had become a vast nature reserve guarded by the Wehrmacht.

The Citroën's tires slid in the soft sand, but the driver insisted upon driving Oberleutnant Bach right to the very door of his quarters. He always did. He opened the door for August and saluted him formally.

"Thank you," said August. "See my Feldwebel and he will fix you up with some eggs." The boy nodded. It was all exactly as it always was, except for one thing. "It's about the Herr Oberst," said the driver nervously.

"What about him?" said August.

"I think the Oberleutnant would like to know that the Herr Oberst has been ordered to join an infantry regiment on the Russian front: Orel. Many officers have. They go on Thursday. We shall miss the Herr Oberst."

"So shall I," said August. "Thank you."

The driver saluted again and walked across to get his eggs.

## 13

"IT UPSET me, Victor, I can tell you that. Couldn't eat a bite of lunch." The Medical Officer shook his head in brief silent anguish. "I've seen it before, Victor. Exhibitionism."

"What do you mean?" asked Löwenherz.

"That surprises you, does it?" Hans Furth, Kroondijk's Medical Officer, pointed to a cupboard which contained his bottle of brandy and glasses but Löwenherz declined. "With all you fit young men a doctor doesn't have much of a chance to show his mettle. My job has become that of a psychiatrist."

"Psychiatry? I thought you disdained that Jewish science, Hans."

Hans smiled. "Go back as far as Henry the Navigator and you'll find that navigation is a Jewish science, but that doesn't mean we can ignore it."

"If you go back far enough, you'll probably discover that gravity is a Jewish science," said Löwenherz.

"That's in order. It's the Luftwaffe's job to ignore gravity." Hans chuckled.

"Himmel, you said, was an exhibitionist," said Löwenherz.

"Life is a game for me, Victor. If you sat behind this desk you'd watch the whole panorama of human life pass: tragedy, humor, honor, disgrace, death and injury."

"And you reported your suspicions to the SIPO?" persisted Löwenherz.

"Mustn't get on the wrong side of the law, Victor."

"But only last week you said you'd never voted for the Nazis and wished Austria had never come under Nazi control."

Hans Furth leaned well back in his swivel chair. A plump man in his middle thirties, he was Austrian by

155

birth, doctor by training and airman by conscription. He affected the smart leather zip-front jacket that the fliers liked and many of their youthful mannerisms. His clothes were clean and well pressed and his thick black hair was freshly washed and combed straight back. His face was ruddy, his eyes blue, and his small, unnaturally red, girlish mouth was always ready to talk and smile. He smoked his cigar carefully without spilling the ash anywhere except into the ashtray and he frequently touched his face, running a fingertip along his lips or around his eyes to be sure that everything was in its rightful place. "You're trying to catch me out, Löwenherz Victor." He smiled. It was a Viennese affectation to invert the names like that and today Löwenherz found it an irritating one.

Furth leveled his cigar like a javelin between finger and thumb. "I'm a working-class lad, you're an aristocrat. Our sort gave the Nazis little or no support in the old days, Victor. Their strength came from the middle-class clerks and unemployed ex-officers: fertile ground, Victor."

"I'm interested in this business with Himmel," said Löwenherz, making one more effort to get the conversation back on his intended lines.

"Damned interesting case," agreed Hans Furth. "I've been through his medical dossier again this morning and I think I've solved the question to some extent." He leaned back like a woman with uncomfortable stays and gave a matronly tug to the bottom of his short jacket.

"How?" asked Löwenherz.

Furth leaned forward and lowered his voice. "I can't prove it, but it's my guess that he's not racially pure. I was reading in the paper the other day that more Jews commit thefts than Aryans do, by a considerable margin."

"That sounds very unscientific," sighed Löwenherz.

The doctor smiled at the window as if he shared a secret with the furnishings. "My dear Baron, you are hardly in a position to deny the effects of breeding. It took a thousand years of breeding to make you what you are. The Jews . . ."

"Everyone in the world has a thousand years of breeding behind them," said Löwenherz irritably. "Perhaps these days Jews have more motive for theft than do Aryans."

"This is my theory," continued Hans Furth. "We Germans have been bred as a systematic nation and this fellow Hitler understands us. . . ."

We Germans, thought Löwenherz, as he listened to the

doctor's singsong Viennese accent, nibbling the German language like *Sachertorte* and showing his teeth at every bite.

". . . Revolutionize a systematic nation by means of political theory and you have an instrument. Harness the military caste to that instrument and you have a weapon. Allow the politicals to have their own armed forces—the Waffen S.S.—and create a climate in which they and the military are in constant and dynamic struggle, and then your weapon will conquer the world."

"There's still a large piece of the world unconquered," said Löwenherz.

"I know," said Furth, smiling and nodding. "It's fascinating to see what will happen."

"Like a game of bridge," said Löwenherz.

"Better," said Furth. "Bridge was never half as exciting. My training as a doctor and as an officer has given me a unique chance to become an expert on the German psychology. Do you know, I can tell what sort of symptoms a man will have according to the rank he holds. For instance, no German N.C.O. would dare to come in here complaining of indigestion, just as few officers come to me with foot ailments. Funny folk, we Germans, eh?"

Yes, thought Löwenherz, and if the Russians get here, then this plausible joker will be occupying some comfortable seat in their military administration amusing the occupying power's officers with these same cynical observations on German character and weakness. And they will be laughing and throwing him an extra box of cigarettes and saying, Gay fellows, these Austrians.

"I don't like any sort of unpleasantness, Victor. All I want is to be left alone."

"And people like Himmel try to involve you?"

"Don't misunderstand me, I like this fellow Himmel. But this isn't an important enough matter for you or me to get involved with. He's an exhibitionist, Victor. Most of the people who get into trouble are exhibitionists."

Löwenherz could think of no response. He looked at Furth, who ran his little finger nervously along his eyebrow.

"I didn't invent the world or any social system in it," said the doctor. His smile endorsed this disclaimer. "Man is a crafty animal and a vicious one. You'll never alter that, Victor. Don't tell me that your ancestors didn't fight, cheat and kill to win and hold your family estates."

"I must get along, Hans."

"I've offended you."

"No," said Löwenherz. "I'm sure you never offend anyone."

Löwenherz didn't bring up the matter of Himmel again. He knew that he would merely be treated to glib and elementary generalizations.

"Speaking as your medical adviser," said Furth, "you could do with a couple of days' rest. I can arrange for guns and accommodation and we'll shoot wild pig. This business has upset me too, I can tell you. I was fond of young Himmel. The mess will buy the meat for sausages. Take you out of yourself, Victor. What do you say?"

Löwenherz laughed, and this puzzled the doctor. "I've arranged all the shooting I can handle at present, Herr Doktor," he said. "Thanks all the same." He got to his feet. Perhaps there was a more direct way to handle this business.

The Alert Hut was littered: chairs empty, newspapers abandoned, amendments to operational orders unread, fur-lined jackets unneeded in the warm afternoon sun. By now Löwenherz had had a chance to think about the dossier. How many influential Luftwaffe officers would be needed to make a protest legal, or at least difficult to punish? The Medical Officer was obviously scared stiff by Blessing and Starkhof, but how many protests had already been made about the experiments? To what extent was opinion already being rallied? Perhaps the document was in the doctor's office because the Luftwaffe Medical Inspectorate were circulating it for comment.

Starkhof could answer all these questions but Löwenherz was determined to give no information in return. The phone was best; after all, one could always hang up if the fellow became objectionable.

Even from the first moment that he lifted the telephone he was nervous. His father would have known how to handle this situation but Victor didn't. On the other hand, his father would not have handled it; he would have left it very much alone.

"Herr Doktor Starkhof, please," he told the operator. There was a short pause. "Hello, von Löwenherz," said the old man. He always used the "von." He knew that Löwenherz would think it uncouth but that amused him. "I thought you might give me a call."

It was startling that Starkhof had guessed who was

calling, and Löwenherz needed a moment or two to collect his wits.

"It's about the stolen dossier, of course," said Löwenherz.

"Sent you one through the post, has he? Dear me, can't think why our people failed to intercept that. Well, you make fifteen. Any idea how many others he sent?"

"No."

"Pity. Any letter?" said the old man.

"No."

"No matter."

"Are you going to come here and collect it?"

"Nervous, eh? Well, that's all right, Baron. Hold on to it until tomorrow. There's no hurry. I have fourteen copies here on my desk."

"There's nowhere really secure that I can lock it, unless I give it to the Kommandeur to lock in the safe."

"No, no, my boy, don't worry about it. There were nearly three hundred copies of that report circulated throughout the medical services. In Nuremberg there was a conference of ninety-five scientists discussing the report. Each of them had a copy and at least four were mislaid, so there's no need for you to get too excited about that one copy."

"So it's been circulated? Did anyone else ... I mean, was there ... ?"

An airplane flew low overhead, rattling the windows; Löwenherz was glad of a chance to stop speaking.

Starkhof said, "Ah, the Baron has been speaking with young Himmel, I can tell. No, of course there was no reaction, except that Doktor Rascher was sent Göring's thanks on behalf of the Luftwaffe. He also received a letter of thanks from the Medical Inspector of the Luftwaffe and many congratulations from his medical colleagues."

Löwenherz felt lonely, degraded and sick as his hopes drained away. Was this the way Himmel had felt when talking with him, in the cool crisp clean air? If so, Himmel's resolution had not faltered. "Did you read the dossier, Herr Doktor?"

"I did, von Löwenherz. I did."

"And ... ?"

"What do you want me to say, von Löwenherz? If you use your brains for one moment, you will realize that I can provoke you with any treasonable or scurrilous statement that I care to invent. Afterward I should merely plead that I did it in my line of duty. Now stop being so foolish. Go back to your airplanes and leave this business to me."

"You are not interested in my opinions?"

"Not in the slightest, my boy. If you know nothing important, then I shall be wasting my time. If you know something important, I prefer to hear it tomorrow, when the dossier has been officially passed to my department. A dramatic breakthrough today would simply mean promotion for our friend Blessing. While wishing him all the good luck in the world, I am not going to work to secure a promotion for him. Tell me tomorrow."

"You are returning tomorrow? To arrest Himmel?"

"Correct. It will be very quiet and discreet. My paper work will be in order and by tomorrow morning you and your friend Kokke will have had time to reconsider your attitude. You'll see the wisdom of cooperating with the law."

"What will Himmel get?"

"Punishment? Well, that depends. If he recants, pleads guilty, cooperates with us in respect of helpers, instigators and fellow plotters or leads us on to a whole network of conspirators, then he will get ten or fifteen years."

"You don't believe it was a conspiracy?"

"No, I don't. But if he wants to persuade me, I'll listen. He has some Dutch civilian friends in Kroonsdijk that I'm not entirely happy about. They have more than enough butter and schnapps down there in Kroonsdijk village. Some of it is filtering back to your air base. Himmel could provide me with the chance I need to open up a big black market racket."

Löwenherz found the Abwehr man's frankness disconcerting.

"What if these documents bring Himmel support from influential Luftwaffe officers?"

"We live in a society where influence can be a trump card," said old Starkhof cagily. "But I'd wager that they'd face execution along with Himmel." Dryly he added. "Although I've heard of cases where suicide cheated the law of a high-ranking victim."

By now Löwenherz's carefully prepared arguments had gone dry in his mouth. He felt a strong distaste for this cynical old man who had confidence enough to say things that other men only whispered.

"You seem very sure of that."

"My boy, this is what I do for a living. I am not as

ambitious as you; I don't want to reform the law or judge its transgressors. I merely bring lawbreakers to justice. If tomorrow your friend Himmel is making the laws and my colleague Blessing breaking them, then I will deliver him to justice with the same calm objectivity." There was a trace of self-mockery in old Starkhof's voice.

"Smug complacency, you mean," said Löwenherz.

"My very sentiments," said Starkhof. "I so wish I had the Herr Oberleutnant's fine vocabulary."

"Good day to you, Feldwebel Herr Doktor."

"Good day, my dear Baron."

# ✦ 14 ✦

THE teleprinters in the Operations Block had been clattering since lunchtime. The message from Bomber Command H.Q. had gone to the Group H.Q.s and from there the messages reached the airfields, including Warley Fen.

CONFIRMING TELEPHONE ORDERS FOLLOWING ARE EXECUTIVE ORDERS FOR THE NIGHT OF JUNE 31, 1943

There followed a gibberish of abbreviations and code words that defined the nature of the attack: flare colors, air and ground marking, cascade heights and times, turning points, assembly areas, bombing heights and times, bomb loads and met. forecasts giving the predicted winds at the bombing heights and conditions at base airfields at the time of return.

Hurriedly the technical officers began to build the plan into lectures and diagrams that would constitute the afternoon briefing. Flight Lieutenant Giles, the Bombing Leader; Flight Lieutenant Ludlow, the Navigation Leader; and John Munro, the Squadron Commander, conferred. The meteorological expert expressed the doubts that forecasters always have about other men's predictions.

The executive orders were as yet communicated only to those who had to know. As an added security precaution, the guardroom had been told to close the main gate and forbid personnel to leave the airfield except with the written permission of the Station Adjutant. In spite of the gaping holes in the perimeter fence the embargo was observed by everyone—partly because there was so much work to do that no one could find an opportunity to get away for a lunchtime beer in The Bell.

Deprived of the noise and movement of the airmen, the

village became as quiet as the airfield was busy. When an attack was being prepared even the public bar of The Bell maintained a decorous sobriety.

Cynthia Radlett, the barmaid, had wiped the tables, rinsed and polished the glasses, fetched more bottled stout from the cellar and swept the floor. She looked enviously at the four farmers who had been drinking and gossiping ever since lunchtime. Now it was almost opening time again. Those who complained of women chattering could never have listened to farmers' talk. It was a good thing that the village policeman was busy out on the green facing Mr. Wate's spin bowling, or he'd be complaining about them drinking after closing time. At last one of the men came to the bottom of his glass. He put it down with a sigh and wiped his lips.

"Beans, I told him, put in beans. Anything else and the wireworm will eat them." The three men nodded and stole a glance at Ben Thorpe.

Old Ben's voice was rasping and slow. "Ten Acre was always full of wireworm."

"Are you sure you don't want to walk up to Parson's Meadow, Ben?"

"Nah," said the old man and blew his nose loudly. They could not tell how upset he was, for an old man's eyes are always wet.

"After the war you'll never know the difference."

"Nah," snorted Ben. "It's the finest piece of grazing for a hundred mile. My dad weeded it and dunged it himself for nigh on fifty years and his dad afore." The old man was crying now, there could be no doubt of it. "I shan't watch them plow her up and sow their damned 'taters there. I'll not live to see her back to grazing again."

"Weorf" is the Old English word for draft animal. Warley meant a place where such animals could graze. Now the War Agricultural Committees had given grazing to the plow and one of the few patches of grassland left was the lower end of Trimmer's Meadow, which the village used as its cricket field. Today it was only a knockabout match, but toward opening time a small crowd of airmen and villagers gathered outside The Bell. They applauded the batsmen, advised the bowlers and dozed in the afternoon sun.

No previous cricket season could equal this one: Royal Engineers Norwich Depot versus R.A.F. Warley, A Flight versus the village; teams from all over East Anglia came to play cricket on the green, shove-ha'penny and darts in the public bar, and drink The Bell's warm bitter. The cricket pitch was smooth and flat, although since it was slightly below sea level it was muddy in wet weather. The R.A.F. had sent carpenters to rebuild the old scoreboard and the station artist—L.A.C. Gilbert—had supervised its repainting. Sammy Thatcher's shed had been moved and rebuilt. Although it could hold only one team at a time, there were no smiles when it was referred to as the pavilion.

Today Bill Beacham, village policeman and domino champion, was the last man batting for the scratch team the village had put up. He hadn't scored for nearly a quarter of an hour but none of Mr. Wate's spinners daunted him and he stonewalled with grim determination. The war had brought Police Constable Beacham promotion to sergeant and when the R.A.F. moved in he had been officially told to "cooperate with the R.A.F. police in matters affecting service discipline and national security." There was even talk of him having a police constable to help him. "Help him home from here on a Saturday night," said Cynthia, and everyone laughed because like most good jokes it wasn't a joke at all.

The Group Captain proudly boasted of an unbroken record of friendship between his airmen and the people of the village. Like most official thinking, the Group Captain's was purely negative. He meant that there were no instances on paper of physical, social or legal hostilities. On the other hand there was no great affection either. When a villager announced the arrival of a lorryful of airmen outside The Bell with the remark, "Here come the Wehrmacht," this too was a joke that wasn't a joke.

There was still another half hour before The Bell was officially open, but Cynthia took a pint of bitter outside to where Sam Thatcher was working at the base of the ancient oak tree that marked the boundary line.

"How is it going?" asked Cynthia.

Sam took the head off his pint before answering. "Same as that tree behind Percy's house. It's rotten inside."

"What a shame." She wiped her wet hands on her apron.

"It's getting old, Cynthia. It's probably stood here for a hundred and fifty years or more." Sam had been drilling deep into the tree and pushing bonemeal mixtures into it to feed the wood. He put down his glass and finished plugging up a hole.

"Will that save it?"

"It will give her another fifty years, Cynthia."

"You'd better do my guvnor after you've finished this tree."

"Now, now," said Sam Thatcher, "don't start." He had no wish to be drawn into the feud between Cynthia and her employer. He looked across the pitch to where Police Sergeant Beacham was still blocking the frantic bowling, and beyond him to the airfield. "They're off again tonight."

"Looks like."

"And that old wind's going to change," said Sam.

"Rain?"

"No, not yet awhile, or my feet would tell me. But during the night that wind will swing round and they'll be coming in right over our heads just about the time I'm turning over."

"Don't say that, Mr. Thatcher. I can't get back to sleep when they wake me."

There was a flutter of applause as Bill Beacham was clean bowled.

"What I don't understand," said Cynthia Radlett, "is what they do all day. I mean, they don't go raiding until after we close at night. I know they have to test their airplanes in the morning but what do they do there all day?"

"They have to work out their navigation and decide where to drop their bombs. They do a lot of talking up there at the aerodrome."

"Well, I don't know," said Cynthia Radlett, "but it's terrible for our business when they go off raiding." It was five-thirty. She walked back to The Bell and started serving drinks.

The most literary and sophisticated officer at Warley Fen was, by common consent, Flying Officer Longfellow. He was, appropriately enough, the Intelligence Officer. A tall blue-eyed man of thirty-eight, he had been in his youth an amateur boxer of some repute at Cambridge, where he studied Classics. After Cambridge he had worked on a small newspaper in the Midlands and graduated from that to a national daily. He had never excelled at newsgathering but had always been able to provide, at short notice, a couple of thousand words on the College of Cardinals (at the death of a pope), helium (airship disaster), or surrealism (record price at Sotheby's). Nor was Longfellow too proud to cover a wedding or review a film. In 1936 he left the newspaper's full-time staff and went to live in Cornwall. He became the science correspondent. A few thousand words a month earned enough money to keep himself, his young wife and two kids in a small cottage with a view of the sea while he labored on a book. It was a murder mystery, set in a Cornish tin mine, and although he modestly referred to it as a whodunit he had inserted the description "a psychological study in depth of the mind of the criminally insane" into the publisher's blurb. The *Scotsman* found it promising, the *Observer* thought it had grip, but a left-wing weekly said that "handmade, and thus readily identified, cigarette ends have become a careless vice among the sort of villains who people this year's mediocre detective fiction." He was stuck halfway through a sequel about a carefully organized bank robbery when the war began. Longfellow volunteered.

An Intelligence Officer's special responsibility was the Briefing Room. At Warley Fen it was a large wooden hut that could seat one hundred fifty air crew on benches. There was a stage at one end and behind it a map of Europe that stretched the width of the hut. Covering the map there was a red curtain that swept aside at the pull of a string. It had become usual for the Station Commander to pull the string.

Along each side of the hut there were windows. They should have been shuttered at briefing time but lately the weather had been so fine and warm that they'd been left open. There were the usual "Careless talk costs lives" posters and a notice board with intelligence memos fastened to it with bright red pins. Specially arranged by Flying Officer Longfellow were the "This is your enemy" displays: photos and threeview drawings of Bf 110 and Junkers 88 night fighters as well as some speculative Air Ministry diagrams of what the newer German fighter planes might look like.

From the ceiling hung models of both enemy and allied aircraft, each one clearly marked with its designation and wing span. Then there was the Accident Board, with photos of airplanes drunkenly askew after sliding off the runway or with a prop blade eating up a tail plane after a taxiing collision. At one side of the stage there was the easel standing ready for the Met. Department's Cloud Board (icing cloud in red, non-icing cloud in blue, all stacked to show altitudes). On the other side of the stage, reaching to the ceiling, there was the Photo Ladder. This didn't denote a proficiency in photography but showed the accuracy of the bombing, bomb explosions being plotted from the flashlight photo that each bomber took as its bomb load landed. Lambert's crew were in the top quarter of the ladder but Flight Lieutenant Sweet's crew were well down.

Longfellow was proud of this Briefing Room, upon which he and his clerks had spent so much time and energy. It embodied all the freshness and appeal of a commercial display or a newspaper layout. It was kept up to date every day and on the notice board there were a world map and a bulletin with a first-class summary of the war on all fronts, as well as a note on yellow paper in which Longfellow attempted to predict the strategic aspirations of the fighting powers. This supposition was clearly headed "Intelligence Guesswork." Often during the day air crew would wander into the Briefing Room, looking at the new displays or leafing through newspapers or copies of *Flight, Aeroplane Spotter, Tee Em* or one of the other technical magazines. Longfellow often claimed, "There's not another Briefing Room in the whole of Bomber Command where the crews pop in and look round when there's no briefing. Even if most of them only want to see Jane in the *Daily Mirror*, doze for half an hour and scrounge a coffee, by the time they wander out again they could have seen something that will save their lives."

Cozily full of bacon, beans and fried eggs—a rare luxury—none of them now dozed. The room was full with the crews of all sixteen bombers. The men, sitting stiffly upright and white-faced with tension, were waiting for permission to smoke. As the time of danger approached men grew lonely and the fliers were dividing into their assigned crews. They exchanged comments and smiles with men they didn't like and had only briefly seen since the previous operational flight four days earlier. For now men were drawing close, not to their friends but to six men who for the next few hours would share their good or fatal fortune.

Lambert's two gunners, for instance, Binty Jones and Flash Gordon, had a deadly feud dating from over two months before, but now they were exchanging jokes just as they'd done in the old days. They had met at the gunnery school and promised each other that they would insist on being in the same crew. They were thick-set young men chosen, like most air gunners, for the short stature that enabled them to fit into the power-operated turrets. Flash was a dark-complexioned, gap-toothed Nottingham miner, a real pitman who'd worked at the coal face on the trickiest seam. His hair was very long and with the aid of generous amounts of hair cream he arranged it in long shiny arabesques. For fear of disturbing its patterns he would avoid wearing a uniform cap. His liking for gold-plated identity chains, skull-and-crossbone rings and white silk scarves and his unmilitary bearing had given him his nickname. His wide mouth smiled easily. Digby had said, "He hasn't got a mouth but a small hinge on the back of his neck." He was, in fact, proud of his white teeth. In spite of being exempt from military service, he'd volunteered on his twenty-first birthday. He hated the pit; his only ambition was to survive the war and get an office job with a local tobacco factory. He was a cheerful boy with lots of energy and endless questions. He always wanted to know what his fellow airmen did in civvy street and he was not too shy to ask how much they earned doing it. Flash Gordon manned the rear gun turret.

Binty, a Welsh milkman—Jones the Milk—was also twenty-one. He usually manned the mid-upper turret, although a few times when Flash had a head cold they swapped. Flash often got head colds because, he said, the rear turret heater didn't work properly.

Binty had joined the R.A.F. when he was seventeen, which made him a peacetime airman by a few weeks. He believed that the superiority of the peacetime recruit was manifested by his very short hair, shiny boots and buttons, and razor pleats that he made by treating the inside of each crease with a layer of soap. His smartness was thus virtually unique among the air crew N.C.O.'s. He was not beyond reprimanding airmen and even corporals for minor faults like having a pocket unbuttoned. This made him very unpopular.

He affected the old soldier's vocabulary, sprinkled with mispronounced Arabic and adapted Hindi. Bint was his word for young girl and he used it frequently, for in spite of an unappealing face he was a womanizer of renown. He had quick eyes and a brain which he described as shrewd but which the rest of his crew knew was cunning. However, none of them would allow an outsider to describe Binty Jones as cunning and they all appreciated that his cleanliness and efficiency extended not only to his sex life and motorbike but also to his Browning machine guns. Artfully he had laid a claim to the upper turret, for which there were only two guns.

Binty and Flash had flown fifteen operations, all with Lambert. They had been close pals for nearly a year, drinking, whoring, fighting, and sharing girl friends, gunnery exam answers, cigarettes and a 350-c.c. B.S.A. motorcycle, until they met a woman named Rose in a pub in Peterborough. Her husband was a corporal in the Eighth Army fighting in the desert. Flash Gordon said they shouldn't see her any more but Binty said she was a sure thing and now spent more nights at her apartment than he did on the base. "No one can have their wives within forty miles of their base," said Binty, "but Station Standing Orders don't say you can't have someone else's wife." The two gunners hated each other but now you would never have guessed it. Binty sat reading a tightly wadded *Beano* comic and nodding while Flash told him about a motorcycle that an electrician on A Flight wanted to sell for fifteen pounds. Flash admired Binty's knowledge of motorcycles.

A fat fly buzzed and settled on Digby's hand. Even a finger prodded at it failed to move it. "Lazy old bugger," said Digby.

"Put him out the window," said Lambert. "He's probably just finishing his second tour." But Digby tipped it onto the floor and Jimmy Grimm put his boot on it.

The briefing was running late. It was already 1705 hours by the big clock but half of the chairs on the platform were still empty. The Assistant Adjutant, Jammy Giles, was there, of course, tipping back in his chair until it nearly fell over, laughing noisily and joking with a group of fliers in the front row. The Intelligence Officer, Longfellow, was also there. He always arrived early to be sure that his precious charts and diagrams were set up and to check that the route was correctly taped on the big map and the curtains closed upon it. He stood behind Jammy and steadied the chair each time it teetered too far back. But Jammy never toppled over. "Jammy" was another word for easy or lucky and Flight Lieutenant Giles was lucky.

Outside in the corridors of the Operations Block there was the clatter of a Telex machine as more orders arrived from Group. There was a pungent smell of floor polish and sweet tea and the clerks were hurrying with last-minute orders and modifications for the briefing officers. Standing in the corner of an empty office in the same block was Wing Commander John Munro, the commanding officer of the squadron. While the Group Captain had

control of the entire airfield from Dental Surgery to
Smithy, John Munro commanded the bombers and their
crews. Not that either of them would be likely to get into
an argument about how things should be done. Air Ministry had carefully delineated their respective areas of responsibility.

If there was one man who had stamped this squadron
with his personality it was John Munro. Its faults were his
and its virtues were his and its skills were his too. Now
Munro was tired. There was no need for him to fly on so
many raids, but he felt that he must. He flew and he kept
his desktop clear and tidy. He was not among the most
popular officers on the station. He knew that but he was
unconcerned. Airmen brought before him knew that they
could expect just punishment but little sympathy. He knew
that the men called him Himmler but he was perceptive
enough to know that there was a paradoxical element of
respect and affection in the nickname. Munro's most cel-
ebrated virtue was that he spoke to the men coming
before him for judgment with exactly the same tone of
voice and listened to them with the same degree of attention that he gave the A.O.C. As one of his gunners had
said after they had been badly shot up over Duisburg,
"He's not as cool as a cucumber, he's as cold as a bloody
iceberg." One night in the mess Jammy Giles, full of thin
beer and hoarse from singing, had pronounced loudly,
"Munro is a gentleman and gentlemen are now obsolete.
This is the age of the technician."

"The age of violence," P.O. Cornelius Fleming had
argued.

"Then we should be all right, old cock," said Jammy.
"Seeing as we are the technicians of violence."

"But Munro's a good type, isn't he?" asked Fleming.

Jammy suddenly sobered up. "He's all right, Fleming
my boy. Men don't come straighter than that tall, thin,
humorless, toffee-nosed old sod."

Now Munro was in the vacated office leaning on his
walking stick and puffing at his pipe. Around him there
were the Engineering Officer and three senior ground staff
N.C.O.s including Flight Sergeant Worthington.

There was a problem. Carter's airplane—*Joe for King*—
which had dropped the bomb that afternoon had developed an electrical fault and would not be serviceable in
time for the raid.

"Our only reserve is the one that came in this afternoon," said Worthington.

"Could do, Mr. Sanderson?" the C.O. asked the Engineer Officer, who in turn raised a quizzical eyebrow at the three N.C.O.s.

"She'll have to go without an air test," said Worthington.

"Get your best chaps on it and keep me in the picture, would you?" Sandy nodded assent.

"We'll be putting the new flame traps on the exhausts. Permission to bomb her up in the hangar while we work?"

Munro looked at his watch. "No choice, Mr. Worthington. And rip as much of that armor plate out of her as you can manage."

"It's a long job, sir," said Worthington.

"Group's boffins say we get an extra foot of altitude for every pound of weight we lose."

"We'll leave the armor behind the pilot, sir?"

"I don't think any one of the crew will want you to take that out, Mr. Worthington," said Munro with a smile.

Worthington saluted and hurried away to round up his bods and break the bad news that they would be working frantically through their mealtime and on through the evening.

"Carter to take the new kite, John?"

Munro raked a match into his pipe and spoke with it still in his mouth. "Seven trips, or is it eight? Average pilot; what's his flight engineer like, Sandy?"

"Ten trips actually, sir. His engineer is Gallacher. Apprentice toolmaker, argumentative, thin on theory but practical enough. They'll be all right."

"That's settled then."

"Shall I tell him?"

"I'll tell him," said Munro. "He'll probably be a bit needled."

Munro's own ground crew chiefie was still standing nearby. "What is it, Chief?"

The old N.C.O. saluted gravely. "What time will you be doing your air test, sir?"

Oh, Lord, he had quite forgotten that he still had his own N.F.T. to do. His poor crew; they had been hanging around all day, and now they would probably have to fly while the rest of the squadron were enjoying the evening meal. "Immediately after briefing, say 1815 hours."

"Very good, sir."

Munro reached into his pocket and looked at the list he had written on the envelope of the letter from his wife. He'd forgotten to put the N.F.T. on it. If he'd seen another officer behaving as he had done over the past two

months he would have grounded him without argument.
But a commanding officer can't ground himself, in spite of
those little talks the quack had given him. There were the
lads in the crew, of course, but then they might have been
flying with some chap straight from an Operational Training Unit, which would have endangered them even more.
It was a problem that would solve itself; tonight would be
his last operation. Next week he was to hand over to a
new C.O.

By the time Munro reached the Briefing Room everyone was there and the Groupie was hovering at the door
waiting for the crews to come to attention. Munro walked
to the platform and waited until the room was silent.
"Gentlemen, Station Commander," he called.

The crews got to their feet as the Groupie's footsteps
clicked smartly down the center aisle. He sprang agilely
up onto the stage and tossed his gold-encrusted cap into a
chair. He smiled, smoothed his white hair and looked at
the great crowd of men as though wondering why they
should be standing at attention.

"O.K., chaps," he called breezily. "Sit down and light
up."

Near the front he saw Tommy Carter's bomb aimer,
who had completed twenty-nine trips. Tonight would be
his last, for if he returned safely he would be screened to
some safe job for a few months. He was nineteen.

"Collins, have one of mine," said the Groupie and flung
him a packet of cigarettes.

Collins caught the packet, took a cigarette and passed
them along the line to Carter and the rest of the crew of
*Joe for King.*

"Thank you, sir. I'm passing them down the line."

"You saucy bastard," said the Groupie. "No wonder
they call you Tapper." The sergeant gave a shy smile.

There was a roar of delight from the crews, for Collins
had earned his nickname from his constant pleas to borrow a few shillings until payday. The Groupie smiled.
Napoleon, he knew, had used the same simple device to
endear himself to his soldiers. And this brilliant fellow in
Africa gave away cigarettes by the cartload, so it was
said. Not that the Group Captain was a cynical man. On
the contrary, he was imbued with a simple desire to have
his air crews like and respect him with the same intense
feeling that he had for them. He would have given almost
anything to fly with them to bomb Germany. Twice he
had flown unofficially as an extra crew member, but the

A.O.C. had heard of it and warned him against doing it again. The Groupie described himself as a Hun-killer. The crews mostly thought of him as a harmless eccentric. In fact he was a lonely man desperately trying to believe that the company of youth would offset the approach of old age. He swept the laughter away with a movement of his hand. The crews sat silent, waiting to hear the name of the target.

In the few moments before the curtain rises at the opera there is a sound, a presence, an indefinable and unique mood. The audience are hushed and expectant, their throats are tight and even the nervous coughs are shrill and have an overtone of hysteria. Imagine then the mood that would prevail if—like these crews—it was the audience that were about to mount the stage: mouthing their dialogue lest they forget it, noting their cues, worrying about lights and timings and fussed over by a dozen stage managers, who will take the blame should the performance become a disaster. It was a complex theatrical drama that this audience were about to stage and one mistake would bring them not a boo or a jeer or a poor review but a sudden, nasty, fiery death.

The Group Captain tugged the cord and the curtains parted with a squeak of metal rollers.

"The target for tonight," said the Group Captain, "is Krefeld in the Ruhr."

The captains and navigators had already been briefed, so it was no surprise to them. Many of the engineers had guessed from the fuel loads and some of the remainder had heard by now, but there were still enough wireless operators and gunners to greet the news with a soft sincere groan. There had been rumors and bets that it would be a pushover target. Krefeld was no pushover. Happy Valley was Happy Valley: the best-defended target zone in Europe.

Lambert, Cohen and Micky Murphy had arrived together from the previous briefings upstairs. Seated behind them were Flash and Binty, the two gunners, and Digby, who was smoking a small cigar. Cohen had his notebook open in front of him. The raid was detailed there in neat handwriting with times in large numbers down one side. Lambert had some notes on the back of an envelope but he knew he would never refer to it. The routes and details that seemed so baffling to the newcomers were second nature to him; he had seen the techniques grow from the

days when they had little more briefing than the name of
the target and time of takeoff.

On the stage the technical officers were seated in a line,
with the Groupie standing like a vicar opening a church
fete. Beside him, on a table covered with a gray blanket,
there was a carafe of water and a glass. He moved it aside
as he always did and turned to the map. Beribboned gaily
with red and white tapes, the route to and from the target
made a squat diamond shape centered upon the North
Sea. The enemy coastline was defaced with ugly red
blotches of flak around the cities of Amsterdam, Rotterdam and The Hague, while the right-hand tip of the
diamond poked into the biggest red patch of all, the
heavily defended heart of Germany's heavy industry—the
Ruhr.

"Krefeld: heavy industry, textiles, light industry, com-
munications," reeled off the Groupie. "It's a big show
tonight: over seven hundred Bomber Command aircraft
operating, with leaflet dropping by Operational Training
Units. Zero 0130 hours. Takeoff 2420." The Group Captain eyed the five journalists and the Flight Lieutenant
from Air Ministry Press Office who had seated themselves
quietly at the rear of the room. He spoke to them rather
than to the air crews, who had heard it all before. He
spoke slowly and deliberately and avoided jargon, as much
as one can avoid it when dealing with a series of new
techniques that have been named as they were invented.

"Any target in the Ruhr is difficult to identify. Even
though the met. man tells me there will be little or no
cloud and a full moon, there will be industrial haze lying
over the target area; there always is. Take no chances,
chaps. No guesswork. Tonight we are flying as part of the
pathfinder element and it's important that we put up a
good show. Don't bomb or mark out of sequence. One
plane can spoil the entire raid and that means they'll send
us back to do the job properly next week. So let's get
there and mark it accurately so that Main Force can hit it
once and hit it bloody hard." The Groupie sat down while
a ripple of agreement ran round the room. No one wanted
to go back next week.

Flight Lieutenant Ludlow, the Navigation Leader, stood
up. The shy ex-bank clerk from Guildford had become an
actuarial curiosity. He was now on his third tour. Only
two percent of airmen survived three tours. Some called
him "the immortal Lud." He had briefed the navigators
upstairs an hour before but now he outlined the route for

the sake of the others. As usual he mumbled so quietly that the crews at the very back couldn't hear properly, but the ones who chose to sit at the very back usually didn't care. "Assemble over Southwold on the coast. You'll need little or no change of course until the turning point at Noordwijk on the Dutch coast. There will be yellow markers at the turning point but don't come back and complain that you didn't see them. They are for the Main Force boys and as pathfinders you're now expected to pinpoint places like that without the markers. Met. says there will be no cloud, but if he's wrong there will be sky markers above the cloud.

"From there it's straight run down to the target. I'll be placing a yellow fifteen miles from the target and you must go in to bomb over that yellow datum-line marker. If you don't you'll be crossing the bomber stream. By the time you reach the datum marker navigators must have their ground speed calculated so that captains and bomb aimers have an exact time to the aiming point. That's all. Anyone with queries can see me afterward."

Some of the new boys were scribbling away furiously. Cohen could see P.O. Fleming and his officer navigator checking and rechecking every word of the briefing. The rest of Fleming's crew sat close and watched approvingly as he prepared the spell that would bring them safe through the night. Not all of the crews were together. Sweet always sat at the front with a group of officers. His engineer, Micky Murphy, sat next to Lambert just as he had always done. On the other side of Lambert sat Battersby, studying the oil and grease on his hands. He noted with pride that they were fast becoming real engineer's hands like Murphy's.

Digby leaned forward to Murphy and Lambert. "Faith, Hope and Charity are writing their memoirs," he whispered.

"Yes, I remember what it was like on my first trip," said Lambert. "I was more frightened of making a mistake on my log than of tangling with a night fighter."

All of the new crews had arrived in the Briefing Room at least five minutes early. For fear of taking some veteran's allotted seat they had all stayed close together near the back of the room. Like new boys at school they were anxious not to attract attention, but when Jammy Giles stood up it was to this part of the Briefing Room audience that he addressed himself.

Flight Lieutenant Giles was the squadron's Assistant

Adjutant and also its Bomber Leader. Thirty-three years
old, he had joined the R.A.F. during the Munich crisis. He
had first flown as a gunner, when any erk standing around
at takeoff could become an air gunner without training or
brevet or sergeant's rank. At that time he had been an
L.A.C., almost the lowest form of air force life. Later,
when his job had been made official and he'd got three
stripes, he had delighted in swapping jobs with other air
crew. He had flown as gunner, as wireless operator, and
even as second pilot. He had proved particularly skilled
at bomb aiming; so much so that at the end of his first
tour he had got the D.F.M. and a job as instructor. The
discipline at the training school had been so irksome that
he had applied for a commission and to his surprise got
one. Now that the importance of his job had been recognized by the creation of the air bomber category, Jammy
had become an important man in Warley.

The eleven men in the room who had already completed a tour of operations were quieter and more intro-
spective than the newer crews. Jammy was a notable exception. He was noisy, balding and inclined to plumpness;
all due, he boasted, to the vast amounts of alcohol he
consumed. Amid a less stringently selected group of men
Jammy's physique would have gone unremarked. Among
these air crews, however, his slight paunch was Fal-
staffian, his pate Pickwickian and his cheerful nose
Cyrano-like.

This was emphasized by the build of his pilot, Roddy
Peterson, a tall thin doleful Canadian. He had a dry,
savage brand of humor that Jammy had taken to immediately and now excelled in. Laurel and Hardy they were
often called. Before joining up Jammy Giles had lived
with his mother in a three-room basement in the London
suburb of Morden and worked as a clerk for a building
contractor. Now he was a bemedaled officer; a flight
lieutenant. It was a transformation beyond his wildest
dreams and he refused to think of what he would do when
the war was over. In any case he didn't expect to survive
it.

"All right. Belt up there and listen," said Jammy. "I
don't care how many times you've heard it before." Several times in the past Jammy had brought some inattentive
crew member up onto the stage and asked him to repeat
the briefing. Jammy knew how to make such a man feel
like an infant; the crews became quiet and attentive.

"First the P.F.F. Mosquito aircraft will mark the target

with red markers. Their gear is much more accurate than anything we have, so their reds are what the Finders must look for. The Finders will put long sticks of flares over the reds. Mixed in with the Finder aircraft there are Supporters—and these are mostly crews on their first couple of trips—who are carrying only high explosive bombs. That's because incendiaries could be mistaken for red markers. Remember, all you Supporter crews, it's your job to shake up the defenses with your H.E. aim at the reds; if you don't see them I'd rather you brought your loads back here than made a mistake. And don't go round again, save that for the experienced crews. All right. Next over the target are the Illuminators—they will be dropping short sticks of flares right on the aiming point, which they will identify from the light of the Finder's flares. Lastly, the Primary Markers will arrive and put yellow markers down upon the aiming point which will be lit by the Illuminators' flares. Aircraft with Y equipment will check by radar and visual means because the whole main bombing force will be looking for those yellows. It's been carefully planned, lads, so it's up to you to check and double-check before you mark. We don't want any more Pilsens and there won't be if you all pull a finger out."

On April 16, 1943, a mistake by the pathfinders resulted in an attack being centered on a huge Czechoslovak lunatic asylum at Dobrany instead of the Skoda arms factory at Pilsen. The horror was compounded by the loss of thirty-six R.A.F. airplanes and Pathfinder Force was still smarting from the shame of it.

There was a flurry of coughs and affirmative grunts. Lambert passed his cigarettes among his crew. Micky Murphy took a cigarette. "What do you think, Sam?" he asked.

"It sounds carefully planned," said Lambert guardedly.

"That's what they say about contraception," said Micky, and he smiled to reveal his gap teeth. He smiled at Battersby too. The boy grinned back, pleased to be included in the joke.

Up on the stage Jammy continued. "All right. The last wave are Backers Up. You are carrying green T.I.s. First look for any remaining reds because they are from the Mosquitoes. If there are no red T.I.s look for yellow ones from the Primary Markers. I'll be there watching you with my beady little eyes and if any of you mess up my pretty pattern of colored lights I'll have your guts for garters. All right?" The crews laughed and Jammy gave a brief guffaw. He always said that at the end of his briefing. A new joke would have worried them; at this time they preferred things that were old and familiar.

"All right, one more thing," said Jammy. "Jettisoning of bombs. In recent months there's been a greater tonnage of bombs dropped on Britain by us and the Yanks than by the whole bloody Luftwaffe." There was a pandemonium of whistling and catcalling. Jammy waved it down. "Yeah, it's a real laugh at briefing, but when you are holding up a mainline train service or asking the poor buggers at Bomb Disposal to clear up your mess, it's not so funny. If you must jettison I want exact times, map reference and fusing details immediately after landing. It's easy to get away with it by saying nothing"—he smiled—"and that's why I'll press for disciplinary action against the whole crew that doesn't report jettisoning."

They were all in a good mood now. "That's it, Jammy, give 'em hell," shouted someone. Again Jammy gave one of his sneezelike laughs.

As the Intelligence Officer got up it was quiet enough to notice the sounds of the countryside: outside the window a chestnut tree moved abrasively, swifts called, a blackbird sang and thrushes were learning how to fly, the scent of newly cut hay came on the warm breeze. It was hard to believe that here in this pastoral backwater plans were being made to destroy a town.

Longfellow had been watching and listening to the briefing with the close attention of a journalist. The drama of the scene moved him. This was history being made. Last week he had sent these men out to destroy Cologne. Cologne, why, it was beyond belief: a thousand years of history shattered into fragments in less than two hours by these young kids. Like a chapter he'd written for his second book: his criminals had sat around in easy chairs drinking brandy and discussing in matter-of-fact tones their plan to rob a bank. He'd rewrite that chapter, because now he knew that it hadn't been matter-of-fact enough! This was how it really should be: young fellows, some still in their teens, offering each other cigarettes and making notes about how many tons of high explosive they would plant in a city center.

Longfellow got to his feet slowly to make sure he had their attention. He ran his hand through his thick black hair. "Can you see me at the back?" he called. There was an affirmative murmur. "I'm surprised to hear it; I can't see you through this damned fug." There was some polite laughter. The room was blue with tobacco smoke and yellow lights, he noticed, glowed through the swirling fumes like distant igneous planets. He made a note of "distant igneous planets." That would do for the book. Longfellow's clerk pinned up a bombing-pattern diagram headlined CREEPBACK. It was a long blob of bomb hits extending to meet an arrow marked "Bomber Stream, Line of Flight." Longfellow put on his spectacles and stared at the diagram. This made his whole audience look at it.

"Tonight," pronounced Longfellow slowly and clearly, "we are attacking Krefeld. The heavy industry ..." He was unable to continue because of the noise, which was getting louder. There was a shrill laugh from Kit Pepper— one of Sweet's gunners—and a sudden hand clap from Roddy Peterson next to him. Longfellow held up his hand and then loudly corrected his error. "Tonight, gentlemen, *you* are attacking Krefeld." There was another sort of noise now; quieter and mollified. He decided to skip the build-up description of the target and go on to the matter of his real concern. The one that the Intelligence people at Group were complaining of so bitterly; in a word: creepback.

"Now, you Backers Up crews," said Longfellow, turning back to them. "It's your job to drop your new flares into the center of the existing flares. I've said this a thousand times but I will repeat it once again. When you see the marker pattern on your approach you are seeing it in perspective. That foreshortening is an optical illusion, so don't drop short of center. Creepback is this tendency to fall short and then shorter still. So don't do it." He paused long enough to give importance to his next few words. "Now you chaps know as well as I do, there is another reason for creepback. One that people are reluctant to mention." He paused again. "Plain old-fashioned cold feet."

The room was silent; no one coughed or murmured. Longfellow had their fearful attention. The Groupie looked toward the journalists but the smoke was too dense for him to see their reaction. Longfellow continued, "When the flak is coming up hard and heavy, you get itchy fingers. What you want to do is to get rid of your bombs and get the hell out of there. Of course you do, but if you are going to drop your bomb load in a field of potatoes then what the hell are you going all the way to Germany for? That last few hundred yards to your aiming

point, gentlemen, is the difference between tearing the
Hun's guts out and throwing in the towel." He took off his
horn-rimmed spectacles and replaced them in a theatrical
gesture.

Longfellow had theories about briefings. The cold accusation of cowardice, followed by a manly understanding
tone, a logical argument and the final sporting allusion,
was calculated to shock, stimulate and reinforce the determination of his audience.

"Rule Britannia!" shouted someone at the back.

"These armchair warriors," murmured Digby. "They'll
fight to the last drop of our blood." Battersby giggled
nervously.

Impulsively Flight Sergeant Lambert stood up. It was
the first time he'd ever asked a question at a briefing.

"What are the guts of Krefeld?" asked Lambert. "What
are we aiming at in that city center?" He had a target
map in his hand; he waved it.

This wasn't so good, thought Longfellow. He ran his
fingers down the back of his hand like a man adjusting the
fit of a pair of chamois gloves. He peered forward to
decide what sort of man this was. He tried to see his eyes
but the ceiling lights threw the fellow's eye sockets into
darkness and masked his expression as efficiently as a pair
of dark glasses. He smiled nervously at Lambert and
remembered the standard answer he'd prepared for this
sort of question. Sometimes the crews got fidgety about
dropping their bombs right into the center of crowded
towns. It was natural that they occasionally needed bolster-
ing up a little. Longfellow held up a target map of
Krefeld and tapped the center on it. "A Gestapo headquarters and a poison gas factory—that's your aiming
point. All right?"

He felt the mood of the room change as he said it;
there was a suppressed muttering and a heightened excitement. The element of anger that a moment ago had
been directed so unjustly at him was now turned upon the
real enemy: Krefeld.

The Group Captain preferred not to wear his spectacles
except in the privacy of his office. He didn't look at
Lambert directly; he closed his eyes and nodded wisely, as
though he had known about that city center too.

Other technical officers continued the briefing. Sandy
Sanderson, Squadron Engineer, was wearing an expensive
blue lamb's wool rollneck and as he spoke of the fuel
loads he kept peering to see if there were any women

among the journalists. "The Gunnery Leader said that Lancasters were still coming back with damage by .303-inch bullets. British bullets. That means trigger-happy gunners firing at shadows. Keep awake, keep alert and keep the turrets moving so that the oil stays warm and thin, but remember that there are two-motor bombers with us tonight, so don't open fire until you positively identify the night fighter."

The Signals Leader gave details of the splasher frequencies—a rapid change of frequencies for bearings from beacons—and then the met. man gave them an outline of the weather situation. His curving line of cold front was in places two hundred miles in error and his prediction of its midnight frontal positions was even more inaccurate, but it would make no difference to these crews, who were going only as far as the Ruhr. There they would find anticyclonic weather as predicted.

"Moon full, rising 0030 hours at target: one hour before zero. Sunrise is 0546 hours, so you won't have to worry about sunup. Now the cloud: along the enemy coast there'll be some well-broken layer cloud. The residual thundercloud will have followed the cold front and won't affect you. Over the target area you'll have a very thin layer of medium cloud between 1,000 and 20,000 feet. Sorry I can't be more precise than that, but it will probably have cleared by 0100 hours."

"Jesus!" said Digby without lowering his voice. "We're going to be dancing naked in the full moon and he consoles us that we needn't worry about sunup." Loudly he said, "Anyone want to buy my wristwatch?" There were a few laughs.

Even if the met. man didn't hear Digby's exact words he interpreted the sentiment without difficulty. Hurriedly he added, "You'll have enough stratocumulus at 2,000 to 3,000 feet to give you some cover; visibility moderate. The bases will be the same: stratocumulus at 2,000 to 3,000 feet; visibility moderate. You've had your winds, navigators. Northwest wind over target, remember. See me afterward if there's anything else."

The last man on his feet was Wing Commander Munro, the Squadron C.O. Young Tapper Collins wasn't the only man who was completing his tour of operations that night. John Munro was also embarking on his final trip of the tour, with the difference that this was Munro's second tour; tonight was his sixtieth bombing raid.

Munro spoke in the carefully modulated tones of the

British upper class. "Not much to say tonight, gentlemen. Flak concentrations: the map speaks for itself. You are routed to bypass these unfriendly regions, so don't wander off or invent some new route that you believe to be better. Keep in the stream and you'll avoid most of these red patches."

Sweet called out, "What about a route that avoids that big red patch?" The big red patch was the Ruhr, so everyone laughed. The Wing Commander smiled as broadly as he knew how to. "Keep in the stream, chaps, and watch your bombing heights. The only collision danger is over the target and if you keep to your height band it is almost eliminated. Don't run across the target except from the northwest, where the datum marker is. It's rather like driving a car in traffic: keep on your side of the street and you are perfectly safe, but drive across the traffic stream and the chances of colliding are considerable." His audience, few of whom had ever driven a car, nodded knowingly.

"And no evasive action over target. There'll be no night fighters there when the flak is firing. Once you're clear, keep to the return route and timing. This is a well-planned show, chaps. It's a big raid—about seven hundred aircraft—with Lancasters, Wellingtons, Halifaxes and Stirlings."

"Hooray," shouted a dozen old-timers from the back of the room. Munro looked up and smiled. On recent raids 12.9 percent of the Stirlings had been lost compared to only 5.4 percent of the Lancs. If it comforted them to know the poor old Stirlings would be with them, lumbering slowly along at their feeble ceiling and drawing the brunt of the flak, why should he spoil it? But his young brother was piloting a Stirling this night, and the smile was a mask.

When the briefing ended there was a clatter of boots and a buzz of conversation as the fliers shuffled out through the door and into the golden world of the afternoon sun, where the air smelled of newly cut grass. Munro buttonholed Flight Lieutenant Sweet near the door. "A word to the wise, Mr. Sweet. These crew reshuffles: bad biz. If any of them want to change crews tell them to come and see me."

"You mean Cohen and Digby?"

"I mean Cohen and Digby."

Sweet smiled winningly. "They were requests. Digby asked if . . ."

"Before you go on, old chap, let me tell you that this

afternoon I had Flight Sergeant Digby, Royal Australian Air Force, on my neck, flushed with the exertion of hard-pedaling around the peri track, flatly refusing to leave Lambert's crew. These chaps get superstitious, you know."

"We can't win a war on superstition."

"Oh, I wouldn't go so far as that. Old Hitler's been using it pretty strenuously and gaining quite a bit of ground. The old torchlight processions and secret signs, eh? No, if these chaps get comfort from their toy bears and lucky lingerie hanging by the windshield, let them have it, I say. That goes for crewing too."

"But that's mutiny, isn't it? Surely Flight Sergeant Digby should have come to me in the usual way if he thinks he's running B Flight."

"I can see you haven't had much experience of our Australian allies, Mr. Sweet. I'm damned lucky he demeaned himself to mention it to me. There are quite a few of his countrymen who would have been on the blower to Australia House and done it via their Prime Minister and ours if they thought they were being victimized."

"You're joking, sir."

"I wish I were. Don't know how, in fact. My trouble, I suppose. Anyway, Mr. Sweet, forget Digby going to your crew even if he is the best bomb aimer in the squadron. And even if your bomb aimer is by far the worst . . .";

Sweet smiled again. "Oh, it wasn't for that reason, sir . . ." Sweet touched Munro's arm in a gesture of reassurance. Munro shrank away. He had a horror of men patting his shoulder or grasping his arm.

"Whatever reason, Mr. Sweet, forget it," he said coldly.

"Take Cohen, forget Digby?"

"Take Cohen, forget Digby; that's the spirit."

Ashamed of his reaction to Sweet's gesture, Munro leaned a little closer to him. "Perhaps your idea is to pile all the B Flight duds into one crew in order to get them reassessed as unsuitable for pathfinders and transferred. But why, Sweet, why in the name of God choose Lambert's crew? Lambert's one of the best pilots on the squadron."

Sweet smiled at Munro. He felt sure that he would be able to convincingly refute this unfair suggestion. "All I'm interested in, sir, is flying maximum ops with maximum bomb loads and killing maximum Huns."

"Really?" said Munro.

"I just want to get the war over," said Sweet.

"Quite a few of us feel like that," said Munro and before Sweet could reply added, "Another question, Sweet. Has Lambert had a portrait of Stalin painted on his aircraft?"

"Stalin, sir?"

"Stalin, that's it."

"No, sir, that's Sergeant Carter's aircraft: *L Love*."

"Umm, that's what I thought. Group Captain came your way this P.M. to see the aircraft with the bomb-release malfunction. He saw the Comrade's portrait on it. . . . He's fretting."

"I'll have the riggers paint it out."

"And have one of your chaps write to the *Daily Mirror* about it? No, I wouldn't advise that. As you know, it's unserviceable tonight. Do nothing until the Group Captain mentions it to you directly. Then you will have a problem."

"I'll think of a way to deal with it, sir." Sweet smiled.

"I'm sure you will," said Munro coldly. Who could say that youth was rebellious. Why, chaps like Sweet would do anything to avoid a harsh word. Munro sighed. After the war, he felt, the world might be full of Sweets, selling their vacuum cleaners, parrying political questions and entertaining millions on television. Eventually everyone in the world would become expert at the modest words, kind smiles and bland assurance that gloved the iron hand of ambition.

Man, frightened that machines might dominate him and overawed by mechanical performance, was becoming mechanical in his emotions and reactions, thought Munro. His gestures, jokes and obedience were robotlike. Lambert's foolish and provocative question, much as Munro deplored such behavior, was at least human by the very nature of its error. That smiling little Flight Lieutenant Sweet would never do such a thing.

Sweet wasn't the only person to be buttonholed. All over the room men were giving last-minute warnings, greetings, advice and information to friends and strangers.

The chaplain was a member of the Socialist Party and secretly regarded himself as a rather dangerous reformer. In his opinion this was why his bishop had been so keen to get rid of him into the air force. Compulsory church parades, some articulate atheists in the Officers' Mess and an inherited stutter had made his task harder than he'd expected. Still, it was his duty to seek out the troubled and he found the man with the lined eyes who'd almost spoiled the whole briefing by disquieting his comrades.

"Are you troubled, Flight Sergeant?" he asked Lambert.

"Why doesn't the Church stop the war, Padre?"

The young chaplain had listened carefully to his archbishop, so, like the Intelligence Officer, he had the answer ready. "The war is due to the sin of mankind, including our own. And so we have got to do it and be penitent while we do it."

"So I'm the right hand of God, am I, Padre? I wonder if the Germans have padres telling them they are."

For one moment the padre's resentment and anxiety almost betrayed him into praying that he would not stutter. He did stutter: "I ... I ... I ... hold the King's commission, Sergeant, and I'll ask you to treat me with the respect my u ... u ... u ... uniform deserves."

"Come on, Skip," called Digby loudly. "We've got some killing to do." The padre glared at them both. Why should these men insult me? he thought; they know I can't stop the war.

"Pay no attention to them, Padre," said Longfellow. "They couldn't care less about decent people's feelings." He wondered whether it was either of those two who had laughed at him when he made that slip of the tongue at the start of the briefing. Once Longfellow had hero-worshiped the young air crew, but that was long ago during the Battle of Britain. That was before he encountered the arrogance that constant danger granted the young. "Intrepid birdmen," he said scornfully after all the birdmen were out of earshot.

# 15

WALTER RYESSMAN often recalled the day when his name had been put forward for the job of Burgomaster. It was a job for life, but he anticipated that two hours a day would be more than sufficient to supervise the civic activities of such a small town. That was before the war, of course, when the world went at a slower pace. Decisions about slum clearance and extensions to the gasworks were referred to subcommittees and the answers were seldom in dispute. Walter Ryessman had been made Burgomaster because of his long and faithful membership in the Party. Now that the nation was at war his primary job was to ensure that Altgarten played its part in winning it, and that took him eight hours a day of paper work and meetings, with frequent visits to anywhere and everywhere to be sure that the air raid precautions were provided as the law demanded. At first the hospital authorities and the TENO engineers' commander had resented his sudden unannounced arrivals. Soon they realized that Ryessman had influence in the Party far greater than his post as Burgomaster of Altgarten would suggest. He also had an honorary rank in the S.S. So they learned how to put on a show of welcome when the tall white-haired man appeared like a ghost in the middle of the night. It was a part of the briefing of any new sentry, night watchman or caretaker to be on the alert for the Burgomaster.

The Rathaus was a red brick building that faced Altgarten railway station across the grassy, tree-lined Bismarckplatz. From his office the Burgomaster looked down upon the war memorial. The fountain splashed brightly in the afternoon sunlight. On the face of it were the names of forty Altgarten men who had died in the First World War. Already the side panels were almost full with Second

World War casualties and the Burgomaster wondered
whether the base of the fountain would be suitable for
carving more names. He decided it would have to be.

The Burgomaster had seen many changes in the
Rathaus since he had taken office. The basement, which
had once housed the birth, marriage and death records,
had been turned into an air raid control room. There was
a gas curtain at the door, emergency lighting with its own
generator, a large-scale map of the town and a smaller-
scale one to show its position in the district. Phones
connected the room to the police, fire, gas, electricity and
water officials in various parts of the town and there were
special lines to the rescue and repair service and to the
senior air raid precautions officials in Dortmund. Official
visitors to Altgarten were always taken to see the control
room and Herr Ryessman was very proud of it, although
some of the ruder clerks called it "the eagle's burrow."

His office had been moved up to the top floor along
with the marriages, births and deaths registry and the
housing department. Artfully they had put benches in the
corridor outside the marriage registry so they had been
able to convert the waiting room into the office of the
Burgomaster's clerk—Andi Niels, a solemn young man
with a gastric ulcer which, together with a certain amount
of string pulling by the Burgomaster, had released him
from army service. Downstairs there were the tax, street
cleaning and ration card offices, and the east wing of the
building was given over to the police, although the Oberwachtmeister had his office on the same floor as the
Burgomaster so that he was available for conference.

The Burgomaster went next door to his assistant's
office, noting with satisfaction that in the corridor sandbags and a rope, ax and stirrup pump had been placed
according to his most recent order.

His clerk's office was smaller than the Burgomaster's
and was crammed full with filing cabinets, but he envied
his clerk the view he commanded. From this window he
could see the tall spire of the Liebefrau rising from the
medieval roofs of the town center. Beyond, where the
open country began, there was the Wald Hotel tucked into
a patch of dark woodland, and to the north, catching the
sun, were four long greenhouses that were a part of
Ryessman's own property.

He was still enjoying the view when his assistant came
into the room. He was startled and to Ryessman's surprise
he flushed.

"Herr Ryessman," said the clerk politely. "Is there something you require?"

"No," said the Burgomaster, watching with amusement as the clerk hurriedly pushed the files he was holding into the nearest filing cabinet. By the time he turned back to the desk he was more collected.

"Today is my birthday, as you well know since you have been sending the invitations. I wanted to ask you to join our party this evening at Frenzel's."

"The Herr Bürgermeister is very kind," said Andi Niels. "I shall be honored."

"It's a small affair," said the Burgomaster. "This is no time for ostentatious display, but there will be smoked eel to start and Frenzel's special roast duckling to follow."

The Burgomaster was puzzled by the young man's behavior. Usually a relaxed and self-composed fellow, today he seemed anxious and neurotic. He straightened a picture on the wall, wiped dust from a shelf and moved around the room. Perhaps his ulcer was playing up, thought Ryessman.

"If you will excuse me, Herr Bürgermeister," he said. "You have an appointment with your tailor and I have a meeting too."

"I was forgetting the time," said the Burgomaster. He nodded to Niels and left the room. Outside in the corridor there were five people. At first the dark clothes of the older people suggested that they had come to register a death. Probably, thought Ryessman, they have these same clothes for weddings, births and deaths. It was the young couple who showed that this was a wedding. There was no doubt about them. They were so clearly in love that they were oblivious of everyone and everything around them. The young man was dressed in a dark well-cut suit with a small spotted bow tie. He was a handsome boy with big eyes and a strong jaw. There were not so many young men like that still in civilian clothes, thought Ryessman. The girl was pretty. She did not have the wide pelvis, heavy bones and strong arms that were common to the local girls. She was petite, with jet-black hair cut short and a heart-shaped face that was pale and doll-like. The parents shuffled uneasily as Ryessman walked down the corridor. Here in the country older people had never lost their fear of authority, thought Ryessman, and that perhaps was a good thing. Young people were less respectful and as he passed he heard someone whisper and the young man looked up and stared him straight in the face.

Perhaps if the Burgomaster had been busy that afternoon he would have never pursued the matter or come across it in the first place. But the afternoon was quiet and sunny as he sat at his desk idly turning over the carbons of letters passing between departments in the Rathaus.

Dear Sir,

The Burgomaster thanks you for your letter of the twelfth of May and confirms that MEYER, Hans-Willy, of Rheinprovinz Altgarten Florastrasse 36 is now officially downclassified to Jew of two-thirds Jewish blood.

Your department will ensure that his employer is informed and that any privileges that he had due to his former status as a Jew of one-third Jewish blood should now be withdrawn.

A. NIELS
*for the Burgomaster*

Niels had initialed the carbon as was his usual practice. Acting on impulse, the Burgomaster phoned through to police records and asked them for their file on this man Hans-Willy Meyer.

"You have it already," said the police constable.

"You are sure?"

"I am certain, Herr Bürgermeister. Herr Niels came down for it personally. He said you had asked for it."

"Thank you."

"Is everything in order?"

"Yes," said the Burgomaster. He knew the man with whom he had spoken, an elderly constable who had been put in charge of records after being badly injured in a fight with two drunks at the beginning of the war. He was a man of experience and would have made no mistake. The Burgomaster picked up the phone but replaced it and walked along to Niels's office instead. The wedding party were still waiting in the corridor.

Niels was not in his office and although at first Ryessman was about to dismiss the matter from his mind he had second thoughts and went through the cabinet to find Meyer's police file. It was not there. There were in fact none of the gray-covered police files anywhere in the cabinet. It was then that he remembered that Neils had been carrying a gray file when he had come into the office and found Ryessman behind his desk. Yes, there it was,

stuffed into a cabinet of purchase agreements so carelessly
that its cover was bent double.

The Burgomaster read through the file of documents.
Meyer was a twenty-one-year-old Jewish farmworker. He
was not permitted to serve in the Wehrmacht. His file was
a very ordinary one that could have been that of any of
Altgarten's two dozen Jews. Ryessman had hoped that his
data card with its identity photo and fingerprints would
have been there, but it was not. Perhaps police records
filed them separately.

Meyer had been downgraded because his grandfather, a
butcher from Lübeck hitherto listed as an Aryan, had now
been classified as purely Jewish. This made Meyer's father
two-thirds Jewish like his mother, and, as everyone knew,
the offspring of two such Jews was a two-thirds-Jewish
son, not a one-third Jewish son. What puzzled Ryessman
was where the information had come from. Usually in
cases of this sort one found in the file a short unpleasant
note from a neighbor or fellow worker—typed sometimes,
or written in block capitals to conceal the writer's identity. Often they contained obscenities, sometimes they ended
with Nazi slogans instead of a signature. This file had no
such note. The grandfather had been dead since before the
Party came into power and these documents had originated with the Lübeck police records office. It seemed
unlikely that they would have made a mistake but then
perhaps in 1933, the first year of Hitler's power, they had
been overworked, for that was when all these Jewish files
began. Before that the police had dealt only with criminals.

It was time to go for his fitting. He replaced the file as
he had found it, even bending it as before. As he left his
office he saw the wedding party again. They were no
longer tense and the bridegroom held his wife's hand
protectively. Herr Holländer, the registrar, brandished a
huge bunch of keys and used them to unlock the cupboard
on the landing. He reached for one of the hundreds of
black-bound volumes that lined its shelves. The ceremony
was not yet complete and Holländer looked the groom in
the eye warningly. They were hushed and solemn as
Holländer handed the official edition of *Mein Kampf* to
the bride, as was mandatory in all Reich weddings. The
Burgomaster nodded approvingly at them as he passed.

The sun now shone from a clear blue sky and Ryessman
enjoyed the walk up Dorfstrasse past the ruined windmill
on the corner. As he crossed Vogelstrasse he could smell

the sweet, freshly cut timber in the carpentry shops where as a young child he had lingered on his way to school. He tried to forget the business of Meyer but he could not. Even as the tailor—old Herr Voss himself—supervised the fitting of his fine Party uniform he remembered it again. What sort of spiteful motive was behind the reclassification? Not that Ryessman had much sympathy for Jews; it was simply a matter of procedure. If there was a reclassification, then the file should show the evidence for it. If the reclassification had been upward instead of downward then Ryessman would have suspected corruption. It did happen, it was useless to deny it. There were such large sums of money involved. Some of them would offer a fortune rather than go into a concentration camp. It wasn't fair that these Jews put that sort of temptation to loyal policemen and Party workers, but what could you expect from such people?

"Raise your arm," said Herr Voss. "Too tight?"

"Exactly right."

"Bend forward and straighten up."

The Burgomaster did so and Herr Voss fussed around the back of his collar, slashing at the soft brown cloth with his chalk. It was a smart uniform; he wished it had been ready this morning when the family had had its group photo taken. How fine his mother had looked even at eighty-six, and the children in their best suits had been transfixed and silent in case the photo should show them as having moved. For their parents had promised them dire punishments if this photograph for grandfather's birthday was less than perfect.

"Sit down. Clothes must look as well on a man seated as upon him standing." Again he applied the sharp edge of the chalk. It was an honor to be fitted by Voss himself. Voss was among the wealthiest men in the town. In 1930 in an upstairs room in this very building he had first tried his hand at making a uniform. It was for an old and valued customer who had just joined the S.A. One of his fellow officers had admired it and by 1933 Voss uniforms had become famous for miles around. One wealthy S.S. officer came from Berlin and had previously been a customer of the famous Stechbarth, Göring's tailor. It made Voss very proud. Some people said things against them, but the Nazis had done wonders for the uniform business, whatever other faults they might have. There were so many part-time organizations that many Germans had two or three uniforms. Voss's greatest complaint against the

Nazis was the way they had deprived him of his skilled
Jewish staff. It was all very well, these arrogant young
men complaining about stitching and the cut of the
breeches. They didn't seem to understand that there were
secrets to tailoring a pair of breeches that were known to
very few cutters, and they were all Jewish.

"Stand up."

It was almost as though the Burgomaster had read
Voss's mind. He said, "Are there many Jews still in the
tailoring business?"

"Yes, Herr Bürgermeister," said Voss. "I still have one
cutter downstairs and there are certain lining materials
which can be obtained only from Jewish concerns in the
Netherlands. Now take this lining in your tunic . . ."

"I don't wish to know about it," said the Burgomaster
hurriedly. "I was asking in case you have heard of a
person named Meyer: Hans-Willy Meyer."

"I don't recall the name, Herr Bürgermeister, but my
cutter Jakob might know. Shall I fetch him?"

"Yes," said the Burgomaster.

Poor Jakob; he came into the room in answer to old
Mr. Voss's call and found the Burgomaster in his full
Party uniform. For a moment he completely forgot that
this was the very garment he had been handling only an
hour before and went white with horror.

"There's nothing to fear, Jakob," said Voss. "There's
nothing to fear, Herr Bürgermeister, is there?" he added.

"Nothing," said the Burgomaster. "I merely wondered
whether you knew a young man named Hans-Willy
Meyer. He lives in Florastrasse."

"No. Herr Bürgermeister," said Jakob.

"It will not mean trouble for him," promised the Burgomaster. "I promise it upon my word as a German officer."

"You are sure, sir?"

Voss said, "Of course, Jakob." All these Jews were
suspicious; why couldn't they behave like patriots?

"The fellow has been denounced," declared the Burgomaster dramatically. "Tell me what you know of him; it
can only help."

There were so few Jewish families still left in Altgarten
that it was foolish to deny that he knew young Meyer.

"He is a fine young man," said Jakob. "His family
comes from Lübeck. He works on a farm. It means
catching a bus at 5:30 A.M."

"When did you first know him?" The Burgomaster
offered Jakob a cigarette. The Jews didn't get a tobacco

ration—or a meat ration either—and Jakob dearly loved to smoke.

"I lived near his parents in Lübeck," said the old tailor. He took a cigarette but stored it carefully away.

"His father's parents were Jewish?"

"No, both his father's parents were Aryan. It was just his mother's mother who was Jewish."

"Are you quite sure?"

"I am quite sure, Herr Bürgermeister. There was so much talk about it." Jakob gave a short laugh. "His father was one of the most prosperous pork butchers in Lübeck."

Ryessman smiled. "So this fellow Meyer is only one-third Jewish."

"For you perhaps, Herr Bürgermeister," said the old tailor. "For me, he is not Jewish at all."

The thing that still puzzled the Burgomaster was the way in which this Jewish fool Meyer had signed the reclassification form. It was almost as if he wanted to be down-classified.

"See the shoulder, Jakob: high when the Herr Bürgermeister is seated, but straight when he stands."

Ryessman was irritated that they should talk of him as though he was deformed. Like surgeons rather than tailors, and that's the way they looked at him too.

"Are you finished?"

"Yes, thank you, Herr Bürgermeister. The day after tomorrow for another fitting. We must have it exactly right."

"My secretary will phone," said Ryessman.

"Is he well?" asked Voss.

"Niels?" said Ryessman. He smiled. "He was when I left him an hour ago."

"I thought I saw him going into the front entrance of the hospital," said Voss. "I wondered whether he was sick or just visiting."

"You were mistaken," said the Burgomaster, but his voice lacked conviction. Young Niels had not been his usual self today, and there was the strange business of the hidden dossier. Perhaps he was sick, perhaps he was in hospital. From the window of Voss's office he could see the gray brick Saint Antonius Hospital and beyond it the flat roof of the Annex building. For a moment he was tempted to use the phone and ask the reception if they had admitted Niels, but he decided that if Niels was in

hospital the Rathaus would have phoned him here at the
tailor to report it.

The Burgomaster was wrong on both items. At that
moment Andi Niels, personal secretary to the Burgomaster of Altgarten, was occupying a bed in room 28 on
the top floor of the silent Annex building.

Originally the Annex had been intended as an overflow
for Saint Antonius solely to cater for Altgarten's increased
population, but under the new hospital zoning arrangements it was used to receive air raid casualties from badly
bombed cities in the Ruhr. From here they were dispersed
as soon as possible and the beds made ready for the next
contingent of casualties. It was a stroke of genius to build
the training center for Samariter nursing assistants between the hospital and the amputee camp. The poor little
girls worked until they dropped. Especially on those awful
days when convoys of the new buslike ambulances were
jammed along Joachimstrasse so that air raid victims from
the Ruhr were lying in corridors for want of bed space.
Samariter with only a couple of weeks' training found
themselves working in the operating rooms or casualty
wards. On the days when there were no R.A.F. raids the
Samariter worked almost as hard in the Amputee Center
across the road. At any time of day or night the nurses'
accommodation wing of the training center was dark with
a silence marred only by the snores and nightmares of the
exhausted girls.

There were many young girls in Altgarten: Red Cross
nurses, Frei sisters, Brown sisters and Samarittas. The
tearooms and hairdressers vibrated with their chatter and
the inhabitants of Altgarten were never at loss for a story
about their shameless activities. Once a month there were
dances at the training center. TENO officers, S.S. men
from the Wald Hotel training camp and certain local
residents received neatly penned invitations and displayed
them like honors. All three of the town's hairdressers
could be certain of one ticket; so could the haberdasher
and an old man named Drews who regularly obtained
bolts of silk and linen from some secret source over the
border. For obvious reasons the senior staff at Kessel's
brewery were asked and the Burgomaster's office received
a ticket as a matter of courtesy. Andi Niels used that
ticket.

Tonight there was to be a dance at the training center.
The girls had decorated the assembly hall with colored
papers and cardboard representations of Mount Fuji. On

the tickets it had hopefully said "fancy dress with a theme of old Japan" but only the most enthusiastic girls had sewn together a costume.

"The old fool invited me to his birthday dinner," said Andi Niels. "What the devil can I do?"

"Couldn't you get away early?" said the nurse. She was a short plump sexy girl who giggled readily at any situation. She giggled now.

"There'll be toasts to his father, the regiment, officers who fell in the first war. Then we'll listen to speeches and sing old war songs. You've no idea what it's like."

"There'll be food at the dance. The girls have been saving their rations for three weeks."

"No matter," said Niels sadly. "We'll go to Düsseldorf this weekend and stay in a fine hotel."

"And share a room?" said the nurse. She giggled. "They will ask for our papers."

"I can fix that."

"Have you inherited some money?"

"As a matter of fact, I have," said Niels. He turned over in bed and reached down to her. "You've left your stockings on," he accused.

"Just in case."

"The door's locked, and no one will come up to the top floor during the day."

"I'll take them off," said the girl. "But I must be back on duty by five." She climbed out of bed again.

"By five I must be in my office," said Niels. "I've left lots of work there." He watched her take off her stockings and garter belt. She knew he was watching her and she moved in a deliberately provocative way, knowing that his impatience would put an edge on his appetite.

Niels breathed heavily. My God, he thought, I'm going to miss all this next week.

After August Bach had driven away, Anna-Luisa busied herself in the house and garden. She scrubbed the kitchen floor, boiled down oddments of soap and cleaned out the chicken house. At four o'clock she met Hansl at the Volkschule and walked him past the fire station. Both of the Magirus fire engines were outside and he watched intently as the equipment and paintwork was shined to a high gloss. The firemen were accustomed to the Volkschule boys and Johannes Ilfa, the Gruppenführer on the number one engine, recognized Hansl and lifted him up to see the driver's seat. For months he had seen Anna-Luisa

meeting the child from school. One of his friends had
teased him about concealing a secret passion for the girl.
He would be teased even more if seen speaking to her.

"My name is Johannes Ilfa," said the fireman, offering
Anna-Luisa a cigarette.

"My name is Johannes too," said Hansl.

Anna-Luisa waved the cigarette aside. "We call him
Hansl," she explained.

"We . . .?" said the fireman. "He is your son? I thought
you were the nurse."

Anna-Luisa enjoyed his obvious discomfort. "You
mustn't jump to conclusions."

"Do you ever smoke?" he asked, the packet still open in
his hand.

"Not in the street. Have one yourself."

"It's forbidden." He brushed his fine moustache with the
back of his hand.

"Lift me up again," called Hansl, and Johannes Ilfa did
so. The little boy fingered the shiny steering wheel and
then looked at his hero in wonder.

"We mustn't be a nuisance," said Anna-Luisa.

"You couldn't be a nuisance." He looked at her for a
long time trying to find something to say. Something that
would make her delay and make her smile at him again.

"We must go." She smiled at the fireman.

"Make Mutti bring you again, Hansl," called the fireman.

"Yes," said Hansl, and he gripped Anna-Luisa's fingers
in his warm hand as though he was part of a conspiracy.

"Say good-bye to Herr Ilfa and thank you," she told the
child.

They both waved when they reached the corner. At
Mauerstrasse they turned right. This was the main road
that joined Kleve to Krefeld and followed the ancient
walls that marked the edge of Altgarten. On the other side
of Mauerstrasse a wide stream moved sluggishly southward. Hansl liked to throw pieces of paper into the green
water and run to each of the wooden bridges to see them
move underneath.

Much of the wall still remained and Frau Birr's
tearoom was built into the massive stones. From the
second floor there was a view as far as the high ground
upon which stood the Burgomaster's greenhouses near the
waterworks. In the other direction there was a view of the
Wald Hotel, now taken over by the S.S. and garlanded

with tall barbed-wire fences and endlessly patrolled by guard dogs.

Smart *Hausfrauen* of Altgarten gathered in Frau Birr's tearoom each afternoon, accompanied by their daughters in neat dark dresses and well-kept shoes. That's why TENO officers, army doctors and administration officials from the Amputee Center liked to have tea here. Sometimes cavalry officers and veterinary surgeons, complete with spurs and riding crops, came all the way from their depot near Kempen and set the ladies' hearts aflutter.

Hansl and Anna-Luisa shared a slice of *Apfelstrudel*. The coffee wasn't too bad and Frau Birr could usually find a small glass of milk for the boy. The people in the big cities didn't live as well as this, thought Anna-Luisa. Life seemed unbelievably sweet. Soon she would be Frau Bach, and the ladies in the teashop with their fruit-filled hats would have to nod in a way different from the condescending smiles they gave to the R.A.D. girl.

Frau Hinkelburg, the architect's wife, was just as condescending as any of them but at least she was affable. This day she sat with Anna-Luisa and Hansl and told them all her news.

There were always stories about the Russian prisoners of war in the disused factory beyond the brewery. The citizens of Altgarten were fascinated and a little afraid of these strange Bolshevik men from the far side of the world where so many young Germans were being sent.

"They put two fierce guard dogs to keep the Russians inside the fence at night. Even the dog handlers were wearing thick protective gloves. By the next morning the dogs had been cooked and eaten. Only the bones remained, they say. And those they carved into crucifixes."

Frau Hinkelburg paused long enough to cut a piece of cake and hurry it into her mouth. Anna-Luisa felt that she was expected to add something, but she kept her own wonderful news to herself to be gloated over and devoured slowly. Even before she'd swallowed her cake Frau Hinkelburg smiled at Anna-Luisa and began again.

"Frau Kersten is going to put apple trees in the field behind the cemetery and she's bought the land she leased from Richter. The money she must make from the potatoes." Frau Hinkelburg opened her fine new patent leather handbag so that Anna-Luisa could clearly see its Paris label. From it she took a small lace handkerchief and brushed a cake crumb from the corner of her mouth. "I heard that Frau Kersten has a leather box full of money hidden in her bedroom. She can't bank it, they say, for fear of the tax department."

"Her farmhouse is being replastered."

"By the French prisoners of war," added Frau Hinkelburg. "Have you noticed the tall one with the tiny moustache?"

"The one giving orders?"

"He's giving more than that, my girl, if the stories about him and Frau Kersten are true."

"But Frau Kersten is nearly fifty."

"Many a fine tune is played upon an old violin." Frau Hinkelburg laughed loudly and clamped her hand over her mouth in a gesture she believed refined. The diamonds on her hand caught the light. "Before the Frenchman, they say she was casting her eyes farther afield."

"What do you mean?" said Anna-Luisa.

"Your employer, my dear."

Anna-Luisa laughed good-naturedly.

"You think that's funny?"

"But Herr Bach and that fat old Frau Kersten . . ."

"Yes, Frau Kersten would be a lucky woman to have Herr Bach as a husband," admitted Frau Hinkelburg as she thought about it.

"Any woman would be a lucky woman."

Frau Hinkelburg looked up sharply. Her ears were attuned to chance remarks and she never missed an innuendo. "*Ach so!*" was all she said, but Anna-Luisa knew that one part of her secret was a secret no longer. Frau Hinkelburg put a freckled bejeweled hand upon Anna-Luisa's thin white arm and smiled at her.

"You were not here when the Wald Hotel was really a hotel. What a wonderful place! The chef was French, from Monte Carlo. People came from all corners of Europe—and from America too—to dine there and to stay in the suites that face onto the gardens and the forest. There were floodlit fountains and an orchestra outside in the summer. They used to dance until two or three o'clock in the morning and the sound of the music could be heard right across the town on a still summer's night. When I was a young girl I would open my bedroom windows and listen to the music and the voices of the fine people who left their motorcars and chauffeurs waiting down there in Mauerstrasse. It will never be the same again."

"When the war is ended, perhaps . . ."

"No, the world has changed since then. There is no

place for romance now. Why, look at what the Wald
Hotel is now used for."

"No one knows what it's used for."

"I know," said Frau Hinkelburg. "My husband is an
architect and he heard it from someone in the Burgomaster's office." She leaned closer to emphasize the confidential nature of her theory. "It's a human stud. Young
carefully chosen Aryan girls are sent there to"—she hesitated—"to have children by selected S.S. officers."

"How awful," said Anna-Luisa. She said it mechanically, for she did not believe it.

"Awful," agreed Frau Hinkelburg, "and yet fascinating.
Is it not?"

"There are so many stories about the men in the Wald
Hotel."

"Because they so seldom emerge from the place."

"Probably," agreed Anna-Luisa.

"Well, it's understandable," said Frau Hinkelburg.
"They have everything they want there, don't they?" She
laughed coarsely; Anna-Luisa smiled.

"Are you going anywhere tonight, Anna-Luisa?"

"I have so much ironing to do."

"I thought you might be going to the Burgomaster's
birthday party at Frenzel's. They are having Russian caviar and roast duckling. I am going."

"Herr Bach scarcely knows the Burgomaster."

"But his cousin Gerd knows him." She watched the girl
carefully. "And you are a friend of Andi Niels, the Burgomaster's secretary."

"He's no friend of mine," said Anna-Luisa. "He's horrid."

"He has a reputation," agreed Frau Hinkelburg, "but he
wields a great deal of influence in this town. The girls with
extra clothing-ration coupons ... you'd never believe."
She laughed again.

"I have heard stories about him," said Anna-Luisa.

"There are stories about everyone in this town. Small
towns are always full of gossip. There are stories about
you, even ... you would laugh if you heard them."

"About me?"

"It means nothing, child. A beautiful girl is bound to
have stories told about her. ..."

"In connection with whom?" interrupted Anna-Luisa
angrily.

The woman smiled and Anna-Luisa knew that she
wanted her to be angry.

"Whom?" repeated Anna-Luisa. "What lies are being spread?"

"I never listen to scandal," said the old woman haughtily. "It's all stupid nonsense. I have told you that."

"With whom?"

"With everyone, child; you would have to be the most energetic courtesan since Pompadour." She patted her arm again and the bejeweled rings flashed in the sunlight.

Fischer was a young man—twenty-four last birthday—but his bloodshot eyes and the black rings of tiredness around them made his appearance deceptive. Now that he had had a steaming hot bath and washed the Russian dust out of his hair he shook away some of his fatigue. He found a last clean set of underclothes and a reasonably clean shirt in his baggage. An orderly had just returned his boots to him brightly shining, although there were deep scratches that went right through the leather in places. His long leather overcoat hanging on the door was also beyond salvage. Its lapels were scuffed white and the sleeve seams had been ripped and resewn so many times that it was crookbacked. He put the Knight's Cross over his head and tucked the lady's garter to which it was attached under his collar out of sight.

In the front line no one any longer wore their conspicuous Leibstandarte cuff band but now Fischer put it on his sleeve. The words "Adolf Hitler" shone bright and new compared with the faded fabric of his jacket. Fischer stroked the armband. The number one S.S. division, and he was to join number twelve. Ugh! He feared it might be like this run-down S.S. training depot where even the sentries were improperly dressed and the slow-witted young officers only half trained. It depressed him to think about it.

He looked at himself in the mirror: a tall slim man with a yellowish complexion that never altered no matter how long he spent in the sunshine. His eyes were black, intelligent and attractive. His brows were bushy, meeting above his large hooked nose to make a straight line across his face. At school he had been chosen to play Julius Caesar when his teacher said that he looked exactly like a Roman emperor. Adolf Fischer liked that idea and even now he would sometimes have too many drinks and surprise the other officers, who knew him only as a zealous and consistently savage warrior, by long quotations from Shakespeare's play.

These rooms on the first floor with balconies overlooking the lake had once been the finest rooms in the hotel. The bridal suite, perhaps. Now they were used for officers in transit and they had been left unaltered, even to the china jug and basin on the marble washstand with an enamel jug of boiling water delivered each morning to the rooms without baths. The pictures too remained: stag hunt, dawn in the mountains and Napoleon after Waterloo. There was a knock at the door.

"Come in," bawled Fischer. He was surprised to find that his visitor was an old man who outranked him considerably. Embarrassed by the manner in which he had shouted, Fischer came to a stiff position of attention and waited with unseeing eyes until his visitor bid him relax.

"Standartenführer Wörth," the old man introduced himself. His voice was quiet and his manner hesitant. Fischer had to watch his lips to understand his words. "I'm the commanding officer. Please continue with whatever you were doing. I only wished to offer you my greetings as I shall not be dining in the mess this evening. The Burgomaster here in Altgarten is an old Allgemeine S.S. officer and he's having a rather formal dinner party."

It was frightening, thought Fischer. The German Cross medal on the old man's pocket showed that he had been a fighting soldier in this war and yet now he'd become a mere vegetable, wrinkled and bent like an old turnip and so pale that Fischer felt positively tanned beside him.

"I have acquaintances nearby, sir. It was my intention to call upon them this evening."

"Splendid," said the old man. "You're going to this new 'Hitler Jugend' division."

"The division commander was with me in the Leibstandarte. He's asked for me."

"Reich Germans?"

"Yes. All of them born in 1926, volunteers from the Hitler Jugend."

"It will be an elite division."

"Yes, my tame *Untermensch* will look out of place."

"So I hear."

Fischer felt obliged to answer the unspoken question. "He's a first-class gunner and mechanic. I had him assigned as a personal servant only in order to keep him."

"You're a tank man?"

"Tigers; I volunteered for the first tank company the L.A.H. got."

"Cavalry man myself." He flinched from some secret

pain. "Left a hand behind in Rzhev; can't hold a rein and
fight with one hand." Fischer noticed the stiff glove.
Cavalry; that explained everything. These old fogies are
from another world.

"Cavalry Brigade Fegelein?"

"Yes."

"It's largely *Volksdeutsche* now."

"In my time it was just Reich Germans. It was an elite
unit then."

"I know that, sir."

Wörth looked at Fischer's cuff band and then again at
the young man's face. He saw his own youth there. Wörth
was with the Leibstandarte in 1937. What fine fellows we
were! Our average age was eighteen years one month.
*Liebchen aller Herzen* they called L.A.H. in those days.
Heartbreakers we were too. Handsome fellows. The
volunteer ahead of Wörth at the medical was failed for
having one filled tooth. He could scarcely believe it now,
when he looked at some of the odds and ends they had
sent him. Dutchmen some of them and Flemings too.
Keen, of course, but he couldn't understand a word they
said. Somewhere nearby a guard dog barked and then
another one. There were shouts and a yelp of pain before
the dogs became quiet. "Those damned dogs will drive me
mad," muttered Wörth.

"I can well believe it, sir," said Fischer. "Why don't you
get rid of them?"

"Why indeed," said Wörth and smiled as though Fischer
had made a rather good joke.

Leibstandarte, this old man, was it possible? "Rzhev?"

"January '42, the Rzhev pocket." It was months since
he'd last spoken of it. "My company of cavalry were
trying to find Ivan. Our artillery found us." In the snow,
horses and riders moved like ghosts, silent and invisible in
their newly issued white smocks. Wörth was riding
Rosenknospe, a light-footed horse as fast as any other in
the company and with a gentle disposition.

They were in the Valdai hills where the Volga rises,
north of Rzhev. They had come over the rise cautiously,
Hentschel first on the black mare that he'd had all the way
from the training school in Warsaw. At the bottom of
the rise there was a T34, its turret askew and a black circle
round it. Hentschel waved them on and then went close to
the sooty burned-out tank, but there was no sign of life
there. It was snowing slightly and the horses were fidgety,
tossing their heads and missing their footing as they en-

countered debris, bodies and goodness knows what under
the snow. "It was our artillery." They must have had the
old T34 zeroed in; by getting close to that we were asking
for it really. "A T34 might be very different from a Tiger
tank but Russian cavalry looks just like us, eh?" Then
there was the noise: deafening thuds and the screams of
horses and men. Instead of a black and white silent film it
became a noisy color film. The black mare racing across
the snow, dragging young Hentschel—his second in command—by his foot, with horse and rider spilling blood as
they went. Hentschel, Hentschel. "No horses survived,
four men did." Rosenknospe, his favorite, threw him and
then kicked wildly. It was frightened, its eyes dilated and
mouth open. Then he saw that its belly was split open and
its kicking feet entangled in its own entrails. Damn you,
Rös'chen. Get up! "Crawled back three miles on hands
and knees." The pain. "Took twenty-eight hours." Why
the devil should he remember it all today? He pushed it
back again deep into a recess in his mind.

"You were all right?"

"Only survivor. The other three died of wounds in
hospital. I was there for three months, discharged myself.
But only on antipartisan work after that."

"That's important duty." Must the fellow relate his
adventures? That little scuffle wouldn't merit a mention
nowadays.

"Strong stuff; a whole village sometimes. Old men, old
women, and then there's the problem of one's own soldiers
with the girls. You take a hundred villagers . . ." His voice
faded before he described their fate. "Strong stuff. I was
glad to leave it."

"Necessary stuff, sir. We must never let up on any of
them," said Fischer.

Wörth looked at him and nodded, confirming not Fischer's opinion but his own opinion of Fischer. Wörth grim-
aced involuntarily. "Gangrene; pain recurs more frequently
lately. My foot and hip too. Without the sunlamp I can't
walk."

"It was bad luck, sir."

"Mustn't bore you with my stories."

"No question of that, Herr Standartenführer." Not
much!

The old man suddenly became tired. "Witting," he
called in a voice no louder than the rest of his conversation, and from behind the door came an N.C.O. "Leave
you now, Fischer. Don't see you again, luck."

"Thank you, sir." Fischer came rigidly to attention and averted his eyes as the bent old man was helped out through the door. Moving ever more slowly, he inched his crippled feet forward. Witting closed the door gently.

> "This is a slight unmeritable man,
> Meet to be sent on errands . . ."

quoted Fischer softly to himself. On the table there were the remains of his meal. He'd eaten two frankfurters and a dish of boiled potatoes but had left the dehydrated cabbage and powdered soup. German army frankfurters, by some miracle of logistics, tasted the same in Danzig as they did in Paris. He wondered how his driver was managing the repairs on the Kübelwagen. It would be ready by 10 P.M., he was sure of that. He'd ordered it for ten and his driver would have it in good order even if he hadn't eaten, bathed or slept and was still wearing the same stinking underwear. Still, you can't have everything.

From his pocket he took a small notebook. Written there was the name of Herr Voss the tailor, followed by his private address. There were four other names and addresses, in Münster and Dortmund, but they had been ticked. Fischer went out on the balcony to have a cigarette and stare at the placid lake and the ducks. Soon he would phone.

Andi Niels, the Burgomaster's secretary, got back to his office at five-fifteen. There was a note waiting: the Burgomaster wanted to see him urgently. He sighed irritably; already the doorman and the typist next door had given him the same message. He went to check that Meyer's file was still where he had hurriedly pushed it. Only when he was sure it was there did he go next door.

"Niels," said the Burgomaster, "you have been signing documents and borrowing police dockets in my name without proper authority."

Herr Höllander from the marriage registry was standing in the corner with a look of satisfaction on his ratlike face. He had always been jealous of Niels, who he knew could win any argument by invoking the Burgomaster's name. Now he was delighted to be in at the young upstart's undoing.

Niels had not responded to the Burgomaster's statement, so he spoke again. "This file on Meyer, Hans-Willy."

Meyer, Hans-Willy, thought Niels; the old buffoon spoke like an official document.

"Explain the downgrading," said the Burgomaster.

"It's all in order, Herr Bürgermeister," said Niels, smiling in one final hope that Ryessman would let the matter drop.

"I didn't ask you that, Niels."

"He wanted to be."

"What do you mean?"

"He wanted to be."

"Don't raise your voice to me, my boy. You know very well that what he wanted has nothing to do with it. You made entries on the documents; why?"

"So that he could be married."

Ryessman remembered the dark-eyed boy and girl. "Was he married this afternoon?"

"That was him," said Niels. "You frightened the life out of him."

"I did?"

"He thought you were about to stop the ceremony. It can't be altered now, you know."

"I still don't understand," said the Burgomaster.

Herr Holländer said, "I understand, Herr Bürgermeister. Marriage between two persons with one-third Jewish blood is forbidden, but marriage between a person with one-third Jewish blood and a person with two-thirds Jewish blood is permitted under certain circumstances. The man Meyer wanted to be downgraded so that he could marry the girl."

"But she must be mad," said the Burgomaster, trying sincerely to comprehend it. "A girl with only one-third Jewish blood could have married an Aryan."

"They are like that," said Herr Holländer. "I get them coming into the registry for advice. It's hard to believe, but some of them would sooner marry one of their own kind than one of us."

The Burgomaster shook his head in wonder. He looked up at Niels. "What did they pay you?"

"Nothing; I did it to help. They were in love."

"Must I hand this matter over to the Gestapo?"

"Three thousand marks."

"When I think of what I did for you, Niels . . . It was my influence that secured your discharge from your regiment when your mother told me of your stomach ulcer."

"Well, your influence didn't last long, Herr Bürgermeister. I didn't get a discharge. I was placed temporarily on the reserve. My papers came this morning. I rejoin the 15th Panzergrenadier Division in Sicily next week. They are awaiting the invasion. I shall never come back." That little bastard Holländer was smirking gleefully.

"You would do well not to come back, Niels. Give your mother a hero for a son; you at least owe her that."

"More than I owe her money to pay the rent and keep her from starving?"

"I would rather starve than have a son like you. You are an enemy of the state, a thief and a liar."

Niels stood waiting for the Burgomaster's wrath to diminish.

"Get out," he said after a long silence. Niels was pleased to get away so lightly.

"And ..." said the Burgomaster. Niels turned. "You will pay the three thousands marks to the Winter Help Fund and show me the receipt. I shall not withdraw my invitation for dinner tonight, but I shall not be unhappy if you fail to turn up."

"Yes, Herr Bürgermeister," said Niels, trying to look sad. That was wonderful. He had far better things to do tonight: the dance, and providing the terror fliers stayed away, perhaps a visit to the fourth floor of the Annex. There was a tall Viennese nurse whom he rather fancied. She would be tastier than the Burgomaster's roast duckling.

Niels had been responsible for the eighteen invitations to the Burgomaster's dinner at Frenzel's. He had done the job carefully, remembering all sorts of obscure cousins and business colleagues. In fact, only one invitation had gone astray; the one to Frau H. Pippert, widow of a building contractor, had been typed with the wrong street name and the postman had guessed, wrongly, that it was intended for Fräulein G. Pippert, a teacher at the Volkschule.

Gerda Pippert knew from the moment she opened the envelope that the invitation was not intended for her. On the other hand she also knew, unlike the Burgomaster, that Hanna Pippert—Johanna really, of course, but no one called her that—had died over six months ago. Hadn't she received more than a dozen wrongly addressed letters of condolence from brick merchants, timber firms and manufacturers of stoves and boilers. And hadn't she forwarded them to the brother-in-law of the dead woman at some address in Krakow. Gerda Pippert deserved the invitation.

In the circumstances surely no one would begrudge her
honorary membership in the Burgomaster's family for one
festive evening. It was over three years since she had
eaten a meal at a fine restaurant, and as for being recognized, if they didn't even know that old Hanna was dead,
what chance was there that they would remember her
face? Anyway, old ladies looked alike. She could put some
new lace on her black dress. One of her ex-students—now
an artillery officer—had sent her an antique lace ta-
blecloth from Brussels. She had never risked a teapot on
it, but as a collar for the black dress it would be most
chic. She decided to gate-crash the dinner, or, as she
rationalized it to herself, attend as a friend of the family.

She had written a brief acceptance, carefully smudging
the initial. She looked at herself in the full-length mirror
of the wardrobe. It made the dress look quite new. Her
white hair was drawn tightly back and fastened with a
black ribbon. She would wear just a touch of face powder—
it was a special event, after all—and leave her spectacles
off. Then she remembered the old lorgnette. It was in the
bottom of her sewing box, a splendid device with an ivory
handle and gold rims to the glasses. She could no longer
see very well through the lenses, but held up to her face it
looked most distinguished. What's more, it would give her
something to do with her hands. In the sewing box there
was an old ivory cigarette holder too. She put it in her
handbag. Tonight after the coffee and speeches and cognac she would try a cigarette again. If only her handbag
were a little more elegant and the handle weren't so worn,
but if she held it low against her skirt it wasn't so notice-
able. She paraded up and down the bed-sitting room practicing well-born gestures. The dress looked fine. Tonight
Gerda Pippert, fifty-six-year-old spinster and schoolteacher, was to dine with the Burgomaster! It was the most
exciting prospect she could remember since her holiday in
Heidelberg in 1938.

Gerd Böll may have been the town wag but he was no
fool. Sometimes he regretted that he had left the university, for the young people there had a sense of humor more
nearly tuned to his than had the people of Altgarten. In
spite of disapproving eyes Gerd continued to act the fool,
for he knew that it was his particular strength that he
could endure the supercilious remarks of his neighbors
without wishing them ill.

Of all the people of Altgarten, Gerd's best friends were

among the TENO engineers who manned the camp on the
Krefeld road. Many times Gerd had taken his van and
gone with them into the Ruhr after a big R.A.F. attack.
He had seen the TENO's digging for hours into burning
wreckage and finding only shriveled corpses. He'd seen
them lifting steel beams in their bare hands and he'd
noticed that some of the most pugnacious and disreputable
roughnecks among them could be the most gentle with the
injured. None of them were young, for the young had all
been screened off to provide TENO battalions for bridge
building and demolition with front-line fighting units. Each
man had a technical skill and their easy discipline reflected
this, for theirs was a job where a few minutes could mean
a cellarful of people saved from flames or drowning. They
were a strange breed of men, new to Gerd Böll. They
took a drink when others would need a night's sleep, they
settled for a cigarette instead of a meal and swore when
lesser men would have wept.

In addition, Gerd liked their equipment: the tractors,
lorries and mobile cranes, the pumps and generators, and
the winches that could topple an office block.

It was five-forty, almost time for Gerd to report his
movements to the Burgomaster's control room. This evening of all evenings it was scarcely necessary, for he would
be at Frenzel's with the Burgomaster. For a birthday gift
he had bought a small humidor, inlaid with ivory and
mother-of-pearl. One of the Russian P.O.W.s had made it
for him. He wondered if the Burgomaster would disap-
prove if he knew its origin. Perhaps he would recognize
the style of work, for the madonnas they sold from door
to door had the same design on the skirts as the humidor
had round its lid.

Dark suit? Well, Gerd didn't have a dark suit. Apart
from this green suit he didn't have one at all. And this one
had long since ceased to fit him. He unfastened the jacket
buttons and breathed out with a long sigh of relief. Well,
he'd leave it open. It would never show when he was
sitting down. He sat down now at his antique desk and
cleared aside the accounts and unanswered correspon-
dence. From this window he had the ugliest view of
Altgarten. The cramped slum tenements crowded together
between brewery siding and gasworks as did the people
inside them.

In the cobbled street a group of children, some of them
in Hitler Youth uniform, were kicking a ball around. Gerd
watched them with interest but eventually the moment he

had been putting off arrived. He pulled a piece of paper toward him and sadly began a letter to his cousin August.

June 31, 1943

Rheinprovinz, Altgarten
Bahnhofstrasse 33

My dear kind August,

Perhaps you will despise me when you have finished reading this letter and yet, try as I have, I can find no alternative to writing it. This afternoon when I met you with Anna-Luisa and you both looked so radiantly happy it seemed clearly my duty (and my joy) to keep silent. Now I once again think otherwise. Think of me and my predicament as I write this letter. As unhappy as you may be, spare a moment to remember that I too am as sad.

The test of friendship is the extent to which a man will expose the friendship to total destruction by doing something he believes is in the best interest of his comrade. The girl is beautiful and to be sure has been a loyal employee and a fine guardian of little Hansl. But a young girl like Anna-Luisa has a life different from us, different too from any style of life we can remember. Like any beautiful girl living alone in a town filled with young men, the temptations put to her are unreasonable, but it would be dishonest of me, and foolish of you, to pretend that she has not succumbed to those temptations in a way that has made her notorious.

As your housekeeper, her private life is of only limited importance to you, and of no importance to me. But when marriage is mentioned, my dear good cousin, how can I not speak? At first you will dismiss my letter as gossip. Perhaps you will be tempted to ask for details. Do not do that, August. It can only cause you deep and lasting pain. Again I repeat, August, it can only cause you more pain than you already know.

Your cousin,

GERD

# ✦ 16 ✦

OBERLEUTNANT AUGUST BACH, who knew nothing of the letter his cousin had written to him and would in fact never know of it, walked along the soft beach in the evening light. One thousand suns bounced upon the wavetops and the sound of the sea was harsh and constant.

It was the coldness of the sea that formed the water particles in the air—twenty thousand of them in every cubic inch—by cooling it to dew point. So along the shoreline the incoming air became cloud and moved inland and became warm enough for the cloud to disappear. Patches of mist brooded in the cold trees and made the taller dunes into tiny desert islands. On the strand where August walked the mist was churned by the wind to reveal the golden horizon and then wrap him again in its cotton wool.

Deep-rooted yellow poppies and sea sandwort struggled for life against the shifting sand that exposed their roots one day and buried their heads the next. Along the high-water mark nature's usual debris had collected: edible urchins like battered shaving brushes, cuttlefish bones, channeled wrack, some of it dried and blackened, and mussels pounded loose from the endless steel stakes that extended out into the ocean and pointed at England. There was other flotsam too: pieces of packing case with cryptic stencil marks, a few dozen squashed oranges and a burned piece of yellow life jacket. Over everything there was thick shiny oil that added a sour smell of decay to the brisk salt breeze.

Bach tapped the loose sand from his boots, climbed a short flight of wooden steps and opened the door of the shack in which he lived. At first his men had thought him

mad for commandeering this ramshackle hut perched high
upon the dunes. It had been an equipment store for the
Dutchmen who had planted the dune grass and maintained
the seawall. Bach had had it lined with insulating material
and supported on new metal beams to make it dry and
free of rats. Inside there were books, a stove, a simple
Luftwaffe bedstead, an old armchair and a table at which
he worked. The few men under his command privileged to
see the place at close quarters recognized now the wisdom
of his choice. His Luftwaffe signals company numbered
one hundred fourteen men, with him their only officer. He
was quite happy to live and eat with them, but men who
obey orders need a chance to complain without an officer
to overhear. His little hut, half a kilometer from the other
buildings, gave them that chance. He unlocked the door
and let himself in. His desk was placed near the window,
from which he could see the beach and ocean when the
weather was clear. Willi, his second in command, had lit
the stove, for even on a fine summer's evening there was
dampness in the air that made the bedding cold and edged
the lenses of his binoculars with tiny spots of moisture. He
filled a kettle from the tap at the washbasin. The pipe
rattled like a machine gun and the water was warm from
its journey through the hastily laid water pipe that went
along the sunny dunes to the main building.

He treasured these few moments alone as he came to
terms with this environment. He remembered Anna-Luisa
and felt a warm contentment at his memory of her. He
knew that once the Stabsfeldwebel arrived and work began he would no longer be able to give himself to these
sentimental emotions. He wiped the lenses of his field
glasses and walked to the rear of the hut. From this
window he could see back across the dunes to the radar
buildings and, when it was not misty, all the way along the
coast to the tip of the tall radar aerials of the next
Himmelbett station.

He focused the glasses upon a clump of grass and
waited for the mist to move. Just a fidget of wing and a
stretch of long neck was for a moment higher than the
edge of a nest. The gray herons were still there on the
dune side. They usually stayed close to fresh water, especially in the summer, but since this coast had been made a
prohibited area the wildlife had become more active.
These had laid their eggs in May. Now it was almost time
to go. He wondered whether they would return next
winter. He felt that they were an omen.

Satisfied that all was well with the herons, he began to change from his uniform into old, more comfortable clothes. He pulled off his high boots, using the homemade wooden clamp behind the door. When the kettle began to hum gently he called Willi on the phone.

"A cup of chocolate, Willi?" he said.

"Thank you, Herr Oberleutnant," said the man at the other end. August chopped the coarse chocolate pieces into chips, melted them in the boiling water and beat the mixture until it was frothy.

August was watching his Stabsfeldwebel marching along the dunes when the heron returned. It was a huge ungainly bird with curiously slow and mechanical wing movements that made it seem man-made. Its legs trailed behind it and from its beak there hung an eel. The bird in the nest gave a croak of pleasure and raised its head to look. Always one or the other of them remained at the nest. "Kroink"; it circled the main buildings. Perhaps the great radar aerials attracted the birds, thought August, as it flew across the face of the Freya. White mist wove through the intricate metalwork like skeins of soft raw wool through a comb and the aerial moved gently, scanning as far as, and farther than, the enemy coast. Sometimes it even detected R.A.F. planes that never left the English sky.

Willi Reinecke knocked briefly and waited for permission before he entered. He carefully brushed the wet sand from his jackboots and stood correctly at attention. The steaming cup of chocolate waited for him on August's desk but first the two men enacted the ritual of salutes and greetings of rank that was a necessary prelude to all military intercourse.

Willi Reinecke was a tall, thick-set man of indeterminate age. Born in Hessen-Nassau, he was drawn north as a young man by the promise of work in the steel industry of the Ruhr, but, unemployed and desperate, he had finally joined the army. He still had a lot of hair. It was graying at the sides in a distinguished way that would have looked right on a banker. As a youngster he had been quite a ladies' man, but a grenade had exploded on a parapet while Willi was still looking over it. His nose had split open, his cheek was a maze of scars, and one ear was missing altogether, which is why he grew his hair long. A veteran of the Moscow battles, August had guessed when he had first been posted here, but the Stabsfeldwebel had growled "Verdun" and only then did August realize that his second in command was a lot older than he liked to admit.

They had disliked each other on sight. Reinecke was a senior N.C.O. of the old school. Twice August had seen him kick a man who had dawdled and he would not hesitate to clobber anyone who looked as if he might argue. These incidents had made the first trouble between them. At first August had tried to explain that the personnel he commanded were Luftwaffe technicians, not cannon fodder, but that had no effect. Finally August had decided to fight with Reinecke's weapons. He gave the amazed Reinecke a blistering dressing down and ordered him to parade each shift an hour before their work commenced. At that time there were six shifts—manning the radar machinery was tiring for the plotters working in darkness and grueling for the men exposed to the sea breeze—and so Reinecke found himself on parade six hours out of the twenty-four.

The lesson was not lost on the stubborn old man and, after a month of the new regime had convinced him that August was quite prepared to continue the same schedule for the war's duration, he called for a truce. He did this when August was away on a two-day course in electronics. The Oberleutnant returned to find that the drafty little hut in which he had elected to live had been completely remade. It had been equipped with furnishings stolen or borrowed from goodness knows where and a large doubleglazed window had been fitted to facilitate August's birdwatching. From that moment the two of them had tried to work together, and in the curious way that happens sometimes to people with such contrasting beliefs and backgrounds, they had become very close. When August Bach understood the man better he realized that his tyranny was matched by a concern for the welfare of his men. Willi Reinecke was not above stealing, lying and even falsifying documents to ensure that his men were properly clothed and fed.

Even more surprising was the skill that Willi Reinecke had shown in the plotting room. For the first week or so August had used one of the younger technicians to help him plot the bombers, but Reinecke always appeared whenever there were enemy planes in the sector and finally August worked with him one night. Incredibly it was that night that the thousand-bomber raid upon Cologne passed overhead. Willi Reinecke didn't have the lightness of touch for which the training school would give high marks. He stumbled up the steps of the ladder to the plotting table and swore loudly when August needed silence. It was a rare night in which Willi didn't drop his Kneemeyer measure two or three times or kick the table as he hastily gauged the speed of the bomber that the radar held in its beam. Willi's value was in the way he could guess the intentions of the quarry. Some of them had a device that told them they were held in the invisible radar beam. These would jink and turn desperately. Willi would poise his marker over a point where he expected the bomber to go while August guided the fighter pilot to it. It was surprising how often Willi outguessed the *Tommis*.

Willi Reinecke had a wife and two children. He didn't smoke, rarely drank alcohol and lately he had shown an interest in August's bird-watching. He was very proud of his first attempt at taxidermy and prouder still when August put it in a place of honor on his desk. In short, Willi Reinecke was a conundrum and that, more than any other thing, was what drew August close to him.

Willi removed his belt and special flak service greatcoat with its wool lining and the stripes on both cuffs that, in the Wehrmacht, marked the company's senior N.C.O. He hung it behind the door. August remained in his armchair and Willi sat erect in the seat at the desk. He nodded his thanks as the chocolate was pushed toward him. He sipped it and held his scarred hands around the cup for a moment before giving his report. He unfolded a piece of paper and read the names.

"Two men sick since you left on Friday: one of the plotting table orderlies—Gefreiter Path—said he had tonsillitis, but I took a look at him." Willi looked up. "He's running a slight temperature but it's only a sore throat. I've put him on light duties outdoors. That should do the trick and meanwhile he's not breathing sore-throat bugs all around the Seeburg table." Again he referred to his paper. "The other case was Gefreiter Kick—the cook with the handlebar moustache. He complained of stomach pains. Too tender for indigestion and the wrong side for appendicitis. Regular colicky stabs of pain. I sent him into Rotterdam with the ration lorry; the hospital is holding him for observation. Meanwhile Unteroffizier Zewlinski will work the last shift until Kick returns or we get a replacement. There's not much work on that shift except counting the stores."

"And you think Zewlinski can count the stores unaided?"

"I'll be keeping an eye on him."

"You are quite a physician, Willi. I'm very impressed."

"I've had a lot of cavalry experience and men are just like horses. I could always tell the horse pox or colic, which just needed isolation and a rest, from the lymph cases and the strangles, which have to be sent back down the line as fast as possible."

"To the slaughterhouse?"

"Sometimes, sir."

"And you sent Kick back?" Bach grinned but Reinecke didn't.

"We shan't see him again," pronounced the old man grimly. "But I let Unteroffizier Zewlinski think he'd only be doing the extra duties for a day or two."

"I understand, Willi."

Willi peered at his piece of typed paper again. "Two men to divisional signals course, three on the gas course, six men guarding the unoccupied gun site near the village with Rimm in charge of them. The cook that H.Q. borrowed is still there." Willi looked up. "He plays the accordion," he added significantly.

"He wasn't much of a cook," said Bach.

"We should try to write him off and ask for a replacement." Bach nodded. "Three in hospital in Rotterdam including Kick, ten on leave, four on day pass, three on ration detail: one hundred and fourteen men present and correct."

Bach nodded.

"Two more bicycles stolen," said Willi Reinecke.

"This time they are in for it."

"The men who lost them are on open arrest. I thought you'd probably sentence them tomorrow after the cashing up is done. Then they can go into Rotterdam tomorrow afternoon as soon as the second shift go on."

"You have informed the local civilian police? They got the last one back, didn't they?"

"Yes, sir, but riding a Wehrmacht bicycle is a risky business for a Dutch civilian. To get home one night after curfew perhaps . . ."

"Yes, if you spot one outside a bar, unlocked and waiting to be stolen. It's just carelessness."

"Exactly, sir. Either that or they are going farther afield in the back of one of the wagons. I have informed the military police office in Rotterdam."

"I will sentence them tomorrow. Air activity?"

"Little or nothing."

"They are expected tonight."

"We had the alert. I have assigned Lemmers' crew to the Freya and I have rearranged the shifts as you ordered. The best crews will take over their radars at 0000 hours."

"It's a short night for them. Let's hope it's to be the Ruhr; then they might cross this sector on the outward as well as the return."

Suddenly August realized that Willi's family lived in the Ruhr. Confused and embarrassed, he searched for something else to say. "Moonrise is . . ." He tried to see the time from the chart.

"Moonrise tonight is 0030, sir. Yes, it will be nice to get two cracks at them."

"And sunrise is 0546. They will have come and gone by 0300, I would say."

"I told the crews that if the target is in the Ruhr it will be a four-hour shift. If the *Tommis* go farther than that, the number two crews will stand them down for a break and we'll put them back on for the return."

"Good, Willi. You outthink me every time."

Willi smiled. They both knew it wasn't true, but it was nice to hear the Oberleutnant say it. They drank the hot chocolate. Willi knew that there was no more official business.

"A good weekend, sir?"

"Wonderful, Willi."

"Your small son is well?"

"He runs me into the ground. I don't know where he finds the energy."

"My two are the same. I'm glad to get back here for a rest."

Willi looked round the Oberleutnant's room. He felt privileged to be allowed into it. Even the senior officers who came on visits to the radar station were seldom invited here. On the wall above a desk cluttered with glue, wire and soldering equipment there was a sheet of white card upon which August Bach had been reconstructing the bones of a gull's wing. Alongside it were pasted reproductions of Leonardo drawings of a wing and some photos of gulls, avocets and harriers in flight.

"The sparrow hawk came back."

"Photo?"

"I'm not as quick as you are, sir."

"It's just practice."

"We got some interesting movements on the radar last night."

"Birds?"

"No doubt."

"Log it all, Willi. We're in a unique position that could make a real contribution. Until now the ornithologists didn't know that birds flew at night."

"The operator made a note of the time."

On the desk there was the blackheaded gull that Willi had wired and mounted. He hadn't mastered the trick of folding the wings and he wouldn't permit August to help, so like many an amateur taxidermist before him he had finally fixed them outstretched—gull at moment of alighting. Under the gull's red feet he had put a nest with three blue-green eggs. Whatever its faults. as August had told him, "No one would guess it was a first attempt." Willi turned it round proudly.

"You saw the heron just now?"

"I'm going to get married again, Willi."

"That's good, sir."

"To my housekeeper."

"That's wise, sir. At our age a man wants a sensible woman, not a flashy piece of skirt."

August smiled. "I'm afraid that many of my friends might say that she is a flashy piece of skirt, Willi. She's an R.A.D. girl, not much older than my son."

It was Willi's turn to be embarrassed, but August didn't care about anything. He was enjoying the warm feeling of being in love. He opened a drawer of his desk and took out a bottle of German brandy. He poured a slug of it into the Stabsfeldwebel's chocolate.

"Drink up, Willi," said August Bach. "Let's think ourselves lucky that we are not flying with the *Tommis*. For tonight, I have a feeling, we shall have a remarkable success."

"Success," echoed Willi and drank his chocolate and brandy.

For some time they sat in silence, drinking and watching the shadows lengthen and the blurred sun drop toward the misty ocean.

"There was no mail?" He knew there was none. Had there been any, it would have been placed upon his desktop as it always was. "None," said Willi.

"He's an inconsiderate little bastard."

"He'll be all right: bright lad, lots of combat behind him. You know how quickly you'd hear."

"He can look after himself; I was thinking only of his promotion. He's been a Sturmmann for over a year and the lowest ranks live like pigs in the front line."

"Promotion is slow in the Waffen S.S. units."

"I wish like hell he wasn't in an S.S. unit," said August.

"I'd feel the same if it was my boy."

"Only because they don't get enough rest between combat."

"Of course," said Willi. "I understand." He got to his feet and stood correctly at attention again. "If the Oberleutnant permits ... there are the personnel and ration returns." The old N.C.O. had moved from intimate chatter to the absurd third person of the Kaiser's army.

"Carry on, Willi. I'll be along soon."

He spent a few minutes looking through a trayful of paper work. It could all wait until tomorrow, he decided. He put on his long black leather overcoat. The wind whined gently as he opened the door.

The sea was blood red by the time Oberleutnant Bach walked along the wet sand to start work. He walked as slowly as he could. He picked up pieces of seaweed and a tern, stiff with diesel oil. Once he thought he saw a hedgehog among the dunes and waited five minutes for it to reappear but it didn't.

From the sea's edge the futuristic shape of the radar aerials was awesome even to him. He could easily pretend that he had just emerged from this sea upon some Atlantis where the technics were a century ahead of anything he had known. The metal graticule, as big as a large house, that swung gently from side to side was code-named Freya. August remembered that Freya was a Nordic goddess whose watchman could see one hundred miles in every direction by day and by night. It was a fair description of the Freya radar device and August reasoned that if he could work that out, then so could the British Intelligence. (In fact he was correct. Dr. R. V. Jones worked it out and reported to the Chiefs of Staff accordingly.)

Not far away were the two shorter-range, but more precise, giant Würzburgs. They were like electric bowl fires as big as windmills. They too swung gently around the horizon but always returned—like the Freya—to point westward to where in East Anglia the Allied bomber airfields were but half an hour's flying time away.

Gently August put the dead tern back on the sand. It was 2200; the *Tommis* were not even in the air yet and when they were the Freya would give warning. The sand

crunched underfoot. He kicked a hole in it and the sea
appeared there as if by magic. Eggs for tea and a walk
along the silent beach in the evening sunlight; Hansl and
Anna-Luisa would love it here. After the war they would
live somewhere remote. This was a fine rich country. Even
with a hungry Wehrmacht gnawing at it for years there
were still eggs and milk and sometimes cream. A few
months ago Willi had come back from Zuidhorn with a
whole sheep. August had checked the ration returns and
the petrol sheets but had found no discrepancy.

From the tops of the dunes one could see fields of
vegetables and greenhouses just like Altgarten. But here in
the spring they had eaten them. The soups had been
brimful of vegetables and meat and he had not complained, nor even investigated. He told himself he would
have found nothing amiss anyway. The truth of it was that
he was a bloody awful officer. That's why he had never
risen above Oberleutnant. And that was why he was
strolling along the strand with a pair of Zeiss 16 x 40s,
soft shoes and an old sweater, instead of besieging Leningrad in full battle order.

Still, thought August, one war is enough for any man.
In the first basinful also he had been happy. Flying his
Albatros twice a day and living on good food and wine in
a fairy-tale château on the Meuse. Wouldn't any spoiled
young brat fresh from university give his life for a chance
like that? That's just what a lot of them did give. Who
knows why any survived, except that suddenly the brain
feels anew the prick of self-preservation that deserts
young men for a few years and so makes heroes possible
and wars welcome.

He raised his glasses to the naval gun bunker. Upon it
sat a tern. He flicked the binoculars into focus and
watched with pleasure as it searched its wings and preened
itself. Suddenly there was the rumble of the emergency
generator being tested. The bird rose alarmed and flew
out to sea until August lost sight of it.

The sea mist had thinned considerably but the light was
going fast. Reluctantly he put his glasses into the case and
entered the T-shaped hut and its plotting room.

Had August been able to see eighty-five kilometers to the
north he would have seen the coastal convoy and the
antiaircraft light cruiser *Held* continuing steadily on their
course. The guns they had fired at Löwenherz and Himmel were long since cleaned and readied for action but

there had been no other interruptions and, as "Admiral"
Pawlak had predicted, they were now halfway to the
Hook. The convoy had moved closer to the coast here, for
the danger from wrecks was lessened and the danger from
Allied aircraft increased.

This piece of coast was still enveloped in a thin streak
of mist but the sunset had turned it bright gold, "like a
Turner."

"Like a what?"

"A painting by Turner; just a swirl of golds and reds
and orange, a sort of land of ghosts."

"You give me the creeps, you do, Dikke. You know
what your trouble is? You read too many books, and
books will get you nowhere. Now come away from that
porthole and listen to what I'm saying and we might get
ourselves another ring round the gun."

The plump boy from Königsberg went and sat on the
bunk where "Admiral" Pawlak, with his mouth full of
cheese, was explaining about gunnery. On the wall of the
storeroom there was a bright disk of light moving upward
as the sun sank lower and lower.

"It's rhythm. No one ever teaches you that but that's
the secret of a high rate of fire—rhythm." He broke off
another piece of cheese and put it in his mouth. "Now
take that starboard number two gun. That loader waits
for the breech to clear and then leans in with the next
shell just like they teach you at gunnery school. That's all
very well for demonstration work or target shooting but
when you have a plane taking evasive action like this
morning's one did you've got to anticipate."

"When I was at training school, one of our crew caught
his hand in the breech."

"Well, he must have been a slow-witted fool, Dikke,
like you."

"That's right, he was. That's why I don't try these tricks
of yours."

"You're a fool, Dikke. Do you want to stay a K3 all
your life? Tonight I'll take the loading. We'll be under
control from the bridge so you can be number one; I
don't care."

"Thanks, Admiral."

"Forget it, Dikke. If we are going to get our third
*Tommi* tonight we'll have to get a lot of shells into the
air."

The ships in the convoy were lit by the sun like golden

toys on a black velvet sea. Inside the cabin the light grew
redder and redder.

"Put on the light, Dikke. I can't see to eat my cheese."

The plump boy did as he was told.

"And close the port covers. You know the blackout
regulations. Do you want to get us bombed?"

# 17

THE NAAFI closed at ten o'clock but the Salvation Army canteen was open until ten-thirty. By leaving the station cinema early and sprinting across the parade ground it was possible to get a cup of tea before bedtime. Mrs. Andrews, who served in the Sally Ann, judged the films by the number of hot drinks she sold last thing at night. "It's not a very good film; fourteen teas Monday and I had to make a second pot on Tuesday night."

The previous week there had been a flying film. The hero made love with a sober intensity and flew with drunken abandon (the complete reversal of the activities of the R.A.F. boys). A cowardly pilot ran amok, was ostracized and finally flew sobbing into an enemy plane. The C.O. ruled with his fists and cried glycerin tears each time one of his boys failed to return. The R.A.F. greeted this film with jeers and catcalls. The projectionist had phoned the Orderly Officer about it.

"Shouting at the film are they? And you want me to come over there so they can shout at me? Not Pygmalion likely. I saw it last night. It's about time you got some good films."

They had no contact with this film or its makers. R.A.F. selection boards had ensured that none of them ever experienced such extreme emotions. No one at Warley had ever publicly sworn vengeance upon the Germans (unless you counted the C.O.). No one here endured a crash so lightheartedly, took off into thick fog or swigged whisky round the mess table, toasted absent friends with song and threw their glasses into the fireplace. Here grief was measured by what was paid for the auctioned, worthless personal effects of the casualties. Tears were for actors. Here cowardice was their common conceit and all

222

had their own favorite acts of cowardice of which to boast. The fliers of Warley were men of even temperament who, for better or worse, did not react profoundly to the work they did.

Tonight there were no crews in the crowded cinema. No one left early nor did they make a noise. It was an old Charles Laughton film—*Rembrandt*—and so many turned up that they had been forced to get folding seats from the Operations Block and sit latecomers along the aisles.

The Music Circle meeting in the Education Hut had assembled nineteen assorted ranks to listen to Georg Kulenkampff and the Berlin Philharmonic play Beethoven's Violin Concerto. The performance was virtually faultless and their pleasure was marred only slightly by having to turn the records every few minutes. The Education Officer had the irritating habit of conducting, but when the music had finished and he produced a few bottles of beer all was forgiven. They were there until almost midnight talking about music. There were very few places on the aerodrome where all ranks could meet on a completely equal footing, let alone drink and smoke together.

The Station Dance Band had been in existence for six weeks but there had been only two rehearsals with every member present. Two of the band were working tonight. Sergeant Tommy Carter, a keen amateur saxophone player, was flying, and a corporal who could play the piano relatively well was on duty in Flying Control. This night the fellow on the piano could only play from the singer's line and the trumpet player was all over the place. It wasn't his fault, for although he had studied music for two years, his instrument was the violin. The seven musicians practiced together at the far end of the NAAFI, but when the canteen began to fill up they stopped playing and sat around drinking tea. The leader, an L.A.C. clerk from Southampton, said that if they couldn't do better than this they should tell the dance committee to bring in a civilian band for the Sergeants' Mess dance next month. By the time the NAAFI closed they were all a little depressed.

Musically, however, Warley Fen was dominated that summer by a simple but subtle melody. Erks whistled it as they bicycled to dispersals. Fitters hummed it as they replaced the spark plugs on the Merlins and a big-breasted blond NAAFI girl named Veronica played it on the piano with lots of improvised vamping. A slim-hipped M.T. corporal with a thin moustache impersonated Al Bowlly and sang it word-perfect with every inflection of that singer's voice. In the Officers' Mess there was a gramophone record of it that someone had brought back from London.

Every lunchtime of that hot summer the cadences floated across the even, bright green lawns of Warley Manor and made the tea roses tremble. The Sergeants' Mess had the same record and it had become the custom for returning air crew N.C.O.s to call into the mess for one last nightcap after leaving the tension and excitement of the debriefing. That record was always near the gramophone and usually the first arrivals would put it on. Sometimes after a grim night when there were a few missing faces they would play it repeatedly until dawn shone.

> Easy come, easy go. That's the way,
>    if love must have its day, then as
>    it came let it go.
> No remorse, no regrets. We should part
>    exactly as we met; just easy come, easy
>    go.
> We never dreamt of romantic dangers
> But now, as it ends, let's be friends and not
>    two strangers.
> Easy come, easy go. Here we are, so, darling,
>    au revoir. Easy come, easy go.

A quarter of a century later, men who knew Warley Fen that summer when the bombers went out night after night remembered nothing more clearly than that little melody. It needed only the opening trumpet notes, the wire brushes and guitar to transport them back there again.

Not all spare time occupations were musical. Flight Sergeant Bishop, the station blacksmith, was sergeant of the guard. He was sitting in the guardroom assembling a large picture of a galleon in full sail from candy wrappers and colored paper. It was a painstaking hobby and the portrait of Joe Louis on the wall in his quarters represented nearly three hundred man-hours of tearing, cutting and pasting. People who saw the pictures wondered that the clumsy muscular hands of the blacksmith could work in such meticulous detail.

Aircraftman First Class Albert Singleton, an Officers' Mess waiter, did that evening, with the help of Aircraftwoman Janet Marsden, motor transport driver, steal from the aforesaid mess one seven-pound tin of butter, three seven-pound tins of marmalade, eighteen pounds of bacon and twenty-eight eggs. These stores, the property of His Majesty King George the Sixth, were taken to Peterborough in an R.A.F. Hillman van, also the property of His Majesty. The foodstuffs were delivered to a restaurant owner against payment of seven pounds ten shillings. By ten-thirty Singleton and Marsden had visited several public houses and consumed a considerable amount of alcohol.

It was nearly eleven o'clock when they came down the blacked-out country lane from Ramsey and parked near the perimeter fence. It was warm in the front seat of the R.A.F. van and the windows grew misty with their breath as they kissed and cuddled in the dark. After a few minutes one of the lorries carrying air crew came past them along the peri track. They paused to watch it.

"It's a new driver we've got," said A.C.W. Marsden, nodding toward the crew bus. "She's straight from the training school; talk about keen."

"Not like you," said Bert Singleton

"I'm keen sometimes," said the girl, and they kissed again. As the crew lorry got to the far corner they heard the crews shouting remarks about blackout to some house in the village but they didn't stop kissing.

Binty Jones folded up his comic and began speaking in his mock American accent. "Eleven o'clock, guys," he said. "Let's get this little old show on the road. I've got me some heavy petting in Peterborough before sunup."

Digby zipped his flying boots and looking up in surprise said, "Are you still sleeping in Peterborough, you mad bastard?"

It had become fashionable among some of the crews to have their names written across the front of their flying helmets. A bottle of light pink nail polish was going the rounds. Cohen was writing "Kosher" on his.

"That I am, feller," said Binty. "A quarter of an hour from billet to bedroom. That's all it takes me on the motorbike."

"Quarter of an hour," said Lambert. "I'd rather fly the operation twice than go that last ten miles on your banger."

"Fifteen miles," corrected Binty. "Ah well, I'm a professional, you see."

"Professional crumpet chaser?" said Digby.

"Milkmen all are," said Cohen, "aren't they, Binty?"

"Some of them." He grinned proudly. In spite of his carefully pressed clothes and shirt, starched like card, he was not much to look at: cropped hair, bad teeth, short stature and pockmarked face. None of which was an impediment to his frantic motorized sex life, in pursuit of which he journeyed constantly across East Anglia. "It's the bike that gets them, man, the rhythm, you see. They hear that in the middle of the night and they quiver like a jelly."

"You still with that married sheila?" asked Digby. He knew the answer but he wanted to draw Flash Gordon into the discussion. He liked to hear them argue.

"She's a smashing piece of crackling, man."

"Why don't you find yourself some piece of single skirt?" said Flash.

"You know why, man. All the best single crumpet in Peterborough has been taken over by the Yanks."

"Well, I don't think it's right. Her old man fighting in the desert. I just don't think it's right."

"I'm just keeping it warm for him, man."

"I hope he comes back and knocks the daylights out of you."

"No danger. I've seen his photo; a tiny fellow he is."

"A judo instructor."

"Sheet metal worker with a REME unit in Alex."

"He'll come back and clobber you," warned Flash.

The conversation had taken the same lines that it always took and after it they were silent as they always were. Binty opened his comic again. "What's the time now?" asked Digby.

"Three minutes later than the last time you asked," said Cohen. Again he checked the contents of his green canvas bag: torch, rice paper message pad, radio notes, protractor, dividers, colored pencils, course and speed calculator, logbook, target map, star tables and ruler. It was all there.

"That's quite a watch you've got there, sport," said Digby.

"My uncle's. My ma gave it to me this morning."

Cothen returned the nail polish to Digby, who put it on the shelf of his locker and padlocked the door. "Come on, Maisie," said Digby quietly. They looked across to the far side of the room where a line of air crew were waiting for Maisie Holroyd to issue them with flying rations. Batters was next.

"Four Bovrils, three coffees."

"Four Bovrils, three coffees," she said, and the clerk gave Batters the required vacuum flasks of hot drinks as well as seven packets of sandwiches, chewing gum, hard candy and chocolate.

Sergeant Jimmy Grimm, the wireless operator and standby gunner, was a cheerful beardless man of twenty-three. He would have been acutely embarrassed to know that among Warley's WAAFs he was known as the "blond bombshell," for although he was married with a two-year-old child he was absurdly shy in the presence of women and was easily shocked by the sort of jokes that the crews related with such proud maturity. Sometimes, balanced over his radio, he'd write long, long letters to his wife, Mollie, in large looping handwriting and always in green ink.

An average wireless operator, Grimm was a dedicated amateur photographer, and the billet that he shared with Digby and Cohen was a disordered muddle of enamel trays, film tins and parts of his homemade enlarger. Often both bathrooms were full of prints, with others in the washbasins. Once one had jammed in the drain and flooded four rooms.

These were group portraits of the whole crew that he was passing round. He had a little clockwork device that enabled him to rush and join them after starting the shutter. Handsome lads they all were. Relaxed and smiling like any one of a million young men. Looking at those prints now, it would be easy to say that it was the work of an amateur or that the materials were inferior or unsuitable because they were stolen from Air Ministry supplies. That wouldn't be true. The fact is that the boys were all like that: their faces were not out of focus or overexposed; they were bland and smooth and as yet unformed. Those grinning cherubs awkwardly placed in that wartime snapshot are a high-definition portrait of the men who that night climbed into their flying boots, adjusted their parachute harness, borrowed clean shirts, reread old letters, lost a quick hand of cards, wrote I.O.U.s for half a crown and watched the clock so carefully. And so often.

"Bloody good snap, that, Jimmy."

"Us with the old *Door* behind."

"What a handsome group!"

"Enlarge it yourself, Jimmy? Bloody good show."

"Look at Dig, scowling. He's a card."

"Pockets undone as usual, Kosh."

"Good of the skipper."

"Too serious."

"Well, he is more serious nowadays."

"It's that bloody Sweet giving him the needle."

"Sweet's all right. One of the boys. He's got a good sense of humor."

"Sense of flipping arse crawling, you mean."

"Any more photos, Jim? Is that your garden?"

"Can I keep this, Jimmy?"

"Cost you one and threepence."

"Bloody robber."

"Here you are. I'll send it to my mum," said Battersby.

"Me too," said Binty. "Four I'd better have. No, make it five."

"Who's that bird with the pram?"

"What a smashing piece of grumble."

"Shut up, you berk, it's Jimmy's missus."

Crews were still arriving. There was an endless clang of locker doors, with occasional arguments when someone discovered his helmet missing or his boots borrowed and returned muddy. Flying gear was worn piecemeal according to personal taste and crew position. Usually the Lanc's heating system blew warm upon the wireless operator, roasted the bomb aimer and left the navigator to freeze. So most of the navigators were wearing the whole gear, from leather Irvin jackets to silk undersocks. So were the rear gunners. Most W.Op.A.G.s on the other hand had only the mandatory helmet, boots and Mae West over the same working blue and white roll-neck sweater that they had worn at supper. Some fliers had brightly colored silk scarves and even civilian shirts. Sandy Sanderson wore a fine leather jacket that he'd had made in Cairo.

It was a warm evening and now that the blackout shutters were closed the changing room became smelly as the crews crowded into it. Some of the early comers were playing cards for money while the late arrivals were grabbing their flying boots and filling their shoes with loose change, farewell letters and dirty pictures before pushing them into the back of their lockers. Few were pessimistic enough to leave a spare key behind and all the tin lockers bore scarred paintwork from being forced open many times.

Wing Commander Munro edged his way across the room.

"Mr. Lambert."

"Sir?"

"Last month after the cricket match you paid for both lots of beer. Will one pound ten see me out of debt?"

"It's only a pound, sir."

"Here you are then, old chap." He smiled, gave Lambert the money and was gone.

"Until now he's just paid alternately. That's the way we've done it since the season started," said Kosher.

"He just wants to be out of debt," said Lambert. Thoughtfully Kosher looked again at the Wing Commander, who was on the far side of the room giving an encouraging word to Fleming.

Fleming's crew felt that they were being scrutinized and they were careful to display no sign of excitement or nerves. Fleming had bent and dirtied his peaked cap to make it resemble those that had done a few thousand flying miles tucked behind a pilot's seat. Now he was wearing it at a rakish angle as he finished reading a copy of Routine Orders. He folded the paper up carefully to make a paper airplane.

"What's that, Mr. Fleming, a Lanc Mark IV?" said Munro in an attempt to make a joke.

"That's it, sir," agreed Fleming. He launched the paper wing. Everyone watched as it flew straight and level the length of the room. When it reached the tea urns, where the catering WAAF's were dispensing flasks of hot drinks, it hit a thermal. It nosed up until it stalled and fell like a dead bird to the floor.

"Back to the drawing board," shouted Binty Jones. Fleming smiled shyly.

Batters returned with a vacuum flask and a packet for each of them. Then complicated exchanges began. Binty liked gum—it was part of his Yank posture—so Digby exchanged his gum for Binty's barley sugar. Then Flash Gordon gave his gum to Binty for chocolate. Then Digby passed his extra barley sugar to Flash, who took this, and a contribution from most of the crew, back to his brothers and sisters. There were nine of them. A few months before, Binty had taken him home on the motorbike. After returning he'd hinted that spare rations from the boys would be the only treats those Gordon kids were likely to see.

All exchanges finished, Lambert gave them each a sealed escape kit containing a compass, counterfeit money, a silk map of Germany and some compressed dried fruit. Then they shuffled along the covered walkway to the next building. The parachute section was always clean and shiny, brightly lit and smelling of floor polish like a hospital for machines. Two bored WAAFs tugged parachutes and harnesses from the shelves behind them and threw them onto the counter with a clatter. Pilots' chutes had their parcel of silk fixed to the harness so that it formed a seat. The other crew members carried their silk canopies as a separate brown canvas parcel which before use had to be fixed to their chests by metal clips. Until they returned, each crewman would carry the chute with him wherever he moved. The pilots didn't have to remember the life-saving parcel, but, on the other hand, moving about within the airplane's cramped interior with a pilot-style chute strapped behind one's thighs was difficult. So there were comparatively few bomber pilots in P.O.W. camps.

Tommy Carter's engineer, Ben Gallacher, was having a noisy argument with one of the WAAFs.

"So why wasn't it done while I was on leave?"

"I don't know anything about that," said the girl. "Your chute isn't repacked yet. You'll have to take this one instead."

"I told your chiefie that I was going on leave."

The L.A.C. shrugged her shoulders indifferently. "I just work here."

"I want my own parachute. I've always flown with the same one. It's lucky. Don't you understand?" First he had lost his own reliable airtested *Joe for King* and now they wanted to give him a strange chute.

"I don't know what you are making such a fuss about. This one is just as good as your one and it's just been checked and repacked." Glad of a pause in her strenuous work, she patted her hair into place. "You're holding up the whole queue, you know."

"Get stuffed," said Ben. "I'll go without."

"Don't be a fool, Ben," said Lambert. "Take it." Lambert had been one of Gallacher's instructors at his Conversion Unit.

"Aw," said Ben, walking away.

"Someone will notice," said Lambert. "How will you feel if you abort the trip for your whole crew?"

The boy made a rude noise and then took the parachute. "Perhaps you're right, Chiefie," he admitted. A line had formed by now and someone shouted, "What's up?"

"Someone's brought one back," replied Digby loudly. "Says it didn't bloody work."

Everyone smiled at the joke they had heard so many times. The line moved forward again and the two girls pushed the harnesses and packs across the counter with a mechanical indifference interrupted only when they saw some crewman they knew. Then there would be an exchange of smiles and a hurried "Good luck."

From the other room Ruth came and stood in the doorway watching her husband as he took his parachute.

At the door there was another holdup: two of the lorries were late. Some of the boys went outside and watched the last glimmer of daylight. It was cold and some of them took a drink from their vacuum flasks or bit into the chocolate ration. Almost every crew had a mascot of some sort and teddy bears and rag dolls were cradled in their arms or stuffed into their webbing harness and silk stockings were worn as scarfs.

A muffled cheer went up as the missing lorries arrived. "B Flight here," called the WAAF driver. There was a sudden flurry of activity as some of the fliers punched each other playfully and vaulted up into the lorry. Lambert looked back and gave Ruth a brief thumbs-up sign. She nodded. He only just had time to climb aboard as the lorry lurched forward. The tailboard rattled loudly. The girl driver followed the blue lights that marked the peri track while twenty-eight crew in the back complained loudly about the slow journey and whistled. They bumped over the runway's edge and went across the black smears of rubber where the bombers' wheels first touched the runway on landing. The lights of Warley village were visible to the left. "Blackout," screamed the crews. "Pull a finger." "Put that light out." There was little chance of their voices carrying all that way to the village even on a still summer's night but this way was their chance to let off steam that had been building up since they had first read their names on the Battle Order that morning.

The lorry turned off the peri track onto the double pan, where two airplanes were silhouetted against the dark sky.

"*O for Orange* and *L for Love*," she shouted.

"Good luck, Skip," whispered Micky Murphy.

"Good luck, Micky," said Lambert. Lambert's crew and Carter's crew tumbled out of the back of the lorry, swearing and complaining as helmets were dropped and harness snagged on the tailboard. They waddled away to the two aircraft, the harness constricting their movements.

The eighteen-year-old WAAF driver had been a flutter of nerves since she had arrived late at the crewroom and faced a chorus of whistles and complaints. Now she leaned out of the cab and peered into the darkness. "Is that *Z Zebra*?" she asked Digby.

"Sorry, luv," said the uncaring Digby. "I'm a stranger here myself."

"What's up, miss?" said Battersby in his squeaky voice.

"It's the first time I've done this job. Is the next airplane *Z Zebra*?"

"After you are back on the peri track again, *Zebra*— *The Volkswagen*, we call it—is on the left-hand pan. *Sugar* is on the right-hand one, near the hangar and B Flight Office."

"Thanks a lot," said the girl. She hesitated for a moment. "And good luck, Sergeant."

"Ted Battersby; Batters, they call me."

There was a thunder of stamping from the impatient crews inside the lorry, followed by loud whistles.

"Good luck, Batters," said the WAAF, blowing him a kiss. She let in the clutch and the lorry jerked forward, throwing its passengers off balance. The girl shouted her name back at Battersby but there was so much noise from the crews that he couldn't hear it.

The ground staff of each airplane were standing quietly under the wing. One or two of them had special friends among the air crews and sometimes a conversation would be taken up right from the point at which it had been interrupted.

"Do you ever have trouble with the ears?" asked Binty as he checked the mid-upper turret.

"No, mine have all been very good so far. But I never let them mix with the other dogs in the kennels. That's where all the troubles start." The corporal armorer and Binty went on discussing their whippets. Binty didn't have his own dogs but he had a financial stake in his uncle's and on the basis of his conversations with Corporal Hughes he was now able to return home with many suggestions and criticisms. "You tell your bloody air force mate to stick his advice," Binty's uncle had told him on his last leave, "or I'll come down there and help him with his bleeding airplanes."

"Sternberg did *The Blue Angel*," said Cohen, "but *The Cabinet of Dr. Caligari* was directed by someone I've never heard of named Wiene."

"I could have sworn it was Sternberg. Funny how the memory can play tricks. *The Last Command* was Sternberg?"

"Oh sure. You don't make many mistakes, Mike. I remember seeing that. It was almost a remake of *The Last Laugh* with Jannings."

"A lot of those films were remakes of earlier European ones."

"Ever see *The Salvation Hunters*?" asked Cohen.

"That was early Sternberg. They thought it was a masterpiece at the time. At my last station the Film Society got hold of a sixteen-millimeter print."

"Pretty terrible, I thought," said Cohen.

"It's a long time ago," said the fitter. "A lot has happened since then."

"Yes," said Cohen, who had seen the film in Vienna when he was a child. "You're right."

Flight Sergeant Worthington started another conversation without preamble. "Two fuses and four wiring faults. We'll have to strip the wiring right out of it and renew every inch of it."

"So Carter's taking a reserve kite?"

"It only arrived this afternoon; it's been a struggle to get it ready. Carter's furious and so is Gallacher. It's not my fault, Sam." He kicked one of the tires.

"Everyone knows that, Worthy."

"Carter was bloody rude. There's no need to be rude."

"Nerves, Worthy."

"I suppose so. But we all worked our guts out on *Joe for King*. No one could have got it ready in time."

"Forget it, Worthy. He'll be apologizing and buying you pints lunchtime tomorrow. You know old Tommy Carter; he flares up but he doesn't mean it." Worthington slapped Lambert's arm gently with the canvas Pitot-head cover. He always did that to show it was removed. Lambert scribbled his signature on the R.A.F. Form No. 700. *Creaking Door* was now Lambert's.

"Your new kid knows his way around a wiring diagram, I must say," said Worthington.

"Battersby?"

"Yes, he's a demon on theory. He worked out the position of the short circuit on paper, but it was enough to make a strong man weep, watching him trying to fix it: gentleman's fingers."

"As the actress said to the bishop," said Digby. The bomb doors were open and now he came round to the front, where Lambert and Worthington were standing, to inspect the bombs. He jabbed a finger at each, murmuring to himself as he counted them, pulling each bomb trying to shift it within the jaws of the grip. He clasped a 2,000-pound bomb and lifted his feet off the ground so that the jaws took his weight too.

"I wish you'd come out and do that before we get here," complained Lambert.

"Have a little faith," said Digby.

Automatically Lambert took his wallet from his battle-dress blouse and folded into it the gold fountain pen that had been his twenty-first birthday present from his parents. It was an unspoken arrangement that if anything happened to him the wallet with all his letters and documents, and a last letter that he'd rewritten from time to time, should go to Ruth. The fountain pen was for Worthington to keep and the money was for drinks all round in the Sergeants' Mess. Worthington nodded and looked at Lambert with concern. It seemed to him a bloody awful sort of war. He'd seen a seemingly endless progression of young kids go to war and eventually not come back. Carefully he put the wallet into his inner pocket.

Lambert was just going to climb aboard to start the motors when he saw the Group Captain's Humber coming round the peri track. It stopped beside the plane.

"*O for Orange*; Flight Sergeant Lambert," murmured Flying Officer Griffith, the Admin. Officer, into the Groupie's ear. Griffith ticked his piece of paper.

"Bloody cold, Lambert, what?" said the Groupie, stamping the ground energetically.

"Yes, sir, freezing," said Lambert. He pushed his battered rag doll into his tunic.

Lambert and the Group Captain looked at each other without knowing what to say and yet both were reluctant to turn away.

"Your lucky doll?"

"Yes," said Lambert. Self-consciously he produced the rag doll: a cross-eyed figure in a black velvet suit.

"She's getting pretty old now," said the Groupie.

"Yes, sir; it's the altitude," joked Lambert.

"Really?" said the Groupie. At one time the air crew were bright middle-class boys with style and a sense of fun. Now they were working-class lads with no proper schooling and accents he could scarcely understand. What did Lambert mean about the altitude? So many of these young scoundrels had got their sergeant's rank too easily and the result was a familiarity of manner that he didn't readily take to.

"Not the first trip you've done to the Ruhr, eh, Flight Sergeant?"

"That's right, sir."

Usually the Group Captain listened to the B.B.C. news broadcast at nine o'clock. That gave him something to talk about as he visited the planes.

"I missed the news tonight," said the Groupie.

"I heard it," said Lambert. "An American fortress raid on the Channel ports. And there's a big new German attack upon Rokossovsky around Kursk from Orel and Belgorod. In the first day's fighting alone the Red Army destroyed five hundred German tanks and over two hundred aircraft."

"Splendid," said the Groupie and turned on his heel and hurried back to his car. He wound up the window against the cold night air.

"Bloody Bolshie," said the Group Captain.

"Pardon, sir," said the Admin. Officer, who hadn't heard the conversation.

"Lambert; a bloody Bolshie I say."

"Lambert, sir?"

"Why else would he have 'Stalin for King' written on his airplane?"

"I don't think it's there now, said the Admin. Officer tactfully. He knew it was Carter's airplane to which the Groupie referred.

"I know it isn't there now," said the Groupie sarcastically. "He's had a fresh aircraft given to him today."

The Admin. Officer was about to correct the Group Captain but it seemed such a small matter to argue about. He'd be with the Groupie for most of the night. Why put him in a bad mood.

"I see, sir," he said. He watched the red sparks fly as the Group Captain lit his pipe and puffed at it angrily.

"Just gave me a lecture about his glorious Red Army."

"Really, sir?"

"Well, of course I'm not going to put up with that sort of thing. Take me to see that young officer who's on his first trip tonight."

"Pilot Officer Fleming, sir. *Z for Zebra.* Parked near the trees, driver."

The car turned and crossed the peri track. The Groupie seemed not to have heard. "I'll get rid of him, Griffith."

"Yes, sir."

"Young Sweet was on about him only today."

"Was he, sir?"

"Hinted that he was a Red." The Groupie gave a short humorless laugh. "Only I was too damned stupid to see what young Sweet was driving at."

"He said that Lambert was a Red?" asked Pilot Officer Griffith in amazement.

"No, he didn't. Too loyal to his Flight, too damned fine a young officer to even suspect a senior N.C.O. of such a thing. No, Sweet just reported a piece of Lambert's bloody propagandizing Communist bilge in the mess. As I say, young Sweet was so hesitant that it's not until I had the full force of it myself that I've tumbled to what's going on. What say to that, Griffith?"

"Remarkable, sir."

"Bloody remarkable, Griffith. If the A.O.C. had got wind of it I'd have been remarkable on my bloody ear-hole, Griffith." No sooner had the Group Captain got his pipe alight than he rapped it against the metal ashtray to empty it.

"Indeed you would sir."

"Who did you say this next one was?"

"*Z for Zebra*, sir. Three officers in the crew. The captain is Pilot Officer Fleming. His first operation." The car stopped and Griffith ticked his list of names.

"Bloody cold, eh, Fleming?" boomed the Groupie, striding across the tarmac. The Admin. Officer prodded the smoldering tobacco to be sure it was quite extinguished. With all this petrol about smoking was strictly forbidden.

Voices carry a long way on an airfield, especially at night. Battersby had heard the WAAF driver stop at *S Sweet* on the far pan.

"All change," she called. There were laughs and shouts and then he heard her say, "Good luck, sir," and knew she was talking to Sweet. Battersby felt a stab of jealousy. After all, she had blown him a kiss. He walked around, checking the exterior of his aircraft. Officers always got the pretty ones.

A corporal rigger poured hot sweet tea for all of them. The enamel cups were chipped and smelled faintly of oil but it was hot and welcome. Digby was still leaning against the wheel and dreaming when he heard the distant voices of *Joe for King*'s crew. They were standing around the door of their airplane arguing.

Their airplane smelled new and strange and the ladder still had protective grease on it.

"Why can't we have *Joe*?" Ben Gallacher said.

"Ask Himmler," said Carter. "You've asked me ten times. It's not the fuses; they can't trace the fault."

"What am I, then?" said Gallacher. "Am I the bloody flight engineer or the tea boy? Why aren't I consulted?"

"Can't you get it into your thick head? The kite's duff. For Christ's sake stop binding; you're making me jumpy."

"I want to fly in *Joe for King*," said Gallacher.

Collins, the bomb aimer on his last operation, reached into the inside pocket of his battle-dress blouse and found a piece of chalk. He climbed up two rungs of the ladder and, leaning to one side, he wrote "Joe for King" across the squadron letter. Under that he scribbled just a huge curling moustache.

"Now you are flying in *Joe for King*," said Tommy Carter. "Get in and bloody well belt up." Gallacher swung round and aimed a punch at his captain. The punch sounded very loud and it was followed by a shocked silence. Tommy didn't respond at all; he'd taken the blow on his thick harness and it hurt Gallacher's hand more than Tommy's chest.

*Joe for King*'s navigator was Roland Pembroke, a public-school-educated twenty-year-old from Edinburgh. Watching the two men growling at each other, he was filled with a despairing horror. The engineer and pilot had never got on well together; Gallacher had failed the pilot's course and was still jealous of the ones that hadn't. Tommy, on the other hand, had that exasperating calm rectitude that only policemen display. Roland Pembroke had done everything he could think of to bring the two men closer. He turned to the corporal rigger and asked in a whisper. "Did you get it?"

"It will be waiting; that bird Cynthia in The Bell is saving me a bottle."

"And cups," said Roland Pembroke in his soft Lowland accent.

"Glasses," said the corporal. "She's promised to wangle me some glasses."

"Great," said Roland.

"And I've got sausage rolls too."

Roland pushed his navigational gear into the door of the plane and heaved a sigh of relief. Tomorrow was Sergeant Carter's twenty-first birthday and the completion of Tapper Collins' final operation. Roland Pembroke had planned a surprise party right there on the pan so that the ground staff boys and the crew could celebrate. It had started badly.

"Ten trips done, twenty to go," said Pembroke as he disappeared into the airplane, crossing his fingers to stave off danger as he always did.

There are many ways in which the life history of an air crew can be charted. There would be a simple graph of the odds that an insurance company would offer. The chances on this one began low—the first three trips were five times as dangerous as the average. But as skills and experience mounted so the chances of survival for each trip became better. Another graph, thirty trips with a five percent casualty rate, would be a simple straight line: a mathematical proposition in which each trip held equal danger and the line ended at trip number twenty. There was yet another graph that could be drawn, a morale line charted by psychiatrists. Its curves recorded the effect of stress as men were asked to face repeatedly the mathematical probability of death. This graph—unlike the others—began at the highest point. Granted courage by ignorance and the inhibitory effect that curiosity has upon fear, the men's morale was high for the first five operations, after which the line descended until a crack-up point was reached by the eleventh or twelfth trip. Perhaps it was the relief of surviving the thirteenth operation that made the graph turn upward after it. Men had seen death at close quarters and were shocked to discover their own fear of it. But recognizing the same shameful fears in the eyes of their friends helped their morale, and after a slight recovery it remained constant until about the twenty-second trip, after which it sloped downward without recovery.

The eleventh trip was not marked by crews asking to be taken off flying, getting drunk or running sobbing through the mess. In fact few men asked to be grounded, and their reluctance was fortified by the R.A.F. authorities, who would stamp the words "lack of moral fiber" across the man's documents, strip him of rank and brevet and send him away in disgrace with the bright unfaded blue patch of tunic proclaiming him an officially recognized coward.

No, the eleventh trip was marked by more subtle defensive changes in the crew: a fatalism, a brutalizing, a callousness about the deaths of friends and a marked change in demeanor. Noisy men became quiet and reflective while the shy ones often became clamorous. This was the time at which the case histories of ulcers, deafness and other stress-induced nervous diseases that were to follow the survivors through their later years actually began. The crew of *Joe for King* were on their eleventh trip.

The crew of *The Volkswagen*, on the other hand, were about to do their first trip. Like a young man with his first sports car, they were keen and raring to go. They weren't tired in the way that Lambert was tired; their reflexes were sharp, their eyesight keen, and their hands itched to prove themselves. Lambert was like a weary old businessman climbing into his family sedan to do a trip that he had done all his working life. He was tired, dulled, slow of reflex and frightened. And yet, as any insurance company will tell you, it's the old men in family sedans who pay the least insurance and the kids in new sports cars who die.

Pilot Officer Cornelius Fleming sat at the controls of *The Volkswagen* and tried to hide his pleasure and excitement. He heard the boys making nervous jokes but he was determined to put on a show of bored indifference for the ground crew. One of the riggers, a gruff-spoken Cockney, came into the cockpit with a tin can.

"Here's your tin, sir," he said.

"What's that for?" said Fleming. He closed his eyes in a mannerism that at medical school had affected concentration.

"To take a leak," said the rigger.

Fleming suspected he was being made the butt of a joke and looked at the man suspiciously.

The rigger grinned. "Do you want to put it under the seat?"

"Don't be ridiculous," said Fleming and sighed.

"Suit yourself, guv," said the rigger and walked back through the plane. He climbed down onto the ground and threw the can away under the ash trees. That was the trouble with officers, you could never tell them anything. That pansy-faced sprog officer had looked at him like he was offering dirty postcards to a bishop. The only crew here with three officers in it, and he had to be assigned to them. No matter, they wouldn't last long, the poor sods. *Zebra* was a real duff kite and no matter about cleaning it up and calling it some foreign name; it was just a matter of time before it fell apart at the seams.

Fleming knew that he'd upset the fellow and he cursed himself for his handling of the business, even if it had been a leg pull. Becoming a good skipper was the most difficult thing in the world, and the most desirable. At one time all he'd sought of God was a pilot's brevet. Then he'd fastened his desire upon a commission. But it was all so difficult; a good skipper must be an expert pilot, a classless

gentleman, a democratic commander and, most impossible
of all, an intrepid leader who kept his men safe. Always
there was this damned class business. That chap would
merely have grinned if an N.C.O. had called his bluff
about the tin. It was all right for Lambert; these chaps
with a gong and a tour behind them could do no wrong
in the eyes of their crew.

"Bertie!" Fleming called his young flight engineer, who
before meeting Fleming had always been Bert.

"Sir?" The boy's flying gear was too large, so that he
looked like a child dressed in his father's clothes.

"All O.K.?"

"Yeah, all okey dokey, sir."

"We'll follow Lambert out, Bertie." The engineer
nodded. Okey dokey, thought Fleming; what strange
things they say.

Lambert was the first of B Flight to start up. He slid
open his window. "Clear for starting, Worthy?" Twenty
feet below him the trolley ac. was plugged in and ready.

"Clear."

Lambert put his hand out of the window, pointed a
finger at the port inner and then turned his thumb upward. From the tarmac Worthy pointed his left hand at
the same engine and revolved his right index finger as
though to move the prop with it. Lambert pressed the
starter button. There was the pitter-patter of the booster
pump and a chuffing noise. Then came the opening bangs
of the Merlin, an affront to the still countryside. It caught,
and roared. Then the next one started, and the next, until
the sound of thirty-two engines echoed back from the
trees of The Warrens and the black tin side of the hangar,
like a million frantic drummers marching off to war.

Sam Thatcher was awakened by it. He looked at the
clock: it was 11:23 P.M.

"They're off again," said his wife.

"Third time this week," said Sam. "I'll have to get some
sleeping pills or something."

But there was an hour before takeoff time and as
suddenly as they had started the motors cut. Soon the
night was quiet except for the muttered curses of men
working by the light of torches and the murmured conversation of the crews.

Flash Gordon, the little Nottingham miner, his pockets
bulging with confectionery for his brothers and sisters, was
looking at his turret. He waited until the last engine cut

and the silence was broken only by a few planes of A
Flight from the far side of the airfield.

"You've done a good job there," said Flash. The sergeant armorer deserved the praise; it had been more difficult
than it looked to remove a section of Perspex from the
vision panel of the turret. "I won't be firing at any more
oil dribbles and thinking they are Junkers 88s," said Flash,
and he laughed.

"Did you ever do that, Flash?" asked the armorer.

"Never saw one," said Flash. "Fifteen trips I've done
and I've never seen a night fighter."

Binty Jones, the mid-upper gunner, walked past. The
armorer called after him. "I'll do your turret next,
Binty."

"Like bleeding hell you will. I check my Perspex every
day. There's not a speck or spot anywhere. And if there
was, I wouldn't be such a bloody fool as to fire at it,
man."

"It was oil dribbles giving the trouble," said Flash
angrily, "not scratches."

"I don't care what it was; you won't get me in that rear
turret again, so don't come asking me to swap when you
get another one of your bloody head colds, right?"

"Right," Flash shouted after him. "I won't, don't you
worry."

"You'll freeze if your electric suit goes u/s," warned the
armorer.

"I'm practically freezing now," said Flash.

"It's cold tonight," the armorer agreed and buttoned his
service overcoat up to the neck and wrapped his home-
knitted scarf high around his ears. The motors of the A
Flight planes had warmed and been switched off. The
airfield was silent. There was nothing to do but wait.

In the airplanes men were making secret promises to
God, performing superstitious rituals or finding excuses to
say heartfelt truths. A fly buzzed drowsily on Tommy
Carter's windshield.

"Go home and get some sleep, you stupid bastard," said
Tommy. "You don't know when you're well off."

Lambert placed the doll, named Flanagan, behind his
seat.

"He won't see anything from there," said Digby.
"Throw him down here; I'll put him in the front turret."

"He's seen it all before," said Lambert. "And he
wouldn't find it hard to break the habit."

Wing Commander Munro opened the side window to

inhale the air. Then he placed his walking stick under his seat. As his crew had already guessed, that stick was the C.O.'s lucky charm, although wild horses would never drag the admission from him. Munro looked at the sky and breathed deeply. He noticed that cloud had eaten a piece of the Great Bear and was sniffing at Scorpio. From the trees at Witch Fen an owl hooted loudly.

"Hear that, sir?" said Jock Hamilton, his navigator.

"Yes indeed. It's good luck," he added hurriedly. Jock looked at him, unconvinced. There was a silence then until he heard a train puffing and rattling northward. Soon that train would be in Scotland, near his wife and the boy. He would be in Germany. Munro looked at the sky; it still wasn't quite dark. To the north it was a purplish color, almost green.

The low that had caused the thunderstorms across Europe turned north as it neared the Swedish coast. The air pressure in the low was equalizing and soon it would die. The met. men were rubbing its Chinagraph image from their maps and marking in the progress of the high that had come marching behind it from the west. This mountain of air already pressed down upon England. Its outer layer slid toward Ireland and Biscay and Norway, where the pressure was less. The descending air became warmer and any clouds in its way evaporated. As it got closer to ground level this descending air brushed against the rotating earth and was deflected clockwise so as to form a gently whirling air mass that measured hundreds of miles across—an anticyclone.

It had brought the light blue sky and diffused sunset that promised another fine day. But this starry night was cold, for with few clouds to trap the rising heat the ground became chilly underfoot and the airmen slapped their hands against their sides and complained of the long wait.

It was fifteen minutes past midnight, B.D.S.T., when the first of the Lancasters moved. Last-minute urination took place before the crews were buttoned into their clothes and settled into the seats they would occupy for several hours. A full bladder, or, even worse, wind, could cause pain at high altitudes. Quickly gobbled beans on toast could have a man writhing with pain at a moment when he was most needed. Ponderously the bombers rumbled round the peri track. Some were in a hurry to beat the queue that would form at the southern end of the runway. As soon as Lambert's *Creaking Door* moved, *The*

*Volkswagen* followed. Fleming kept its tail in view as the planes crawled past the dim blue perimeter lights. What greater disaster could strike them now than that he should put a wheel into the soft-going beyond the lights and hold up the whole squadron? He touched the brakes as they came to the corner by the Ramsey road. A Hillman van had parked there with its headlights on or else Fleming might well have turned too wide and clipped his wingtip against the fence. Lambert's taillight moved again. Some of the other bomb aimers were shining a signaling lamp from the nose to help light the way but Lambert preferred to have his eyes accustomed to the darkness. Each Lancaster announced its arrival at the runway by flashing its code letter to control. At the answering green light the takeoff run commenced and the next plane crawled into position.

Lambert glanced toward the crowd of ground crew that were waving from the edge of the runway. Old hands, young girls and even the NAAFI women were there. Even when it was raining they came to see the bombers away. Lambert felt grateful to them.

"Big crowd tonight," said Binty.

"Your harm," said Kosh.

"Ah," said Binty.

John Munro had detailed the takeoff pattern. Moving from their pans onto the peri track, the bombers lined up on both sides of the runway's end. No sooner had one plane got a green than the next one was signaling its code letter. A bored officer in Flying Control logged each takeoff and phoned them to the Operations Room, where, on a wall-size blackboard divided into rectangles, was entered each pilot's name, code letter, takeoff time and time of return. There was also a space for remarks.

Each of the bombers was loaded far beyond peacetime safety limits and getting them into the air was no easy matter. Lambert drove up an invisible ramp as steady as a rock and as perfect as a theorem. Then came Fleming, a slight swerve before unsticking. for this was the first time he'd flown with a full bomb load.

You could recognize any of Tommy Carter's takeoffs: too much throttle, stick back too early and undercarriage retracted before he was over Witch Fen. This night he swung badly too. Angry, and new to this factory-fresh airplane, he'd applied too much rudder. Halfway down the runway he was already askew, pointing at the control tower and traveling too fast to stop before the main road.

He knew he was going off the hard runway only when its white marker lights came racing under him like tracer shells. Beyond that there was earth, damned soft earth after last night's rain. He heaved desperately on the stick with one hand and tried to push the starboard outer's throttle farther forward to correct the swing. He felt one wheel plop off the sharp edge of tarmac. Gallacher braced himself against the bulkhead and cursed.

Tommy wasn't flying the aircraft any longer, he was fighting it.

"Panic boost," he shouted. They might have been his last words except that the propellers hung upon the cold air like finger tips to a crevice. For long seconds he gained no altitude but skimmed the grass with only inches clearing his tires. Then slowly and dutifully *Joe for King* the second sniffed the air.

In the control tower the Duty Officer, the Group Captain and a Flying Control WAAF stood transfixed at the sight of a complex alloy parcel packed with high explosive, phosphorus, fuel and magnesium being steered directly toward them at a hundred miles an hour. No one moved until the airplane roared across the top of the tower, clearing the railing by inches, shaking its foundations and taking an aerial with it.

Tapper Collins always stayed in the nose for takeoffs and landings, even though it was against regulations.

"I saw the bloody bomb aimer," whispered the Group Captain, scarcely able to believe it. "I saw the bloody bomb aimer's face."

And Tapper had seen them too: white petrified staring blobs flashing past not more than thirty feet under him.

"Jesus Christ," said Tapper. "I thought you'd left something behind."

"Bit of a swing," explained Tommy.

"Bit of a swing?" said Tapper. "We've got the bleeding Groupie's hairpiece tangled in the undercart."

"You don't have to bloody sit there," snapped Tommy. "It was your idea."

"I could have touched him," said Tapper. "Could have reached out and tweaked the silly old blighter's hooter."

One after another the giant planes climbed into the darkness and disappeared. The colored wingtip lights thundered over the misty, alcohol-laden Hillman that Singleton and his girl friend had borrowed for the evening. They stopped cuddling until the last plane—Munro's own *D for*

*Dog*—took off. As the sound of it faded away, the countryside became silent.

"It's funny when the planes are away. It's sort of
lonely," said the girl.

"What do you mean?"

"I don't know. You get used to those big planes everywhere you look. Last month when they were all diverted
to Yorkshire because of the fog it seemed funny to see the
aerodrome in daylight all empty. And there was hardly
anyone around in the sections either."

"I wouldn't mind them being diverted for a few days.
It'd make my life a bit easier, I'll tell you," said Singleton.

"I wonder if they'll all come back," said the girl.

"It's a gamble, isn't it?"

"They've been lucky lately."

"*Able* bought it last week, *U Uncle* the week before,
and that Flight Sergeant Lambert brought back a dead
navigator three trips ago."

"I'm glad you ain't in one of 'em, Bert."

"I could have been a gunner, but my feet let me
down."

"I couldn't bear it, Bert. Give me another kiss."

They kissed for a few minutes, then Singleton said,
"Were you frightened tonight?"

"No, of course not."

"Go on, you were."

"A bit."

"It's exciting, isn't it, knowing you might get nicked.
But I spend it too easy, that's my trouble."

The girl laughed.

"You know what I'd like to do one night. Now this
might surprise you, Janet. I'd like to get hold of some tires
or petrol. That's where the real money is."

"Or booze," said the girl.

"You would think that, because you have no experience
of crime," said the mess waiter. "Booze is locked up and
counted. Only a mug goes after booze."

"Whatever you say, Bert."

"I told you I was a villain, didn't I?" he warned. "Don't
keep giggling, Janet."

The girl was tempted to tell him how many times she
had been in trouble with the law and of the final house-
breaking escapade that had sent her to Borstal, but wisely
she smiled and said nothing.

Lambert knew the way from Warley to the coastal assem-

bly points as he did the one from his billet to the mess.
Usually he flew straight to the assembly point using a
course based upon the met. man's estimate of the wind.
Cohen then faked in the Gee fixes from that point back to
Warley. From there onward Cohen did real Gee fixes
based upon the correct wind. Tonight Lambert knew the
wind was wrong from the moment he was airborne and he
steered well to the south, allowing the wind to push him
onto the track he required. "Southwold," announced
Digby. He was lying in the nose of the plane looking down
through the transparent bowl.

"O.K.," said Cohen, who knew he was talking to him.
This was the way they always did it.

Cohen took a fix from the Gee radar and marked the
time at Southwold on his plotting map. "There's quite a
wind, Skipper," he said.

"We'll see," said Lambert. "When we've got a bit of
height we'll have a better idea. The high winds may be
different."

"Permission to test guns?" asked Binty.

"Yes, both of you," said Lambert, knowing that Flash
would ask immediately after. Digby tested his nose guns
too. The sound of the guns rattled along the metal fuselage and from Digby's turret at the front there was a
smell of cordite and scorching oil. Tracer sprayed in a
gentle curve and splashed down into the sea.

Today's pressurized, high-speed, high-altitude, jet-
propelled traveler might find it hard to imagine the very
different experience that flying was to these men. The
whole airplane rattled and vibrated with the power of the
piston engines. The instruments shuddered and the figures
on them blurred. Oxygen masks were mandatory and they
needed microphones and earphones even to converse. At
these altitudes their power-weight ratios made these planes
very vulnerable to the condition of the air through which
they flew. Although now, in the cool of night, the aircraft
was steadier than it had been in the heated turbulence of
afternoon, the air was still full of surprises. They hit hard
walls of it and dropped sickeningly into deep pockets.
They bucketed, rolled and yawed constantly. Their degree
of stability depended as much upon the pilot's strength as
upon his skill, for the controls were not power-assisted and
it required all of a man's energy to heave the control
surfaces into the air stream. And all the time there was
the vibration that hammered the temples, shook the teeth
and played a tattoo upon the spine, so that even after an

uneventful flight the crew were whipped into a condition of advanced fatigue.

Digby sat down next to Cohen. He had his own gadget, the H2S radar set, to operate. It looked down at the world below and gave an X-ray picture which distinguished between woodland, water and houses. Often the set went wrong and even at its best the picture bore only a messy resemblance to a map. Cohen had warmed the set and they both watched the dull green screen.

"What do you know? It works," said Digby.

Cohen pushed his map case to the back of the plotting table and stood it on end. That obscured the neat metal patch. Flight Sergeant Worthington's riggers had riveted it over the jagged shrapnel hole. Through that had come the splinter that had entered a navigator's lung and killed him in this very seat three trips ago.

"Don't do that, sport," said Digby. He pushed the map case aside. The little adjustable desk lamp hit the new metal at an angle that made it shine like a glass eye. "I like to see that," said Digby. "I figure that lightning don't strike twice. You and me have got the safest seat in the kite here."

Cohen looked at the metal plate and felt better about it.

"Is everybody happy?" asked Lambert.

To the tune of "Abdul Abulbul Amir" Flash Gordon in the rear turret sang unmusically:

"Just an old-fashioned Avro with old-fashioned wings
And a fabric all tattered and torn.
She's got old-fashioned Merlins all tied up with strings
And a heater that never gets warm.
But she's quite safe and sound, 'cause it won't leave the ground,
And the crew are afraid of the chop.
One day we will try to see if she'll fly
While mother looks after the shop."

Flash waited for a word of appreciation or applause, but none came. Binty said, "Man, yo' is jes' crazy wid rhythm."

"Oh, shut up," said Flash.

"When you've all finished singing and chatting," said Lambert, "perhaps I could say a word."

"Gentlemen," said Digby. "It's my proud pleasure to introduce to you the captain of our aircraft, your genial

host and raconteur, who has given up his eighty-first
birthday to be with us here tonight. Gentlemen, your
friend and mine, Flight Sergeant Samuel Lambert,
D.F.M."

"Now let's get ourselves organized," said Lambert.

"For a change," said Jimmy Grimm.

"For a change," agreed Lambert.

Jimmy Grimm tuned his radio carefully. "They've given
us new winds, Skip. Do you want them?"

"Give them to Kosh," said Lambert.

They flew higher and higher and for every thousand
feet they gained, the temperature dropped two and a half
degrees centigrade. The crew buttoned themselves into
their suits or moved closer to the hot-air blowers. At
8,000 feet they began to breathe the oxygen that they had
brought with them. Lambert continued to climb. They
entered a cloud bank. There is as yet no way to discover if
ice awaits you in a cloud, except to fly into it with your
fingers crossed. This cloud seemed unending. The cold
chilled the airplane to its marrow and slowed its circula-
tion. *Door*'s port outer coughed not once but twice and
then didn't fully recover.

"Fuel flow?"

"O.K.," said Battersby.

"Give it some fully rich."

"I have already."

"Good boy."

The motor, appreciative of its luxury diet, roared into
full power.

"Carburetor icing."

"Temperature looks O.K. now."

"We'll be out of it in a moment." Lambert put the
aircraft into a steeper climb and Battersby adjusted the
engines to give him more power.

"I hate cloud," confided Lambert.

It pressed against the windows and made the cabin even
darker than before. Battersby fussed over his instruments
and was anxious to prove his expertise to Lambert. The
engines had only just begun to unsynchronize when Battersby reported, "Pressures and temperatures look all
right." The motor began a weary drone.

"Do you know why it's doing that?"

"Oil getting too cold and stiffening the pitch control?"

Lambert nodded and said, "Can you synch them
again?"

Battersby waggled his fingertips upon the levers. After

choosing the wrong motor and then overcorrecting, he finally had the engines back into their regular harmonized roar.

"Bang on," said Lambert. "Micky just can't get the hang of that." Battersby had never felt so proud of himself.

One by one the stars pricked the roof of the cabin and they were above the cloud. Lambert's controls had become slack and mushy now, for *Creaking Door* had reached its normal ceiling and no amount of pulling on the stick would make it climb higher. This was the stage of the journey where Lambert employed a technique that an old-timer had told him about, way back when he was flying Whitleys. By suddenly lowering the flaps fifteen degrees while flying at cruising speed, Lambert and Battersby caused the airplane to hit a wall of air. It shuddered with the impact and the whole airplane leaped 200 feet higher. Each time it did this it held its new altitude. By this method Lambert could add over 1,000 feet of height to his ceiling. The first of a series of spine-jarring thumps ran through the aircraft. "We're going up the steps," said Lambert. "That's what I wanted to tell you."

Flight Lieutenant Sweet stared out into the night. Beneath him he saw a tiny rectangle of flare path and guessed there was another squadron climbing to join the stream. He had above-average night vision and usually saw pinpoints before the bomb aimer saw them. There were no other airplanes in sight. It was odd that no matter what methods of timing were used to pack the bomber stream as tight as possible, the sky was still so immense that he sometimes did a whole trip without catching sight of another airplane. He supposed that fellows with below-average night vision went whole tours without seeing anything.

Ahead of him the front turret moved gently from left to right.

"Bomb aimer. Don't keep fidgeting about with that turret."

"I'm searching, sir. That's orders."

"Then swivel your neck." Sweet's voice rose a tone.

"I'm keeping the hydraulic fluid warm, sir."

"Must you always argue, Spekey?" Sweet made it into a joke. Placatingly he added, "Keep still, there's a good chap."

"Pip" Speke, an eighteen-year-old with a big black

moustache and a reputation as a lucky gambler, ducked out of the turret and got down on the floor behind his bomb sight. Most crews had sergeant pilots and some crews stuck together. Some went off boozing as a crew. Some had decent officers even. The easiest way for any of those lucky ones to make Sergeant Speke lose his temper was to tell him how fortunate he was to fly with such a fun-loving good sort as that modest Flight Lieutenant Sweet, D.F.C.

"Navigator," said Sweet, "how many miles to the coast?"

"About ten," said the navigator.

"Let's not have too many 'abouts' tonight, eh, Billy boy," said Sweet. "Bomb aimer, let me know when you see the coastline."

"O.K."

Sweet looked down. The countryside was dark but in spite of the blackout the faint shapes of towns could be discerned. "Navigator," said Sweet. "I can see Lowestoft below us. We're off course."

"Are you sure, sir?"

"Am I sure, sir? Yes, I am sure, sir. Beyond it I can see a bit of a glim from Yarmouth. We're at least ten miles north of our track."

There was a short silence while the navigator calculated their position on the Gee. "Steer 120 degrees," said the navigator. "The winds are wonky."

"That's just a correction. I want to join the stream at the assembly area over Southwold."

"In that case, sir, turn almost due south, let's say 160 degrees."

"That's more like it, old son." Sweet realized he had upset the navigator and upsetting people was a luxury he seldom indulged in. "This is the Flight Commander's airplane, chaps. We must do things by the book. It's stupid, I know, but if we start cutting corners the other crews will do it."

Sweet flew south humming to himself. Suddenly he said, "Did I tell you the story about the WAAF officer and the sergeant . . . ?"

"English coastline coming up, sir," said Pip Speke. Now it was possible to see how good Britain's blackout was, for beyond the coast the world below them was truly dark.

# 18

THE huge Freya radar aerial swung gently, smelling the cold wind that blew from England. It stopped, began to swing back and stopped again. Willi Reinecke called to August Bach down the length of the dimly lit T hut. "First contact, sir."

And so the battle began: three groups of men using every device that science could invent began to grope around the blackness like gunmen in a sewer.

August hurried up the wooden steps to the plotting table platform.

"Logged at 0035 hours." said the clerk.

"Near Lowestoft. An extreme-range contact," said August. "Congratulations; they are not even over the British coastline. The Freya is working well tonight."

"They seem to have stopped the jamming lately," said Willi.

"Since we made the wavelength band wider. They can't jam the whole width of it."

"And it's the tuning."

"'And it's the tuning,'" said August, smiling. "I said 'Congratulations.'"

"I've told the FLUKO," said the telephonist. "They hadn't had a previous contact.

"Good," muttered August. He put his protractor on the map. He knew all its bearings like the palm of his own hand but still he put his protractor on it as he gave his instructions. Willi admired that sort of thoroughness, especially in an officer.

"The red Würzburg to sweep from Ipswich to Yarmouth, 270 degrees to 290. Don't tell them the range or they won't try so hard."

"Lowestoft," said Willi, looking at the map. "That's

well north of the usual route. Perhaps they are going to Berlin."

"Too early to say yet. Perhaps they are routed south and that one is a few miles off course. That would account for it. We'll have to wait and see, Willi."

Soon Willi said, "You're right, sir, you're right. He's turned almost due south."

"They'll assemble over Southwold." August nodded. "They are creatures of habit, the British."

Out in the cold among the windswept dunes the crew of the red Würzburg became newly alert. They knew that the Freya had twice the range of their equipment, but the Würzburg had a narrower beam and was therefore more precise. It could "see" one airplane and tell its altitude and so bring the night fighters into contact with it. The Freya gave an early warning but the Würzburgs made the kill.

"The Nachtjagdführer is giving us two Ju88s from Kroonsdijk," said Reinecke. He was still on the phone. August nodded.

"Let's hope it's a pilot we've worked with before," said Willi.

"When that fool let the *Tommi* escape last Wednesday I could have killed him," said August. "He must have been right on top of him."

"The blips superimposed," said Reinecke disgustedly.

The T hut was the center of the Himmelbett station, which August commanded. Nearby there were other huts: billets, mess hall, motor transport garage and the radar machines themselves. As well as the Freya there were two identical Würzburgs: great bowls, seven meters across. One (blue) to record a night fighter and the other (red) to follow the passage of one of the R.A.F. bombers. Inside the T hut two plotting clerks sat hunched underneath the big wooden platform that dominated the interior. Each of them wore headphones and was in contact with a Würzburg. To show the progress of both planes, each plotter shone a spotlight upon the glass map that was his ceiling. From their position on the platform August and Willi Reinecke could see the two light-beam spots through the Seeburg table in front of them. One was red, the other blue. Their job was to bring the two dots of light together. After that the German night fighter should be able to pick up the bomber ahead of him on his own radar detector. Or, on a brightly moonlit night, perhaps even see him.

The T hut was dark. There were no blips on the

Seeburg table, for the enemy aircraft were not yet within range of the Würzburgs. August looked at the large-scale map on the wall and every few minutes Willi reported the progress of the R.A.F. bomber stream as it flew across the North Sea straight toward them.

The phone buzzed quietly. "Our two planes are airborne," said Willi.

"Tell the blue Würzburg to sweep from 50 to 70 for them."

Willi Reinecke was biting his fingernails. August smiled. This was the worst time of all. Many nights they picked up the *Tommis* as they assembled over their own coast, but often the bombers were headed elsewhere. Himmelbett Station Ermine was only one small sector of a long coastline and unless the bombers headed straight into the Ruhr they would pass by out of range. In that case they would spend all night gnawing their knuckles and cursing their luck. One thing Willi knew: the best crews were on duty; if the terror flyers came this way they would be certain to pick them up. After that it was up to the night fighters.

"Here comes the jamming," said Willi. Then, more officially, "Airborne jamming on the Freya, a wide band of it, averaging 290 degrees. Constant bearing, increasing in intensity."

"The jamming aircraft must be coming straight for us."

Willi said, "I don't know why the Nachtjagdführer doesn't send some of our boys out to shoot them down."

"How bad?"

"Not too bad. He's still getting a clear blip and if the tube grasses up more he can side-tune to improve it."

"The Würzburg will have them soon."

"Thank goodness they can't jam those."

"Any night now, Willi my son."

From where August stood he could watch the table and the wall beyond it. The map stretched from East Anglia to Frankfurt. The smaller one showed only Ermine's sector and the overlapping circles of the sectors surrounding it. Now that the early warning had been given the other sectors were alerted and lit up bright green on the glass map.

Willi tapped the table with his Kneemeyer measure as he listened to the messages. "First night fighter overhead."

"I want him right out to sea at the extreme range of the Würzburg. Let's see, if they are coming in from Southwold let's say code square Heinz Emil Four. How high is he?"

"Fifteen thousand feet, still climbing."

"As high as possible, Willi. Height is everything."

# ⚜ 19 ⚜

"THAT'S eight million three hundred thousand and eighty marks you owe me," said Löwenherz, setting up the chessboard again.

"It's in my other trousers," said Kokke. On the radio a close-harmony group was singing.

> Everything ends, everything passes,
> Upon every December follows a May.
> Everything ends, everything passes,
> But two who love always remain faithful.

The girls cooed to an end and were replaced by a men's chorus singing "*Bomben auf England*" with appropriate wire brushes and drums. There was a loud raspberry of displeasure and the man nearest to the radio turned the volume down before any missiles were thrown in his direction.

Löwenherz looked round the Alert Hut. The crews were sprawled around the place in the most remarkable poses: hair uncombed, ties loosened and feet resting on chairs. It was as if they were all dead, thought Löwenherz, as if fumes or gas had done for them all, and yet if the loudspeaker sounded the quiet double click that warned of an announcement they could all be on their feet, tugging their helmets onto their heads and draping their bodies with oxygen connectors and microphone and earphone leads that made them a part of their machines.

Klimke—Kokke's radar man—used to spend these hours in the Alert Hut writing interminable letters to his wife, but since she had been killed last Christmas he had taken up knitting. In spite of howls of derision and practical jokes he sat calmly producing endless scarves for everyone he knew. He couldn't master the knack of decreasing, so he could only knit rectangles. Alongside him Leutnant Beer jerked convulsively in his sleep. A mosquito was buzzing round his ear.

"What a Wagnerian body of men," said Kokke, looking around at the dozing fliers. Klimke grinned but did not stop knitting. Kokke moved his piece and they began a new game.

"Not fool's mate, Kokke. You underestimate me."

"Never, Herr Oberleutnant," said Kokke, and Löwenherz lost a knight.

"Damn."

"Experience is better bought than taught," said Kokke, moving forward.

"You lose because you are too reckless," said Löwenherz.

"But I have more fun," said Kokke.

"Probably," agreed Löwenherz.

"Double or nothing on what time the first plane is put up?"

"Very well," said Löwenherz. "One."

"One?"

Short summer night with full moon means a short trip; that means the Ruhr. To get back before first light and allow time for stragglers they will probably time the attack for two o'clock. A Lancaster does 225 miles per hour, so it will pass over the British coast at zero minus 50. A good Freya radar will pick it up then, but by the time they fiddle around talking to the FLUKO and the Nachtjagdführer it will be fifteen minutes past one."

"That leaves us fifty minutes." Kokke had to raise his voice a little, for the radio music was now much louder.

"It might leave us all night. Who knows if we shall be put up?"

"Such modesty, Oberleutnant."

Löwenherz smiled. "About fifty minutes, yes."

"And how was 'die Wurst' bearing up this afternoon?"

Among his close friends in the Officers' Mess the gemütlich Hans Furth was happy to answer to "Hanswurst" (clown). However, he took exception to Kokke calling him simply "die Wurst," perhaps because of its feminine gender. Kokke seldom referred to him otherwise.

"Bearing up remarkably well," admitted Löwenherz. "Everyone who gets into trouble is an exhibitionist and he's going pig shooting to forget it. The mess will make Wurst of his successes."

*"Wurst wider wurst,"* said Kokke.

Löwenherz smiled; "sausage against sausage" also meant "tit for tat." "He knows you hate him."

"And I'm sure he's very mature and forgiving about me."

Löwenherz nodded. "He is."

"What a bedside manner! After the war he'll have an expensive Berlin clinic for old ladies who have too rich a diet."

"I only hope that after the war it's Berlin where the old ladies are wealthy and diets are rich."

Kokke shrugged. "Then perhaps Moscow. Or even New York."

"I was hoping he could help. About Himmel, I mean."

"That *Stoppelhopper* is interested only in helping himself." It was a favorite German nickname for Austrians, who were said to be mercurial, untrustworthy people who leaped around mentally like a man running barefoot through stubble fields. "He could have done something about the documents without calling in the SIPO, but he was pleased with an opportunity to show what a loyal, laughing little Nazi he can be."

"We'll get no help from him," said Löwenherz.

Kokke looked at him, heartened by the plural. "Suppose both of us opened our mouths for Himmel."

"I beg your pardon."

"Suppose both of us supported Himmel and his protest. You're a baron and an ace; I could perhaps swing the old man."

"Redenbacher?"

"I might be able to."

"A slim chance."

"Too slim for you?"

"Look . . ." said Löwenherz. He laughed in protest and embarrassment. "You can't just put this to me, here and now."

"How much longer is there? By this time tomorrow the man who took you into battle when you were a duckling will be in a concentration camp."

"A civilian prison. They will hold him for trial and investigation."

"A nice distinction. And afterward release him with a reprimand?"

"Can't we talk about it tomorrow?"

"Herr Oberleutnant, we can't put off everything until tomorrow."

"That's what Himmel said."

"Exactly." The swarthy Kokke stroked his short beard reflectively.

There was a click as the Operations Room clerk switched on the microphone and a hum as the circuit came alive. Under his feet Bubi awoke, snorted, yawned and nibbled at Löwenherz's boot.

"You should have made your bet, Kokke. I was wrong; the *Tommis* are early."

Kokke didn't answer. Löwenherz looked around the hut; no one had moved but now their bodies were tense. There were only dim red lights glowing in the Alert Hut, not enough light to read, scarcely enough to play chess. At the far end of the hut there was a huge glass aquarium; inside it tropical fish moved in slow motion. Löwenherz remembered the day it had arrived: five men and a heavy lorry. They spent three days fixing it up; it had been supplied by order of the High Command. At the time the whole Geschwader had been desperately short of cannon shells and no amount of pleading would release the aquarium lorry to fetch some.

He remembered the winter battles before Moscow, the men clad in their thin summer uniforms. One of the last airlifts into Stalingrad had brought rubber contraceptives. He remembered too the fuss they had made about salvaging the motor of the ancient wrecked Junkers before finding that it was a British engine. The whole damned Luftwaffe was being mismanaged by political favoritism and political fanaticism. The Freezing Report that Himmel had shown him was just one step away from the aquarium.

I'll stand by Himmel, thought Löwenherz and suddenly realized he'd said it aloud. My God, he thought, that bloody aquarium!

"Thank you, Herr Oberleutnant," said Kokke. "I knew you would."

"I'm a fool," said Löwenherz, and he wondered if he could get out of it some way.

The microphone click came again and the dispatcher's voice said, "*Achtung! Achtung!* Oberleutnant Löwenherz, Major Redenbacher and Leutnant Kokke to instant readiness. Oberfeldwebel Himmel, Leutnant Beer and Feldwebel Schramm are now at alert." The toneless voice ended with an electronic click.

"Thanks," said Kokke as he zipped his flying overall. "We'll beat them, Oberleutnant."

"Why do you think that?" asked Löwenherz bitterly. They were both grabbing at their equipment and climbing over outstretched legs as they moved to the door. Löwenherz saw his radar operator pulling on his boots and made sure that Mrosek, his observer, was also ready.

"Put away your knitting. Klimke," Kokke shouted. He turned back to Löwenherz. "Because we are such an unlikely combination," said Kokke. He grinned.

Löwenherz nodded but was unconvinced. *"Hals- und Beinbruch!"* he said. To express the wish that a friend will break his neck and leg was said to fool the devil and bring him back safe. Kokke waved a grateful response.

"Uniform hats," called Löwenherz to his crewmen, Sachs and Mrosek. They both waved their folding cloth caps at him and Löwenherz responded by clasping his white-topped cap under his arm. If their airplane should be diverted to another airfield, the military police would make the devil of a fuss if they were hatless.

Löwenherz always insisted that his crew carry all the items that regulations demanded. Laden under a signal pistol, a garterful of flares, dinghy, life jacket, parachute, iron rations, Pervitin tablets and a flashlight, they all hobbled to their plane.

It was cold outside and the yeasty smell of the sea was on the wind. The airplanes were warm and ready to go, and their crews were glad of the comparative comfort of their cockpits. Löwenherz placed his peaked cap behind his seat and made sure that his radio leads were fixed to his flying suit, exactly as regulations prescribed. Then he plugged it in and connected his oxygen tube. After that he made sure that his crew had done the same. His hands went through the sixty consecutive hand movements that they had done blindfolded at training school. The green and red panel lamps came alight. The ground crews were fussing around the rudders and wheels.

He looked at his observer seated beside him: Mrosek, a nineteen-year-old Leutnant with long black hair. His pinched face and prominent incisors gave him a rodentlike appearance; a comparison endorsed by his narrow chest, small stature and wiry agility. After the cannons had been fired it was Mrosek's job to crawl headfirst into the nose to wrestle full drums onto the guns. That was difficult enough on the ground, but many times Mrosek had done it while Löwenherz had the plane in a dizzying vertical bank coming around for a second attack.

Mrosek's father was a vineyard manager from Heidelberg. Perhaps the proximity of so much wine had helped to make his disposition cheerful. He gave Löwenherz his quick ratty grin and held up his binoculars before he could be asked if they were aboard.

"Is everything in order?" Löwenherz asked his radar operator formally. He twisted in his seat to look at him.

From the rear seat Sachs smiled a deferential smile and raised his thin white manicured hand. He was a nineteen-year-old Feldwebel from Hanover and, partly because of his nouveau-riche and ambitious father, he remained in awe of the noble Baron Victor von Löwenherz Grawiec and modeled himself upon his pilot's speech, manners, walk and bravery.

Sachs the Saxon; Löwenherz wondered why there were always jokes about their capacity for hard work; it was a commendable virtue.

And that accent: "No, *Junge*. Grandfather's ashes will not go on the mantelpiece. They will go into the hour-glass. Grandfather must work, all we Saxons must work."

Sach's father had been a builder's laborer in 1935 but when the West Wall was started he had gone into business with his brother-in-law, supplying metal clamps for poured concrete structures. By 1940 the company was listed on the Hamburg Stock Exchange. On the day of issue several Todt Organization officials were given free shares in the thriving young company. In 1941 Britain's unwillingness to come to terms meant the beginning of the Atlantic Wall. The most extensive engineering project in the history of architecture was to deface Europe's northern coasts. The project devoured endless tons of prestressed concrete and used countless clamps. Georg's wristwatch was Swiss, gold and as thin as a Pfennig. His cufflinks were jade, his shoes handmade and under his regulation N.C.O's uniform his underclothes were silk. His trips into Amsterdam were made in a new sports car, except on weekends, when his father would send the chauffeur in the Mercedes with its Todt Organization pennant flying.

Georg Sachs, to his father's great disappointment, had become a radar operator after failing to meet the requirements of the pilot's course. He had grown to like his job and was good at it, which is why Löwenherz had chosen him from all the others on the Staffel. During the final minutes of an interception Georg knew that the aircraft was under his command. As he told his father, at the moment of the kill Baron von Löwenherz was nothing more than a machine-minder.

"Everything is ready, Herr Oberleutnant," said Georg Sachs.

Control came on the air.

"Major Redenbacher to Himmelbett Station Tiger; circle beacon at 5,000 meters. Leutnant Kokke to Himmelbett Station Ermine; circle beacon at 5,000 meters. Oberleutnant Löwenherz to Himmelbett Station Gorilla; circle beacon at 5,000 meters."

Each of the pilots acknowledged the order.

"We're going onto oxygen now," said Löwenherz. Some of the crews waited until they were over 1,200 meters but Löwenherz knew that loss of night vision is one of the first symptoms of oxygen lack.

The wreck of the old Junkers 34 was garlanded with red obstruction lights. They came past it round the perimeter track as fast as safety would allow. The ground was soft and he was careful not to cut corners. Across the aerodrome the Flying Control personnel saw his navigation lights, and as soon as he reached the end of the runway they switched the flare path on.

"Clear to take off, *Katze One*," said the Control Officer without waiting for him to ask. There were gusts coming from the IJsselmeer that made his plane falter as it passed over the dijk road. Löwenherz pulled the control column back and the variometer showed a steady climb while holding the airspeed. Now he extinguished the navigation lights on his wingtips. There was no light anywhere except from his instrument panel. The artificial horizon with its tiny green luminous airplane tilted as he came round on a course for Gorilla, almost due south of him. The long rectangle of runway lights passed under him, getting smaller as it went.

Kokke was the next to go. Redenbacher was behind him and perhaps that's why his takeoff was a copybook example of flying skill. The forward window was hinged down the center. Kokke pulled it closed but did not lock it. He left it slightly ajar, for like many fliers he liked to hear the note of the engines as clearly as possible. He enjoyed the sound of the airstream as it whistled through the gap. Gently the tail came up and they were airborne. Leutnant Klimke, the radar man, felt the wind round the back of his neck. He shivered, adjusted his hand-knitted scarf and watched the airport buildings tilt and drift under the port wing.

"It's freezing back here," he said. "Close the . . ."

Until radar was discovered and manned by dedicated

men, few people guessed how many flocks of birds moved after dark. This night nearly one hundred gulls, driven inland by the bad weather, were flying toward the fishing villages on the IJsselmeer, where nets laden with juicy tidbits had been hung out to dry. Only eight birds of the flock hit *Katze Two*. Two were bisected by the propeller blades and three struck the engine nacelles, were mangled and sucked into the air intakes. Two hit the leading edge of the wings and were cracked open like eggs.

It was the one that burst through the slightly opened front window that did the worst damage. By the time it entered the cockpit it had no wings or head. It was little more than half a pound of bloody offal that hit Kokke in the face, plus of course a thousand feathers. But it came in at 200 miles per hour, putting out both eyes, fracturing his skull (with multiple fractures of his right cheekbone and nose) and dislocating his jaw. It was impossible to distinguish where the bird's remains ended and Kokke's face began. He lost consciousness almost instantly, but somewhere a reflex had ordered his hands to pull on the control column and they pulled. Neither the observer nor Klimke realized what had happened even when the cockpit was white with shredded feathers. Kokke was dying, medically perhaps already dead, but his muscular arms strained at the control column with a live man's strength. It was no use. Kokke's radio line was not fastened to his back. The radio plug from his helmet had fallen into the gap in the floor through which the control column passed. To have got the control column back far enough to gain height he would have had to crush a solid metal plug to wafer thinness.

The Ju88 hit the IJsselmeer at a shallow angle. Finishing his sentence as though everything depended upon it, Klimke gasped ". . . window," and was dead. The waves were about a yard high and with a soft crunch the plane was swallowed like a gourmet's oyster. All the crew were dead by then, for the impact snapped their vertebrae. The black airplane slid into the dark water, banking and turning as it had in the sky, until with a gentle thud it struck the sea bed. The tail broke off and the aircraft was enveloped in a cloud of muddy water.

With a thump the yellow life raft, activated by a water-immersion switch, erupted from the compartment in front of the tail. There was a hiss of compressed air and a flurry of bubbles. It inflated, writhing like a demented monster, as the air entered each rubber compartment in turn.

Finally it was a perfect yellow circle and it floated up until it was held by the six feet of restraining cord. It stayed like that just under the surface of the sea: a sculpture-like yellow ring seemingly balanced upon the taut cord. The current sent it spinning gently like a hoop upon a conjurer's finger. For many months it remained there, turning in the sunlight and in the darkness and attracting foolhardy fish until, rotting compartment by compartment, it finally sank to the ocean bed and disappeared. By that time eels had eaten the three fliers.

"I've lost radio contact with Leutnant Kokke in *Katze Two*," said the ground operator.

"Damn these bloody radios," said the officer. "He's only been on the air for two minutes. You'd better reassign Löwenherz to Ermine; they're getting fidgety out there. And tell Kokke to return to base. It's probably only his transmitter gone, in which case he'll still be receiving you."

The operator nodded and tuned to Kokke's wavelength to tell him that his transmitter was not functioning. "Announcing: I am deaf," he said. "Announcing: I am deaf."

Löwenherz laughed when he heard the news. He could imagine Kokke cursing. So they had ordered him to return to Kroonsdijk. Not a chance of Kokke doing that; he would try and get into the stream and find a *Tommi* without radar aid. Löwenherz's radar operator turned their radio to the controller at Ermine.

"Order: Proceed to Heinz Emil Four," said the new voice calling him from Himmelbett Ermine. Let's see, Heinz Emil Four was halfway to England. He'd probably be the first pilot into the bomber stream. Tonight was starting well.

# ♦ 20 ♦

THE bombers were swimming upward. Ignoring their assigned heights, most pilots that night kept their noses trimmed skyward and let the technical limitations of their machines decide the altitude at which they turned the trim wheels back to normal. Some of the older Stirlings could not get above 11,000 feet. Even the best ones at 18,000 were not above the extreme range of the 8.8-cm. flak. The two-motor Wellingtons, however, of even older design, could all do better than this and the best of them, at nearly 24,000 feet, were flying higher than any other planes in the stream.

Lambert had pushed *Door* to nearly 21,000 feet. Now he trimmed the controls so that the plane was flying "hands off" and turned on the automatic pilot. He felt the elevators kick as it engaged. He had corrected course for the changing wind, so they had crossed the British coast at the prescribed assembly point. In his curtained cabin Kosher watched the shape of the pulses on the scope of the Gee and calculated their position from its map. He penciled a dot upon his plotting chart and calculated how much longer it would take until they were over the target. "Fifty minutes to T.O.T.," he announced. They had entered Luftwaffe fighter grid square Heinz Emil Four, although they had no way of knowing that. Now they were at the front of the bomber stream. That was no great navigational achievement; the stream was an unwieldy slab of bombers flying as much as fifteen miles to either side of the penciled route. It was timed to be nearly two hundred miles long. So while *Creaking Door* was over the North Sea the rearmost aircraft was only just taking to the air.

Tonight visibility was poor and only the sound of 2,800

264

high-performance engines marked their track. Each of
those engines required the manufacturing capacity of forty
simple car engines. The man-hours spent constructing each
four-motor airplane would have built almost a mile of
Autobahn. The radar and radio equipment alone equaled
a million radio sets. The total of hard aluminum amounted
to 5,000 tons, or about eleven million saucepans. In cash,
at 1943 prices with profits pared to a minimum, each
Lancaster cost £42,000. Crew training averaged out at
£10,000 each, at that time more than enough to send the
entire crew to Oxford or Cambridge for three years. Add
another £13,000 for bombs, fuel, servicing and ground
crew training at bargain prices and each bomber was a
public investment of £120,000.

Without including the Oboe Mosquitoes, the nuisance
raid on Berlin, the O.T.U. planes dropping leaflets upon
Ostend, training flights, transport jobs or any of Coastal
Command's activities, this bombing fleet cost eighty-five
million pounds.

Six bombers had already landed—the "boomerangs."
Most air crew hated to abort, for unless they bombed the
target the trip didn't count toward their tour. One Lancaster had got as far as the coast when a radiator leak caused
the port inner to disappear in a cloud of steam. A Stirling
had a faulty radio and the pilot of a Wellington was
suffering from stomach pains. The latter turned back just
before the Dutch coast. One Lancaster taking off from an
airfield near Lincoln bounced badly enough to smash the
undercarriage—one wheel went through a barn roof—and
was unable to retract its landing gear when in the air. Its
fuel jettison device failed too. It was still circling its base
under orders from Flying Control. When enough of its
fuel had been used up to achieve Safe Landing Weight it
would try a landing. At Warley Fen, John Munro managed a perfect takeoff in spite of a tire blowout. He'd
corrected the resultant swing effortlessly and two of the
crew didn't notice anything unusual. His problem would
arise on his return.

*Creaking Door, S Sweet, The Volkswagen* and *Joe for
King* were all within half a mile of each other, with
Lambert 2,000 feet above the others, although on this
dark night the only person to know that was the radar
operator at Ermine who watched the blips slide across his
screen. Lambert was as high as the plane would go and
the control column was mushy and insensitive in his
hands.

High above him, almost touching the stratosphere, he could see long wispy cirrus clouds. At the moment they weren't lying along the wind direction, but the wind would continue to back until they were. They heralded rain, but Lambert's interest in the clouds was a more immediate one and warned of a more immediate danger. The clouds glowed white and luminous, spotlighted by a bright moon that had not yet appeared over the horizon. Soon it would appear and the sky would lighten and the mantle of night would start to go at the elbows.

The Freya radar warned the smaller, more accurate Würzburg of the stream's route. Its three-man crew complained of the cold, as they always did, and tilted the mirror until suddenly four blips—*Door, Sweet, The Volkswagen* and *Joe for King*—slid across the hooded radarscope. The number one operator missed three spots of light but held the fourth one and turned to it. Inside the warm dark Plotting Room August held his breath like an angler when the float twitches.

"Red Würzburg has a contact, sir," said Willi Reinecke, "in Heinz Emil Four." It was as August had predicted. He compared the blue spot of light that marked Löwenherz's night fighter. It was about ten miles away from the red one. "Question: Your altitude and bearing *Katze One,*" said August as a double check.

It was Sachs, the radar man, in the back seat, who replied. Löwenherz hearing the call, turned his instrument panel illumination to minimum and leaned close to the black windshield. He could hear the wind buffeting the hinges and fixtures.

"Order: Caruso ten left, *Katze One,*" said August. Lowenherz touched the rudder bar. He knew that he must comply with every instruction immediately after it was given, for the heavy Junkers with its clumsy aerial array was not much faster than a Lancaster. For the same reason its stalling speed was higher.

"It's a parallel head-on intercept," said August. "I'll bring him in slightly to the north of the *Tommi.*"

"Announcing: Boring cinema," said Löwenherz. It was code for poor visibility.

Willi Reinecke gave a little sputter of indignation. "They are always complaining." He followed the moving points of light across the frosted-glass table, marking their progress with a wax pencil so that the converging courses could be seen. In spite of the dimmed lights August could see that the Plotting Room had begun to fill up with off-duty personnel who wanted to see the excitement.

"Prepare: 180-degree turn," said August.

"That's clear," crackled Löwenherz's acknowledgment.

"A starboard turn," August explained to Willi. "If he turns to port he'll pass close enough across his front for the *Tommi* to spot him."

By now, Löwenherz had become a part of the machinery; it was August who was flying the plane.

August looked round the Plotting Room at the expectant faces. Some of the men were in overcoats thrown over pajamas, their hair awry and faces stubbly. They watched him with the godlike and superior impartiality with which spectators judge card games. An orderly elbowed his way through them and came up the steps of the rostrum with a tray of coffee cups. The coffee soon disappeared and he went back to the kitchen for more. August drank his without tasting it. He watched the two colored lights rushing toward each other. They represented a combined speed of 600 miles per hour. He knew that a mistake in the timing of *Katze One*'s turn could cause them to miss the contact. That wasn't an enjoyable thing for the Commanding Officer to do for an audience of subordinates.

"Skip, give me a bit of straight and level for a star shot." Kosher Cohen stood under the Perspex astrodome fixing the stars through a sextant. Kosher was one of the few R.A.F. navigators who was skilled in its use. At the Navigation School he'd handled it better than his instructor. "Where the devil did you learn how to handle one of these, son?"

"My father's yacht, sir."

"And a bloody comedian to boot. Sit down. Next."

There wasn't time for another shot, so he compared his readings with the Gee fix. Four shots with a four-mile-wide cocked hat to show their position. Not bad at all.

Cohen looked at his plotting chart in the tiny circle of his desk light. To make good his track he drew the wind speed and direction and calculated their ground speed from the remaining side of the triangle thus formed. "Eleven minutes to the Dutch coast," he said. No one answered.

Lambert shifted his behind on the hard parachute pack. The heavy unpowered controls required a lot of physical strength to move them and already he had an ache in his shoulder and the usual pain in his spine. He sat upright to stretch his back and rolled his shoulders. "We are within radar range," he warned the crew. "Keep your eyes peeled for fighters."

Like all of the bomber stream's wireless operators, Jimmy Grimm, whose father had a radio shop in Highgate, was tuning his radio to the frequencies between 7050 and 7100 kilocycles, trying to find an enemy voice. Then he could transmit a signal on the same frequency to blot out the conversation between controller and fighter pilots. A microphone was fitted into an engine of each bomber especially for this purpose. Suddenly he heard August's voice.

"Order: Start turning . . . now."

"Turning," said Löwenherz.

Jimmy Grimm was excited. "I've found one of their controllers and a night fighter."

August Bach's voice came over the headphones with the same clarity that Löwenherz heard it. "Order: Steer 097 degrees," said August. "Announcing: Enemy range ten kilometers."

"The plane he's following is on our heading," said Cohen.

"Every plane in the stream is on our heading," said Digby. He was full length in the nose trying to see the Dutch coast.

"I wish I could understand German better," said Jimmy Grimm. "That's the trouble with being a radio ham; in peacetime I used to pick up all sorts of stations and only speak a few words of everything."

"While you types are sodding about, some poor bastard is going to get the chop," said Digby. "Why don't you jam him?"

"Perhaps it's us he's after," said Binty from the mid-upper turret.

"Can we steer onto 080 degrees just to be sure, Skipper?" said Cohen.

"You're the navigator," said Lambert and put the plane into a shallow banking turn.

"He's still a long way behind the bomber," said Cohen, "and the controller keeps telling him to lose height."

"You are still well above him," August told Löwenherz. "Lose another five hundred meters."

Again Löwenherz touched the control column and the fighter dipped. Beside him the observer had his field glasses on his lap; the bomber was too far away and the night too dark for there to be a chance of visual contact yet.

Behind Löwenherz, facing rearward, the radar operator was boxed in with so much equipment that he was scarcely able to move. His three radar screens that showed range, altitude position and lateral position were tucked under his right elbow and to see them he had to cock his head on one side like a sparrow. It was useless to look at them yet, for the equipment wouldn't show the target until they were three thousand meters away.

"Order: Hold it," warned August. Löwenherz throttled back.

Flash Gordon was staring through the newly open part of his rear turret. God, it was cold, but he could see better than he had ever done before. If he bent forward he could almost get his head outside the aircraft. When he rotated the turret the slipstream passing across the barrels of the four Brownings made a gentle screaming sound, like high wind through telephone wires. He kept the turret moving, making the gun muzzles describe little circles as he had practiced at gunnery school with pencils in the muzzles. A good gunner could write his name like that. It was a lonely position in the rear turret, especially when night fighters were about, for then chatter on the intercom was forbidden. Flash Gordon and Löwenherz were staring toward each other with all the concentration they could muster, but the night was too dark for either of them to see anything.

Flash heard Cohen order a change of course and watched the clouds slide past the tail.

August watched the red blip change direction on the Seeburg tablet. Willi marked it with the pencil. "He's turned to port," said August. "Order: Steer fifteen degrees left. He's very close now."

"I think it is us," said Cohen. "He's told him to change direction."

"Jam him," said Lambert urgently. Jimmy Grimm tuned his 1154 transmitter to the 1155 receiver, heard its whistle, sought the silent "dead space" and switched on the microphone that was fixed inside the engine. Lambert banked steeply to change course again.

In the night fighter they were silent. Löwenherz had turned as directed; Mrosek, the observer, had his field glasses to his eyes and was scanning each side of the aircraft where the radar did not point. Suddenly Sachs's radar tube lit up at the end of the range circle: a *Tommi* at extreme range.

"We've got him," said Sachs, trying hard to keep the

excitement out of his voice. Suddenly jamming deafened them, so near were they to Jimmy Grimm's radio transmitter.

"Just in time," said Löwenherz and they tuned the noise to minimum. Löwenherz switched the gun safety catches to "Fire" and a line of red lights appeared on the instrument panel. Suddenly the whole Junkers hit a patch of turbulence. The plane dipped steeply like a horse refusing a fence. A wingtip fell and Löwenherz had to use all his strength to correct the plane's heading.

"The *Tommi*'s slipstream," said Löwenherz, but the others knew what it was. The force of it showed how close they were behind the speeding bomber.

"He's turning right," said Sachs as the blip on his screen started traveling along its base line. "He's turning, keep turning." He watched the tube.

"Level out but keep turning, range still closing. Straighten out, range still closing too fast. Twelve hundred meters." Löwenherz followed the turn until when heading almost due south the bomber straightened out and Löwenherz did too. "Where do you want him?" asked Sachs.

"Slightly starboard."

"He's about 7 degrees starboard."

"That's enough; read off the range."

"Under 1,000 meters, closing slowly."

Löwenherz wanted to move onto the bomber as slowly as possible, for that would give him the maximum duration of gunfire. "Bring me in level with him. I'll lose height when we get a visual."

"It's still very dark; you'd do better to have him against that bright cirrus."

"Very well, bring me in a little below him."

"Nine hundred, left a touch. We're coming in too quickly, Herr Oberleutnant."

"I can't see him."

"Still too fast."

"Damn, why is he throttling right back?" Löwenherz reduced his speed until Sachs grunted, "That's in order, Herr Oberleutnant."

"Still can't see him."

"We're very close, five hundred meters."

"Got him," said Löwenherz, and at the same time Mrosek also gave a yell. Eight yellow dots of exhaust flame pinpricked a horizon across the darkness.

And because all primitive rituals, especially those concerned with death, have their own vocabulary, Löwenherz reported his sighting to Bach with the words "Ket-tledrums, kettledrums."

"Lancaster bomber," said Mrosek, whose task it was to identify the targets before an attack.

"You beauty," said Löwenherz.

Flash Gordon was a mild man, small in stature, humble in origin and quiet of voice, and yet within him was growing a hatred of Binty Jones that he wouldn't have thought possible. Hardly a day went by without a jibe or a word of sarcasm and now most recent and hurtful of all was Binty's scorn of his turret modification. If Binty had publicly recognized what a fine idea it was, then the Gunnery Officer might have ordered the turrets of all squadron planes to be similarly altered. Who knows, it might have been called the "Gordon Panel." Invented by a gunner named Gordon; people say he was one of the greatest gunnery experts the air force ever had.

Although Flash Gordon never told real lies, he had come to realize that sometimes a white lie can be neces-sary for the sake of mankind's progress. If telling a lie was the only way of having an excellent modification incorpo-rated into Warley Fen's airplanes, then a lie wouldn't stand in his way. In ten minutes I'll do it, he thought, but changed his mind. There would never come a quieter time than now: the fighter scare was over and they were quite alone in the sky.

"Fighter, fighter. Corkscrew port, go!" said Flash Gor-don. Without bothering to use the sights, he opened fire into the blank darkness. Lambert, obeying instinctively the command that any crew member was empowered to give, flung *Creaking Door* into a vertical bank and let it drop through the air like a slate.

Binty Jones, not to be outdone by his colleague, also fired his guns. Curves of tracer hosepiped across the sky as *Door* fell faster than its turrets could turn.

"My God," said Löwenherz as the tracer came toward him. Instinctively he shied away, while *Door*'s eight ex-haust flames tipped vertical and slid out of sight under his nose. The little .303 bullets that the *Tommis* fired were seldom fatal against the solidly built Junkers, but still Löwenherz found it impossible to fly through them.

"He's seen us," said Mrosek. Löwenherz swore. He followed the bomber down, trying to bring the flame spots up past the windshield again, but now that he was higher than the bomber he no longer had the advantage of the moonlit clouds.

Lambert was following the classic maneuver of the corkscrew and chanting its litany as he went, to warn the crew: diving port, climbing port, roll, climbing starboard, diving starboard, roll, diving port, climbing port . . .

Many times Löwenherz had seen such an evasive pattern. Four or five times he had been able to execute identical maneuvers in formation with his victim and kill him while they danced together. He could not do it this time. For a corkscrew can be executed in such a leisurely fashion that it occupies ten miles of air space (some pilots corkscrewed like this the whole journey) or it can be the brutal wing-wrenching, back-breaking maneuver that Lambert now put into effect.

"Lost contact," said Sachs.

"My fault," said Löwenherz.

The night fighter's Li C1 Airborne radar projected only a narrow cone of signals straight ahead (between sixty and thirty degrees to be precise). Löwenherz waggled his aircraft through a horizon-searching series of maneuvers. It was no use. He switched on the radio transmitter.

"Announcement," said Löwenherz. "*Katze One,* contact lost."

"*Katze One,*" said August, his voice still badly marred by the jamming. "Order: Steer 200 degrees." August looked at the plotting table and saw that the blip that was *Creaking Door* was at the extreme edge of his sector. "He has luck, that *Tommi,*" said August. "If he'd turned the other way we'd still be able to go after him."

"There are plenty more where he came from," said Willi.

In *Creaking Door* Lambert had stopped corkscrewing. His hands were trembling; so that Battersby would not notice, he kept a tight grip on the controls. Suddenly the pain in his back and shoulder, unnoticed during the time of danger, returned with new ferocity. "Give me a course for Noordwijk, Kosh," said Lambert.

"O-eight-six, Skip," said Cohen. Always the perfect navigator, he had been keeping the calculation fresh while waiting for the question.

"Now do you believe in my clear-vision panel?" Flash Gordon asked the world at large. He had waited long enough for a word of congratulation or thanks.

"Bloody good show," said Lambert.

"I don't believe you saw anything," accused Binty Jones.

"A damned great night fighter, man. In fact, I think I may have hit him."

"Balls," said Binty. "There was nothing there."

"Then why were you firing?" asked Flash. There was no reply. "The Gordon clear-view panel, I'm going to call it."

" 'Just an old-fashioned liar with old ...' " Binty began the fourth verse of the song.

"For Christ's sake belt up, everyone," said Lambert.

*S Sweet* had lost headway by the wind error back at Lowestoft and *Door* had been turning and corkscrewing over the ocean, so that by one o'clock, German time, while both Sweet and Lambert were eight miles short of the coastline, Tommy Carter in *Joe for King* and Fleming in *The Volkswagen* had reached Noordwijk, turned and were four miles along their final leg for the target. About midway between them—two miles off Noordwijk— Löwenherz was moving back over the sea. Twice he had passed within one hundred yards of *Joe for King*. For a few seconds his wingtip was only twenty feet from the tail plane of a Halifax, but none of the crews had spotted these near misses and to them the sky seemed vast and empty.

Noordwijk-aan-zee is a holiday resort on the coast of Holland. In 1943 the sand was crisscrossed with barbed wire, and steel spears were hidden in the sea. The hotels had become convalescent homes and military offices and the wide seafront that in peacetime was crowded with holidaymakers was guarded by armed sentries. The lighthouse stands on the modern esplanade and now its shaded light was switched on while the convoy moved past. The flak cruiser *Held* was leading the line of ships and it located the bomber stream as they passed overhead. Each time the *Held* fired, the sound rattled every window in Noordwijk and flashes lit up the whole seafront. The red fire of one salvo burst uncomfortably close to Löwenherz's Junkers and he climbed away from the flashes. It was the second time within twelve hours that "Admiral" Pawlak had fired at Löwenherz but there was, of course, no way in which either of them would ever know that.

"How nice of them," said Lambert. "They've got the Noordwijk lighthouse switched on for us." He asked Cohen for a course that would take him well short of the nearby town of Leiden with its notorious flak concentrations. Even while Lambert, and Digby in the nose, were looking at the pulsating glimmer of the lighthouse, the whole esplanade suddenly lit up as if the sun had selected

that town for a private dawn. Two pathfinder Lancasters
had dropped flares to mark it as the turning point for the
bomber stream. The lighthouse keeper peered out of the
window at the blinding yellow Christmas trees of flares
that inched slowly downward, crackling loudly and sending up snakes of white smoke. Illuminated by the flares,
the smoke looked yellow. So did all the hotels and the
faces of the sentries and the Luftwaffe air crew staring
out of the windows of the convalescent home.

"Kosh," said Lambert. "Turning-point markers at
Noordwijk."

Cohen pulled aside the curtain that screened his chart
table. The light from his desk was briefly reflected in
Lambert's windshield before Cohen switched it off. It took
him a moment to adjust his eyes to the dark. Then he
leaned across to the window and saw the strip of coastline with its hotels and lighthouse lit by the flares.

"That would be about right," said Cohen and stood
staring for a moment before going back to his charts.

Löwenherz, two miles to the north, also saw the flares.
"Ermine Control from *Katze One,*" he said. "Turning-
point markers going down on Noordwijk. I'll head toward
them until you give me a contact."

At Ermine Willi Reinecke quickly wiped the wax pencil
marks off the frosted glass as the kitchen orderly returned
with more coffee. The wide-eyed young man served Willi
and August and then gave one each to the blip operators
who sat under the table. He gave one to the telephone
man too. Outside, the orderly had seen a big glow in the
sky. "Big fires to the north of here," he confided. "Leiden's
getting it, I should think."

Scornfully the telephonist said, "Nonsense. That's just
the *Tommis* dropping their marker flares to help the
bombers find the way. The raid hasn't begun yet, *Junge.*"
He took the hot coffee and put in three sugars. It was
going to be a long night if they came back this way.

Very, very high in the sky above Noordwijk a fast
R.A.F. Mosquito also saw the flares. The 8.8-cm. flak
could not reach the Mosquitoes because they flew so high;
the Würzburgs had difficulty tracking them because they
were made of wood, and the night fighters had not been
able to catch them because they were so fast. This one
was flying to Ahaus, where he would turn south for fifty
miles and, flying under electronic guidance, would lay four
red markers upon Krefeld for the heavy bombers to
pound. That, at any rate, was the plan.

Meanwhile it was exactly one minute past one o'clock when the flares went down on Noordwijk. Within seconds, reports of them were being phoned to the Opera House at Deelen, where they were marked in on the giant screen. Sentries in coastal watchtowers saw them and so did air raid volunteers on factory roofs. The control room of the flak cruiser *Held* gave their bearing and the Hitler Jugend gunners at Ahaus reported their glow.

In the Flugwachkommando at Duisburg the experts waited to see whether the planes would really turn at Noordwijk. It was an R.A.F. trick to drop T.P. markers, having briefed their crews to ignore them. This had some-times caused the FLUKO to warn the wrong district, and workers lost sleep sitting in damp cellars cursing the Luftwaffe. Still worse, the defenses and people in the real target were left unprepared.

Within two minutes there were enough other reports to persuade them that the stream was turning. Warnzentral's commander needed only to nod to his attentive deputy. P.A.Z.s (pre-alert zones) became A.Z.R.s (alert zones) as the bombers moved eastward. The country over which the bombers moved blacked out completely. Railways stopped, stations went dark, factory workers took shelter.

"A.D. 30 for the whole Ruhr."

Air Danger 30: cities, towns and villages as far as Cologne and Dortmund were told to prepare for an attack in thirty minutes. At the flak sites cigarettes were doused and coffee abandoned as men came grumbling, laughing and yawning out of the rest huts, buttoning their great-coats against the chilly night. The barrels were elevated, searchlights tilted, radar warmed and shells fused. Civil defense workers, police, fire services and hospitals were warned too. Shelters were unlocked and the Nazi Party organization through which bombed-out civilians were cared for began to prepare. Fires were lit under vats of soup, blankets were sorted, shrouds made ready, ration cards endorsed and bundles of secondhand clothing un-tied. Altgarten was now in the P.A.Z.

# ⦚ 21 ⦚

"DID you see the sunset this evening?" asked Gerda Pippert of the man sitting on her left. She had gained confidence by now. No one had guessed that she was not the Frau Pippert on the invitation list, and nowadays everyone was far too concerned with his own life to inquire into hers.

"Ah," said her companion, "we should have been out in Koller Meadow, you and me, holding hands and catching pneumonia on the damp grass."

Gerda Pippert blushed. He was frightful, this bald-headed little man with whom she had sat through dinner, and yet everyone else took his jibes in good spirits, so she was reluctant to object. Although, goodness knows, Koller Meadow, behind the hospital and nurses' training center, had become truly notorious on these summer nights. There was a joke going around town: whenever someone had a bruise or cut they said they had fallen over a nurse while crossing Koller Meadow in the blackout.

The architect's wife, who even on this warm evening had insisted upon sitting through dinner in her fur cape, leaned across and said, "I heard they were going to have caviar."

"I've never had caviar," said Gerda Pippert.

"It's horrible," said Gerd Böll. "I'll take smoked eel every time."

"How lucky you are to have a taste for the common things," said Frau Hinkelburg. She was watching her architect husband at the far end of the table as he talked with a redheaded young cousin of the Burgomaster. Once before she'd had trouble with her husband over a redhead.

"There are certainly enough common things about," agreed Gerd Böll cheerfully. As he reached for a second helping of tart he winked at Gerda and she smiled at him. He didn't care what he said to anyone and she admired that in a man, she always had.

She looked around the table at all the guests, especially the ladies. There was the Burgomaster's mother; what a dignified lady: eighty-six years old with a lace blouse boned high under her chin and freckled white hands glittering with rings. There was the Burgomaster's wife, her white hair drawn back in the severe earphone style that was now considered patriotic. A handsome woman of great charm and kindness, neither of which virtues could truly be attributed to her husband.

"And the lady with the diamond tiara?" asked Gerda Pippert.

"Gräfin von Linck."

"The astrologer?"

"None other," said Gerd.

"People say Reichsführer Himmler consults her. She says victory will come next year."

"Yes, she does; she says that every year."

Gerda Pippert scrutinized Gerd's face in alarm and Frau Hinkelburg tutted her disapproval.

All the waiters were busy attending to the curtains, so Gerd reached to the ice bucket and served both ladies with a little more French champagne. He noticed that the 1937 label saying "For export to England" had been overprinted with "Réservé pour le Wehrmacht." He wondered if that labeling department had already prepared similar ones for the Americans or even the Russians. To drown the thought he served himself an extra measure.

The windows of the Frenzel Stube's private room gave all the Burgomaster's guests an extensive view of the town, which is why the waiters had waited so long before closing the curtains and putting on the lights, but once that was done a different atmosphere came to the party. More intimate and seemingly more private too, the guests— merry with the Burgomaster's carefully chosen and generously supplied wine—settled into their chairs and made ready for the speeches and toasts that would occupy the rest of the evening. Some speechmakers already had their notes before them on the table.

Gerd Böll timed his exit nicely. A second helping of Frenzel's apple tart marked the end of the evening as far as he was concerned. He knew the drill from now on: coffee cups were standing by on the trolley and even before the spoons were in the saucers the first of the

speechmakers would be on his hind legs mouthing a dili-
gently assembled collection of sycophantic and patriotic
clichés. Each would bring lengthy if unenthusiastic applause. It was a damn shame about the cigars—blunt-
ended *Stumpen* from Holland—which had long since disappeared from any sources that Gerd Böll knew, but even
they didn't tempt him to stay. He had explained to the
Burgomaster that this evening he would have to leave
early in case of air raid duties.

"Duty comes first," the Burgomaster had said. Many
years ago he'd been complimented on his fine speaking
voice and he always pronounced his careful *Hochdeutsch*
as though speaking to an imbecilic foreign child.

Actually Gerd Böll was going down to the railway
station buffet for a game of skat with his TENO friends.
He'd promised to be there before eleven-thirty and he
whispered his excuses to the garrulous wife of the architect and to the simple old schoolteacher woman seated
next to him.

"Good-bye, Frau Pippert," said Gerd. "So nice to see
you again, and I'm glad to see your foot is so much
better."

Frau Pippert smiled uneasily. So the real Frau Pippert
had a bad foot. "Yes," she said tentatively, "it's much
better now." She decided to embellish it a bit. "The toes
give a stab of pain from time to time."

"Well, we can't complain about that," said Gerd cheerfully. "After all, there are not many people these days
who can grow a complete new leg after an amputation."

Gerd smiled and kissed her hand. "Have a wonderful
evening, Frau Pippert," he said. "A grocer has to be most
careful about confusing the bills for two ladies of the
same name, but luckily there are no other grocers here
this evening."

Oberwachtmeister Müller was on his feet as soon as the
coffee appeared, but by fast footwork Gerd just made it to
the door. Müller pulled at the skirt of his blue uniform
jacket and cleared his throat nervously. It was an honor to
speak first and yet it was difficult too. The waiters were
still serving the coffee and he noticed more than one guest
looking enviously at that fellow Böll as he practically ran
to the door. Someone rapped upon the table with a spoon
and then, as he began to speak, they gave him their
undivided attention.

The police chief related the Burgomaster's achievements
and Altgarten's role as a war-winning and law-abiding

part of the Third Reich. If it was a story that also reflected the police chief's successes, then that was exactly as it should be. Other officials added their praise; the Gasmeister and the Kreisleiter gave brief speeches.

Some speakers saw this as an occasion upon which they could once again relate Germany's progress from the demoralized nation that emerged defeated from the First World War to the mighty fear-inspiring master of Europe in 1943. Schott—the electricity chief—had known the Burgomaster for the greater part of this time. In 1933 they had worked side by side at a bench in one of the factories that were secretly rearming the newly planned Wehrmacht. Schott spoke of those times. It was not a period of his life about which the Burgomaster cared to be reminded.

"An old man in the paint shed stole one piece of perambulator each day. When he had all the parts he tried to reassemble one in his living room. Funny thing, he told me; every time I try it I end up with a machine gun."

There was laughter and applause and even the Burgomaster smiled primly.

Most of the men were in uniform. A stuttering Party official from Berlin had come in an S.A. uniform complete with ceremonial dagger, commemorative armband "Horst Wessel" and a display of medals and ribbons. He presented an engraved plaque to mark the Burgomaster's service on the committee of a local Adolf Hitler School.

Obersturmführer Berger, senior full-time S.S. official of Altgarten, then stood up. He straightened the knot of his black tie and flicked at his sleeve as if to remove a piece of lint from his gray tunic. Satisfied with his appearance, Berger smiled upon his neighbors. He announced the Burgomaster's promotion to honorary S.S. Obersturmführer and made a witty speech describing the lengths to which the Allgemein office had gone to arrange that the promotion be announced on this the Burgomaster's birthday. He also made a little joke that the Burgomaster had caught up with his own rank and he thought he should now turn the tables upon him by becoming honorary Burgomaster. It wasn't much of a joke, but there were so few jokes made that evening that the guests took that opportunity of having a side-splitting laugh and a cough.

The evening sped past, thanks in some measure to the way in which Frenzel's waiters enthusiastically complied with the Burgomaster's order to "keep the champagne coming until everyone has had enough or I tell you otherwise." The old room smelled of roast duckling, schnapps, candles and good cigars. Smells that went deep into the oak paneling and joined memories of other dinners in other times.

The rehearsed speeches came to an end at five past midnight when the tiniest Jungvolk boy in Altgarten presented the Burgomaster with a huge bunch of flowers on behalf of all of the Nazi youth organizations in the district. There were still some impromptu addresses and the old songs.

"A memorable evening," said Berger, who had taken off his S.S. jacket and was leading a chorus in a voice as powerful as it was discordant.

S.S. Standartenführer Wörth—C.O. of the S.S. unit at the Wald Hotel—smiled indulgently at Berger as he sang the old Party songs. He joined him in a chorus of one that he remembered from his days as an ensign, although the old man's voice was scarcely audible. At twenty to one he declared that it was his bedtime and got to his feet. He was like an overbred Borzoi dog, his limbs thin and spindly and his face the same, with sad gray eyes that looked round anxiously as though fearing unprovoked attack. The old S.S. officer moved slowly, prodding the floor with his stick before committing his weight to it. He gave a nod to the other guests and edged through the door. Behind him Dieter Witting, a burley N.C.O., was ready to support an elbow or pull a chair for him or signal a person from his path in a courteous and unobtrusive way that would not mark Wörth as the desperately sick man that he was.

The car was close to the entrance and the driver wrapped blankets across his commander's knees before closing the door with a considerate click. Wörth sank back into the leather seat and closed his eyes to meet the pain. His missing left hand still tormented him more than did his injured knees or feet.

It was a few minutes after one o'clock when a messenger arrived from the Rathaus and whispered in the Burgomaster's ear. Until that young fellow arrived with his steel helmet, heavy-duty gloves and official overalls, it had been perfectly possible to forget that there was a war on.

"Can I have your attention," said the Burgomaster, and the whole room was alert. The waiters stood at attention, the way they did each morning when Herr Frenzel inspected their hands and nails.

"I have official notification that there is a heavy force

of R.A.F. planes in the air tonight. Our FLUKO in
Duisburg has given us the preliminary warning. They
predict that the Ruhr will be attacked. My guests will no
doubt wish to answer the call of duty at the earliest
possible moment. I will therefore bid everyone good night.
Heil Hitler!"

"Heil Hitler," repeated the guests soberly. The Burgomaster kissed his wife and mother and bowed to his
guests. The first ones to leave saw searchlights to the
northwest. Soon after that the early warning sounded.

Altgarten railway station was noted more for the liveliness
of its buffet than for the liveliness of its train schedules.
The Bahnhofecke had become a favorite hangout for
policemen from the Rathaus across Bismarckplatz and for
TENO engineers, as well as the brewery manager and his
foreman and of course the railway people, who were there
all the time.

It was smoky and noisy all day every day and it smelled
of thin beer, cheap tobacco and synthetic sausage. Sometimes it didn't close until 3 A.M. even though the one
o'clock train was the last one. Many times when the main
line was bombed troop trains had been shunted into
Altgarten and the two old ladies who ran the Bahnhofecke
had served beer, coffee and sandwiches until the supplies
were exhausted.

The buffet was furnished like a Victorian parlor. There
were dozens of plants, glass-fronted cases full of polished
glasses, a bust of Beethoven and a drawing of Wagner, a
colored reproduction of the Führer and an old piano. On
the top shelf of the bar there were school caps donated by
high school students when they went off to the war. It had
become a ritual, and now there were twenty-eight dusty
caps untouched since the day they were flung there. On
that same top shelf there were four ancient empty Scotch
whisky bottles. Never a week passed without some joker
ordering a White Horse or a Black and White but still old
Frau Klein was able to smile as if the joke was new.

The three tables near the piano were the best ones.
From the counter one of the two old ladies could lean
over with bread, beer, sausage and potatoes, but on a
crowded evening customers near the door could shout all
evening and still not be served. The three best tables were
marked with *Stammtisch* flags, so that only regulars would
dare to sit there. This evening the center one was taken by
a group of men playing skat for small money stakes and a

little crowd had collected to watch the card players: Gerd
Böll and his two TENO friends.

Fuchs Ueberall was talking. His TENO jacket was hung
upon his chair. The two stars on its collar patch showed
him to be a Zugwachtmeister, which is a grand title for an
N.C.O. His army braces supported ill-fitting gray trousers
that almost covered his chest. He had a strong Saxon
accent. It seemed especially comical here where the local
people spoke a high-speed dialect like Dutch, but no one
smiled. It would be foolhardy to annoy this amiable giant.

"You'll never get them bowling here in Altgarten," said
Fuchs. "It's too near the Dutch border for the *Tommis* to
risk it."

"If you mean bombing say bombing. I hate these slang
words," said Bodo Reuter, a TENO officer. He asked for
another card. That rumor was resurrected every now and
again. "It's a comforting thought."

"They are forbidden under pain of execution to bomb
targets within twenty kilometers of any frontier of their
ex-allies," said Fuchs Ueberall. He put emphasis on the
word "bomb."

"How do you know that?" asked Reuter. "I hear the
Americans and British never execute their soldiers."

"We are eleven kilometers from the Dutch border here.
Do you know of any bombs dropping as close as that to
the border?"

"Yes," said Gerd. He won the trick and piled the cards
in front of him.

"Oh, I know about the plane that jettisoned its bombs
on Frau Kersten's place. That doesn't count."

"You'd better explain that to Frau Kersten," said Gerd.
Some of the men laughed.

"Play on," said Bodo. Fuchs was a rumormonger.

"She's too busy learning French to let me prove anything to her," said Fuchs, and there was a louder laugh.

The one o'clock train was almost due when Jürgen
Löwe, one of the Hitler Youth bicycle messengers, came
into the Ecke. He wouldn't sit down because he had an
urgent message for Andi Niels and had been unable to
find him.

The H.J. messenger said, "The Ruhr is going to get
pasted tonight; over seven hundred *Terrorflieger*, the
FLUKO message said."

One of the men playing cards said, "That will be the
second heavy raid in a week."

Two brewery workers were playing chess in the corner.

They had their French army helmets and gloves ready and were wearing their civil defense overalls. "Lie-in tomorrow morning," said one of them, for if the alarm went at night they were paid a two-Reichsmark bonus and allowed two hours off in the morning.

"Loser of this game goes back to phone the Rathaus."

"Suits me," said the second one and he brought his bishop to threaten the king's knight.

Herr Holländer, the marriage registrar, was one of the local Blockwarte. He swallowed the last of his beer and hurriedly got to his feet when he heard that a raid was imminent. It was his job to open the shelter and collect front-door keys from local residents in case of fire bombs. He also must make sure that old deaf Frau Klietmann was properly awakened when the alarm sounded. Not all the people from his block would go down into the shelter, in spite of the regulations. Most of them worked in the brewery and no one who had to clock in at a quarter to seven wanted to interrupt his sleep and go into the cold cellar. Blockwart Holländer slipped out quietly.

The one o'clock train came in exactly on time with a whistle, a groan and a hissing of steam. Six TENO engineers who were going on leave left the Ecke to derisory cheers. The doors had hardly stopped swinging when one of the TENO men put his head back round it. "Come and look at the *Tommi* flares going down—somewhere near Neukirchen I'd guess."

The words were hardly out of his mouth when the Public Warning began. The warbling notes echoed eerily across the town. Even then not everyone left the Ecke. The Public Warning was only a preliminary caution for people in the street or a long way from shelter. And even if the more serious General Warning sounded it was purely academic out here in Altgarten; the bombs were destined for one of the big cities of the Ruhr.

Gerd Böll still had his playing cards in his hand when he went out to look at the flares. They were a long way away, sputtering little pinpoints of intense light like that of the old-fashioned acetylene cycle lamps, Gerd decided it was time for him to report with his van to the Rathaus Control Room. Once the FLUKO let them know where the attack was being centered he would head into the bombed town to help. That was the advantage of being single, thought Gerd. He'd never be able to do such a thing if he had a wife and children to look after. That's what led him to think of Hansl and the girl. If the attack

was going to be a heavy one—over seven hundred, the
messenger had said—then perhaps he had better call in at
August's place and make sure the child and the girl took
shelter tonight. They'd object, of course, but he would
insist upon it. He sat down again and took a last look
at his cards. Then he raised his eyebrows to ask what
Reuter thought would happen.

Bodo Reuter played a famous game of skat. He'd
played it when as a fifteen-year-old he'd falsified his age to
go to the first war. He'd played it in the merchant navy
and now after many evenings in the Bahnhofecke playing
Gerd Böll and old Fuchs for Pfennig bets he'd almost
regained his former skill. After a few glasses of Gerd's
homemade schnapps he'd tell stories: around the Cape in
a floating dock, the Grand Banks in a Spanish trawler, the
trenches in the winter of 1917, Paris in the summer of
1940, brawls in Boston, brothels in Shanghai.
Oberzugführer Reuter had done it all, and, as he said,
some of it twice.

He was from Hamburg, a quick-spoken man, tall, with
light-blue eyes deeply set into their sockets, drawn face,
high cheekbones and a big forehead with receding soft fair
hair. He looked more like an art critic than a pioneer
officer; most of Altgarten's TENO battalion were, like
Fuchs, brawny fellows with a noisy sense of humor.

Some of the regulars at the Ecke found it hard to
believe that this quiet-spoken man had done the things of
which he told, but he had a chestful of medals to prove it
and, as he had once told a crowd of angry Bolsheviks, his
hands told the story of his life. Knobbly red angry hands
they now were, shiny with scar tissue and crisscrossed with
calluses from a windjammer's lines.

Bodo threw his hand of cards upon the table to indicate
that the game could not continue. Gerd lined up the edges
of his cards with a neurotic care and Fuchs Ueberall sadly
assembled the whole pack together and put it into its box.
For an hour Fuchs had become a civilian again, but now
that Altgarten had come under attack he was jerked back
into the world of harsh military reality.

"Take my grocery van," Gerd told Bodo. "I will borrow
a bicycle and be with you before you are ordered out."

There was no time for the courtesy of argument. Bodo
caught the keys that were thrown to him and, nodding to
the other men in the bar, hurried out. Fuchs sat in the
front seat alongside his officer and a few minutes later it

was Fuchs who shouted in time for them to avoid driving
into a big crater near the railway crossing.

Gerd borrowed a woman's bicycle from Frau Klein
behind the bar. The tiny slotted blue streetlights had been
extinguished but the luminous paint on the trees and
lampposts helped him find his way through the darkened
town.

As he passed the Nazi Party H.Q., he popped in to tell
them there was a big raid tonight, but one glance told him
that he needn't have bothered. The N.S.V. kitchens were
bustling with voluntary workers in aprons and Party
officials in their fine uniforms. Shrewdly it was a matter
of policy that compensation, clothing, soup kitchens and
emergency aid for the homeless were all provided by Nazi
Party workers. Gerd picked his way past mountains of
potatoes. The raw smell of the freshly peeled ones was
strong. Gerd hated that smell. There were blue fantailed
gas flames under the soup vats and more potatoes were
being tipped into the peeling machines.

"Some coffee, Herr Böll?" said Frau Grundel.

"I mustn't interrupt the good work," said Böll. The
woman smiled. Many years ago they had held hands under
the trees and on summer evenings like this had walked
along the stream as far as the Kersten windmill, long since
broken and demolished. Now she was nearly fifty, wid-
dowed, with three grown-up daughters and a soldier son.
She ran her baker's shop and still volunteered long hours
for the Frauenschaft. Frau Grundel reached for a chipped
enamel mug from the shelf of mugs that stood ready by
the stove. She poured the hot dark coffee and passed it to
him.

"For the Hilfzug?" asked Gerd Böll.

"That's it," said the woman. "The lorries are waiting.
It's strange to think that within three hours poor bombed-
out people in the Ruhr will be drinking our good hot
potato soup." She smoothed the starched white apron of
her uniform.

"We've a lot to thank God for."

"God and the Führer, Gerd," said the woman.

"There are flares dropping to the north," said Gerd.
"And searchlights."

"You are the third one to tell us," said Frau Grundel.
"But there's no need to be alarmed about the *Terrorflieger*; our brave boys will be in the air after them."

"I must be getting along," said Gerd Böll. He swallowed

his coffee and pursed his lips at the bitter aftertaste. Frau Grundel noticed his grimace.

"You've nothing to worry about; our antiaircraft defenses in the Ruhr are the most formidable in the world."

"Good-bye, Frau Grundel," said Gerd. She turned away and switched on the peeling machine, which made a noise like thunder.

Anna-Luisa was brushing her hair carefully, three hundred times as she did every night, when she heard the voice of little Hansl from the next room.

"Fräulein, Fräulein."

"Yes, Hansl. But you must get back into bed." He had pulled back the curtain.

"The pretty lights, Fräulein. Such pretty lights. Like Christmas trees in the sky."

Anna-Luisa went to the window. "Yes," she said. "Exactly like Christmas trees, Hansl."

"Is Daddy doing it?"

"No, Liebchen." The colored lights were close; very close. She picked him up. "You're a weight, Hansl. Soon you will be too heavy for me to lift."

"When I am a man I will lift you, Fräulein."

"That will be splendid," said Anna-Luisa and kissed the boy.

When the knock came at the door she went to it still carrying Hansl.

"Herr Böll, is something wrong?"

"Good, you are dressed."

"Why?"

"I want you to take shelter this night."

"Shelter?"

"Next door with Herr Voss. Last month he told August that he wanted you and the child to shelter there if the air raids came. His shelter is reinforced and has fans for air. Suffocation is the great danger, you see."

"Tonight?"

"The flares are dropping already. They are target markers. You must hurry."

"But they will not bomb Altgarten."

"Please hurry."

"I must get my shoes and a coat for Hansl."

"I can't wait, Fräulein," said Gerd. "Hurry, and knock loudly on Herr Voss's door. I know he's in because his blackout always has chinks in it, but he plays the gramophone and he may not hear you."

"It was kind of you, Herr Böll."

"I promised August," said Gerd coldly. He swung his leg over the saddle of Frau Klein's bicycle and pedaled away toward the TENO camp.

When the first bombs fell it was a sound new to Anna-Luisa: a slippery, shuffling half-whistle, like a heavy parcel sliding down a metal chute. Each ended with a bang. Not the sort of bang that a firecracker or a pistol makes. This was as different from those bangs as a tuba is from a piccolo. These were big bass brassy bangs that slapped ears, shook the ground under foot and kicked urgently at the windows.

"We must hurry, my darling Hansl."

# 22

THE lights of the final Lancaster disappeared over the hedge of Warley Fen airfield. The sound of that last one became fainter until it too was gone. For a few minutes there always remained an unnatural quiet that made even insensitive people speak in whispers. The Group Captain was not an insensitive person. He stopped signing papers and turned out the desk lamp before drawing the blackout curtains and opening the window. A cold wind made the papers on his desk flap noisily. The flare path was switched off and except for the shielded lights on the corners of each building and a careless blackout in the Operations Block the night was dark and still.

It was always the same for him when the airplanes had gone; the Group Captain felt remote. He had a secret fear that one night none of them would come back and he would sit alone on the airfield forever after. This was the twelfth raid this month. It was too many. His men were tired and so was he. He'd pulled every string he knew to be used as a pathfinder squadron, but if he faced the truth, they weren't up to it. They were very ordinary airmen and he was an unexceptional commander.

He wished he could manage on four hours' sleep a night as so many of the young ones could, but missing sleep made him tired, forgetful and easily irritated. In spite of that he always waited until the planes returned. It would be unthinkable to go back to the house and try to sleep. He hated the place; it was far too large and empty for one man. Warley's previous Station Commander had a wife and three children and so much furniture that he'd been pleased to leave half of it behind when he'd heard that Jarman had no furniture of his own to bring.

He wished Helen had lived long enough to see him get

288

his scrambled egg and a station of his own. Some of his comrades and their wives felt sorry for him in that there had been no children. Laurie and Daphne had even said so. That was because they had no idea of the relationship between a commander and his men on a proper combat station. An operational station: how often they had dreamed of it and joked of it when he was a young acting Flight Lieutenant in the tiny peacetime air force. Then it had seemed that promotion would never come. "Roll on death, promotion is too slow," they used to joke in the mess. Now, my God, it was sometimes too fast. They had kids of air commodores throwing their weight about; kids!

As his eyes became accustomed to the darkness he could see as far as B Flight dispersal. In the tin huts, where men would keep vigil through the cold night, tiny temperamental stoves were being coaxed into flame. The Group Captain sniffed the wood smoke and remembered his seven days in the front line in the spring of 1917; it was his whole leave. Those brave gods had thought him crazy but they had no idea what it did to a young infantry officer to incarcerate him in a supply depot for the entire war. And at a time when at the front the average life of a subaltern was three weeks!

His air crews were even more stringently selected than Haig's young officers and yet in this month alone he'd lost three crews on their first trip. One crew had been here only eight days. They had the courage of a thousand lions and no one would be allowed to mar the honor he felt at being in the front line with them. He sniffed loudly, closed the blackout curtains and turned on the desk light again. The adjutant had left a pile of papers for signing and he continued through them mechanically without reading the contents. It was like being the mayor of a little town. Nowadays he scarcely saw his airplanes.

Again he picked up the note from Laurie at Besteridge.

Dear Jar,

What price Saturday now? Still, no matter; I never said, "Sports results are the acid test of skilled command." But you might be able to convert me to your point of view over a pint.

LAURIE

Attached to the hastily scrawled note there was a newspaper clipping showing a famous cricketer in air force uniform with a Wellington bomber behind him and Laurie grinning alongside. The caption said that the batsman was now knocking bombs into German boundaries and was proud to be a member of the finest team of all—R.A.F.

Group Captain Jarman grunted. He'd never regretted anything more than the much-quoted remark he'd made after his cricket side had won the cup, but that was years before the war, when he was a young kid, commanding a small unit for the first time.

It was only since Laurie had got this damned professional posted there that he'd suddenly taken an interest in cricket and started to borrow good players from all over the Command. The A.O.C. loved it, of course. He and Laurie were as thick as thieves lately. Laurie had a devastating memory for indiscretions. Not his own, of course, but his rivals'. God knows what else he'd be saying in the mess on Saturday after they'd wiped the floor with Warley's keen but amateurish eleven. Sweet had taken over as captain this season and had done a pretty good job with them, except that this slow bowler—he looked down at his notebook—Lambert hadn't even put in an appearance for the last few games. The Group Captain filled his pipe carefully and lit it.

There was a knock at the door and his clerk came in. "Corporal Taylor," she announced. She was just going off duty.

"Hello, Corporal Taylor. That's all right, stand at ease. I don't think we've met before." He smiled. "But you've probably seen me about. You're in Safety Equipment, aren't you?"

"Yes, sir."

"And now you are probably wondering why I sent for you."

Corporal Taylor said nothing.

"Sit down, Corporal. As perhaps you know, we have a tradition in the R.A.F. that on certain occasions officers and men talk what we call 'man to man.' You probably know what I mean by that."

Corporal Taylor still didn't speak.

"It means that what we say to each other is informal. It means that you no longer have to weigh each word you say in case it might be what we call 'conduct to the prejudice of good order.'" He smiled paternally. "At times I've had fellows cut up frightfully rough when I've let them do that. Of course they've regretted it afterward, I've made sure of that, but meanwhile I've been able to get to the bottom of something that's troubled them. Smoke, Corporal?"

"No, thank you, sir."

"Now, how long have you been married to Flight Sergeant Lambert?"

"Three months, sir."

"Are you happy here, Corporal? Why aren't you happy there, my girl? What's so different about that aerodrome?" The Group Captain was so like her father.

How could anyone describe it? Low-power bulbs at dead of night, iron beds, dirty linen, damp walls and a door banging desolately. Behind it some bereaved girl is taking an unendurably hot bath and drinking gin. "It's the war, Dad."

"I'm near to my husband."

"Exactly, and meanwhile you've continued to use your single name for WAAF records."

"Yes, sir. I've been meaning to do something about it but . . ."

"But Section Officer Holroyd hasn't chased you up about it and you're frightened that you'll be posted elsewhere if Records hear."

"Yes, sir."

"Well, I've spoken to Miss Holroyd about you and she tells me you're a conscientious worker and she feels that on an operational station efficiency is the main thing."

"Yes, sir."

"Yes, there's nothing more important than efficiency in this day and age. There's nothing more important than killing Huns. The R.A.F. has no Colonel Blimps. It's a young service with young ideas and it's not hidebound by rules and regulations, but there must be a matter of give and take. You know what I mean."

"Perhaps I will have a cigarette, sir."

"Here we are, matches on the desk. But give and take means that the air force expects people to have a similar goodwill in return, Mrs. Lambert, and that's what I want to talk to you about."

"Yes, sir," said Ruth.

"Your husband, Mrs. Lambert, is one of my most experienced captains. There are not many people on this station who were flying in 1937: myself of course, Wing Commander Munro . . ." The Group Captain felt that it was not a good line to pursue. "Anyway, when we've got a chap—a regular R.A.F. air crew bod—painting Communist slogans across his aircraft, what will people think, eh?"

"Communist slogans?"

"Communist slogans, Mrs. Lambert. 'Joe Stalin for King.' You would call that a Communist slogan, I take it?"

"I would call it a joke, sir. When people say that, they don't intend it to be taken literally, I mean, everyone is saying it. I've even heard it on the wireless."

"And that's exactly what we've got to be careful about."

"But that's not painted on my husband's aircraft. That's painted on Sergeant Carter's *L for Love*."

"Allow me to know my own airplanes, Mrs. Lambert. You'll have to allow me that." He smiled, pitying her feminine limitations.

"Is that what you wanted me for, sir?"

"No, it isn't, Corporal. I've sent for you to see if we can't get to the bottom of what's troubling your husband. Mrs. Lambert, he seems determined to challenge authority. And on this aerodrome"—he smiled—"well I'm authority."

"Challenged you, sir?"

He leaned back in his chair, not sure of how to continue. When he began to speak again it was with a new tone of voice as though he had decided to reveal everything to her in a sudden attempt at reason. "As you might know, Mrs. Lambert, I'm a committee man. Can't help it; always have been, always will be. You get a reputation for helping with one set of chaps and each of them will be off trying to get you on some other committee. But if there's one darned committee I'm pleased to be on it's the cricket committee. It was my idea to appeal to the public for used cricket gear. Last year we staged parades, we flew a Lancaster over Peterborough dropping leaflets about it and had collections at the local cinemas whenever there was a flying film running. Got a trainload of cricket gear too. Well, that's good stuff, Mrs. Lambert. Keeps the chaps fit and amused. Cricket's a little like flying in combat, I always say: long leisurely time in the pavilion followed by brief moments when a chap faces some fast bowling. Damned like cricket, saving your presence, Mrs. Lambert. Understand?"

"I don't think I do, sir."

"The cricket match on Saturday, R.A.F. Warley Fen versus R.A.F. Little Besteridge. I want Warley to win, Mrs. Lambert. That's natural enough, isn't it?"

Ruth smiled. It seemed so childish to go to all this trouble about a game. "And you want my husband in the team?"

"Well, of course. We all know he's the finest slow bowler in the Group. With him we'll knock spots off them but without him we've got no bowler worth the name."

"And this match is special? I mean, you haven't minded that he hasn't played much recently."

"Trust you to see right through me, Mrs. Lambert. As my mother once said, there's not a woman in the world who can't see right through me. Yes, the Station Commander at Little Besteridge is a chap I've known for years. He once played for 3 Group. If his dotty little Maintenance Unit at Besteridge beats us he's going to make life hell for me on every committee meeting afterward." He laughed and puffed at his pipe.

"You flatter me by suggesting that I can influence my husband, sir. And even if I could, I'm not sure that it would be wise."

"Come, come, Mrs. Lambert, I'm not that naïve, and neither are you. Give and take, take and give. That's the air force. You are living unofficially with your husband in the village when it's strictly against regulations, but your Section Officer and I don't want to be unreasonable. . . ."

Ruth looked round the room as if seeking a way of escape. It was dark and inhospitable and the air was charged with the herbal scent of the C.O.'s tobacco. Over his desk lamp there was a flypaper, its gum shiny in the yellow glare. There were a dozen flies on it and not all of them were dead. She knew she'd not been brought here to be consulted or even commanded. Nor did his intimate confessions of frailty convince her that he was anything but devious. She had been brought to bear witness that the C.O. was a man of infinite compassion and wisdom, a man devoid of personal ambition or prejudice, reluctant to see her husband punished for his intractable behavior. Ruth's father was like this. She remembered the way in which he'd humiliated her very first boyfriend and afterward pretended to be unaware of having done so.

Ruth put one of her fingernails into the back of her hand until it almost bled; she wanted to be oblivious of everything except that little pain and she knew that if she were stoical about it this frightening old man and his clever questions would disappear. When she looked up he had not disappeared. "I don't know what you want of me," she said. She hoped he would reply, "Nothing."

"All I'm asking of you, Corporal, is to convey an un-official message to your husband." He tapped his pipe into the ashtray. "I'm even thinking of taking him off fly-ing duties." He watched Ruth during this slow and studied declaration but he saw no change in her calm face. He was growing impatient of this foolish girl. A loyal wife would have immediately perceived the trouble that was in store for her husband. Her silliness was almost funny and he permitted himself a trace of a smile. "You know what being taken off flying duties will involve, Mrs. Lambert?"

Ruth had been frightened that the Group Captain would see her hands trembling, so nervous was she, but his smile changed all that. It was the brief smile that some men kept ready for women, babies and respectful beggars. Both patronizing and complacent, it triggered in her a righteous wrath. She tried to keep her voice low and calm as she replied but the anger in her voice could not be concealed. "I know what it will involve, sir. That's the ultimate punishment in the air force. But it doesn't fright-en me. How do you think I feel when I watch his plane take off at night? I'm lying awake full of sleeping pills that have no effect, waiting for a ring at the bell instead of the sound of his key in the lock. When they are diverted be-cause of bad weather it's worse. I stay near a phone all the time waiting in case one of the girls from Flying Control might have heard something about the casualties. Take him off flying, if that's your decision, and then I'll have a husband who will live to see the war over."

He pretended to concern himself with the papers on his desk. "I don't think you understand the disgrace that will go with him being grounded. Have you . . . ?"

She was determined not to raise her voice again. "Dis-grace is only for men. Save talk of that for your schools and your clubs and your old comrades' dinners. Save talk of disgrace until you lose your cricket match, or for the next hesitant hero."

He looked up. "Is that the way you will bring up your children, Mrs. Lambert, without pride and without honor?" He said it as though he thought it most likely.

"Ask the widows of your dead air crews how they ex-plain honor to their fatherless children. Or to the rent collector."

She twisted her wedding ring nervously and looked into the old man's eyes to see what effect her words were having. Like her father, he refused to reveal his discomposure even when, as now, she was promising to stop. Oh well, she would continue: "If you really want to know what I mean by disgrace, it's to hear you talking about killing Huns as though it was a manly duel instead of blowing people and their homes to pieces." How could this old man ever understand? she thought. He has no wife, no children, no home.

"Just make sure your husband knows what's involved, Corporal."

"Don't worry, sir, everyone on this station knows what's involved. We are all playing in your cricket match, aren't we? I wonder what your team will score over Krefeld tonight. And I wonder if my husband will be run out."

The Group Captain said, "I think that will be all, Corporal. We shall be rectifying your present position vis-à-vis your marriage."

"You can decide between making my husband very unhappy or me very unhappy. But one of us will be quite content."

"You are dismissed, Corporal." She stood up slowly and gave a salute of insolent perfection. Level with her eyes a fly buzzed frantically but could not escape from the sticky paper.

One had these hysterical women to deal with and yet there was a limit to the disciplinary action possible. If an airman had even thought those things he would have stripped him of his rank and put him into the greenhouse, but these women couldn't be treated like that. They were just uniformed civilians really and in any case they'd always think of some womanly ailment to excuse themselves. Or else they'd go off and get themselves pregnant. What's the use?

He'd been a damned fool to speak to her in these circumstances, especially at night. A Groupie in Coastal had reprimanded a WAAF sergeant for losing some stores, whereupon she'd cried her eyes out and practically yelled rape. It had finished up with the Groupie apologizing. Apologizing!

When she'd gone he rang the buzzer on his desk. "In the morning I shall want to speak to Section Officer Holroyd."

"Shall I pencil in the subject?" said his clerk.

"No. I shan't forget what I'm going to talk to her about."

He could, of course, be elsewhere when Laurie brought

his damned cricket team here on Saturday. It was damned disgraceful: that hysterical girl going on like that at the very moment when his lads were risking their brave young bodies.

## ♣ 23 ♣

*"Levator labii superioris aloequae nasi."* For no reason at all Pilot Officer Fleming, at the controls of *The Volkswagen*, intoned the words like grace. He had in fact once said it as grace in the Officers' Mess and had got by unchallenged, but he'd taken care not to do it when the Medical Officer was at table.

"What's that, sir?" said Bertie, the flight engineer, who thought it might be a technical matter he'd neglected.

Fleming closed his eyes and tilted his head. "It's the longest name of any muscle in the human body."

"What's the name of the shortest one?" said the mid-upper gunner and was promptly answered insultingly, accusingly and unscientifically by the wireless operator.

"O.K., chaps," said Fleming. "Let's have a bit of hush."

Four of the Leiden searchlights had been on for some time but now another six were switched on. "Look at that," said Fleming.

"Searchlights," said the flight engineer. In every group of lights there was one that remained vertical. That one was controlled by a Würzburg radar; it was called the master searchlight.

"I'm going to steer a bit to the north, Mac," Fleming told his navigator. "No sense in heading straight toward that muck."

"Don't let's even head for the fringe of it," said the flight engineer.

Fleming laughed; perhaps the boy wasn't such an idiot after all. It was a bad system, training an engineer apart from the crew. Fleming had known the rest of them for weeks, but he'd flown only a few hours with this child, his assistant pilot. Fleming wondered if the boy could handle the controls sufficiently well for him to go back

to the lavatory. Next trip he would take that tin can he'd
been offered and be grateful for it. Was it fear that did
it? He'd noticed that the engineer and the bomb aimer
had already been back there. It was easy for them, but
he was strapped into the pilot's seat and getting out of
it was a struggle.

Fear should tighten the rectum and bladder, not loosen
them, or so his medical training told him. In the Briefing
Room he had watched his fellowmen grow pale as fear
diverted their newly thinned blood from the skin and the
viscera to the brain. That's why so many had been unable
to eat their supper. He'd felt his own heart begin to beat
faster as his blood—now red-corpuscle dominated, sugar-
rich and laden with adrenalin—rose in pressure. He
handled the heavy controls with newly found strength and
knew that fear had supplied blood to his muscles and his
liver had released carbohydrate into his veins. His lungs
benefited too, taking more oxygen in breaths that were
both deeper and faster.

The first sight of the searchlights had provided him with
further physiological evidence of his fear: loss of peristalsis
and gastric juice had turned his supper into a hard knot
and his saliva had gone, so that his tongue was rough
against his mouth. Lastly, his scrotum had constricted
tight against his body. Resulting from these changes Fleming believed he could detect a rise in body temperature
as a result of the increased basal metabolic rate. To confirm his theory a trickle of sweat rolled down his spine.
His father—a truly dedicated physician—would be interested to hear of these observations.

"Keep this course, Skip," said the navigator. "We'll turn
five miles inland instead of over Noordwijk. That should
keep us well clear of Leiden."

"Okey dokey," said Fleming and for the first time felt
truly like a skipper.

Robin, fellow officer and bomb aimer, had been sitting
at the navigator's table filling in his log. He collected up
his parachute, target map, log and Thermos flask, disconnected his oxygen supply and came forward. He
pushed the flight engineer gently to one side and, waving
a greeting to Fleming at the controls, bent double to put
his foot downward until it reached the step formed by
the glycol tank. Carefully he ducked his head under the
traversing ring of the front gun turret with its twin
Browning guns. This was his world. It was quieter here.
He spread the map out and lay full length, with his belly

on the exit hatch and his head in the clear-view bowl that
formed the nose of the airplane. Outside, the night was
growing lighter; the moon was coming out. He looked
round with interest but not surprise; he had always known
it would be like this.

To the right, one of the searchlight beams was shorter
than the others and instead of tapering, its beam ended
in a blunt hammerhead. "Look," said Robin, "they've got
someone in the searchlights."

"Poor swine," said Fleming as he watched more searchlights affix their beams to the airplane.

The trapped plane was tilting and twisting like a tormented animal, but although it broke clear of some of the
beams, always at least one of them hung on to it. The
flak had started now; some of the bursts were so close to
it that the smoke obscured their view for a second or two
but still the plane flew on.

"We have him on our set now," said Löwenherz.

"Where do you want him?"

"Just starboard and level."

"Let me put him a trifle high, Herr Oberleutnant."

"Very well."

"We're closing too fast again."

In the searchlights everything was white. Two more had
him now and they were fixing him to the sky like gleaming hatpins holding a fluttering white moth in a black
velvet box. There was a brief flicker under the plane and
it shivered slightly.

"He's hit."

"It's *B Beer*, the Navigation Leader."

"The immortal Lud."

The navigator couldn't see. "Are they getting out?"

"No, he's jettisoning his bombs."

As they watched it the bomber seemed to swell up very
gently with a soft *whoomp* that was audible far across
the sky. It became a ball of burning petrol, oil and pyrotechnic compounds. The yellow datum marker, which
should have marked the approach to Krefeld, burned
brightly as it fell away, leaving thin trails of sparks. The
fireball changed from red to light pink as its rising temperature enabled it to devour new substances from hydraulic fluid and human fat to engine components of
manganese, vanadium, and copper. Finally even the airframe burned. Ten tons of magnesium alloy flared with a
strange greenish blue light. It lit up the countryside beneath it like a slow flash of lightning and was gone. For

a moment a cloud of dust illuminated by the searchlights
floated in the sky and then even that disappeared.

"Jee—sus!" exclaimed Pilot Officer Cornelius Fleming
in horror.

"No parachutes," pronounced Robin from the nose.
The searchlights began moving again.

"Flak did it," said the mid-upper gunner, who had the
best view of all.

Far away near Utrecht, Fleming saw another master
searchlight tilt from the vertical position at which it
rested. The top of its beam seemed to explode as it moved
across cloud patches. Between the patches it reached sev-
en miles into the sky. Unfalteringly it found a victim.

"The stream isn't routed over Leiden," said Fleming to
his crew. "All of those aircraft are off course." It sounded
not only prim but callous, but before he could modify the
sentiment the mid-upper gunner said, "I don't give a
bugger who they are; it takes the heat off us and for that I
am truly grateful. Amen."

"Kettledrums, kettledrums," said Löwenherz.

"Lancaster," said the observer, putting away his field
glasses.

Löwenherz hardly increased speed at all; he inched
underneath the huge airplane very very slowly. He looked
up through the tip of his cabin and he could see every
detail of it. He let its red-hot exhaust pipes pass back
overhead until he was exactly underneath the bomber. The
two planes roared through the sky in close formation
until, in the classic maneuver of the night fighter, Löwenherz pulled the control column back with all his strength.
His nose went up closer and closer to the great bomber.
The fighter shuddered as it neared stalling point, hanging
on its propellers, thrashing like a drowning man but suspended and stationary for a moment. Over him came the
bomber. "Horrido," said Löwenherz to tell Bach what he
was about to do, and he pressed his gun buttons and raked
its belly from nose to tail. The gunfire lit both aircraft
with a gentle greenish light. Löwenherz squinted to
preserve his night vision as much as possible. These Richards were nothing but highpowered gun platforms and the
demented hammering of the big cannons deafened the
fliers even through their closely fitting helmets—just as the
smell of cordite got into their nostrils in spite of their
oxygen masks. Working exactly by the instruction book,
Löwenherz kept his guns going even after the nose of the

Junkers began to fall back toward earth. Suddenly the gunfire ended. The drums were empty.

Three 20-mm. M.G. F.F. cannons were fitted in the nose of Löwenherz's Junkers 88R. In sequence of threes there was a thin-cased shell containing 19.5 grams of Hexogen Al. high explosive filling, an explosive armor-piercing shell with a reinforced point and an incendiary that burned at a temperature between 2,000 and 3,000 degrees centigrade for nearly one second. Each cannon was firing at the rate of 520 rounds per minute and was fed by a drum containing 60 rounds. So in seven seconds all of the cannon drums were empty and 180 shells had been fired at *The Volkswagen*. The target measured 300 square feet, and 38 struck the airplane. Theoretically 20 shells would have constituted an average lethal blow.

"My legs," screamed Fleming. "God! Help me, Mother Mother Mother!"

The first shell that penetrated the aircraft came through the forward hatch. Missing the bomb aimer by only an inch, it exploded on contact with the front turret mounting ring. It dislocated the turret, severed the throttle and rudder controls, burst the compressed air tank and broke open the window-spray glycol container. In the airstream the coolant atomized into a cloud of white mist. One-twenty-sixth of a second later the second shell came through the bomb compartment and exploded under the floor of the navigator's position. In the mysterious manner of explosions, it sucked the navigator downward, while blowing the astrodome, and the wireless operator standing under it, out into the night unharmed. Although without his parachute.

Three shells—one H.E., one A.P. and one incendiary—exploded in glancing contact with the starboard fuselage exterior immediately to the rear of the mid-upper turret. Apart from mortally harming the gunner, the explosion of the H.E. shell fractured the metal formers at a place where, after manufacture, the rear part of the fuselage is bolted on. The incendiary shell completed the severance. A structural bisection of *The Volkswagen* occurred one and a half minutes later and two thousand feet lower. Long before this, another H.E. shell passed through the elevator hinge bracket on the tail and blew part of the servo trim tab assembly into the rear turret with such force that it decapitated the rear gunner. Those six hits were the most telling ones, but there were thirty-two

others. Some ricocheted off the engines and wings and
penetrated the fuselage almost horizontally.

He couldn't hold her, he couldn't. Oh dear God, his
arms and legs! Dropping through the night like the paper
airplane. "I'm sorry, chaps," he shouted, for he felt a
terrible sense of guilt. Involuntarily his bowels and bladder
relaxed and he felt himself befouled. "I'm sorry."

It was no use for Fleming to scream apologies; there
was no one aboard to hear him. He outlived any of his
crew, for from 16,000 feet the wireless operator falling at
120 m.p.h. (the terminal velocity for his weight) reached
the ground ninety seconds later. He made an indentation
12 inches deep. This represented a deceleration equivalent
to 450 times the force of gravity. He split open like a
slaughtered animal and died instantly. Fleming, still
strapped into the pilot's seat and aghast at his inconti-
nence, hit the earth (along with the front of the fuselage,
two Rolls-Royce engines and most of the main spar) some
four minutes after that. To him it seemed like four hours.

The air-conditioning in Ermine's plotting room wasn't
intended to cope with so many off-duty personnel standing
round as spectators. In addition, the tension seemed to
raise a man's body temperature, as does a meal. August
mopped his brow and heard Löwenherz give the traditional victory cry: "Sieg Heil!"

"Sieg Heil!" said August. Willi came to attention and
gave August a formal salute of congratulation in a situation where most men would have shaken him by the hand.
There were shuffles and coughs from the onlookers and
murmurs of congratulation. The loudspeaker crackled.

"He's breaking up," said Löwenherz. "The main spar
has snapped and the fuselage is doubling back like a
hairpin."

Willi wiped the wax marks off the table.

"Order: Go to Heinz Gustav One," said August.

"Please: Via Noordwijk?"

"Announcement: Yes, Katze One." To Willi August
said, "He might get a visual contact if they are still putting
flares down but I can't call the flak to a stop just because
he is overflying them."

"He won't hang around," said Willi. "He's a bright
fellow."

"We're all smart fellows," said August. Willi smiled at
August, his ruddy battered face twisted like a freshly
squeezed orange.

Löwenherz let the Junkers fall from its vertical position and after gaining speed he eased the antlers back and began climbing to fly back through the stream. Mrosek took off his seat straps, lit his torch and crawled down into the nose to change the 60-round cannon magazines on the Oerlikons. Löwenherz held the same shallow climb, but a patch of turbulent air caused Mrosek to blister his hand upon the breech. Changing the drums was an awkward job even on the ground in daytime, but Mrosek never complained. They flew on past Noordwijk without spotting any bombers, although there was lots of flak, including even some brightly colored 3.7-cm. stuff from Valkenburg aerodrome. The Junkers continued right out to the extreme western end of Ermine's range. Those two interceptions had been quick and easy, but next time he might need to traverse the whole sector under August's guidance before he made a contact.

In *Joe for King*, Roland Pembroke, the young Scots navigator, had overcompensated for the wind error. His Gee was unusable owing to German jamming. Now his mistake had brought *Joe for King* to the Dutch coast five miles south of the turning point. Ahead of him, flying through flak and searchlights, there were others who had made the same error of reckoning.

"We'll go south of it," said Tommy Carter.

"South of Leiden?" said Roland, who had worked out his plot carefully and rather objected to abandoning the flight plan.

"South of that muck," said Tommy, waving toward the flak and lights ahead of them.

"O.K., boss," said Roland.

The brand-new airplane had a strong smell of fresh paint and varnish. The controls were hard and stiff under Tommy Carter's hands and as he turned the wheel it made brittle cracking sounds. On the other hand, everything worked properly. On his previous airplane two or three of the instruments were suspect and would stick and lag behind the others. In some ways he liked having this nice new airplane. He wondered whether they'd be allowed to keep it.

Tommy knew it as a bad idea as soon as he changed onto the new heading. It wasn't only Leiden that was alive with flak, it was this whole coast; The Hague under the starboard wing was damn nearly as bad as Leiden. There were Grossbatterien of dozens of guns and searchlights working under radar control. The whole land was asparkle with gunfire. Tommy fixed his eyes upon a black region of countryside beyond the gunfire and pushed the throttles forward.

"Close your eyes and swallow," said Tommy. "It will soon be gone." The motors screamed loudly.

There was an explosion rather nearer than the previous ones. It rocked the wings and made an acrid smell.

"There's light stuff too," said Tapper Collins, the bomb aimer. He was in the nose watching ropes of red and yellow tracer curve toward them and fall away at what he knew to be thousands of feet below but which looked close enough to touch. "Lots of light stuff now, from directly below us."

"That must be the aerodrome at Valkenburg," said Roland Pembroke.

"Jesus," said Tommy. "Leiden to the left of us, Hague to the right of us and now we are doing a straight and level over a bloody Hun aerodrome. What do you think you're on, charge of the flipping Light Brigade?"

"Sorry, Tommy," said Roland politely. He didn't point out that the change of route was Tommy's idea.

Tommy Carter didn't answer, for at that moment all of his attention was taken with a searchlight that, having remained vertical and immobile for some time, had tilted and now moved toward them.

"It's coming at us," shouted Collins from his position at the bombsight.

"You berk, Tommy!" shouted Ben Gallacher, and Tommy Carter was outraged that he should be blamed for something so obviously beyond his control and not of his liking.

"Sideslip down the beam," said Collins. He was a veteran and Tommy respected his experience. This new airplane required extra strength to move its controls. He heaved at them and banked until the light was blinding bright. It had them. The cockpit was so brightly lit that it made his eyes ache and he could see only by almost closing them.

The theory was that is you sideslipped down the beam the seachlight would(by continuing to move along) lose you. This searchlight crew seemed to have seen the trick before, although in fact Tommy Carter's sideslip was not nearly violent enough to test the theory.

"Fire into the light," Tommy shouted.

"Turn more, I can't reach, I'm full traverse and I can't reach," called the gunner.

Suddenly the light went out. Tommy and Ben tugged at

the controls and the bomber eased out of its steep bank. The flak and searchlight had gone and the night was agreeably dark and silent. He began to climb again. It was more than a minute before anyone spoke and then everyone spoke, chattering hysterically and trying to make jokes.

"Everyone shut up," said Tommy Carter in the tone he used when he didn't want an argument—what his crew called his copper's voice.

"Navigator," said Tommy with unusual formality of address, "give me a course so that we'll join the stream beyond Leiden."

"O-eight-five," said Roland in his prime public school accent.

They flew on in a silence broken only by the drone of the motors. "Sorry, boys," said Tommy finally, intimidated by the silence of his crew. "Bloody stupid of me to go south of Leiden."

"That was a master searchlight," said Collins, the expert. "The blue ones are always radar controlled." Because arc lamps seem more blue when angled toward the viewer, R.A.F. crews believed that the ones pointing at them (the bluish ones) were the most accurate, i.e. radar contolled. Luftwaffe crews over Britain believed the same thing, but there were no blue searchlights.

"Then why did the flaming thing go off?" said Ben Gallacher.

"We were a bit small," said Tommy. "They decided to throw us back and wait for a Stirling."

"I'd like to know why," said Ben.

"It's a secret new weapon that some of our planes carry," theorized Collins.

"We'll never know for certain," said Tommy, "so belt up and be grateful."

At that moment on the ground near Valkenburg a young Irdian Feldwebel was shouting abuse in Hindustani, which is well suited for that purpose. He watched three phlegmatic signals regiment mechanics remove the front of his searchlight. In the British army, before capture, they had been separated by caste. The Wehrmacht, however, had mixed their new volunteers together, with only these brightly colored turbans—lilac, ocher, green, and even pink and white with blue spots—to show the difference between himself and the lowest of the pariahs. Again he swore an ancient oath at the mechanics. One of the fools proclaimed it to be an ill omen. It was difficult to

contradict him, for today they had been told that the local
Dutch civilians had protested at the presence of *kaffers*
and they were to be moved to France with all their new
flak equipment.

This was one of the first of the new high-performance
200-cm. lights to be delivered. A beauty—2.7 million
candlepower. Damn! He kicked the cable angrily. It was
just his luck that, after a first-class contact on the
Würzburg and a *Tommi* in the beam, just then the
carbons should go. Sometimes he wished he were back
home in Delhi.

In the potato fields a few miles to the west of Ahaus the
young Leutnant who had spoken to August and Max
during their delay on the road surveyed his Grossbatterie.
The two Hitler Jugend guns were manned and ready;
those boys were always the keenest. Some of the other
guns were not completely jacked up and some were not
even uncoupled from their prime movers. It had been a
long hard day, with many delays on the road and his
Oberst complaining every step of the journey.

The young Leutnant sniffed the air and detected a faint
smell of soot and smoke. Whenever the wind was from the
south it brought the aroma of the Ruhr with it. During
last month's raids the air had also carried the smell of
fouled earth, brick dust, cordite and burning buildings.

The sound of aircraft engines came suddenly. He
phoned to his control room and when the phone was in his
hands he looked up and saw the glint of moonlight upon
a wing. He saw it for only a moment and it was too high
to be more than a speck of light but it was leaving a
condensation trail that glowed in the moonlight. Even had
his 8.8-cm. guns been ready to fire they couldn't reach
that height.

The information was passed to Deelen but already it
was superfluous. Other reports showed that the aircraft
were two Mosquitoes at 32,000 feet.

"They are turning at Ahaus," said the Plot Officer.

The Operations Officer moved his hand to make an arc
southward from Ahaus, pivoting upon the Oboe transmitter at Dover. His thumb swiveled across the open country
until it encountered the shaded pattern of a large town in
the Ruhr. He looked then at the bomber stream's reported
position. The heading of the bombers would bring them
over the same place.

"Krefeld," he said. "I'll bet a week's pay on it."

The other officer nodded. He didn't take up the wager.

The plan was now clear. On their present heading the bomber stream would pass over Krefeld at half past midnight. Moving a hundred miles an hour faster and turning to approach from the north, the Mosquitoes—with their secret Oboe device—would pass over Krefeld three minutes earlier. That would be exactly enough time for the colored indicator bombs to mark the target for the heavy bombers.

The routes were converging like the rays of light through a burning glass and tonight attention was focusing on one town. The leaflet raids over northern France, the lone Mosquito that was causing the alarms to sound all the way to Berlin, and the dog-leg course that had taken the stream to Noordwijk before turning were all clearly seen for the ruses they were; the target for tonight was Krefeld. Deelen Control and Duisburg FLUKO began to arrange the defenses of the Reich accordingly.

In peacetime a complicated electronic device like Oboe would have spent six months more on the test bench and four or five in prototype, and anything up to a year would have passed before they were sold, installed and in use. But this was war and Oboe was in production. It needed nursing all the way to the target and even then it was no surprise to Flying Officer MacIntosh when the set went dead twenty-five miles short of Krefeld.

"Not a sausage. What a nuisance; the signals were clear as a bell—then it went dead."

"We'll turn back then."

"Might as well. We're on a curve but we'll never find the target with a dud set."

"Bloody thing. I canceled a date tonight."

"You shouldn't have joined."

The Mosquito turned abruptly until it faced west to England. There was no sense in going a yard nearer to the Ruhr than was absolutely essential.

"Let's get out of here, Mac."

There were two radio transmitting stations in England from which the signals went to activate Oboe. The stations could handle only two Mosquitoes every ten minutes. The two planes that should mark the target for the very first bombers to arrive were now reduced to one plane. That one was piloted by Pilot Officer Alan Hill; his observer was Peter Hutchinson.

They had done everything according to the book. They

had flown at 32,000 feet, for only at this height were the
signals able to reach over the radar horizon. At a point
fifty miles north of Krefeld they had turned southward.
Keeping the steady beat of the signals in his ears, the pilot
had banked his wing to fly a gentle curve that would—at
the moment the signal from the second transmitter
reached him—bring him at the right distance from Krefeld to allow for the forward movement through the air of
the 250-pound target indicator bombs.

They did not know that the accompanying Mosquito
had turned away with its Oboe device out of action. Nor
did they know that they were accompanied by a German
airplane up in this region of the sky that was almost the
stratosphere. It was a specially equipped Ju88S in which
the GM1 system injected nitrous oxide into the supercharg-
ers and thus provided oxygen that boosted its performance by nearly twenty percent. Its endurance was
measured in minutes and a few nights previously it had
used up its Ha-ha device just as it caught sight of the
Mosquito. Tonight there had been no miscalculation.
Tonight the moonlight had made the upper reaches of the
sky into a floodlit arena.

"Bombs armed," reported the observer. At the speed
they were going, Krefeld was only two minutes away.
There was suddenly a thumping sound and the controls
were wrenched from the pilot's grasp. The panel was bent
and torn and the glass from its instruments flew in all
directions. Two Perspex panels had suddenly gone white
and the sky was no longer to be seen through them. Even
when the bangs stopped, the engines were screaming an
octave above their normal tone. The Mosquito performed
a flick roll, steadied itself for a moment and then put its
nose up and stalled. As he dived the aircraft to regain
control they saw the Ju88 far away on the port beam. Its
wings shone in the moonlight as it turned to find them for
a second attack.

"Fire!" shouted Peter Hutchinson.

"What with?" shouted Alan Hill angrily, until he noticed
that the port engine was coughing blue flame and spitting
orange sparks and his few remaining instrument needles
were collapsing. He wrenched at the tiny jettison box by
his side and tore a nail as he broke the safety wires.
There was a lurch as two 250-pound target indicator
bombs—each almost as big as a man—fell out of the
bomb bay, and then he struggled with the box for what
seemed like hours until the other two went. Relieved of

the weight of its bomb load, the airplane responded more readily to its controls. He kept the nose down and headed desperately for the cloud bank, but it was still 2000 feet below him as the Ju88 came in again. More pieces of wing disappeared as the cannon shells punched holes through the wood.

"To hear you two young fellows talk you'd think the Germans had no fighter plants."

"They don't as far as we're concerned, Dad. We're too high for them."

"Well, I didn't say this in front of your mother, Alan, but mark my words, your Jerry is a damn good engineer and if he wants to get up to you, one of these nights he'll do it."

"Drink up, Dad, we've two more days of leave yet."

"And change the subject, I know. Your job's too hush-hush to talk to your father about."

"Peter, Peter, jump! She's coming to pieces." Peter didn't move. That last attack must have done it. Please God, don't let that Junkers come round again!

In the Junkers the fuel warning lights were on. He'd had his forty-five minutes' fun and now the nitrous oxide was used. He turned away from the Mosquito. It was done for, he could see that. He wondered if Luftwaffe High Command would let him claim it; they were so keen to keep the Ha-ha secret.

Alan Hill held the stick with one hand and shook Peter frantically with the other. There was no sign of life. He grabbed at the flying helmet and turned the head to look into his friend's glassy eyes. As he shook him the oxygen mask fell aside and he had difficulty in refixing it. Peter's face was covered with fresh blood.

Down where the bomber stream was flying it was cold—colder than the coldest of domestic freezers—but up here it was much colder. Sixty degrees below zero and the air was rarefied and its pressure fatally low for a human lung. Alan undid his safety belt and Peter's too before he put the stick over. When the Mosquito was upside down he fell out of his seat. He tried to pull his observer with him but Peter's leg was caught under the bent instrument panel. He tugged at Peter's arm but that too became bloody even as he watched.

Alan took one last gulp of oxygen and then, holding his breath, he let himself fall. He dropped a long, long way before pulling the rip cord but even so he had slight frostbite and lost the joint of an index finger that stuck to the metal handle. Perfectly, the canopy bloomed above him. He landed in a plowed field two miles from the Dutch border. His only other injury was a bad cut on his right hand that must have happened during the first attack. He realized then that the blood on Peter's face and arm was from this cut. He asked himself if he could have saved Peter's life. Alan was interned together with other bomber crews and was thus not interrogated in the way he would have been had they guessed him to be an Oboe pilot. He spent the rest of the war in a prison camp and died aged forty-nine in a motorcar accident in Liverpool, and yet there was not a day when he did not ask himself that same question.

A layer of cold air lay close upon the great district of the Ruhr, untroubled by any wind. This cold still air trapped smoke from the furnaces and factories and held it like a gray woolen blanket. Water droplets had built up against this layer and formed a roof as dense and flat and smooth as a sheet of gray aspic: what today we call smog. One target indicator jettisoned by the Oboe Mosquito went into this layer near the Rhine at Duisburg. The second went into the Rhine. One and half minutes and nine miles later the second two landed on the southeast edge of Altgarten.

Detonated by barometric pressure at 1,000 feet, each marker bomb spewed benzol, rubber and phosphorus for a hundred yards in all directions, so that there were two pools of red-colored fire easily seen by the bomber stream four miles above the earth. It was Altgarten's fate to be on the track of the bombers as they flew from the coast toward Krefeld. Had the bombers passed a few more miles to one side or the other then the stream might not have seen the burning T.I.'s waiting to be bombed. It was an extra misfortune for the town that the markers dropped on its far side, for the creepback would start to bring the bombing right across the town toward the approaching stream. Each crew would bomb as early as they could do so without shame. Then they would turn away before the concentration of guns and searchlights that guarded the Ruhr on Altgarten's far side. Perhaps some of the more experienced crews would not have been deceived by the markers into bombing the little town, except that to the H2S radar the acres of green houses that were Altgarten's special pride appeared on the green radar screen like enormous factories.

The first Finder circled twice before putting flares down

to the southeast of the markers, trying to get a visual confirmation. Then a Supporter—on his first trip—put a string of high explosive between the flares and the red T.I.s and a second Supporter did the same. The last of these bombs hit the Venlo road and set fire to a gas main.

Tommy Carter in *Joe for King* the second was a Backer Up. He arrived five minutes early and put his four green markers onto the reds. One thousand feet above Altgarten sixty pyrotechnic candles were ejected from each marker. Each was suspended under a tiny parachute. Falling in close proximity and according to wind and weight they assumed the shape of a bunch of fiery grapes, or, if bottom-heavy, a Christmas tree.

Within ten minutes dozens of Supporters and Finders had dumped their flares and H.E. upon Altgarten and inevitably the release points were creeping back northwest across the town.

Meanwhile, at zero plus three minutes, an Oboe Mosquito arrived exactly on time over Krefeld and marked the real target with four perfectly placed reds. They burned unseen by the bombing force. By now attention had been centered upon Altgarten and the plan had begun to go terribly wrong.

# ♦ 24 ♦

Afterward there were those who said that the Burgomaster was pleased when the first flares dropped near Altgarten. Karl Keller, one of the waiters from the Stube, said that he'd left there with a smile on his face after the warning had been delivered to him. But, as one of the civil defense messengers said, it was his birthday and he had just finished a banquet in his home; why shouldn't he be smiling?

An official car was waiting outside Frenzel's and the Burgomaster was taken at high speed through the empty streets to the Rathaus, where a policeman saluted him smartly as he descended the steps to the heavily sand-bagged control room. Inside, three civil defense girls were at their desks, and two Hitler Jugend cyclists were uniformed and at attention in the anteroom.

"Red Christmas tree flares one mile to the southeast: 0129." The girl smiled. "That's probably somewhere in Frau Kersten's fields."

"Mark it in on the map, Fraülein."

The telephonist said, "FLUKO reports red markers near Duisburg 0130. The same aircraft, probably."

"Mark that in too," said the Burgomaster calmly. "We must know which way the aircraft are approaching."

The Burgomaster hung up his hat and sat behind his desk. The yellow desk lamp made a rim around his profile. He passed his long white fingers over the three phones, blotter, pad and sharpened pencils as if to reassure himself that all was arranged to his orders. He had never been under air attack before. He was determined to work by the rules. For many months he had studied the instruction books and reports; tonight he would use his store of knowledge. Suddenly he stood up. It was the first

Supporter aircraft putting down his stick of H.E. Six
500-pound medium capacity bombs fell in a line about
seventy yards apart. Had there been an eighth bomb it
would have fallen upon the Rathaus.

"What are they bombing out there?" asked the Burgomaster, looking at the wall of his office as though some
mystic force might allow him to see through it and thus
solve the problem.

"Frau Kersten's potatoes," said the telephonist. "Perhaps they are trying to starve us out."

The Burgomaster froze her smile with a look. The First
World War had left him with the belief that jokes under
fire were only one step away from hysteria.

There was a rattle at the door handle and another
Hitler Jugend boy appeared. He was excited and flushed
with the exertion of pedaling. "The road is on fire, Herr
Bürgermeister."

"What do you mean, the road?"

"A thin white flame as tall as a house," said the boy.

"Fräulein Eva, tell the Gasmeister. *Junge*, give the
exact position of the fire. Fräulein Bertha, prop something under that door to hold it open so that there is free
access to the control room. Tomorrow I want that door
handle mended properly. It's nearly a week since I asked
for it to be done."

"Yes, Herr Bürgermeister," said the girl.

Tommy Carter's *Joe for King* came steadily across
Altgarten and released a bomb load which included the
green T.I.s.

"And connect me to the waterworks master too."

The telephonist pushed the key continuously but the
phone was unanswered.

The waterworks master had hurried away from the Burgomaster's birthday party keen to prove that he knew his
duty as well as the next man, but he'd forgotten the keys
of his office. He walked across to the filter beds and the
great water tank. There was nothing for him to do. He
found the half-finished cigar in his top pocket and relit it
and began a gentle stroll. There were red flashes in the
sky. It seemed very close, but he knew such appearances
could be deceptive. The sound of airplanes grew louder.
He often watched them pass over on their way to the
Ruhr. Sometimes he had seen them hit and burning in the
sky like comets.

The waterworks master was Altgarten's first victim.

When colored marker bombs came down he began to run but he was swamped by cascading pools of green fire. And then came high explosive and his body was thrown into the air and buried in the churned soil among potato roots and splinters of tree.

The raid was no novelty for the Technische Nothilfe Bataillon. They came out of their huts completely equipped before the first stick of flares had guttered and died. Their heavy trucks, with the wide white identifying band painted round them and the white bicycles strapped to the tailboards, were drawn up in convoy order and the men swung aboard in the darkness as they had done a thousand times before. This was just another air raid for the TENOs, with the subtle distinction that this time they did not have to go to it; it had come to them.

First the car decelerates and moves slowly enough for the driver to see the house numbers. Finally it stops. The men's voices are low in tone and volume and their rhythms imply orders and assent. Doors slam gently and metal-studded boots click loudly in the night air. The door knocker rat-a-tats.

All over Europe in 1943, ears had become sensitive to such a sequence of sounds. At eleven-forty-five on the night of June 31 old Herr Voss the tailor cocked his head and listened fearfully.

Herr Voss was a short plump man of fifty-nine. The crown of his head was bald, but a natural wave gave him curls across the ears and over his collar. He was a talented amateur baritone and as recently as 1940 he had performed at a local concert. His wife had once been a noted Lieder singer. They liked music of all kinds and had a large collection of records ranging from American jazz to Beethoven quartets and of course many choral works. Each evening he dressed in his black velvet jacket and tasseled smoking hat. His daily housekeeper left them a simple cold meal and after finishing it he smoked his pipe and he and his wife listened to music, often until one or two o'clock in the morning. At present his wife was visiting their only daughter and son-in-law in Freiburg. Although alone in the house, he kept to the usual ritual.

Voss turned down the music on the radio. For a moment he stood listening, then he shuffled down the hall in his carpet slippers to open the front door. Even before he got there the knocker sounded again. "All right, all right," called the old man irritably. "Everyone is in such a hur-

ry." It was dark outside and he could just make out the
silhouette of a steel helmet. "It's the front-room curtain
again, is it?" said old Voss, his voice changing into a soft
apology. "It's the cat that moves it."

"Voss?" said the man. And now old Voss looked at him
a second time. By the shaded light he could see that it was
a Wehrmacht steel helmet the man was wearing, not a
Luftschutz pattern.

"Voss?" repeated the soldier. His voice was strange.

"Yes," said Herr Voss. He tried to say it doubtfully, so
as to retain the option of denying it.

"This is the house, sir," called the soldier in the thick
throaty Russian of the Caucasian mountains. Another man
came out of the darkness.

"Get the bundle," he said in halting Russian. He was
taller and slimmer than the HIWI, with a leather overcoat
that was badly damaged on the elbows and lapels. "I'm
the one who telephoned," said the tall one. His voice had
the singsong lilt of the Rhineland. "Come in," said Voss.

They both came into his sitting room. The Hilfsfreiwilli-
ger—auxiliary volunteer—was loaded under three long
sacking bundles. He had them upon his shoulder and they
sagged with their own weight.

"On the floor," said the tall one. He was a pale-faced
young man with tired eyes and a hooked nose. Like an
owl, thought Voss. The man opened his coat to search for
cigarettes and revealed the black S.S. rank patches on his
collar. The foreign volunteer was a Feldwebel; his uniform
was at least a size too small for him. On his sleeve there
was a yellow dragon on a bright blue shield. "Galician—
14th S.S., eh?" said Voss.

"How do you know?" asked Fischer, taking off his coat.

"I tailor uniforms. I probably know more about army
insignia than you do. And you're Leibstandarte, eh?" The
old man smiled, noticing the L.A.H. epaulets and new cuff
band on Fischer's arm. He thought them the trappings of
a poseur. Now he looked more closely at Fischer's
Knight's Cross.

"We're posted to Hitler Jugend Division," said Fischer
angrily. He threw his leather coat over a chair. He hadn't
wanted the old man to know which unit they belonged to,
but lying was complicated. Still, there wasn't much danger
that this little crook would dare complain about an S.S.
officer.

The HIWI dumped the bundles on the floor, unsheathed

a bayonet and neatly sliced one open. He unrolled it with the toe of his boot.

"From the National Museum in Kharkov," said Fischer.

"Caucasian?"

"Kuba." The officer nodded. "Nearly three hundred years old. It could tell a few stories."

The HIWI flipped back the corner like a professional carpet dealer. "Look at it," said Fischer. "Notice the warp threads on two different levels. Look at the border."

"Kufic," said Voss.

"Exactly," said Fischer. "You know a thing or two about carpets."

"I've bought them before."

"So I heard," said Fischer dryly. "You'll be a fool not to buy this one. It's a museum piece."

"Everyone says they've got a museum piece," said Voss, rubbing a corner of the carpet.

"Yes," said Fischer, "but not everyone takes it out of a Russkie museum at the point of a gun." The HIWI watched them carefully as they spoke, trying to understand Voss's fast guttural *Plattdeutsch*, as much like Dutch as German. Suddenly comprehending, the HIWI laughed and revealed a set of bad teeth.

Fischer watched Voss's face as he examined the stitches. "See how thick the base is."

"How much?"

"Ten thousand."

"Reichsmark?"

"No, Pfenning," said Fischer sarcastically.

Voss ran his fingers across the flowers and birds. Soft reds and greens. The colors shone in the electric light. "It's worth it," admitted Voss.

"Worth twice as much," said Fischer. He went to a silver box on the coffee table. "I'll take a cigarette," he announced.

"Please do," said Voss. He looked at the other bundles. "What are the others?"

"Modern Shirvans. They won't interest you; you know too much about carpets.

The old man smiled at the compliment but the smile was frozen on his face as the first stick of bombs came down. Immediately after that they heard the second bomb load go. The farthest one was a quarter of a mile behind Frau Kersten's but the last one was upon the slum housing behind the gasworks. Voss and the two soldiers hurried to

the door. Outside, the night was as bright as day. Tommy
Carter's green marker flares were hanging in the sky, each
cluster spread out toward its base like a Christmas tree.
There were other Christmas trees, one over the brewery
and another near the church. To the southeast the sky was
still glowing red from the Mosquito's T.I.s.

"Markers," said Fischer. "Those green flares form the
corners of a square into which the other planes will drop
their bombs."

It was a common mistake, made because people on the
ground didn't realize the big margins of error within
which the bombers operated. Actually Tapper Collins was
trying to put all of the green Christmas trees onto the
same aiming point.

Fischer had no sooner spoken than a salvo struck the
northern side of the town. Among the 500-pound bombs
there was a 4,000-pound cookie that made the ground
rock. The echoes rolled through the narrow streets of the
old town and Voss and the two soldiers found themselves
full length on the road without remembering how they got
there. Another Lancaster started its bomb run. Voss saw
the two soldiers holding their hands over their ears to
protect their eardrums. He did the same. They waited
until the next ear-splitting explosions had rocked the
earth.

"Have you got a cellar?" called Fischer.

"Yes," said Voss.

"Let's get into it."

Voss eyed their Kübelwagen parked at the curb. He
had half hoped that they would decide to hasten away but
on the other hand he coveted the carpet. He had never
seen one quite so fine. Except in museums.

The window of the next-door house rattled open. "Herr
Voss, is that you?"

"Yes, it is," said Voss.

"Are they bombing us?" asked Anna-Luisa. The officer
laughed.

"They are, my dear," said the old man. "You'd better
bring the child into my cellar."

"Thank you, Herr Voss."

"And hurry," called Fischer. They scrambled to their
feet and hurried indoors. The Lancaster of Sandy Sanderson, Engineer Leader and squadron dandy, released ten
canisters of incendiary bombs exactly at the aiming point.
From each canister tumbled ninety magnesium sticks. For
a moment nine hundred incendiary bombs hung together

in the gaping bomb doors like a cluster of iron filings
dangling from a magnet. Then the airstream punched into
them and they sprinkled out over the town all the way
from Mauerstrasse to Party H.Q. near the church.

Each 4-pound incendiary struck the ground with a
sound like the crack of a whip and a white flash. Then
they burned and flared fiercely. The three men watched
from the door. One of the incendiaries hit the ground only
a yard ahead of the Kübelwagen and the HIWI Feldwebel ran back to kick the bomb along the gutter and
then kicked after it the red and white fragments of burning magnesium that it had scattered.

"Where's the cellar, Herr Voss?" said the officer and
old Voss produced a heavy ring of keys and unlocked the
cellar door, his keys jangling in his nervous fingers. The
three men ushered the girl and the little boy down the
stone steps. Once they were there the soldiers could see
why the old man had been reluctant to allow them to see
his air raid shelter. It was a treasure house. There was a
glass-fronted case full of silver and a box full of
glassware, all wrapped carefully in newspaper. Squeezed
among the antiques and boxes of goodness-knows-what
there were four comfortable old chairs, and even a telephone extension. Calling it his air raid shelter was a
convenient rationalization for arranging a room in which
the old man could survey his loot in privacy and comfort.
Voss lit the oil lamp but the electric lights were bright
enough to make it unnecessary.

Anna-Luisa laid the child Hansl upon an armchair. He
was sleepy and she arranged a blanket round his head to
muffle the noise.

It was the 2,000-pound high explosive bomb from Tommy Carter's plane that hit the corner of Mönchenstrasse
and Postgasse only a block away from Voss's house. In
the cellar it shook the dust from the shelves. Old Voss
coughed and the HIWI sneezed and then laughed uproari-
ously. Outside, the dark street was clouded in brick dust.
The bomb had sliced thirty yards from the apartment
block like a segment of cake, leaving brightly colored
layers of wallpapered rooms exposed. Sloping up to the
second floor there was a mound of rubble with bricks,
broken furniture, an upturned bath and slabs of unbroken
wall poking out of it. There were freak escapes: a mirror
on the wall, pictures unscathed and a parlor maid found
stark naked but quite unharmed in the garden at the rear.
She had been asleep on the top floor.

Old Storp, the Blockwart, an overcoat over his pajamas, came wide-eyed through the dust and darkness to meet the TENO engineers. He had a scrap of paper in his hands and he shouted loudly to make himself heard above the explosions.

"Eighteen people altogether. All of them sheltering in the cellar."

The TENO man eyed the tall mound of bricks and rubbish. "We'll never get them out," he said briefly. With a terrible finality he chalked "18" on a piece of masonry and turned away.

"You must," shouted the Blockwart. "My wife's in there."

"It's no use," shouted the TENO man. A bomb exploded nearby and he crouched down. "It's the water pip that we must fix."

The Blockwart started to lift one of the heavy wooden beams aside but finding it unmovable he grabbed at loose bricks. "I'm coming, Bertha," he shouted. "Don't be frightened, my love." He seemed no longer to hear the bombs dropping. He worked feverishly to clear a way to the cellar, but inside it they were all dead.

It was the sound of that same high explosive bomb that brought Herr Voss back up from his cellar. Its blast distorted the nine-inch spun-iron water pipe that ran past his house and its lead-wool caulking had cracked badly enough for a steady flow of water to run into the Voss cellar. At first the flow was no faster than a kitchen tap but the water pressure opened the gap and did further damage to the caulking so that soon the water had formed a large pool and ran in streams under the easy chairs and wet the bottoms of the wooden boxes. There was no drain in the cellar and Voss knew that unless the engineers got to the pipe soon it would be completely flooded. He hurried up the steps, anxious about the damage the water might do to his paintings and carpets.

The two soldiers remained in the cellar with Anna-Luisa for ten more minutes. Above them the bombs were shaking the house to its foundations. Hansl awoke and began to cry gently.

"We'll go soon," said the officer. He got to his feet and began to unwrap some silver and glass that was packed into one of the boxes. He selected three Georgian silver teapots and a cream jug and placed them carefully on the armchair. Although not a word passed between them, the Feldwebel found a sack and put the silver into it. The

officer selected an ancient flintlock pistol from the wall
and found a red silk Kashan rug wrapped in newspaper on
the shelf. He rolled it into the bundle of carpets they had
brought with them.

"What are you doing?" asked Anna-Luisa. She smiled as
she said it, hoping that they were only joking.

"We are old friends of Herr Voss," said the officer.
"These are things we have bought from him."

"I don't believe you," said Anna-Luisa. She walked
across the cellar to the steps and called to Herr Voss, but
no answer came.

"He's probably dead," said the officer.

"Let's wait for him," suggested Anna-Luisa, standing in
his path and holding up her arm to prevent him from
passing. Fischer drew back his fist and punched her in the
face as hard as he could.

She knew he had broken her front teeth even before she
felt the pain of the blow. The force of it threw her back
against the wooden boxes. She twisted her ankle and an
antique decanter fell and smashed on the stone floor. She
moaned in pain and, holding her face in her hands, she
rocked to and fro trying to comfort herself. When Hansl
began to cry loudly she gradually opened her eyes. The
man had gone and so had the sackful of silver and the
carpet. She pulled Hansl close to her. "It's all right, baby,
everything will be all right." Her mouth was swollen and
her voice was strange because of her broken teeth, but she
went on saying it in order to comfort herself. The water
was still gurgling into the cellar, but she no longer cared.
No one did.

Upstairs the two soldiers moved briskly through the
house. There was a moment's pause in the gunfire and
bombs after the first bombers passed over. It was dark
and there was a foul smell of brick dust and disturbed
sewage. They put the bundles into the back of the Kübelwagen and drove away. In the gutter only a few yards from
the house was the body of Herr Voss. The soldiers didn't
recognize him. There were other bodies in the street too;
they hardly glanced at them. They had seen many dead
bodies.

# ⚓ 25 ⚓

DESCENDED from Norsemen, the Munros of the Isle of
Nichuish were a fierce God-fearing tribe of fighting men.
It was said that they'd never sat down to a meal without
thanking the Lord and opening the gates to the hungry,
but they'd done so with their swords close to hand. Old
Andrew's purse and sword never left his side from the day
he first strapped them on until he died on the far-off
battlefield of Lützen commanding one of Gustavus Adolphus's Scottish brigades. There, a silver damascened
wheellock pistol pushed under his breastplate opened purse
and belly and spread guts and gold across the battlefield.
His brother Ian fled from Cromwell after Dunbar wearing
the clothes of a crofter. Another Munro Americans
buried—in four separate parts—under the cold soil of
Lookout Mountain before the battle of Chattanooga had
properly begun.

Andrew, a captain in the Scots Fusiliers, was in 1704 at
Blenheim the first Munro to fight on the same side as the
English. Since then there had always been one of the men
of Nichuish in the British army. The history of the Munros reads like battle honors on a dusty standard: Fon-
tenoy, Waterloo, Inkerman, Abukir, Koodoosberg.

In 1918 John's uncle had fought the Turks from Basra
to Kirkuk and his father had spent four long years in
France and collected a D.S.O. at Ypres. They had both
come back to the estate at the war's end. Uncle Ian had
attended to the paper work right up until the week he had
died of some unidentified tropical disease. His father on
the other hand had delighted in working on the land and
with livestock. So many times, arriving on vacation with
his friends from school, they had mistaken his father for a
cowherd. Now they were both gone, and with John and

his young brother Ian both in the R.A.F., the whole place was being run by Sarah. This is where the family's military tradition might end, thought John Munro.

He would advise his son against going into military service of any kind. Last week two airmen had come before him for creating a disturbance in the Airmen's Mess. One was reported to have said, "After this lot you wouldn't get me to join a Christmas Club." It was alleged that the other replied, "You won't get me to bloody well join hands even." Munro had given them three days' jankers for "conduct to the prejudice of good order" but the sentiments were his exactly. Perhaps someday after the war he would see them on the street and tell them how much he had agreed. Although deep in his heart Munro felt sure that there would be no "after the war" for him. He'd never before had such a premonition of death. He told himself it was merely because this was his last trip, but he could not convince himself of that. Last night he had written checks for his tailor, his dentist and the mess, written a letter to his wife and the child and propped it on his pillow, and revised his will. Everything was done except this; he corrected the course with a touch of rudder.

Munro looked calmly down upon the dark landscape. Although for the newer crews the searchlights and explosions were a confusing maze of danger, for the old hands the flak concentrations provided a grim series of familiar navigational pinpoints.

"Some silly blighter's drifted off over Nijmegen," said Munro, watching the twinkling flak to port.

"Arnhem's pretty active too, sir," said the bomb aimer. "But not so many searchlights as there used to be."

"The Jerries are pulling back into the Ruhr. I suspect they're letting their night fighters have a go over the target nowadays and using the lights to help them spot the stream."

"It makes the navigator's job easier," said the engineer. Jock Hamilton, the navigator, was always fair game but this time he pretended that he had not heard them.

"There's a buzz going round that they are going to do away with them," said the bomb aimer. "We'll be taking extra incendiaries instead."

"You'll no' bluidy get back then," Jock warned them.

The others grinned, but for Munro the threat reawakened his fears. He watched and noted the changing patterns of the air defenses. It was amazing how far one

could see from this height. On other, clearer nights he'd
been this close to the Ruhr and still been able to see the
English coastline. Tonight, thank God, he couldn't, but the
cloud was breaking up as they got farther inland. He
didn't like that. There was no sign of searchlights or
gunfire ahead of him where the target should lie. He
called the navigator. "Are you getting a picture on the
H2S, Jock?"

"It's no' so bad."

"Can you see the River Maas?"

"Aye, sir. Just about. I make us level with Cleve." The
landscape was dark and featureless except that Munro
could see the river far below them. The Maas curved
gently away.

"Big bugger, that one to port, sir."

"Yes, that's what I call a searchlight. Makes the others
look like a Toc H lamp."

It wasn't far now.

Keeping a proper all-round watch in a top turret was a
tiring procedure. It meant rotating the head in a manner
for which human anatomy was not designed.

Lofty, Munro's gunner, did his series of horizon search-
es and ended each with two visual sweeps overhead.
That's when he saw the shape. One piece of darkness with
a horrifying slowness detached itself from the night sky
and reached out to grab them in its black grasp. A man
can't scream into an oxygen mask but, not knowing this,
the gunner did scream. He almost choked, gasping for air
with a force that gave him chest pains. He switched his
microphone on to tell Munro what had happened, but had
difficulty in speaking. In a shaky voice he reported, "A
Lancaster just about parted my hair, sir."

"Direction?" asked Munro.

"Same bearing as us, sir, but only a few feet overhead.
How we missed him I don't know."

"So long as the stream are keeping on course," said
Munro. Jock grinned to himself. It was typical of Munro
that so close to a midair collision he should be concerned
whether the other plane was on the correct course. "Sure
it was a four-motor job, Lofty?"

"Yes, sir."

"Good, but keep your eyes peeled."

No one aboard Lancaster *Q for Queen* had seen Munro's Lanc come so close to them. The only crew member
who might have seen it—Jammy Giles, the bomb aimer—
wasn't full length in the nose looking down; he was sitting

in the pilot's seat grappling with the controls. He'd never taken over the controls on an operational flight before. He was reluctant to do it this time until the pilot—a Canadian Flying Officer named Peterson, known to his friends as Roddy—made it an order. In spite of Jammy's superior rank the pilot, a taxi driver from Montreal, was the captain. Jammy said, "O.K., you drunken Canadian bum, but I should be couchant by now."

"Bum" and "couchant" were two of Jammy's very favorite words, and just as the former was applied to his crew and his sex life, so was the latter applied to his job and his sex life. It wasn't as easy to change pilots as they both thought. A stray boot hit the control column and for a time there were no feet on the rudder bar, both of which put the bomber into some unusual flying attitudes.

At first it had been a bit of a joke. Jammy had been sympathetic about Roddy's diarrhea because it was undoubtedly the result of a drinking party that Jammy had insisted he join. Closer to the target, however, Jammy was getting more and more anxious. "Roddy, do you know what's got an I.Q. of one hundred?"

"No, what?"

"Ten Canadians. All right. Now get your flaming arse off that thunderbox, Roddy, and come back here and start driving."

"I'm ill."

"Canadian twit."

"Limey berk."

"I'm serious."

"I'm serious too."

"I'm the Bombing Leader, Roddy."

"And I'm goddamn ill, feller."

"All right. How long are you going to be on your bum?"

"You take her over target, Jammy."

"And who will be couchant, you transatlantic twit?"

"Let Al bomb; he was always better than you." The incapacitated pilot scored a shrewd blow with that suggestion, for Alun Davies, the navigator, had remustered from observer and knew almost as much as Jammy about bombsights, drift, markers and selector switches.

It was Jammy's strict instruction that the target should be identified both on radar and visually before bombing. "Can someone hold *Queenie* straight and level while I do the couchant bit?" asked Jammy desperately.

Whoever was at the controls would suffer Jammy's

wrath as they tried to comply with his steering directions over target. They all knew this and no one volunteered.

Jammy sighed. "All right. Alun, forget the H2S, have a go at the bombsight, will you?"

"Certainly, sir," said Alun, ex-public school, ex-cinema manager from Ffestiniog. He gathered together the maps under his lamp and took a closer look at them.

When Alun had last bombed, the target maps had been gaily colored, fully detailed ones of the sort that a hiker would take on a cross-country stroll. Now the target maps were somber things: inflammable forest and built-up areas defined as gray blocks and shaded angular shapes. The only white marks were the thin rivers and blobs of lake. The roads were purple veins so that the whole thing was like a badly bruised torso. On the old ones the rivers were bright blue and the trees green and hospitals were marked with a neat red cross. But now the urban conglomerations were just shapes like the ill-defined blurs that passed across the H2S radar tube. That, of course, was the whole idea. The old maps were as ancient as the idea of looking over the side of the cockpit to see the enemy you bombed. The new gray faceless maps were just one aspect of a new kind of war.

Alun Davies switched off the H2S radar set. That was Jammy's toy; Alun had never like it. He gathered his maps and notes together and moved forward. It was dark. He saw Jammy's helmeted head rigid and silhouetted against the Perspex and groped for handholds as the plane lurched to Jammy's inexpert touch. As he passed the pilot's seat Jammy spared a hand long enough to pat his arm in encouragement. "Don't forget the fuse switch, Al, and look for the red Oboe T.I.s first, then the greens. All right?"

"Very well, sir."

"How are you back there, Roddy?"

"Goddamn miserable, Jammy." It had taken the pilot several agonizing minutes to undo his flying clothes in order to use the Elsan chemical closet. Whoever decided that the flying meal should include beans had never suffered from wind at high altitude. The distension of the stomach and bowel that at ground level is merely painful becomes agony at 16,000 feet. Roddy Peterson had the added pain of an inflamed intestine. Originally he'd wanted to vomit and then a wave of shivering had hit him, followed by an urgent looseness of the bowels. Here at the back he'd plugged in his intercom and oxygen, but at 16,000 feet, with his trousers round his ankles, he was very cold indeed. In spite of being chilled to the bone he was sweating and could feel the perspiration trickling down his neck and back. He still felt sick and inside him there was an empty feeling of misery. Back here in the tail every trace of Jammy's inexpert piloting was magnified into rolling motion and sickening drops through space.

He'd never realized before how dark and lonely it was for the rest of the crew. Looking forward from the Elsan all he could see was the feet of the mid-upper gunner as the turret traversed with sudden purrs. When they flew near cloud there was enough reflection for him to see the gunner's arms too. Beyond that the tunnel of aluminum formers and ammunition runways seemed to extend for miles. Sometimes, like day at the end of a railway tunnel, he saw a pinpoint of yellow from the navigator's desk-lamp. It was noisy here too. The roar of the engines was much louder from behind and the wind buffeting the tail bumped and groaned and curious little clinks came from the girders around him. Now and again there was the explosion of a flak shell nearby and once there was the pitter-patter of spent shrapnel knocking upon the metal skin. All the time he felt a desperate frustration at not knowing what was going on.

"You left your parachute on the seat here, Roddy," said Jammy Giles over the intercom. "One of the boys will bring my harness down to you. The chute is in the rear stowage. All right?" Roddy nodded.

"Hear me, Roddy?" Roddy was racked by another awful pain and a bowel movement that drained the life out of him. He groaned and scarcely summoned the energy to switch his microphone. "I don't want a chute. I just want to die."

At the controls Jammy saw an extra-big searchlight moving across the sky toward them. It looked very blue, as he'd been told the master searchlights were, and he pushed the rudder bar urgently. Without any bank the plane simply yawed sideways, skidding through the sky and lurching as the propellers tried to renew their grip upon the air.

"Yes. All right, hold on to your Elsan," said Jammy. "This might be your big chance." Jammy gave a characteristic mirthless guffaw modified by the oxygen mask he was wearing.

Himmel saw the same big searchlights. As they swept

across a patch of cloud they lit it like frosted glass. Conspicuous upon that white patch, like a cockroach on a counterpane, was the black silhouette of an airplane, and then came a second bomber, slightly smaller.

"Announcement: Kettledrums, kettledrums." He thus dispensed with his radar station's services. Himmel had already followed one contact right across the zone of the Würzburg without success and was about to fly back along the stream and begin again. He switched on the Revi sight and an engraved cross and circle lit up on the glass before him. He put the Junkers into a steep dive, turning onto the same course as his quarry. The bomber had been at least a thousand feet below him when he'd spotted it and he watched the next patch of cloud hoping that he'd see it again closer to. At 15,000 feet he leveled off but continued on the same bearing. He'd only seen the bomber for a second or two and he might have misjudged its heading. Then the observer saw it again. One hundred yards away, much larger and just above the starboard horizon. "There he is." Himmel stole a glance at it. Too fast.

The speed of the dive was still affecting their forward motion and even throttling back drastically didn't help much. It was damned near. Himmel pulled the nose up. They slowed. It would put them above the horizon for a moment or two but it was better than showing them his exhausts.

"Corkscrew port go," shouted Lofty Lee from his upper turret and began firing as Munro slammed the stick over and stood the bomber on its wingtip. Lofty's machine guns tilted high above him as he tried to keep the night fighter in his sights while his own plane banked vertically and slid down. It was impossible. Munro grabbed the throttles and reduced the forward speed (and exhaust flame) to minimum and had the satisfaction of seeing the Junkers pass rapidly over him. Its exhausts glowed brighter and brighter as the angle narrowed and he was right ahead of them.

"Don't fire, anyone," said Munro. "He's lost us." He'd seen his bomb aimer dodging under the ring of the front turret. It was tempting, of course, for now positions were reversed: Himmel's Junkers was silhouetted against sky and moonlit high clouds. Munro kept in the blind spot behind the Junkers' tail and vanished against the dark background of earth. Himmel banked for a better view

around him. Munro watched the plane ahead as it searched
for them and held his breath lest they hear him.

"Everyone all right?" asked Himmel.

"One bullet starred the cockpit glass," said the observer.

"Those piddling things don't do much damage," said
the radar man.

"Not to you, buried under all that machinery," grum-
bled the observer.

"Keep looking for him," said Himmel.

"We'll never see him in that muck," said the observer.

"He knew what he was doing," said the radar operator.

"My fault," admitted Himmel. "It's so seldom the *Tommis* spot us that I've grown complacent. I climbed. I
should have dived and circled behind him."

"They're lucky, those *Tommis*. Not many get away as
easily as that."

"Probably old-timers."

"Someone else will get them," said Himmel. "Keep
looking." They kept looking, but finally Himmel had to
tell his controller that he had lost contact.

"Good work, Lofty," Munro said to the tiny upper
gunner who had warned them of Himmel's approach.

"I thought he was a Wellington in the stream at first.
Then he went a little higher and I got a good silhouette of
the bastard."

"It was good work," said Munro. "Keep your eyes
peeled, everyone. They'll put up every night fighter they
have on a night like this."

Cautiously Munro put the nose up and began to climb
to his assigned bombing height.

Some bomb aimers were seeing a town under attack for
the first time. In Jammy's plane, his navigator, Alun Davies, had done so many operations hidden behind his
curtain that he'd almost forgotten what a target looked like.
Battersby, in *Creaking Door*, stared down at the fires and
flashes and for a moment forgot his duties. He'd expected
the fires and markers to look much bigger, as they had in
the training films he'd seen, but they had been photographed with telephoto lenses. From four miles high even a
whole city block on fire was nothing more than a pimple
of red in a vast bowl of darkness. A tiny red glowworm
was all that could be seen of fires that stretched from the
gasworks to the brewery sidings. It was such a muddle
too. At the briefing the plan was so clear: red markers,
then greens and yellows accompanied by the H.E. Illuminators scheduled to arrive before the Finders. Now, look-

ing down, only the most experienced crews knew what was happening. Battersby couldn't distinguish a fire from a descending marker, or the flicker of an exploding bomb from the slower photoflash.

Wrong wind predictions had thrown the weight of the stream northward and would have made the timings wrong even if they hadn't mistaken the target. Altgarten was nine miles closer than Krefeld and the immortal Lud's yellow had marked neither. Main Force Stirlings were arriving even before Illuminators. Some Primary Markers had had doubts about the correctness of the markers and had circled several times looking at H2S, thus making themselves late. Altgarten now was a meaningless chaos of greens and yellows, fires, photoflashes and explosions.

"The H2S is acting up, sir. I'm going to bomb the central fire," said Munro's bomb aimer.

"O.K., bomb aimer," said Munro. "She's all yours."

"Left, left, and a bit more. Now we're nice. Steady. Left, left."

The fires were like little furry animals, their edges softened by the smoke. And like animals they seemed to breathe, expanding and contracting as the flames inhaled the surrounding air currents. Sometimes it was possible to see the tiny flicker of dozens of incendiaries as they landed and glowed pink. Much larger, the H.E. bombs flashed and were gone. From each aircraft came a photoflash bomb, which exploded above the target with seven million candlepower of light that lasted longer than the bombs and threw enough light upward to illuminate the bombers. One of these was going off every three or four seconds. Munro, listening carefully to his bomb aimer's instructions, saw by the light of one photoflash eight airplanes close around him and was so frightened that he made himself stare at his instrument panel.

"Left, left, steady." There was no mistaking the instructions since the word "left" was always said twice. Adding "steady" without pausing was his way of telling Munro to touch only the left rudder. "Steady, steady." Plenty of flak now; the row of tiny fires crept along the bombsight wire with agonizing slowness. The Volkschule fire, the gasworks fire, the Nehringstrasse fire, the Altmarkt fire pulsated like red embers on a sooty fireplace. The bomb aimer waited for the largest one—the hospital annex. Left, left, steady. The wire crossed the edge of it. "Bombs gone." The selector was at salvo. The whole bomb load dropped away so that the Lancaster leaped into the air. Munro let the

nose come up. For thirty seconds more they flew on
straight and level, waiting for the photoflash to explode
and the F24 camera shutter to turn over to record the
accuracy of their bombing.

'O.K." Munro turned gently. "Let's go home."

Only a hundred yards behind him Jammy Giles was
doing his best to follow his bomb aimer's instructions but
he consistently overcorrected.

"Left, left," said Alun. "Right. Too far, left, left.
Steady. No, too late. Right. Steady. Yes, that's good. Hold
her like that. Steady. Left, left. Jammy, left, left, more."
The plane yawed across the target. The yellow markers
slid past, well to the left of his bombsight mark. Under
him came the Liebefrau church. The control column kicked
against Jammy's sweaty grasp.

"Bombs gone, Jammy. Jettison bars across. It wasn't
awfully good, I'm afraid."

"Let's get out of here," said Jammy. He tipped the wing
down and with the engineer's help increased the airspeed.

"Wait for the photoflash," shouted Roddy as the plane
tilted.

"Bugger," said Jammy, "I forgot. Oh well, give me a
course for home, Alun."

Alun was looking back through the clear view panel
into the bomb bay to make sure that the racks were
empty. The 2,000-pound H.E., the incendiaries and the
1,000-pound H.E.s had all gone. He tried to visualize the
plot in his memory. "Steer 280 for exactly four minutes,
Jammy. By that time I'll have a new course for home."

"Close your bomb doors, clot."

"I forgot that."

"But that you really forgot," said Roddy archly.

"Now listen, Roddy, you bum. I didn't turn off like that
to avoid getting a photo."

"Flanneling limey bastard."

"Deserter."

"Have you been drinking, Jammy?" said Roddy.

There was a moment of hesitation. "Only a couple,"
said Jammy guiltily, and suddenly his crew had discovered
an awful secret about Jammy's lively indifference to danger. No one spoke for nearly five minutes; they were all
silently vowing that no one else on the squadron should
know. It was now a family secret. In the pilot's seat the
first red flush of embarrassment had faded from Jammy's
cheeks. It was better that they knew.

# ◖ 26 ◗

In the Rathaus the Burgomaster's telephones were ringing continually: "0139. Florastrasse. High explosive. Fifteen wounded, two dead. Mains intact. Road blocked."

The telephonist bit her lip as she impaled her written message upon the spike with the others. She lived in Florastrasse.

"0140. Railway line near brewery. High explosive. No casualties. Railway blocked."

"0141. Saint Antonius Hospital. High explosive. Unknown casualties. Mains intact. Road blocked."

Munro's cookie hit the Saint Antonius Hospital. It landed squarely upon the front steps of its neoclassical façade. The fine columns and the great pediment collapsed and some of the girders followed it. Luckily the front of the hospital consisted of offices, the main staircase, the lift, the inquiry desk and storerooms. One of the operating theaters was severely damaged too, although the boiler house below ground escaped. The heating system and hot water supply were in full working order as soon as the broken pipes had been cut out of the system by screwing up the valves. The doorman lost one of his legs and a doctor suffered bad scalds on his upper body from the broken central heating. Two theater nurses had to be treated for shock and small multiple injuries. Four patients were cut by flying glass. At the time it seemed a miracle that so little damage had been done to the hospital by such an enormous bomb.

On the other hand the raid had scarcely started yet and the damage to the steelwork had made the whole structure unsafe. More immediately, since the sloping ramps and the big—bed-size—lift shaft had gone, it meant that there was no way of evacuating the bedridden patients from the

331

upper floors. In the wards the flashes of bombs and guns
were lighting up the frightened faces of the trapped patients. The markers painted the sheets bright green and
yellow and the shadows moved eerily across the floor and
up the walls as the flares floated down upon the town.
Everyone wanted attention: bedpans, sleeping tablets, a
drink of water or just a word of comfort. The ones that
could walk insisted upon going to the toilet even though
that was forbidden once the night shift began. They
huddled at the window, these frightened, privileged, mobile few. One of the A Flight Lancs dropped a salvo near
the Liebefrau church. Then Jammy Giles came across the
town. "Bombs gone, Jammy. . . . It wasn't awfully good,
I'm afraid." The explosion shattered more of the hospital
windows and threw a dozen patients full length to the
floor. The far end of Dorfstrasse was just hot rubble.

"Get two dozen nurses from the dance," ordered Matron.

"They are in the shelter," said the ward sister.

"We need them here," said Matron.

Throughout Altgarten a special burden of responsibility
had fallen upon men of experience. Luftschutz officials,
transport workers, gas engineers, electrical fitters and telephone linesmen had all began to take their orders
from the men who had experienced in other towns air
raids of this ferocity. The fire chief, for instance, was
depending upon Johannes Ilfa's eighteen months' duty in
Cologne to provide solutions to the problems that arose
this night, but Ilfa knew that for many of the problems
there were no solutions.

Altgarten's population was about 5,000. For each person there was 30 gallons of water per day. A sum based
upon a 15-hour day shows a total need for 10,000 gallons
per hour. A town's fire capacity was the margin of extra
water for its fire brigades and for Altgarten this was
calculated as double the normal rate. So Altgarten could
produce 20,000 gallons of water per hour through its
arteries until high explosive bombs sliced those arteries
and incendiary bombs by the thousand produced fires on a
nightmare scale. To supply its water most of the town's
pipes were of 25-cm. diameter, but the expensive new
houses along Dorfstrasse and Mönchenstrasse all had bathrooms and so the next size of pipe had been fitted in those
streets, and the next size was 35 cm. Small by big-city
standards, but tonight the large-capacity pipes along Mön-

chenstrasse and Dorfstrasse had become a vital defense
in the battle of Altgarten.

As soon as the 2,000-pound high capacity bombs fell on
Mönchenstrasse at the Postgasse junction it was the Burgomaster's strict order that the water pipes must be attended to before casualties or trapped survivors. The
TENOs had arrived within four minutes and decided that
the eighteen persons in the cellar were too near the center
of the explosion to have survived and they immediately
brought out the large-girth canvas pipe sections. They
kept a thin supply going until a bomb on Liebefrauplatz
severed the junction. Still they continued with the repairs,
working down the deep hole in shifts of four, each only
being able to stand the work for five minutes at a time.
They had dug down beneath the cracked pipe, slipped
supports under it and hoisted it into position and then
bound it with tape and glue. The men had been virtually
immersed in liquid mud created by the water flow, for it
would have taken the turncock half an hour of walking in
a tight circle to close the main. Since water was coming
from the pipe during the work, the mud became more and
more liquid and only by the quick-witted action of the
winch operator on the standby lorry was Gerd Böll
pulled out of the mud into which he had gone up to the
armpits.

It was 0146 when Jürgen Löwe, the Hitler Jugend
messenger boy, arrived at the Rathaus. He carried his
bicycle down the steps and propped it inside the sand-
bagged entrance.

"The Mönchenstrasse water pipe has now been repaired."

The Burgomaster nodded.

"Heil Hitler," said the boy.

"Heil Hitler," said the Burgomaster.

The waterworks master was dead. Now that the main
pipeline was repaired the Burgomaster had to make a
decision for which he had no training. The city stream
passed near the waterworks and then curved back to
become what had once been the inner moat of the old
town. Nowadays it was one of Altgarten's most decorative
features. Swans on the stream came majestically past the
old timbered houses and a patient photographer could be
rewarded by one of the most beautiful tourist views in the
whole region. In summer the stream dwindled to little
more than a gutter and in the last few rainless weeks there
had been little more than damp weed there. But at least

the stone canal was intact, if his most recent reports were
to be believed. What was more, the irrigation valves could
isolate the town section of it. If the Burgomaster deliberately pumped the water supply into the moat then the
firemen would have a meandering supply of water right in
the heart of the old town where the fire hazards were
greatest. Each pump could take from the part of the
stream nearest to the fire.

He looked at the map. There were so many fires: the
Liebefrau church, the houses near the gasworks, the Volkschule, Nehringstrasse, the old market and the hospital
annex. Most of them would benefit from the stream being
flooded. Now that the Mönchenstrasse pipe had been
repaired they could take water out of the moat at one end
of that street, pump it through the large-capacity Mönchenstrasse pipe and use it at the other end where the
hospitals were.

On the other hand, the stream water was not fit for
drinking and if he pumped it into the clean pipes of the
town supply at Mönchenstrasse he would have to order
all drinking water to be boiled for twenty minutes before
use. That would be a great encumbrance to the hospital,
soup kitchens and every living person in Altgarten. Furthermore, the water pipes would have to be cleaned next
week and he would be called to account.

That was just one of the problems. He shuffled the
memo slips on his desk. The Gasmeister had stopped
sending messages by now. The gas was turned off at the
gasholder. The oldest parts of the town, where they still
used gas lighting, were in darkness. Here and there pockets of gas in the broken pipes were still blazing fiercely,
but they would soon burn out. There would probably be
no gas in the town for three days. Four times the N.S.V.
had phoned to tell him the vats of potato soup could not
be ready because of the gas cut. "Then let them have cold
soup," he finally snapped at them.

Ryessman called Schott, the electricity chief, whose
report was brief and unequivocal. If the Florastrasse fires
didn't spread toward him and if the hospital generators
kept going, the supply on the central net, i.e. the city block
to each side of Dorfstrasse from the hospital to the
brewery, would be working. The rest of the town would
stay dark except for the Wald Hotel and the TENO camp,
which had their own generators. "At least that will
guarantee the blackout for eighty percent of the town,"
added the electricity master facetiously.

"I don't know when you last ascended from your cellar," said the Burgomaster coldly, "but half of the town is on fire. You could read a newspaper by its light, even as far away as Frau Förster's sheds."

"If you would prefer me to be reading a newspaper at Förster's sheds, Herr Bürgermeister, I will go there. But at present I am trying to keep the electricty supply of this town going in spite of losing my senior engineer and my most experienced foreman."

"Continue to do that, Herr Schott," said Ryessman angrily.

Actually Schott was being most restrained in his answer, for his chief engineer and foreman were laid out in his office. To get to his plans chest he had to step over them. They had both been killed by the blast from one of Jammy Giles's 1,000-pound medium capacity bombs. They had fallen backward and landed in a heap in the doorway of his room. With only a Hitler Jugend boy to help him, Schott hadn't been able to get them up the steep cellar steps. So he had pulled the bodies into his office until a stretcher party could be spared.

In the Rathaus the Burgomaster ran his fingers along the course of the city stream: a blue mark on the map. A Luftschutzpolizei girl marked the map with a wax pencil as the reports came in: the southern part of the Nurses' Training Center was alight and they had had no reports from the Amputee Center for some time. He suspected that the phone connection had gone and hoped the TENOs would be stringing an emergency line. If the fire jumped to the old buildings, then the Saint Antonius Hospital would be alight and that was packed with sick people. Some of them would be very difficult to move. He remembered that the electricity chief had made the hospital generator a condition upon which the supply of the central net would depend. Also he had said that the fire must not approach closer to the electricity station.

Electricity was still reaching most vital sections of town: his control room at the Rathaus, the police station, the emergency TENO command post they had set up next door, Party H.Q. with its soup, ration cards, blankets, money, etc. for the homeless. As long as the electricity on the central net worked, the phones would work, and there would be a chance for his town to survive.

He turned to the girl. "Put the city stream into the Mönchenstrasse pipes," he said. "And pump from the waterworks to keep the pressure going." The TENOs were at the waterworks. He was confident they could manage.

The Luftschutzpolizei girl at the phone nodded. She had never expected him to do otherwise. So many decisions were like that. She was talking to the TENOs almost before he'd finished saying it. They had already sealed off the junctions at Mönchenstrasse and Zillestrasse where the mains were severed. Now they began to pump the water into the moat. The surface started to move the way it did in winter. One TENO man was stationed up near the cemetery to watch in case the flow began to reverse. That would be dangerous, for from that point the sewage effluent was in the stream. An H.J. cyclist went to tell the firemen at the hospital to run out more hose. Then he told the men near the cinema that they too could use a hydrant. Until now it had remained unused so that the hospital complex should get the pressure.

For nearly one minute they were rewarded with a high-pressure jet that reached far into the fires of the Nurses' Training Center through the third-story window. A muffled cheer went up from the firemen and police but it turned into a groan. What the Burgomaster could not have known was that the 2,000-pound bomb from Tommy Carter's plane, which had landed on the corner near Voss, had caused concussion all along Mönchenstrasse. The cobbles made it difficult to see how much the camber of the street had increased. It was always a curved and bumpy surface but now some of the stones had been squeezed from the street like seeds from a lemon. Under those cobbles at seven places the water pipes had opened at the caulking joints. These splits were now being made larger by the water from the city stream. Without a sign to show its going, Altgarten's precious water was soaking into its sewers and draining away. The hoses went soft, limp and finally flat.

Even as the newly found water supply was failing and a fire messenger was running back to halt the pumps, H.J. boys were pasting up typhoid warnings on the lampposts. All citizens must boil their tap water and milk before drinking it.

Now for the first time the sweet smell of the newly dead perfumed the warm streets. Few of Altgarten's residents recognized it and some thought it might be a new sort of disinfectant, but old soldiers and TENO men glanced at each other and prepared the drums of chlorinated lime.

# ❧ 27 ❧

ALTGARTEN was an awe-inspiring display that could be seen by airmen a hundred miles away. A flare crackled loudly and left a crooked trail of white smoke. It painted one side of the Liebefrau's steeple gleaming white and made a knifelike shadow across the Platz. Five of Jammy's 4-pound incendiaries had gone through the church roof and twelve others had straddled Frenzel's Stube opposite, some falling harmlessly in the roadway and others burning insidiously in neighboring attics. Seen from the air all the fires were soft elongated red blobs. They were shaped by the direction of the speeding bombers from whose bellies hundreds of incendiary sticks tumbled, ignited and burned until the fires joined. Once there was a great mauve flash as an electricity line short-circuited.

In spite of the flak, Redenbacher followed the stream, judging its direction from the shape of the fires. He knew the radar controller would be annoyed with him for not keeping to his assigned Würzburg zone, but if he bagged a *Tommi* there would be no complaint. There, and another. Fast, very fast. He was in the stream. They were all around him: plump brown *Tommis*, full of fuel and explosive.

Major Redenbacher turned slightly to starboard to bring himself under and behind the nearest of them. A thump and a shudder told him that he'd passed through its slipstream turbulence. A Stirling. He was so close that he decided to attack horizontally from behind and low instead of attacking under it. Here over the target the Stirling's rear gunners would mistake him for another *Tommi*. Redenbacher reached back with his left hand and switched on the Revi sight. He turned the illumination low. He had modified the sight with strips of gummed paper so that the

337

range-estimator ring surmounted with a cross was merely
four dull red T shapes pointing inward. He was so close
that two of the Ts cut the wingtips off the plane ahead.
Skillfully he adjusted his speed to that of his target and
switched his guns to "fire." He pressed the gun button and
the cannons and machine guns hammered away like road
drills, their trails scratching the sooty night sky.

Redenbacher watched the shells entering the bomber
with a detached interest that frightened even himself. The
light from his gunfire illuminated the tail of the Stirling.
The rear turret revolved and a piece of it became
dislodged. It sped toward him, growing larger at a frightening speed until it filled his windshield and with a terrible
thump that shook the Junkers it turned the windshield
glass black. Redenbacher was unable to see; his flier's
instinct took control. He climbed steeply up through the
stream. More shapes, that might have been bombers, were
seen as dim blurs through the dark dribbling fog that
eclipsed his forward vision. "Oh my God!" said Redenbacher.

There were several thumps and a vibration from the
prop and a rattle against the fuselage. The engine temperature needle crept toward the danger mark. That was the
trouble with the air-cooled B.M.W.s.

In the Stirling, Flying Officer Ian Munro, on his fourth
operation, pulled the bomb jettison lever. The port outer
was vibrating and it felt as though an aileron had been
ripped up. Coolly he pulled back the pitch control, closed
the throttle and pushed the feathering button. The broken
propeller blades turned until they were edge-on to the
airstream and thus wouldn't be forcibly revolved by it.
The propeller stopped. If they got back that engine would
be salvageable. He called up the crew. There was no reply
from the rear gunner.

"Captain to rear gunner. I repeat, are you O.K.?"

"This is Monty, sir. I'm back at the rear turret now. It's
been rotated and is empty."

"You mean Chris fell out?"

"Bailed out, I'd guess, sir."

"Bad show. I thought he was a bit edgy tonight. Can
you get into the turret?"

"Afraid not, sir. It's fully rotated with the rear doors
flapping open. I can see into it but I can't move it."

"Leave it, Monty. We'll just have to keep our fingers
crossed, chaps."

Not far away Flight Lieutenant Sweet's Lancaster began its bombing run.

"Left, left. Steady. Steady. Steady." Sweet put his head into the transparent blister that enabled him to see the ground below. "I don't want them there, bomb aimer. I want them in the dark patch to the west. Let's shake up his fire fighters. You know the drill."

"Very good, sir," said the bomb aimer hurriedly. "I think I can still make it. Right?"

"Nothing doing. We'll go round again. We've come all this way, now let's do it according to the book, eh?"

Sweet put the plane into a steep bank. "And don't let's have any moaning, chaps. Moaning gets me down. Do the job properly and then we can go home and not come back to this one again."

Sweet cautiously watched the Lancaster ahead of him as he pulled across the stream to go round in a circle. There was enough light from the fires and photoflashes exploding below them to see other aircraft quite clearly; flickering like an old silent film.

Enviously Pip Speke, Sweet's bomb aimer, watched the exhausts of other planes now going home. Sweet continued a flat turn across the farmland to the south of the fires. It was silent and dark here, but a few miles away he could still see the fires and sticks of bombs flashing, one after the other, in little straight lines like some prize-winning score on a pinball machine. The light threw shadows of Pip's head upon the inside formers of the aircraft. He watched anxiously as the explosions and fires came round to the front, leveled off and began to creep toward him like lava. None of the other crewmen realized how much more vulnerable a man felt lying full length, watching the gunfire come slicing at his belly. Speke moved his parachute pack so that it covered his genitals. It was stupid, he knew that, but he always did it.

"You know where I mean now?" Sweet asked him.

"Yes, sir, the dark patch to the west."

"Exactly. Fuse switches on? Salvo selected? We're coming in from the west this time."

"Yes, sir."

"Very well, bomb aimer. See if you can't do a very good job this time."

The compressed air, released by electropneumatic valves, made a nose like a sharp intake of breath and there was a slight jar as the breech blocks of three Oerlikon cannons and the three MG17 machine guns retracted and cocked.

He turned the safety switch to select "All guns." The red panel lights winked.

"Kettledrums," said Himmel. There ahead of him was an airplane.

The hammering of cannon shells interrupted Sweet's conversation. Himmel had placed himself beautifully. His assigned Würzburg patrol area came right up to Altgarten and a sharp controller seeing Sweet's blip had guessed he was going round again to bomb.

Sweet's rear gunner fired only 146 machine gun bullets before the power supply to the turret ceased. A damaged engine supplied its power. Slowly the gunner began to turn it, using the hand control. He tried to see the Junkers through the glare from the incendiary bullets and shells coming at him. The turret's Perspex shattered into sharp angular pieces and sparks flew from the gun barrels. The rear gunner was the first to die.

Himmel's incendiary shells also hit S Sweet's port outer engine and its coolant burst into flame with an audible spasm. Sweet flipped the throttle forward and then fully back. "Close mastercock for port outer," he told Murphy.

"It's off," said Murphy.

Sweet pushed the control column forward to maintain airspeed but there was no response. He pressed the feathering button and closed the radiator. They waited for the propeller to stop turning. There was enough light from the fire to see it clearly.

Sweet struggled with the controls. The ailerons were badly shredded, which tipped the Lancaster fifteen degrees from level, and bent rudders caused it to steer to port. All the while there was an awful vibration threatening to shake the plane apart. Sweet joggled each of the throttles and found that the vibration slowed with the starboard outer's one.

"Close master fuel cock for starboard outer," ordered Sweet.

"Starboard outer off," said Murphy. The vibration slowed but only a little.

"It won't feather and I can't get her to fly level."

"We're losing fuel from the port tanks. That's unbalancing the trim," said Murphy. "A broken blade is causing the vibration." The two men looked out at the fire. It began in a perfectly straight line along the wing near the trailing edge and ended in a wispy ragged edge far behind. So far only the petrol spray leaking from the broken fuel tank was alight. Sweet pushed the button to operate the Graviner extinguishers but there was no visible difference.

Sweet leaned forward on the control column and gradually the nose dropped. "Don't dive, Skipper," said Murphy, but Sweet had heard too many pilots boast of dousing an engine fire by diving to be persuaded against it. Unfortunately many pilots had found that increased speed only fanned the flames and sometimes the metal itself caught fire. But these pilots did not return to the mess to relate their stories.

Micky Murphy stared at the blazing engine with a fearful attention. He'd seen alloy burn and now he watched for the intense white glare that heralded it. Using the toe of his boot he pulled his parachute bundle nearer to him. The airstream, speeded up by the dive, was spreading the fire from the exhausts smoothly across the upper surface of the wing in a fantail that flicked sometimes toward the cockpit.

It was a steep dive: the airspeed needle jumped to 390 m.p.h. without warning. Sweet wound the elevator tab control back and heaved at the stick but managed to move it only after Murphy added his weight. The airplane gradually flattened out and then rose a little. The airspeed needle fell back drunkenly to a dangerous 100 m.p.h. and then flicked between 80 and 120.

"I'd not be trusting the airspeed. The Pitot tube is likely bent or perhaps its heater's gone and it's icing."

"The heater's gone," grunted Sweet. "That's a laugh." There was so much noise from the engines that, now they could spare a hand, they were both pressing their phones to their ears to converse. The altimeter showed a height loss of 2,000 feet but Murphy no longer believed any of the dials. The bottom of the "turn and bank" was fixed to one side and did not move.

Sweet had got her straight and level now but at the lower speed the vibration increased. The engine cowling glowed dull red. The alloy weld on a clip gave way and the cowling began to bounce violently in the slipstream. Each bounce gave them a chance to glimpse the bright yellow furnace inside. The gap provided a superfast channel of air that fanned the flames to a lighter color until a second clip weld gave way. For a terrible moment the whole cowling flapped above the burning engine like the bright red wings of a bird of prey. It bent backward, slammed against the leading edge of the wing three times, broke free, lifted, slammed down heavily upon the upper

surface of the wing and then, lifted clear by the aerodynam-
ics of the airflow, it flew off over the tail flapping gently.

"A piece of wing. Jesus, it's fallen off. It just went past
me like a vampire," called the wireless operator.

"Calm down, everyone," said Sweet. "I can handle it."
To Murphy he calmly said, "Cowlings are your check,
engineer. Did you inspect that one before takeoff?"

Murphy looked at him. There was plenty of bright
yellow light in the cockpit and Murphy could see Sweet's
face glistening with sweat as he fought the controls. "It
was fine, sir," answered Murphy, "and the port outer
wasn't afire either."

"I don't want any of your damned sarcasm," said
Sweet. Now that the cowling had gone the engine flames
had lessened a fraction but the missing cowling caused a
braking and spoiling effect upon the airflow which made
the Lancaster buffet and bounce. Sweet had both feet on
one rudder bar trying to prevent it from yawing sideways
across the sky.

There was a sharp crack, a whine and a smell of cordite
as a shell burst nearby. They were attracting flak now.
"The flame on the trailing edge is looking very nasty, Mr.
Sweet, sir. She might explode her tanks."

"Scientifically impossible, engineer," said Sweet, smiling.
"Even in an empty tank the fuel-air mixture is too rich to
ignite and explode."

"I've seen it happen," persisted Murphy.

Sweet looked back over his shoulder and then gave
Murphy a prim shake of the head to calm him. He was
holding her now and, although the flames were just as
bad, they weren't getting worse as far as he could decide.

"And, Murphy," said Sweet. "You'll remove that name
from your helmet. My crew don't steal each other's equipment."

Murphy called to the rear gunner to ask if the night
fighter was still there. "See him, rear gunner?" Murphy
asked.

"David's dead," said the Canadian upper gunner.

"Can you see him from your turret, Kit?"

"The fire's so bright I can see the tail all right but
bugger all beyond it. It's dazzling from here. But how the
Christ could he miss us, Micky? We're blazing like a
bonfire. Both rudders are shot up and the port one is
leaning sideways."

"We are going in to bomb," said Sweet. "Bomb doors
open."

"You mad berk," said Kit Pepper, the mid-upper gunner. "Haven't you jettisoned those bloody eggs yet?"

"Bombs gone," said Speke. The aircraft lurched to confirm his words.

"You stupid fool," said Sweet. "Who told you to jettison?"

Murphy watched the feathered propeller blade come to a stop. "Port outer ignition off, sir."

"It won't count toward your tour," warned Sweet primly. "Jettison is the same as an abort trip."

"Who said we jettisoned?" said Kit Pepper.

"I aimed at the target," said the bomb aimer obligingly.

"Liar," said Sweet. "We're miles off target." There was no reply. "That was sabotage and I'm going to put you on a charge when we get back."

"If we get bloody back," said Speke, "I'll not complain."

"Bomb doors closed," announced Sweet.

"Navigator, give me a course for Warley. Since you're all too frightened to do your job properly, we may as well go home."

"Steer 283, sir," said Billy Pace, the quiet ex-architect who was their navigator.

"The compass is dead, sir." said Micky Murphy.

Sweet noticed that for the first time. "I'll steer by the stars then." He leaned over for a better view of the bomb aimer. "What the devil are you doing down there, bomb aimer?"

"Getting bloody out," replied Speke, struggling to undo the forward escape hatch. "They may give the Victoria bleeding Cross to pilots who press on in flaming Lancasters, but not to bomb aimers they don't."

"You'll be court-martialed."

"And you'll be dead," said Speke. Murphy watched him. Once hit, these Lancs had a bad reputation for escaping crews: only eleven percent of air crew survived compared with twenty-nine percent of escaping Halifax crewmen. Pip Speke got the hatch open and, as if frightened that Sweet might leave the controls and grab him, he dived headfirst through the hatch. There was a thump as his legs hit the side of it and one flying boot remained inside the nose. A rush of wind coming through the hatch jolted Sweet.

Toward the rear of the Lancaster the wireless operator and Kit Pepper, the upper gunner, were unable to open the entrance door. Bravely they had struggled to dump

hot flares and signal cartridges down the flare chute. One
of Himmel's cannon shells had bent the door lock but they
hammered at it with the fire ax and kicked it open a little.
Ax blows vibrated through the fuselage. Sweet had felt the
weight of the two men move back toward the tail and had
revolved the trim wheel to compensate. He guessed what
they might be doing. "No one leaves the aircraft, and
that's an order. I don't care if I court-martial all of you."

"O.K., Cap," said Kit Pepper, but he didn't pause in his
efforts to open the fuselage door. Kit signaled to the
wireless operator that he was going to squeeze himself out
through the bent door. The other boy nodded agreement.
The plane lurched under his feet so that he grabbed at the
nearby turret to steady himself while he carefully clipped
his chute to the chest of his harness.

"We are going to make it, chaps," said Sweet. There
were sparks from the starboard outer as he spoke. "I'm
holding it on 283."

"The compass is u/s," shouted Murphy. "We are going
round in circles. That's the target coming up to starboard.
The rudders are warped. We'll never get her home. She's
well alight too. Can't you see?" They were lower now and
the Altgarten fires seemed both fiercer and larger. Most
were lemon or pink in color, but now there were deep red
ones too where the fire had got out of control.

Himmel came in for another pass. The explosions of the
cannon shells echoed inside the Lancaster's metal fuselage
like a cricketball in a biscuit tin. Three of Sweet's windows starred and the engine fire was seen through them as
only a pink glow. Near Murphy's feet there were three
black disks like bent gramophone records. Wondering
what they were, Murphy saw a searchlight beam pass each
in succession and realized they were gaping cannon shell
holes in the aircraft's stressed metal side.

Still the shells were exploding. Murphy heard someone
scream and there was a whine of flying metal fragments.
To the starboard side, high, at about four o'clock, he saw
another Lancaster flying straight and level. The flaming
port outer of S Sweet illuminated the other bomber from
underneath in an unnatural way that made it like a model
used in a film. It kept too still and flew too perfectly
straight to be real, thought Murphy. The flames shone on
its propeller blades like four silver disks and Murphy could
see the little white patch that was the nose and eyes of its
pilot and he knew he was saying, "It's them that are about

to die and not us and I thank you truly O Mother of God."

Murphy tapped the oil gauges: eighty-nine degrees, not too bad, and seventy-pounds-per-square-inch pressure was normal. The temperature and pressure readings for the windmilling outer starboard was almost normal too, but that was just a momentary mechanical freak. He expected it to seize up very soon and that would put even more strain on Sweet's abilities, both physical and mental. Bang, bang. There were more hits; he could feel each one shake the metal floor. He decided it was hopeless, but he'd always had this petrifying terror of parachuting and even now it didn't leave him.

Fighter pilots either made a kill soon after being assigned to a squadron (as Himmel had downed a Polish bomber near Lodz) and then went on chalking up kill after kill, or else they never even damaged the paint on an enemy plane, no matter how often they went into combat. For this second sort of flier just staying alive for fifty sorties was a notable achievement.

The *Experten* were easily recognized: they were alert and had remarkable reaction speeds. They were excellent gunners who were able to aim off correctly for deflection shots, estimating the enemy's speed and predicting his course. An *Experte* could control his aircraft to get very, very close to the enemy and hold that gun platform rock steady long enough to kill. Three seconds could be enough.

Himmel was an *Experte*, while pilots like Beer would never make it. Driving his racing car had called for boldness but not this degree of judgment. Beer hosepiped his fire all over the sky while his plane was yawing and skidding. By the time he'd corrected his flying, the enemy was already into another evasive maneuver. Given an enemy flying straight and level ahead of him, then Beer might have shot him down, except that he probably wouldn't allow his plane to get close enough for more than ten percent of his gunfire to strike home. But unfortunately for Sweet and Murphy it wasn't Beer who was attacking them, it was Himmel.

He watched the Lancaster growing in his gunsight as he came in as steady as a freight train. As if seeking its own destruction, the target's wingtips reached out for the range rings.

Bang. Bang. Bang. During the four-second burst, forty-

seven pounds of steel and high explosive left Himmel's
guns and much of it hit *S for Sugar*.

Both the men levering at the exit door saw Himmel's
Junkers closing upon them from the starboard quarter for
his third pass. Kit switched on his microphone to warn
Sweet, but all anyone heard was the beginning of a
scream. A shell hit his belly and blew his shoulders from
his legs. It atomized his trunk into a spray of red foam
that covered the inside of the fuselage as far as the rear
spar. The wireless operator standing beside him regained a
brief consciousness drifting through the air under a
parachute canopy. He felt cold and sleepy and a little
drunk. His femoral artery was severed and he was losing
blood as fast as his wildly beating heart could pump it into
the night air. He died four thousand feet above Altgarten.

The plane gave an agonizing lurch. Until that moment,
Billy Pace, the navigator, had not been frightened, but,
having survived Himmel's third pass, he urgently needed
the reassurance of a solid, earthlike, well-built platform
under his feet. But *Sugar* sagged and dropped fifty terrifying feet through space before regaining stability in a sickening groan of straining metal. The rear part of the
fuselage was being wrenched from side to side by the
airstream over the badly bent rudder. Each waggle made
more rivets ping loose. Air rushing across the torn metal
edges of two dozen holes in the fuselage made a loud and
constant flutelike scream.

Billy Pace tried to climb out through the escape hatch
on the roof above the main spar even before he had
consciously decided to jump. He had clipped his parachute
to the metal clips on the chest of his harness but could not
get through the small hatch. Patiently Pace eased his
shoulders back inside the aircraft and unclipped the
parachute. Then he climbed out through the roof holding
the parachute bundle in his hand. The airstream hit him
like a hammer. It smashed against his face and chest at
230 m.p.h. and pinned his legs against the edge of the
hatch. Inch by inch he dragged himself into its overwhelming force. It crushed his body and prevented him from
inhaling properly. Suddenly the airstream overcame the
strength of his arms and threw his upper body hard
against the fuselage, twisting his knees in doing so. Then it
plucked him out of the hatch.

The fire from the port outer enabled him to see as if it
were daylight. He grabbed for a handhold but there was
none. The slipstream slid him along the rough paint work

like a shove-ha'penny. He hit the upper turret hard and grazed both knees badly before tumbling off the fuselage top with his parachute bundle still in his hand. Beyond there was just space and into that he fell. He dropped, bowling over and over, and saw the airplane, and then the moon, pass over him. The tail wheel was only a yard away from his face, and because for a moment his speed was almost equal to that of the airplane, it seemed to move very slowly. He knew that his parachute was useless unless fixed onto the metal clips and cried tears of desperate rage as he fumbled for the metal rungs. He had fallen 4,500 feet before he realized that he could look down at his hands to see what he was doing. Then he was able to affix one hook with no difficulty, but he could not get the other one fastened. He did not dare look toward the ground but out of the corner of his eye he noticed the searchlights and the Altgarten fires circling slowly around his feet and growing bigger every second. He decided to hold the parachute across his body with one hand and pull the rip cord depending upon the single clip. When he pulled it there was a jerk that spun him sideways suspended from one strap. The canopy opened with a slap of air and Billy Pace, whole and unharmed, drifted gently into the zephyr-like warm winds of Altgarten.

Only Sweet and Murphy remained alive in the aircraft now. After the bomb aimer went, a gale of great intensity blew through the open hatch into the cockpit.

"Abandon," said Sweet. "Clear off, Murphy. I know you are only waiting for me to say it."

Micky Murphy nodded. Sweet said, "Use the forward hatch. Wait for my command."

Murphy took an oxygen bottle and edged his way forward. He gripped the underside of the pilot's instrument panel and swing himself under it. He had to use all his strength to move against the 200-m.p.h. wind coming in. He got down onto the step and then straddled the open hatch. Through it he saw fires and searchlights. He plugged into the intercom and said, "I'm ready to go, sir." Sweet grunted.

The aircraft rolled alarmingly as the starboard side aileron trim cable snapped and wrapped itself round the aileron hinge, locking it in a tangle of shredded wire. She kept rolling now until the starboard wing was tilted upward at 40 degrees. Uncertain whether to jump, and devoid of his intercom, Murphy poked his head low and saw Sweet with his shoulders against the fuselage side, red-faced and straining at the control column. It was only after he gave up the struggle that the coiled trim wire fell from the released aileron to droop in the slipstream. The controls were free again. Aware that some miracle had saved the plane from rolling over and over all the way to the ground, Sweet corrected the bank. Infinitely slowly the Lancaster came back to straight and level flight.

Murphy slammed his intercom plug into the bomb aimer's station and said, "Aren't you going too, sir?"

"I took it up and I'm taking it down."

"Not to Warley?"

"Onto the deck somewhere."

"You'll not do it alone."

Sweet grunted again. "You might be of use, I suppose."

Murphy was frightened to jump out through the hatch. The burning airplane was almost like a home to him. "Better the devil you know . . ." said Murphy. He turned to climb up on the step and the airstream blew him back to his engineer's position. He clamped his huge hand around a metal girder. "Use the hand trim."

"I was just going to," said Sweet.

"And bring the revs up. We'll not be trying to save fuel."

"Shall I detonate the secret gear?"

"I've done that," said Murphy.

"What shall I do now?"

"Can you remember what the wind was?"

"No, I'm sorry. It's that bloody navigator. He's gone, I suppose. He was always bloody useless."

"Never mind him; there's just the two of us left."

"What about the night fighter?" asked Sweet nervously.

"Ah, I was forgetting him," said Murphy dryly. "Yes, there's three of us really."

Himmel was very close to them, watching the blazing bomber with a fear and fascination. "Poor fellows," said the observer. It was clear that the crew were struggling to keep her flying.

"They burn our cities and bury our people alive," said Himmel. He moved into position for the coup de grâce. He had come up a few points to starboard now and was dazzled by the burning engine. A flak shell burst near the Lanc's starboard wingtip and both airplanes jolted.

"The flak will probably claim her," said the observer.

"They claim everything," said Himmel. He still did not open fire on the stricken bomber. He throttled back and suddenly there were bright blue and yellow flashes from his own exhaust.

Himmel knew the revs were dropping before he looked down at the gauge. Perhaps it was the vibration through the control column or a slight modulation of the engine's sound as the plugs began to oil up. Just the starboard motor: boost and oil pressure too. The valve was seating badly and again the mixture ignited in the exhaust manifold and gushed flame. That damned motor. If Kugel had changed the engine instead of trying to save Luftwaffe money by fobbing him off with a new set of piston rings there would be another *Tommi* downed.

"Tighten your straps," said Himmel. "It's a piano out of the fifth floor." So as not to alarm his crew he used the slang term for a forced landing. Neither of them replied, but he saw the observer touch his parachute as if he could not depend upon his eyes to tell him it was to hand. She would cut at any moment. And when she does, that radar array will grant her the aerodynamic perfection of a broken brick. He put the nose down steeply, for he needed every bit of airspeed he could muster if he was to get them down in one piece. The variometer needle sank. Above them the blazing *Tommi* was straightening out and flying level again.

"Butterbrot from *Katze Four*. Butterbrot from *Katze Four*. S.O.S. engine failure. Map reference . . . "

"Ludwig Nordpol Six," supplied Himmel's radar operator hurriedly from the rear seat.

"Ludwig Nordpol Six," said Himmel.

"Order: Steer 180," came the reply. Himmel was already heading that way; he knew they would want to take him as far away from the route of the enemy as they could. Anxiously he watched the cloud patches. To port the Ruhr was under its usual blanket of smog, although here and there he could see the dull red smudge of a steel furnace. He steered away toward the flat, open country.

The Liaison Officer at Deelen was referring to his distress map. On its airfields with blind-landing apparatus were distinguished from emergency strips. High ground, obstacles and high-tension cables that would prove a hazard to a crippled plane were all indicated. Quickly he chose an airfield. Selected searchlights over which Himmel was flying tipped their beams almost flat along the surface of the ground. From 15,000 feet they were like gray roads, all of them pointing to the distress airfield.

"I can see them now," said Himmel.

"Announcement: Radishes and shroud too," promised the Liaison Officer.

"Yes," said the observer.

"We see it," said Himmel. The starboard engine coughed twice and cut. Himmel feathered it and switched it off. Ahead of him a searchlight beam held upon a piece of cloud. That was the promised shroud, then came the radishes: white rockets and red rockets exploding above an airfield where ambulances and fitters, fuel bowsers and ammunition supply lorries were waiting for him.

"Shall I fire a red?" asked the observer.

"Why not?" said Himmel. "We'd better contribute something to the party." He tuned in to the blind-landing frequency and heard a single high note They were exactly on course. Himmel was about to lower his flaps but on impulse he defeathered the propeller and switched on the ignition. The airstream spun the blades and it fired and roared into life.

"You bastard," said Himmel. Neither of his crew spoke; they could almost taste the hot coffee that was awaiting them. He pulled the stick back and turned toward the bombing to look for the airplane he had half killed.

# ♦ 28 ♦

WHEN the water supply dried up, Bodo Reuter—the TENO officer—took an H.J. boy's bicycle and cycled through the bombs and shrapnel to report to the Burgomaster at the Rathaus. He hurried through the sandbagged entrance and pushed past the police chief. Impatiently he waited while a messenger from Frenzel's Stube completed his report. A bomb there had killed twenty-five people including eight of the Burgomaster's guests who had been having a few final drinks in the bar. The ground floor of the Stube had been converted into an emergency mortuary.

"Next," said the Burgomaster, turning his blank eyes to Bodo Reuter. It was as if he had not heard the report, thought Bodo, and perhaps he hadn't. Perhaps he was waiting until tomorrow before coming to terms with such news.

"Why didn't you phone?"

"The phones have gone, Herr Bürgermeister. The western half of the power net is out of action. I could have phoned you from Party H.Q., but that journey was almost as long as coming here directly."

"The western side?" said the Burgomaster. He looked at his telephonist; she nodded. In the part of town near the old market the electricity supply was carried on overhead wires from building to building. Some of those streets were now tangled with broken wiring, impeding pedestrians, blocking traffic and injuring cyclists.

"Report," commanded the Burgomaster.

"The city stream is flowing well, Herr Bürgermeister. And the broken pipe on Mönchenstrasse has been repaired but there is hardly any water coming through it."

"Why?"

"They have had four or five bombs on Mönchenstrasse. Only the first bomb made a crater in the road and
severed the pipes but the others have cracked the joints.
There might be a dozen leaks along the length of the
street; it would take many hours to dig down to repair
them."

The Burgomaster listened to Bodo with an almost inhuman calm. He turned back to his map. At first he had
placed a big red pin into the site of each bomb but it was
ten minutes since he had run out of red pins. He fingered
Mönchenstrasse and without turning round said, "Voss's
house was hit?"

"Voss is dead, Herr Bürgermeister. He was putting
sand upon an incendiary bomb when he was killed by the
blast. Some of them contain an explosive charge."

"The fool," said the Burgomaster. Outside there was no
respite from the bombing. "Run hose the whole length of
Mönchenstrasse. Take your water directly from the city
stream."

"Do you realize how much hose that is?" objected Bodo
Reuter. "And what will it give us? One single branch. We
may as well pee on the fire."

"There's no alternative," said the Burgomaster. His hair
was standing up from his head. His stiff wing collar had
come unclipped from his collar stud and it waggled in the
air, making him look like a music hall comic.

Reuter turned to leave but the Burgomaster took his
arm and dragged him roughly toward the map of the
town. There was a tremendous explosion nearby and
although the others in the room ducked these two men
seemed not to hear it.

"Where?" said the Burgomaster. "Show me where." His
voice was not his natural one, and for a moment the
fireman was afraid of this comical-looking wretch with the
scarecrow evening suit and white brick dust down his
waistcoat.

"We'll string out the hose, Herr Bürgermeister," said
the fireman.

"No alternative," said the Burgomaster. He said it as
though it was a little dictum that he lived by, and indeed
for the last half hour he had.

A Luftschutz girl finished typing a short note and
passed it to the Burgomaster for signature. He called an
H.J. messenger. It was little Jürgen Löwe, the barber's
son.

"Cycle quickly to Nehringstrasse, the fire at the bakery.

They must demolish the houses behind it to create a fire break. The senior TENO officer will need this written order."

"I've no bicycle, sir."

"How dare you come here without it? The safety of the town depends upon a good messenger service."

Jürgen was only fourteen. This was his first week of official duty and he was downcast by the Burgomaster's scolding.

"You'll run all the way. And next time you come on duty, don't dare forget your bicycle."

"I didn't forget it, sir," said the child. "I was blown off it at the corner of Dorfstrasse and Zillestrasse. I could only find a wheel and that was badly bent."

"Get along with you," said the Burgomaster. "And be careful." The little boy ran out of the room clasping his blue-painted messenger's helmet as though it were an Iron Cross.

"It's finished," said the telephonist. "The bombers have gone." She logged the call from the observer post on the Venlo road and soon there were more calls confirming the report.

Scarcely believing it, the Burgomaster climbed the steps from his control room like a man whose joints had aged overnight. The others followed him and as they emerged through the sandbagged entrance the glare made them half close their eyes. The fires were dragging the air across the flat farmland and creating a warm breeze. The more air consumed at ground level, the higher were the flames and the greater was the heat at the fire's center and the lighter its color. Apart from the spectacular sight of the gasholder, the highest flames were from the Nurses' Training Center. Thank God that, at least, was evacuated without casualties. They could feel the heat of the fires and hear the roar of them, but the hum of the aircraft had all but disappeared. Suddenly from the Liebefrau church there was a tremendous crash. A sheet of flame rose and sprinkled white-hot sparks across the roofs of the town.

The firemen had been expecting it. Half of a canister of incendiaries jettisoned by Munro's young brother Ian had been the deciding factor. Molten lead had been dripping onto the firemen below for some minutes. As soon as the men on the church roof saw the trusses buckling, they hurried back down to the ground. The bells fell soon after that with a monstrous din. The stonework of the outer walls was expanding and it made angry growls and sudden cracks. The nave of the church was ablaze and the great stained-glass window had never shone more beautifully than it did in the Liebefrau's final agony. A buttress fell with an awful crash. The stonework continued to expand until, with an earthshaking roar, it released the roof upon the burning interior. Sparks flew into the air for a thousand feet and the windows flashed red.

The fifteenth-century altarpiece, the carved pulpit and the painting of the martyrs that was said to be a van der Weyden were gone forever. The firemen turned away from the church. For some time their hoses had been directed upon the old houses and Frenzel's Stube on the far side of the Platz. One of the priests had become almost violent when the firemen refused to put their hoses upon the church. He had refused to believe that it was too late.

That sly fool Frenzel had stored five barrels of black market schnapps and fifteen sacks of sugar in his apartment above the restaurant. The heat had fired the sugar and was exploding the schnapps barrels like high explosive bombs, squirting burning alcohol onto TENOs and firemen in the street and as far as the neighboring houses In the cellar sat the Frenzels and their three young daughters. The firemen urged them to go to the shelter round the corner in Studentenacker, but the girls would not leave their mother. Frau Frenzel in turn would not leave her husband and Herr Frenzel would under no circumstances leave his cellarful of French wines. It was bad enough to sit there with the smell of his black market Westphalian hams scorching. He cut another slice of Frau Frenzel's *Schlumperwerk* and bit into the sweet apple filling. It was always like this when he was worried; he ate without even being hungry. The firemen hoisted another hose up the face of the building to a second-story window and tried to prevent the fire from moving downward. Frenzel's restaurant had become an emergency mortuary and the firemen were picking their way between rows of corpses laid out on the floor of the bar and awash with water from the hoses.

The hardware store on the other side of Liebefrauplatz was a similar fire hazard. Eight drums of paint had caught fire and were pouring down the staircase like molten lava, trapping and endangering twenty people in the cellar. The TENOs were digging toward them through hot masonry.

Near the gasworks a crowd of over a hundred civilians

had formed a human cordon across the road and beaten
up the crew of a fire engine who were on their way to the
hospital and would not attend to their blazing homes.

In Florastrasse Herr and Frau Meyer, who had been
married that afternoon, were sitting in a cellar under her
parents' house together with a dozen guests. A Rumanian
cantor was singing the ancient songs of the wedding feast.

Herr Holländer, the man who had married the couple
that afternoon, was at that moment opening the heavy
door of a deep shelter in Kaiserin-Augustastrasse. He
looked in every few minutes. It was a grimy street, not far
enough away from the gasworks to be disassociated from
the slums that surrounded it. Correctly garbed and with
dimmed torch to hand, he looked around and then noted
the time. Most of the occupants were brewery workers
who on account of their early rising resented bitterly being
told to take shelter. It was the law, as Holländer told
them this night. It wasn't a decision of his, it was the law.

Most of them were snoring and there was a smell of
stale breath and unwashed bodies. None of them would
thank him for his concern. Hollander believed that they
all hated him. He believed that they thought him a rodent-
faced bureaucrat who used his job as Blockwart to inter-
fere and pry into the business of his neighbors with the full
backing of authority. Holländer's wife was a meek little
creature—the rat and the mouse, someone had once called
them. She did not believe that anyone could think such
things of her husband, let alone say them. She was wrong
and he was exactly right.

He closed the door behind him and hurried up the
stairs. He had the keys of all of their apartments in his
bag. Perhaps he should make sure that no fire bombs had
fallen into any of them. His was a grave responsibility and
he met it with diligence and thoroughness. Perhaps the
first apartment should be old Frau Klietmann's.

Andi Niels had succeeded in persuading the tall Viennese nurse to leave the dance hall "for a breath of fresh
air," but she wouldn't go to the annex with him. So they
had gone out across Koller Meadow and had been lying
on the grass in a state of semi-undress when Tommy
Carter's Lancaster arrived. One of his T.I.s splashed fire
upon them so that they had assumed the strange boxer's
pose that burned bodies take up. Both of them had shrunk
to four-and-a-half-foot lengths of carbon.

For all the people in Altgarten the departure of the
bombers brought a merciful quiet for which they had al-

most ceased to hope. Although warm winds roared through the narrow streets to feed the fires and carry away the cries of the injured, dying and trapped, at least most of the town was still intact.

Two hundred sixty bombers had attacked Altgarten in the twenty-eight minutes between 0124 and 0152, which is an average of 9.3 aircraft per minute. Of these aircraft, 156 bombed within three miles of their aiming point. Only eight aircraft ignored the Altgarten fires and passed over them to bomb Krefeld by means of the H2S apparatus.

Most of the aircraft had a bomb load of 14,000 pounds and although twenty-five percent of the R.A.F.'s high explosive bombs were duds, it still meant that for several minutes at a time in Altgarten it was no easier to distinguish between the explosions of individual bombs than it is to identify those of a fast-revving car engine. Now that the bombers had gone the silence was curiously oppressive. When the Burgomaster spoke his voice seemed unnecessarily loud.

"Thank God," said the Burgomaster. The others turned to look at him. It was not a National Socialist sentiment. The Burgomaster did not care. "Thank God," he said again.

There were clouds across the moon: cirrostratus thickening to become altostratus. Half an hour ago the moon had been a sharp-edged disk with a halo, but now it had become a soft white blob. For a moment the moon darkened behind the thickening cloud. There were chunks of fractostratus too, scudding across the town so close to the rooftops that they glowed bright red and flickered like little private hells in the sky.

"Filthy swine," said Oberzugführer Bodo Reuter.

"The Mönchenstrasse pipes," said the Burgomaster.

"Immediately, Herr Bürgermeister," snapped Reuter. He took his small bicycle and found it difficult to ride. Odd that he had had no difficulty riding it when the bombs were falling. "All of your hose to Mönchenstrasse," shouted the Burgomaster after him. Miles to the west there was the rumble of antiaircraft fire as the returning bombers passed over the massed batteries near the Dutch frontier.

The diesel pump in the TENO yard had been destroyed and the tank below it was afire. A thin snake of black smoke crawled through the back streets near the railway, bringing oily smears, motes of soot, reddened eyes and a

taste that reached into the back of Bodo's throat. He bit
into the wet handkerchief tied across his face and pedaled
faster. At the corner of Neustrasse he stopped and stared.

A curtain of dust eddying and swirling in the air
currents, moved toward the fires on Dorfstrasse. Those
fires—Schmitt the butcher's, the old insurance building
and Becker's dress shop—shone through the smoke as a
fairy ballet through a theatrical gauze. By their light
Reuter could see shop window dummies—broken, stiff and
denuded by blast—scattered among the debris on the
pavement. Except that where the fires burned most brightly it was clear that they were not dummies.

But it was not the fires or the bodies that made Reuter
stare: it was the absence of the entire city block that until
tonight had separated Dorfstrasse from this corner. Over
one hundred yards square and four stories high, it was
now a tangled mess that, apart from a couple of chimney
breasts, stood nowhere taller than a man. The 2,000-
pound bomb from Jammy's aircraft had exploded there.
Yet elsewhere this night there fell bombs four times as
heavy as that one.

Bodo climbed back onto his tiny bicycle and hurried to
Gerd Böll near what was once the house of Voss.

"You keep looking across there," said Bodo Reuter.

"It's Voss's place. My cousin's housekeeper is in the
cellar." Bodo noticed that his friends's eyebrows had been
scorched and he could feel that his own were too, and his
lips were cracked and raw.

They both looked at the pile of rubble where another
1,000-pound M.C. had demolished Voss's house. Neither
of the men spoke; there was nothing they could do.
Finally they walked to the hole in the road. Their torches
probed around the crater with the deft professional touch
of surgeons examining an open belly.

It had been neatly done. The gas pipes were plugged
with wedges and, farther along, the twisted, brightly colored electricity cables were roughly clamped across the
charred ends as if with artery forceps. The special fire and
police phone lines had also been given first aid.

Lower than those, so that the water could not leak and
cause a short-circuit, there were the small-capacity street
water supply pipes, but the torches did not linger upon
that side of the crater. The problems were all in the center
of the street. A layer of cobblestones had been scattered
for yards and the paving and broken stone under it had
collapsed into the crater. There the gas pipes bent drunk-

enly and the 35-cm. water pipe was leaking at its joints. Deepest of all, and along the very center of the street, just exposed at the bottom of the crater was the main sewer. It received the street's strong (i.e. domestic) sewage as well as weak sewage from gutters and rainstorm water from the street drains. The sewer pipe was lower than the water pipes so that it would receive any water that might leak from them. This, like many of the main sewers through the oldest part of town, was simply the medieval gully. Now water from the broken mains was coursing through it, moving southwest toward the sewage works.

"A few sandbags would do it," said Gerd.

"It's worth trying," agreed Bodo.

"Find the sewage manhole on Dorfstrasse, block up the outlet with a few sandbags, wait for the water to fill the sewer and then use the manhole as a sump from which to pump water."

"Suppose the water level gets high enough for the sewage to get into the town supply?" said Bodo. "It will be the devil of a job to clean."

"Then you can blame me," said Gerd.

For a moment Reuter was silent. Then he said, "Very well, Gerd, you are the doctor of engineering." The group of TENOs were waiting for their next orders. Meanwhile they had been giving the distracted Blockwart Storp a hand to dig down toward his cellar.

Reuter said, "Find the Dorfstrasse sewer inspection manhole and block the outlet with sandbags. Then tell the senior fireman at the hospital that he can take water from there."

"'raus!" shouted Reuter, and his men leaped aboard their lorry. The Blockwart called upon them to come back. "There are eighteen people under here," he shouted. The lorry lurched forward.

"There are three hundred people in the hospital," said Gerd gently. "Your wife will be all right until we put that fire out."

The Blockwart nodded. Under the ground the water from the mains was still splashing away.

Just a few yards away from where Gerd Böll and Reuter were standing, Anna-Luisa and little Hansl were trapped in old Herr Voss's cellar. The bomb had exploded above them at the third floor. Like most of the thin-walled H.C. bombs it had spread its shock wave sideways. In the cellar it had not sounded as loud, or made as much disturbance, as the earlier medium capacity had done, for that one had penetrated the road before exploding.

Anna-Luisa was not frightened when she was unable to open the cellar door. She suspected that the Waffen S.S. officer who had stolen Herr Voss's carpet and silver had locked it to prevent her giving the alarm. She pushed against it but it would not move. It was a solidly built door that Voss had selected specially to guard his subterranean storehouse. Anna-Luisa did not suspect that there was a couple of hundred tons of shattered masonry piled upon it.

It was very quiet there, apart from the gurgle of water. She didn't move around much. There was only the glow of the oil lamp now that the electricity had gone off. The light glinted upon the water that at the lowest part of the ancient stone floor was three or four inches deep. This didn't worry her either, for at its present rate the damaged pipe would take a couple of weeks to fill the cellar deep enough to drown them.

It wasn't until the TENO men had blocked up the Dorfstrasse sewer outlet that she became alarmed. For soon the combined sewer in the street outside began to fill. Half a dozen leaks along the whole length of the street were draining into it and the level backed up until it crept along the sewage pipe to the house. At Voss's house it reached the broken pipes above the cellar and then these too added to the flooding. For ten minutes she was horrified by the amount of water coming in. One side of the cellar was six inches deep in water but after that it virtually stopped.

It stopped because the firemen began to pump water from the Dorfstrasse manhole, which by how had formed a sump. At last the firemen at the hospital had a reasonable supply of water to fight the fire. For them the fire had become a live enemy. With their newly found supply of water they were able to take their revenge upon it. Six branches were in operation on the Dorfstrasse side of the hospital. Now that the patients had been moved along to the intact wing of the building it could only be a matter of a couple of hours before the blaze was completely under control, i.e. surrounded and reducing in area.

Of course it was uncomfortable for the patients. At first they had been close to panic and there was a time when the Oberstarzt from the Amputee Center had brought ten armed soldiers to the hospital and told them to be ready to restore order in the wards at pistol point. The turning

point in hospital morale was when Frau Thorn had
thrown the contents of her bedpan over a burning chair in
the surgical ward. The story had gone through the hospital like lightning. Everyone knew Frau Thorn and everyone had laughed. It seemed to have restored the stoic
German calm. The beds were crowded, with hardly an
inch between them. Patients were mixed up, women and
men were crowded together into corridors and
storerooms, but no one complained. In one ward they
were singing.

Across the road at the Amputee Rehabilitation Center
the Oberstarzt gave a sigh of relief when the bombing
stopped. Already the hut nearest to the hospital fire had
burst into flame. The radiation had heated the flimsy
woodwork to a temperature where sparks falling upon the
roof set it alight. There was no panic; there were enough
soldiers among his patients to quell the spoken fears of the
civilians. The nurses, helped by patients with only arm
amputations, wheeled the beds out of the huts just before
the walls ignited. Unfortunately those patients had to be
left out in the open fields and already metal fragments had
injured three of them and this had caused the others to
become uneasy. But, as the Oberstarzt said, some of the
patients in the huts were also being injured by fragments
and broken glass.

It had been a trying time for the Oberst and he was no
longer young. It was natural that people should think that
the trainees in nurse's uniform were skilled enough to
handle casualties, but many of them were shopgirls and
domestic servants with only a few days' training behind
them. Even the fully trained girls were really only to be
trusted with dispensing of drinks and emptying bedpans.
Goodness knows what damage the trainees had done this
night!

"Put all the patients out on the field," said the Oberst.
"We'll cool the huts off with buckets of water."

Meanwhile on the other side of town at the Wald
Hotel a crisis of another kind had occurred. It was a fine
Edwardian building set in two and a half acres of park-
land. Because of the high walls and the barbed wire, as
well as the constant howls of fierce dogs it was widely
believed that the Wald Hotel was a secret S.S. center of
considerable importance. One rumor said that it housed
Jewish millionaires who had bribed the S.S. to get them
out of concentration camps and now lived here in luxury.
There were stories about it being a stud farm for S.S.

men on leave, as Frau Hinkelburg had suggested. Another rumor said that Stalin's son, captured on the East Front, was held prisoner here. In reality it was simply a Waffen S.S. dog-training center and the screams heard at night were the yelps of hungry dogs.

The dogs began to bark from the moment that the first H.E. bombs fell near the waterworks and the excitement of the sentries communicated itself to the dogs, for they were trained to respond to human intentions. Ian Munro's Stirling had jettisoned its bombs when Redenbacher opened fire. Then it came low from the south across the bomber stream. Only two of its motors were still functioning; one of the others had run away and the crippled engine was tearing itself to pieces and screaming like a dental drill. It disappeared over the rise in the ground beyond the waterworks, still trying to gain height. The eager Heimatflak boys from the brewery had a go at it with their 2-cm. batteries and the sky above the trees was crisscrossed with tracers and the smell of the firing drifted through the dog cages. The sounds and smells added to the excitement of the dogs and the barking increased until the dogs were running up and down their compounds in great agitation.

It was the 8,000-pound H.C. Blockbuster—the largest size of bomb dropped that night—that demolished a row of new houses near the cemetery and that sent the dogs berserk. In one compound the dogs threw their bodies against the wire netting of their compounds, uncaring of the pain and blood. The netting tore open and the dogs ran through the hotel garden. Mausi Scheske was on guard duty; he shot one dog but was set upon by the rest of them and badly savaged. His brother opened fire and killed two of the dogs, but galvanized by fear, five other dogs escaped over the gates. Poor little Mausi died of his wounds twenty minutes later, whereupon Hannes visited each of the dog compounds and shot the dogs. In twenty-five minutes he killed eighty-seven dogs, some of them fully trained and already assigned to a mountain regiment in Yugoslavia. Hannes was arrested by the guard sergeant, disarmed and locked in the old wine cellar. There was no wine there.

Standartenführer Wörth cursed the noisy dogs, but as the bombing stopped he returned to a pile of paper work. He was sitting at a writing table in his suite on the first floor. He had chosen this room not because of its proximity to the lake but because it had thick walls and was as far from the dog compound as he could live. His orderly entered the room at 0200, bringing with him a young N.C.O. with torn trousers and a bleeding leg wound. The N.C.O. delivered a report about the Scheske brothers and the maddened dogs.

"Tell Hentschel," said the Standartenführer.

The N.C.O. knew no one of that name. He exchanged a quick glance with the orderly, who nodded and moved his head to indicate that they should leave. "Heil Hitler," said the wounded boy.

"Heil Hitler," said the Standartenführer without looking up from his desk. It was ten minutes later when the orderly came to tell him about the horse and he hurried downstairs and out into the chilly winter's night to see if it could possibly be true.

"Rosenknospe," he said. There were sugar cubes in his pocket. He'd never ceased to carry one or two since he was a child. "Rose." If only young Hentschel could have also been sewn up and put together again like the horse. Who in the regiment remembered him and had recognized the horse? Someone assigned to a veterinary farm, perhaps. "Rosenknospe. You're not as young as you used to be, old girl." The horse whinnied: the smell and the voice had helped her recognize him. How long since he'd ridden? Such a fine horse. She'd be well cared for now.

Dieter Witting, the Standartenführer's orderly, dozed for a few minutes after the last bombs. He was awakened by the bell and looked at the clock. It was a closely guarded secret that the C.O. could not go to the toilet without the assistance of his orderly. Witting put his overcoat over his pajamas and took the case containing the syringe and tablets just in case they were needed. He went in without knocking, as was his usual practice when answering a summons. Wörth was sitting upright in his chair staring straight at the door. Witting wasn't frightened. Wörth tried to speak and his orderly bent close to his mouth.

"Rosenknospe," whispered Wörth.

"Rosebud"; Witting had seen many men die and often their last words were incomprehensible.

"It's going to be all right now, sir," said Witting. "Yes," said Standartenführer Wörth, and died of frostbite and wounds suffered eighteen minths before.

The Burgomaster did not return to his control room. The planes had passed over and anyway all of his phones were out of order. From now on the air raid services must work on their own initiative. He took one of the portable stirrup pumps from the entrance and walked toward the red glow of the old town.

He walked through his town in horrified disbelief. By the lights of the big fires near the gasworks he could see a whole row of slum housing that was simply a one-wall façade like a film set; the houses themselves had disappeared. Alongside the railway station a locomotive had jumped its tracks and was now several feet away from the railway lines. As he turned north onto Nehringstrasse the whole street was a blizzard of flying sparks. The first time he saw a body—just beyond Tornow the printer's—he stopped to look at it. It was Tornow's son, dressed in his naval officer's uniform. Quite dead. He recognized the body of a girl clerk too. After he'd passed fifty bodies he no longer glanced at them.

Only three minutes after he'd left his control room an N.S.K.K. motorcycle messenger arrived. The FLUKO at Duisburg had tried to get through by means of every official phone in Altgarten but when none of them could connect to the Burgomaster's control room they ordered that a messenger should go from Party H.Q. The message simply said that the second wave of R.A.F. aircraft, numbering approximately four hundred planes, was approaching Altgarten. All fires must be extinguished and nonessential personnel ordered to take shelter.

# ◄ 29 ►

LAMBERT had seen six bombers since leaving Warley but he'd had only a glimpse of them. So far the trip had been uneventful. Sometimes he'd returned from trips to find other crews describing all manner of pyrotechnics and mayhem while he had seen little or nothing the whole trip. Other sorties had proved to be the very reverse.

"Changing tanks," said Battersby.

"O.K.," said Lambert.

The flight engineer let the tank drain to the final empty cough before changing over. That was the most efficient way to log the fuel consumption and avoid air locks.

"Look to port," said Binty. "The searchlights have coned some poor bastard and the flak is coming up like confetti."

Instinctively Lambert touched the rudder to steer away from the flak.

Digby was still in the nose. The target was full of colored lights flickering and winking as the heat rose. There was smoke too. The flares and fires under it made it glow and the heat and blast made it ripple and bubble like milk boiling out of a saucepan. There was black smoke too from where the TENOs' diesel tank had been hit. Once Digby saw a shock wave expand across the brightest fire and wobble it like red currant jelly. "I'd like to bomb those flak bastards. What say, Skip, that I save a couple of thousand-pounders for the flak? We could . . ."

"Fighter, fighter, port beam," screamed Flash Gordon. His four machine guns were joined an instant later by the upper turret's two guns.

"He's attacking someone else," said Binty. Just a couple of hundred yards to port the thin line of incendiary shells turned like the sweep-second hand of a clock as the night fighter closed upon his victim, changing his angle of attack, and then climbed away into the dark.

"Bomb doors open."

It had begun. They were fixed on the tramline course that would take them across the center of the target's fires and into its flak. It looked like a child's birthday cake, half a dozen yellow candles flickering in a darkened room. A kid's birthday cake. Left, left. Steady.

The plane ahead was on fire. Its propeller blades slowed as they feathered, but the flames were getting brighter by the second. Steady. Right, hold that, nicely, nicely, hold that steady. The night fighter would come in again as sure as God made little apples and when he did *Creaking Door* would be brightly illuminiated by those damned flames. Brighter still. Its cowling is breaking apart. Steady, left, left. Please God make him go down! He doesn't have to crash, if he'll just go down. Please God, just a thousand feet! Right. Steady. Five hundred, then.

A crash of flak made the wing lift. There was a patter of shrapnel. "Come in," said Jimmy.

You're veering, Skip. Left, left quite a bit. Even if it's Micky Murphy. Make him go down! That night fighter must be behind us at this very moment. Steady. Even if it's my mother. The light from the burning Lancaster was worse. They'll never save it now. Jesus Christ, that's another pass! That's the night fighter's cannon shells punching those pieces out of him. Get out. Jump, jump, jump. You bloody fools. The rear turret is hanging in shreds like a bundle of bent wire. So where are the parachutes? She's leaping about like a punch-drunk boxer. The propeller blades must have broken on the other side. Left, left. Smoke everywhere, Skipper, I can't bloody see. O.K., hold her like that.

The pilot in the burning plane was throttling back. The distance between them narrowed and the tips of the flames seemed to be trying to get into their own airstream. Closer. So don't look. Look at the instruments and look at your engineer. Battersby was staring at him in horror. Lambert nodded encouragingly and Battersby turned back to his panel. He thinks I can save him. They all do. Why the hell should they pick on me? Steady, left just a fraction. Steady. That's good. She's well alight, said Digby calmly. He was only speaking of the target. Target; I'd forgotten the target. They're having trouble to hold that blazing coffin and in a moment it's going to stall and we'll fly into it. Steady. God, it's coming closer still!

"Drop the bastard bombs," someone shouted. It was a high-pitched anxious voice, not recognizable as anyone of the crew until the cry was repeated and Digby identified it.

"Here she comes, Skip. Keep your hair on," Digby told him calmly.

Is he so glued to that bombsight that he can't see that the whole sky is ablaze with this bloody great dying Lancaster almost touching our wingtip? Make it go down. Shoot it down. Anything, but just darkness, please. Just darkness. Nothing should hold on like that, it's obscene. Perhaps they're all dead in there and it's on auto pilot and it will fly in the stream on auto pilot all the way to England with us. Who says you'll get that far, Lambert? Perhaps this is it; good night, nurse. Blow out the candles.

"Bombs gone," said Digby. His voice was completely relaxed, until he too saw the bomber losing height alongside them. "My flaming oath."

The other Lancaster's fuel was atomizing as it left the trailing edge of the wing and burning like a gas flame. A flare caught fire as it fell out of its flare chute. So white it seemed almost blue in a world colored yellow and pink and red.

"Hold her steady, Skip, for the photo," said Digby.

Lambert saw green-and-red pistol flares make a string of brightly colored beads as they were jettisoned, already alight. He looked at Battersby, who was occupied at his panel. The cockpit was golden with the light of the flames while thirty of the longest seconds in the history of the world ticked past.

"You cow. Flare chute's bent, Skip. The bloody flash is jammed in it." Jimmy's voice.

"Kick it out," said Lambert. "I'm not holding this forever."

"It won't budge."

"Make it bloody budge," said Lambert. All that and they hadn't even got a picture for the photo ladder. He sighed as he banked the bomber over and slid into the darkness, away from the fiery airplane that Murphy and Sweet were trying to coax back to earth.

"That aged me ten years," said Jimmy Grimm, who had been watching the burning bomber.

"Any luck with the flash, Jimmy?"

"Still trying, Skip."

Grimm had echoed his thoughts but captains just don't

say that kind of thing. That would be the second time this month he'd come back without a photo. On the Intelligence Officer's board the three rows of target photos arranged in chronological order would include one print that was merely a shiny blank card. Nor would there be caption detail either. It would be as if *Creaking Door* and its crew and its bomb load did not exist.

"Watch for night fighters, everyone," warned Lambert.

"Okay, Skip," the gunners acknowledged dutifully, although they had not ceased searching the sky for one instant.

Lambert tasted the stink of rubber in his oxygen mask and knew that he had broken into a flush-sweat of fear. He unclipped his mask and wiped his face. His jaw was stiff and his chin was stubbly.

"Only one H.E. All the rest were incendiaries and phosphorus tonight," said Digby.

"Glad I didn't know that on the run in," said Battersby.

"Concentrate, chaps," said Lambert. Here was the moment of maximum peril. The tension of the target was suddenly replaced with a relaxed relief and a surprise of being still alive on the far side of the flak. Now came a terrible tiredness and with it a lack of fear, an inability to concentrate and an almost overwhelming desire for sleep. Men had returned to tell stories of crewmen—even pilots—who fell completely asleep on the return journey. Other crews did not return to tell the same story.

"Concentrate," repeated Lambert. "There are fifty million dedicated Germans trying to kill us. Concentrate."

Lambert always said that or something similar. Jimmy Grimm nodded over his radio set and to help him stay awake he poured a cup of coffee from his Thermos flask and sipped it. It was scalding hot. From his rear turret Flash watched the target burning: a scattering of pink blobs. Suddenly one blob swelled and went white for a moment. It was the roof of the Liebefrau collapsing.

Lambert's head ached. He slipped an aspirin into his mouth. Binty took his Benzedrine. Battersby entered up the fuel change in his logbook. In his navigator's log Kosher wrote "Unidentified four-motor aircraft on fire over target."

By now the moon was high. It wasn't the golden orb that dust particles color for men on the ground. From here they saw it as it really was: a cold blue cipher in the sky. The landscape was blue and black and it was possible to distinguish dark patches that were towns and the edges of fields and trees. He saw the River Maas glint in the moonlight and then on the river a dark patch that was Venlo winked as its flak opened fire. The ground was often obscured by grayish-blue patches of cloud that drifted past only five hundred feet below.

"Steer 271," said Kosher. "That will take us a shade south of the stream, with Eindhoven to port and Tilburg and Breda to starboard. That O.K.?"

"If Eindhoven turns nasty, you must steer me farther north of it."

"Wilco, Skip. I'll come up and watch if I may."

"Bring a friend."

Eindhoven— a notorious flak concentration—was quiet as they flew across the outskirts. It wasn't until they neared Tilburg that they saw intense flak again.

"The colored-light stuff is Gilze-Rijn airfield. Breda beyond it. Fifty miles to the Dutch coast. . . . With this wind, say sixteen minutes."

"I'm going to start losing height," said Lambert. "We'll put on a bit of speed if we put our nose down."

North of Breda the flak was concentrating upon one section of sky while the searchlights moved busily through the flashes. Suddenly there was a reddish flash. Larger than the others, it stayed bright longer too. "Scarecrow shell," said Digby. Everyone in Bomber Command knew about scarecrow shells; they were designed by a German flak expert to look like an aircraft exploding in midair. Even today survivors swear they could tell the difference between them and the real thing. But there were no scarecrow shells, only exploding planes.

"Yes, scarecrow shell," said Lambert.

Satisfied with his identification of Breda, Kosher went back to his navigator's table behind the curtain. Battersby watched Lambert's hands as he kept the compass steady. Battersby had been trained to hold a Lancaster upon an even course, although landing one had actually been one of his recurring nightmares while he was training. The controls were tremendously heavy to move and yet Lambert seemed to use only his fingertips. Now he watched him ease the controls forward.

"Beginning descent, Skip?" asked Battersby.

"I want the cloud on my belly," said Lambert.

Battersby nodded blankly. Lambert said, "Nothing can get under our backside then."

"What about radar?" asked Battersby.

"No, they need a final visual," said Lambert. "All O.K., gunners?"

"Sure thing, boss," said Binty.

"This clear-vision panel is fantastic, Skip," said Flash.

"Good boys," said Lambert. They were all good boys; Lambert was lucky. He let the Lancaster settle gently until it hit the grayish-blue bank of cumulus. Shreds of it poured across the wings and tufts made the windshield opaque. He let the airplane wallow in the cloud, churning it up and sliding under it like a child hiding in bedclothes. Make the most of it, thought Lambert; ahead there was the Dutch coast. There this ragged cloud, like the land below it, ended. A vast plain of inert black treacle stretched below them, glinting in the moonlight. That was the North Sea.

# 30

WHEN the second and much larger wave of bombers began to attack Altgarten it wasn't fear that dominated the minds of its citizens. Nor, although this was in many minds, was it simple anger or a feeling of being victimized by fate. It was a neurosis of a kind that comes from being asked to do something beyond one's mental and physical capability. Life had got out of control. For the professionals, their jobs had got out of control. The fire service officers had spent their lives handling one fire at a time with a plentiful supply of water and the telephones in working order. Tonight they faced over a hundred fires, many of them large and out of control. They were hampered by broken water mains, disconnected phones and exploding bombs. Now, just as they had the emergency power and phone lines almost complete and the water was pumping from the Mönchenstrasse sewer, it was going to start all over again.

There were many symptoms of this neurosis, and for some survivors it was the beginning of a mental breakdown from which they would never recover. One senior fireman was singing an old music hall ditty over and over again as he worked at the pump. Several of the firemen at the hoses were speaking to the fire, swearing at it in a confused obscene mumble. At the Volkschule a Block-wart, after warning a group of people of the dangers of throwing water on a burning incendiary bomb, had picked it up as though it were a demonstration dummy and inflicted upon himself very severe burns.

When the second wave of bombers began their attack, both Gerd Böll and his friend Bodo Reuter knew that it was going to be even bigger than the first wave. This was the way the *Tommis* worked and the fast-revving British

engines were as loud as a swarm of hornets. Salvos of
bombs were centering on the fires. The noise hammered
their eardrums and the blast plucked at their bodies. They
both knew that a sensible man would take cover, but they
moved up Mönchenstrasse toward the hospital fire in
leaps and runs punctuated by long waits flat on their
faces. There were several damaged lorries in the street;
one—an army lorry—was on fire. They passed it cautiously and then kept close to the walls until the last block
before Dorfstrasse, where conscientious civil defense men
were throwing burning bedclothes and furniture into the
street from a fire on the top floor.

Even before they turned the corner into Dorfstrasse
they could see the fire at the hospital reflected in the wet
roadway. The main street seemed to be running in blood
as the brightly lit water rippled along the gutter. The air
was full of sparks and the ground so littered with burning
wreckage and incendiary bombs left to burn themselves
out that Reuter stepped into a patch of phosphorus. The
goo burst into flame as he tried to scrape it from his boot.
It was an evil, frightening substance that clung like glue.
Reuter put his boot into the water-filled gutter, which
extinguished the flame, but immediately afterward it ignited again in the air. Finally Gerd used a piece of broken
brick to scrape it away. Then they resumed their journey. Now they were stepping more carefully around
the burning timber and white-hot magnesium fragments
from the incendiaries.

They passed more than a hundred fires in their short
journey and seven times threw themselves full length to
the ground as high explosive bombs dropped nearby. Five
times they were implored to give assistance in rescuing
trapped people, but they refused, and even the angriest of
civilians knew better than to argue with a TENO officer.
Some of them, seeing Bodo's high collar, cuff band and
black rank patches, thought he was in the Waffen S.S.

During the second wave's attack the fires got out of
control. Even the most heroic fireman cannot survive a
barrage of high explosive bombs and the bomb loads of
the second-wave bombers had been planned with this in
mind. Even after the last of the bombers had departed the
effectiveness of the fire-fighting and salvage teams would
be hampered by the delayed-action bombs. They would
continue to explode for two more days.

Gerd Böll and Bodo Reuter always stayed together.
They had defused bombs and tunneled under masonry and

walked across planks high in the air, each confident that
the other would never let him down. Gerd Böll stayed
with Reuter and Reuter's place was with his men at the
hospital.

"Two hundred at least, sir," said Reuter's Hauptwachtmeister. "Perhaps more, and that doesn't include the nurses who are up there with them."

"And the basement?" asked Gerd.

"Another hundred. They can get out but there's
nowhere to take them and they aren't exactly mobile.
Some can hardly walk, let alone run."

"No one on the top floor?"

"That's gone; it's just ashes up there."

"What's that sound, like singing?" said Reuter.

"Screaming," said the old N.C.O. "When there's an
explosion nearby or they see an incendiary they call out
together. There's no panic, but being bedridden up there
with a view across the city must be rather sobering
tonight." He gave a grim smile.

"The structure?" asked Reuter.

"All the front has gone and the steel went with it. The
top floor is tilting, according to one of the men who've just
come down."

"You've been up?"

"Half an hour ago, Herr Oberzugführer."

"Let's go up and take another look. Bring a couple of
messengers and a couple of strong fellows with ropes and
axes."

The journey up to the fourth floor was slow and circui-
tous but not dangerous. They used the service staircase
as far as the second floor and although it was pitch dark
and littered with large pieces of debris, it was intact.
They passed through a crowded children's ward on the
second floor and down a corridor littered with wet burned
blankets. Through an office door on the left they glimpsed
a surgeon carrying out an operation. Rembrandt-like
lighting was provided by two oil lamps, an electric torch
and five candles. They went through the broken doors to
the old building and up the winding staircase. That was
tricky, for in places the cantilevered stone steps had brok-
en, leaving only broken stumps for toeholds with a nasty
view downward that included sharp stonework projections.

Now and again they were splashed. Jets of water were
striking the top of the stairwell and falling upon them in a
fine spray. They waited patiently while another squad of
TENO men and firemen lowered a door down the stair-

case shaft. As the door twisted Gerd saw the white face of an old man strapped tight against the board. His arms were slightly extended like those of a wooden doll. In short jerks he was lowered past them without a sound. Revolving gently, his face transfixed, eyes wide and mouth open, he was trying to remember how to scream.

Since Bodo's N.C.O. had last visited the top floor, the roof had collapsed on one room, killing four radiographers. The floor tilted more now and there were cracks in the wall large enough to see through. Every minute or two the whole building groaned like an old man who had sat too long in one position, and like an old man it leaned a little more to one side. Always to the same side.

"Stay close to this wall," Reuter ordered his men.

The floor lurched under them. The walls were bulging as the bricks expanded. The metal girders expanded too; pressed against the ceiling, writhing in the heat, they fired hot rivets across the room like bullets.

"How fast are they getting these people down?" asked Bodo.

"One team down the staircase, one by the airshaft. They are each taking about seven minutes."

"Get the nurses out of here," said Bodo.

"And the patients?"

"Get the nurses out."

His Hauptwachtmeister gave a perfunctory salute and turned to bellow at the men. "You heard what the Oberzugführer said; evacuate all nurses to ground level. We will start on this floor." Without delay the TENOs hurried after the N.C.O., rounding up the nursing staff and ordering them to leave their patients. The nurses began to argue, but orders are orders.

"How long do you think, Bodo?"

"Not more than ten minutes, Gerd."

Neither Bodo nor Gerd saw the first row of beds go. One of the TENO messengers swore and a nurse screamed and then the far end of the ward was empty. The light of the fire lit the ceiling, for there was no longer any wall; it had exploded out into the courtyard along with the beds and people. The second row of beds screeched as they slid across the tilted linoleum, for the wheels had the safety brakes on, but gravity was too much for that device. The beds collided and interlocked. Thrashing blanketed bundles grabbed at pillars and lost their fingernails. A nurse overbalanced and she toppled over. She slid on her bottom across the highly polished floor, trying to hold her flying skirts down all the way until she fell off the edge and into the courtyard two stories below.

They were screaming now. Hysterical screaming which neither alerts nor implores. Fatalistic yells and high-pitched cries were the final denunciation of an unjust world.

The TENOs linked hands. Gerd, Bodo and one of the TENO men had each grabbed a patient out of bed and, sharing the weight of their limp bodies, the six TENOs and Gerd inched their way from one handhold to the next along the hot bulging wall. Outside, the bombs were exploding and flares were lighting the streets as bright as day. Shadows moved drunkenly and there was the continuous whine of shell fragments. The building was creaking and groaning now that the far end of the steel structure had collapsed. They felt the whole building sway with each explosion like a house of cards being blown upon. Each time dust and plaster fell noisily from the ceiling and sent up clouds of dirt. The abandoned patients were making more noise now, but the TENOs tried to close their minds to the distant cries.

They roped each of the three patients at the top of the circular staircase and two of the men went down to receive the lowered bodies. The stairwell was dark. The heat was coming up it like a chimney and there were bits of charred cloth and paper whisked skyward past them as they searched with their boots for the stone toeholds. For a moment a green flare directly above them lit the stairs like daylight—for there was no longer any roof—and then it drifted past, leaving them in an even more baffling darkness.

"Let me die," one white-haired old man said repeatedly as they passed the rope under his arms. The stone was hot to his bare feet and he danced painfully upon the top step. "Let me die, just let me die."

"Shut up, you old fool," Bodo shouted finally. "I'll tell you when you can die."

"*Jawohl*, Herr Leutnant," said the old man in a clipped obedient voice that he hadn't used since 1918.

The TENOs worked without haste, testing each knot and examining each handhold, but their faces were flushed and sweat dripped off their chins. One of them took off his steel helmet and tried to clip it to his belt but in the darkness he fumbled and the helmet fell down the stairwell, ringing like a cracked bell as it hit the broken steps and bounced from wall to wall.

One by one the nurses from the top floor were coaxed, helped and handed down the stairwell. Then the patients were lowered on ropes. At last it was time to lower the last of the survivors. It was a woman scarcely conscious and whimpering softly as they fastened the rope around her. "Soon have you down, mother." Gerd encouraged her. She smiled in friendly disbelief. The steadying rope burned through when she was halfway down and she spun slowly round as the support ropes shrank with the heat. Gerd was halfway down the staircase, his steel-tipped boots wedged against the remaining inch or two of broken stair and his hands searching for a handhold. He spared a hand to grab at her spinning body and managed to slow the dizzying movement as she was lowered past him. She was still smiling. "Nearly there," said Gerd.

It was the TENO at the bottom who called up that she was dead. His voice echoed in the slim stone stairwell like some gatekeeper of the Lower World. That was when the whole of the old building collapsed, throwing beds and bedridden into the courtyard in one great heap of broken people.

"Six minutes," said Gerd.

"Yes," admitted Bodo. "Damn them, we could have cleared those wards in another fifteen."

On the ground floor one of the storage rooms for X-ray plates was on fire. Thick smoke was rolling down the stairs into the basement and many of the nurses were wearing wet masks.

In the courtyard torches flashed over the bent iron bedsteads and bloody blankets that were heaped upon the stone flags. It was senseless to worry about the blackout when the whole town was burning bright and visible for a hundred miles. Here and there the nurses and men were extricating a still living body. "Stretcher party," they called, but it wasn't easy for a stretcher party to pick its way through the heap of two hundred bodies without treading on others that were still moving and groaning.

"Bombs gone," said Digby, his voice completely relaxed.

When the two 250-pound phosphorus bombs from *Creaking Door* hit the old building, the quick dropped flat upon the dead. The phosphorus bombs threw their showers of white sparks sixty feet into the air and they came down as pretty as fireworks with large fragments of burning phosphorus. A cluster of fragments struck Johannes Ilfa's legs. He knifed it away from the fabric and flesh but some

were deeply embedded. Around him men screamed and
fought and burned and sometimes survived. They wriggled
like live bait and a few regained their feet like ghosts
arising from a mass grave. Water had no effect upon
phosphorus. The official instructions were to cover it with
sand. Can you put sand upon a man's face?

Already Ilfa was finding it easier to reject the pleas of
those too far gone to be saved. It was right to do so and
logical too, but Ilfa told himself that it was one more step
on the journey to inhumanity.

Ilfa, with most of the phosphorus splashes cut away,
came coughing and spluttering through the smoke and
heavy phosphorus fumes. The trim young fireman looked
at the elderly TENO officer before saluting.

"Have your people got breathing apparatus, Herr
Oberzugführer?"

"It's ten minutes away," said Bodo. His false teeth hurt
him and he bit hard on his knuckle.

"Then, with your permission, we'll put my fellows in to
sort through the bodies." Ilfa coughed again.

"If only we could damp them down."

"There's not enough water for that unless we abandoned the post office," said Johannes Ilfa.

"What about the swimming baths?"

Ilfa wiped his moustache, which, like his face, was
glistening with water from the hoses. He'd used all the
water from the municipal baths when they first ran short.
Now he looked at the thin old TENO man and grinned.

"Sorry," said Bodo Reuter. Like members of a secret
society the two men recognized in each other the skills
and judgment that were in such short supply this night.
They looked up to the building opposite, upon which
most of the water was being sprayed in an effort to
prevent the fire from spreading to that block. "It's quite a
mess," said Ilfa tentatively.

"It bloody well is," said Bodo. "I don't envy you trying
to sort out that heap if the bodies ignite."

"My firemen are only kids," said Ilfa.

Bodo nodded, but how old could this fireman be? His
middle twenties perhaps, and yet now he walked across a
dozen bodies without a trace of hesitation in his step as
limbs flaked underfoot like charcoal logs.

There was a hesitant cough. Fuchs Ueberall was at
Bodo's elbow; his flushed face and dilated eyes gave a clue
to his suppressed hysteria. His voice was comically high-
pitched.

"I can't go on, Bodo. Can't. I picked up a child and it came to pieces in my hands. Bobo. Can I go and give a hand with the digging? I'll send one of the boys back here. He came to pieces."

Bodo Reuter grabbed his drinking companion by the collar and turned it to squeeze his throat. "I'm not Bodo, you *Narr*. I'm Oberzugführer Reuter and you'll call me sir, and you'll stand with your feet together and salute. And you'll do what you're told without argument and discussion or hesitation because, Ueberall, I swear to you by anything you can find to hold sacred right now that I will take a gun and blow your brains out if I so much as see you pause long enough to wipe the sweat off your big fat face. Now go." He threw the man back toward the heap of bodies. Ueberall stumbled and fell and as he got to his feet Reuter screamed, "Understand?"

Like some young recruit, Ueberall sprang to attention and yelled, "Yes, Herr Oberzugführer. Heil Hitler."

"Heil Hitler," said Bodo Reuter and to himself he said, "They're not bowling, my friend."

"No, they're not bowling," said Gerd Böll

Everywhere there were pieces of phosphorus. It lit up the whole place and gave off enough heat to ignite body fat. Dead and dying were exploding with the same surprising flash with which a frying pan ignites in the hands of a careless chef. Hair burned even more readily and the phosphorus and burning hair and flesh produced dense black smoke that attacked the eyes and mucus of the nostrils and made men choke and splutter. The heat was unimaginable and even the veterans were daunted by it. The largest pile of bodies was now blazing and no one could approach it.

"Breathing apparatus," said Johannes Ilfa. He put his own on and it hurt him as he knew it would. He needed to inhale deeply to bring the air through the filters and each breath hurt his damaged lung.

The fire squad with its breathing apparatus moved slowly, like deep sea divers. The nurses and the TENO men and the medical students and the firewatchers, the policemen and the Blockwarte and the soldiers and the cripples who had tried to help the dying withdrew. They climbed over the hot debris: a fabric woven of wood, brick and bodies. Their steps were lit by pieces of blazing phosphorus. Still chunks of brickwork and liquid roof lead fell into the courtyard, but all the rescue workers reached the road except for eight nurses and seven men who were near the west wall of the old building when the chimney complex of the annex collapsed upon them.

Johannes Ilfa had manned hoses, operated pumps and climbed over burning roofs. Splashes of phosphorus mottled his legs and, in spite of his knife work, were eating deep into his flesh, burning with a foul smell. One of the youngest trainees reported Ilfa's wounds and he was ordered to a first aid station.

Neither Gerd nor Bodo spoke of the two hundred men and women who had died in the courtyard. It was a taboo subject not subsequently mentioned except perhaps to a new recruit by someone who was there. Even then it was only after too many drinks and men spoke of it in whispers.

What was left of the old wing of the hospital had been pressed into use as a treatment center. Here the dim lights of the emergency generator threw the scene into extremes of light and dark. Most of the patients were known to the doctors as they were wheeled in for surgery.

"Hello, Doktor Maurer," said a girl who had been brought into the hospital for tonsillitis.

"We're going to have to take that arm off, Fräulein. You'll feel much better then, believe me."

The out-patients' waiting room had been converted into a multiple operating theater in which eight doctors worked at once. A policeman with a bucket and pump hosed down the blood from the lino and a garbage can for severed limbs was wheeled through the ward on a tea trolley.

In the corridor Johannes Ilfa, still cherishing his secret passion for Anna-Luisa, was ignoring his pain. He had been arguing stubbornly with a nurse who wanted to cut away his trousers to examine the phosphorus burns on his thighs. Now that he had rested for a while he began to realize how weak he had become. His lung hurt him more than ever. The nurse was a young trainee and she had no idea why the fireman was making such a fuss until a middle-aged ward sister came along. She had a piratical array of surgical instruments stuck into her belt and her hair had been frizzled by fire. She pulled her face mask down. "Don't be so stupid," she said angrily. "Do you think you're the only one here who has soiled underwear?" Many had involuntarily emptied their bowels that night, but for Johannes Ilfa his decorum was to prove fatal. By the time his trousers and underpants were cut away he had died.

Along the corridor came two nurses in fancy dress:

homemade kimonos and colored sashes. One of them had
been badly splashed with blood. Bodo Reuter watched the
nurse tip Ilfa's slim body off the bench to make room for
the living. Bodo took it by the hand as if to say good-bye
and heaved it over his shoulder in a fireman's lift. "We'll
put him somewhere," said Bodo.

"Yes, let's get out of here," said Gerd. "It gives me the
creeps."

Outside in Dorfstrasse they put the body on the front
seat of his Magirus fire engine before walking back along
the hose lines.

"He knew his job," said Bodo.

"Yes," said Gerd. That accolade served as his epitaph,
for he got no other.

The sump constructed by blocking the sewer was still
the main supply, but paper and sewage continually clogged
the filters and the firemen had to pick them clean every
few minutes, which left the hoses squelching air until the
filters went back into the stinking water again.

The night air was hot but the men handling the hoses
were shivering with cold and their hands were white, numb
and stiff. A group of TENOs had three hoses on the far
side of the courtyard dousing the neighboring buildings
that were not on fire. They soaked the walls of the post
office and killed the deadly sparks. But the pump's five
hundred gallons per minute was falling in shallow curves
short of the post office roof.

"Disconnect two of those hoses," said Bodo, "or you'll
never reach the next roof." The men hurried to obey.
"And bring the pressure up to ten kilograms." Gerd and
Bodo waited while they disconnected the junction. This
was difficult to do while the water was pumping but a
young fireman from the town fire service helped them. As
the new pressure moved through the hose it bulged like
a maddened snake, lashing from side to side in a frenzy
that needed four TENOs to control. The new jet of water
made a freezing draft that punched a hole through the
black smoke, and the firemen ducked their heads close to
the nozzle of the hose to see through the tunnel of fast-
moving clear air that fanned their faces.

The air was full of flying sparks like luminous locusts,
with larger red embers floating more gently downward
from the nearby fires. Each flash of light from the bombers' photoflash bombs, or from the explosions, illuminated the airborne flotsam. Some of the citizens of Altgarten were to survive to tell a story that the R.A.F. dropped

leaflets that night. Stories circulated of dire and ugly
warnings of more raids to come, but, although leaflets
were dropped upon northern France that night, Altgarten
got only bombs. The air was full of charred paper, some
of it a thousand feet in the sky, but it had all come from
the town itself. There were bills, wills, manifests, invoices,
handbills, bonds, shares, love letters, warrants, carbons,
dockets, leases, passes, deeds and misdeeds. Their scorched
shapes floated on the warm wind and fell back upon
the town like black snow.

Filing cabinets, deed tins, safes and mailboxes were
among the night's casualties, and one letter that journeyed
a quarter of a mile into the air upon the thermal of the
Nehringstrasse bakery fire had been posted by Gerd Böll
that afternoon. His letter to August Bach came down in
Liebefrauplatz and was run over by a TENO lorry, ripped
by a fireman's boot, then it floated down a gutter into a
drain and was lost in the sewer. It reappeared in pieces
and was plucked off the hose filter several times until it
softened and shredded and went through the wire mesh. It
was only tiny specks of gray pulp when it came out of the
hose nozzle and was sprayed into the heart of the fires
that, in spite of all efforts, had started on the post office
roof.

"Look!" shouted someone from the darkness as, high in
the black air above them, a Lancaster was hit and exploded in a red oily ball of flame. There was another bomber
on fire too, but it kept steadily on its bombing run. Four
spots of radar-controlled flak burst in a line under and
beside it and finally, as its bombs fell away, the flak blew
it to pieces right over the target.

It is impossible to forget the smell of a bombarded
town. Under the sudden strange whiff of spilled perfume,
chemicals or food, there is the constant stale aroma of wet
cloth, charred wood and spent explosive. But dominating
all else there is the smell of the compacted earth that has
cradled the sewer pipes and the acrid stink of the dust
from ancient bricks. Many of the rescue workers had tied
wet handkerchiefs across their faces and had to drag them
away in order to speak. "Don't take the child away. He
must tell us where his family were sheltering or we'll be
sifting through this rubble for weeks."

Herr Holländer had a busy night. He'd visited twenty
apartments to be sure that no fire bombs were burning
there. Between times he had put his head into the dark
cellar where his flock were sheltering. He logged each visit

and on the last one he had seen the bomber in flames
above the city. As usual he called, "Raid is still continuing
but our brave fighters are giving the swine something to
remember," and as usual no one replied. The bombing was
heavy enough to persuade him to stay there for a few
moments. It was dark and fetid and since the 4,000-pound
cookie had dropped across the road the fans were no
longer working. Not that anyone had complained about
Holländer. They made good money in the brewery, for
the Wehrmacht would buy all the beer that could be
brewed. On overtime even a laborer had a fat pay envelope at the week's end. Some even had more pay than he.
It was disgraceful. Now they were not even polite enough
to make room for him to sit down.

He looked at their coarse hands and dull bovine faces
and the way their thick bodies had slumped against the
support beams or fallen upon their neighbors' shoulders.
One young girl had her head thrown back and her mouth
wide open in a most unattractive manner. Sometimes he
wished he could find a house in the Altmarkt or Mönchenstrasse—the nice end—or even the new estate. On the
other hand his place in Kaiserin-Augustastrasse was so
near his place of work, and so cheap.

The electricity had gone off and the oil lamps were
spluttering in the foul air. He flashed his torch around to
be sure that no one was smoking; that was strongly
forbidden. It was as silent as a tomb. When Holländer
realized exactly what had happened he let out a little yelp
of fear. Or was it pain? Or perhaps compassion? Everyone
in the shelter with him was dead, and had been for a long
time. He had been visiting corpses. Eighty-six men, wom-
en and children with ruptured lungs had died without so
much as gasping for breath. The human lung is a delicate
device; even a pressure of seventy pounds per square inch
will damage it beyond repair. The cookie near the brewery had done it, one of the first bombs that dropped.

Terrified, Holländer backed toward the door and
tripped over some sandbags. He fell heavily. He was an
old man; his brittle thighbone fractured and the torch
went out. The shadows from the oil lamps flickered eerily,
but Holländer knew enough first aid to realize that dragging himself to the door could tear a jagged edge of bone
across the femoral artery and bleed him to death. He
remained where he was. The rescue workers said he had a
narrow escape. Two days later an astounded doctor made

an X ray of Holländer's lungs ·and sent it to a medical school in Cologne.

Firemen with breathing apparatus were salvaging the living from the mountain of dead in the courtyard. Now there was enough water to spray the hoses upon the workers. Their clothes were so hot that the water hissed and steamed as it fell upon them.

At Kaiserin-Augustastrasse 94 a man had insisted upon reentering his blazing home to get his insurance papers and had burned to death. At one o'clock on the northern section of Dorfstrasse three men found with suitcases full of new shirts and sausages were summarily executed by a policeman. It was glass splinters in the sausage that made him certain they were looters. Frenzel's Stube had proved impossible to save and although the Frenzel family were finally forced to evacuate the place, forty-three bodies laid out there were incinerated when French brandy in the cellar exploded.

Frau Pippert, who had walked home along Nehringstrasse, helped to extricate a young policeman from a burning building and held him while a medical student amputated his trapped arm with a penknife. The policeman later recovered.

Four 4-pound incendiary bombs had hit the police station next door to the Rathaus and had been discovered and extinguished—although not before a senior fireman, who should have known better, had directed his hose onto a high-voltage cable and killed himself and rendered two other firemen unconscious for fifteen minutes. The shock shredded their trousers into rags and for the rest of the night they worked bare-legged.

It was a police motorcyclist who picked his way through the littered streets looking for Bodo.

"Herr Oberzugführer Reuter?" He saluted, and almost before Bodo returned the salute he was relaying his message and already eyeing the debris, deciding where there was sufficient space to turn his motorcycle.

"A *Tommi* has landed on Frau Kersten's farm. It is of vital importance that the crew do not destroy their aircraft before it can be examined." Bodo nodded. He knew that certain parts must be sent to the special electronics laboratory that the Luftwaffe had set up in Dachau concentration camp. Jewish scientists were trying to discover the R.A.F.'s most cherished secret: the magnetron valve of the centimetric radar. "Immediately," he acknowledged.

"I shan't go with you," said Gerd Böll. "I'll get back to my cousin's house. His child and the housekeeper are in the cellar."

"This is important," urged Bodo. They both knew that Gerd would say, "Not to me it isn't."

Gerd nodded. "A moment, please," Bodo called to the policeman. "Take this man to Mönchenstrasse."

"Yes, Herr Oberzugführer," said the policeman. Gerd climbed into the zeppelin-like sidecar and using his powerful torch he helped the driver around the piles of timber and bricks. He looked back to Bodo and impulsively gave him a simian wave and pulled a face. Bodo waved and turned away.

In the center of the street outside the hospital annex there was a TENO lorry on fire. The fire inside the building was so strong that the flames from the lorry were drawn horizontally toward the building. The motorcyclist drove round the lorry and by the light of it could see fifty yards down the road. As they reached Zillestrasse the lorry's fuel tank exploded with a tremendous boom.

Entombed in the cellar, Anna-Luisa heard the lorry explode but was still not afraid. She had the child to comfort and in doing so she stilled her own fears. This basement had once been a kitchen and near the steps she found a small service lift. Its shaft was filled with rubble but alongside it on the wall there was a speaking tube. She shouted into the tube too, but there was no answer. She could still hear explosions and she decided that most people would be sheltering from the bombs. "We're safest where we are, Hansl," she said. "There is no hurry to go anywhere." She fingered the fine silver and Meissen figures but without coveting them.

"I shall always love your father, Hansl."

The little boy smiled. Everyone loved Daddy.

# ♦ 31 ♦

HAD Sweet been able to inspect his own complexion at close quarters at that moment, he would have detected the faint bluish skin pallor that warns of anoxia. His connection had torn and he was getting very little oxygen into his face mask. The symptoms are an ebullient feeling of well-being and optimism far beyond that warranted by circumstances. Anoxia is a little like being cozily intoxicated.

Theoretically Sweet was right about the burning wing: at normal temperatures the fuel-air mixture in any partially full fuel tank is too rich to ignite. But the port outer tank of his Lancaster was not at normal temperature. At 20,-000 feet, this summer's night was very cold and so too were the aircraft and its fuel load.

The ragged edge of vapor fire trailing aft of the tank had done nothing to raise its temperature. Inside the tank the less volatile particles of fuel had condensed and thus weakened the fuel-air mixture. This is where the theory went wrong: the fuel was not only inflammable but highly explosive.

The rubber seal at the damaged aft edge of the tank had been on fire for several minutes. As it melted, burning rubber dribbled through the broken seam. The petrol splashing about inside (in spite of the baffles) doused the first few smoldering dribbles but finally an extra-large one was sucked in by the vibrating seam. It produced the perfect conditions for an explosion.

Sweet thought that it was a direct hit by a flak shell. He would never change his mind. The concussion smashed much of the canopy Perspex and threw him sideways against his harness. The control column and rudder bar were momentarily wrenched out of his hands. Sweet was not sure what damage had been done, but Murphy, who had been expecting such an explosion, guessed exactly what had happened.

When the 114-gallon fuel tank exploded this broke the wing at the port outer engine. At the same time it fractured that engine's main girder at its point of attachment under the wing and partially severed a support at the wing's leading edge. Lacking that support, the burning engine began to buffet violently and within fifteen seconds it too tore itself away from what remained of the main plane. When the section of wing broke away the Lancaster continued for half a minute in an only slightly curving line. Then, the engine gone, its balance changed drastically. Lightened by the loss of the great twelve-cylinder Merlin, the port wing tilted upward. Gathering momentum, the huge bomber was beginning a roll. Sweet and Murphy put all their weight behind the control column but the port aileron and the section of wing attached to it had floated off into the darkness. The starboard aileron was little more than rags. Without ailerons to correct their airplane's antics, Sweet and Murphy watched thunderstruck while half a dozen tiny orange spiders crawled up the starboard window and continued their movement over the clear Perspex roof and, faster now, hurried down the port window. That was Altgarten on fire. Each spider was half a city block blazing furiously. The huge airplane had rolled completely over.

Murphy had grabbed for his parachute and clipped it on as the plane began its roll. He knew that it must continue now. It would roll faster until centrifugal force made it impossible to escape from the bomber. Already his knees had buckled and he felt his whole weight pressing against the cockpit floor and forcing him down toward the step in the nose positon several feet below. Gripping the edge of the trunking around the throttle controls and projecting formers and metal edges, he dragged himself toward the black rectangle of night, kicking the fixtures of the folding seat to help him along. Once his broad shoulders were pinned over the edge of the bomb-bay housing, centrifugal force threw him head first into the bomb aimer's position. His oxygen tube and microphone lead were throttling him. He tore them off his head but not before hearing Sweet say, "No need to panic, I've got her."

Already the Lancaster, with engines roaring, was beginning its second roll. It was moving faster now. The col-

ored lights and flares came nearer the transparent nose;
she was tipping over into a spin. Frantically he bent his
knees to get his boot heel against the flat front of the
bomb bay. Panic-stricken, he kicked himself against the
stiff airstream that smashed at him like an invisible sledge-
hammer. Inch by inch and using every ounce of strength
his leg muscles could give, he forced his body lower. The
edge of the hatch bit into his body and caught every belt
and buckle of his harness. Sweating and almost exhausted,
he was taken by his last kick into the black cold night.
The centrifugal force threw him in a curve. As the curving
fall flattened he found that he himself was spinning head
over heels in a crouching position, his face close against
his knees. He knew that he must not open his parachute
until the spinning body stopped, but it did not stop. He
waited for what seemed like an hour, until the lights flashing past him were dangerously close, and then he pulled
the rip cord anyway. The canopy and lines tumbled out of
the brown canvas cover, striking him in the face. He
recoiled with the shock of the blow so that on the next
revolution his feet did not go right through the support
straps. Instead he was caught up in the harness by one
boot. He kicked at it again but was unable to get free. He
was frightened to kick too energetically in case he fouled
the lines of the parachute and "candled." Cradled in his
tangled harness like a baby in a stork's bill, Murphy
floated gently down toward the stricken town. Once a
searchlight passed across him and for a moment the silk
canopy was blinding white. Murphy remembered a childhood prayer and said it aloud.

Sweet saw no reason for the engineer to go groveling
across the floor in abject panic. Sweet had been in plenty
of spins. At Elementary Flying School it was a mandatory
exercise. He didn't worry that the rate of spins was increasing, for he knew that the faster the spin the more
airspeed he had and therefore the easier it was to regain
control. He let the orange spiders come round again. By
now they were dancing across the windshield and he knew
that his dive was almost vertical. Calmly he put his weight
on one side of the rudder bar with both feet. He guessed
it would need a lot of muscle, so he jabbed hard. There
were no port ailerons and precious little port wing by now.
Sweet fell forward, barked his knees and cut his knuckle.
"Damn," he said mildly. He knew now beyond a shadow
of a doubt that he must get out. The huge airplane was
spiraling earthward, it's structure rattling and screaming.

There were sounds of snapping metal. The altimeter needle was revolving backward at a frightening speed. His hands were heavy weights that pressed upon his chest but he managed to remove his torn gloves to get at his harness and slowly undid the strap. He checked that his parachute was correctly fastened and decided to get out by the nose hatch. Statistically the nose hatch was safest.

It was bloody silly, but he couldn't get up. He pushed and pulled and wriggled, but he couldn't get up. The force of gravity was pressing him to his seat so that his weight was beyond his strength to lift. There was a weight upon his head that gave him a double chin and made him feel sick. His blood, pressed downward out of his brain, dimmed his vision. Ridiculous. He had so much to live for: fit and handsome, he had a medal, two girl friends (one with a flat in London), a little private income (his shares were doing nicely), promotion due in August, lots of good friends among the chaps. Why couldn't he get up out of his seat? His vision grew even darker as the increasing gravitational force of the spin drained his brain of its blood.

When Lancaster *S for Sugar* hit Frau Kersten's farm it made a crater thirty feet across and in places eight feet deep. The largest remaining part of it was the tail section, which landed two hundred yards away. The rear gunner— killed in the initial attack—was still in his turret which broke off before the impact. The forward part of the fuselage had hit the side wall of the farmhouse and demolished the whole building. Broken bricks and chunks of plaster almost covered torn and scorched paper money and coins that glinted in the light of torches. Saucepans were mixed with altimeters, bed heads with fuel lines, and pieces of Frau Kersten and her French soldier were intimately mingled with Flight Lieutenant Sweet. There were tattered ailerons, bent flaps. One hot twelve-cylinder engine had drawn a scorched furrow across the grass and lopped a tree. Another had turned the cowshed into a butcher's shop. There was a stink of burned oil and hot carbon and the red-hot metal pieces tinkled like sleigh bells. Among the personal effects found in the wreckage there were an ivory-handled knife with a cigar-cutting device, a warm bunch of keys, the bomb aimer's left boot and a torn flying helmet with "Murphy" written on it in nail polish.

Bodo Reuter and his lorryful of TENO men arrived on the scene of the crash fifteen minutes after it had happened. He organized a search to be sure that no diaries, log books or radio equipment had fallen clear of the main impact points. Fuchs Ueberall and another TENO man found an R.A.F. flier tangled into a tree only a hundred and fifty yards from the crash. He was a burly figure who smiled nervously when challenged. The two TENO men killed him with their spades.

# ◗ 32 ◗

WHEN the illuminated glass map had been in use for an hour the light bulbs, warm varnish and painted metal gave off a smell that mingled with that of floor polish and tense bodies. All Luftwaffe T huts had this same smell when the air battles were at their peak. The smell, the tension and the glare from the Seeburg table combined to give August Bach a dull headache. It always did. When the raids ended early, or when the bomber stream's return route was over some other sector, he liked to stand outside the door, sniff at the ocean and let the night breeze refresh his tiredness and the darkness rest his eyes. The red blip turned gently and headed toward Utrecht. That was at the extreme eastern range of this sector. August corrected the fighter's course.

"He's getting away," said Willi Reinecke. He followed the light dots with his wax pencil. He had traced a twisting record of inexpert attempts to intercept wherever the two lines intertwined. Now the two lines were converging once more and Willi's pencil hovered, trying to will the fighter on to its quarry.

"Order: Increase speed, *Katze Eight*," urged August.

In the darkness Leutnant Beer was staring ahead, trying to see the target. He glanced enviously to the north where the sky was lighter. If he had them that way he might be able to see them but heading eastward toward the banks of cumulus that made the horizon ragged and ugly there was little chance of getting the *Tommi* silhouetted. If any of those fellows had ever been in an airplane at night they would have more sympathy than this edgy bad-tempered fool who, just because he could see the red blip clearly upon the table, thought that it must shine clear and visible up here in the sky. It was so lonely here, almost like being

389

at the bottom of the sea with only a distant flicker of light
to indicate that the world is awake—or even alive.

On the port quarter there was a battery of ten searchlights that moved aimlessly, slowly changing their abstract
patterns from vertical bars to a gray ghost of a pyramid
that even as soon as it was built was demolished and
became Vs and Xs. A lot of help they were! Beer knew
that should he wander near those beams they would try to
kill him.

On the starboard quarter, eighty miles away, he could
see the target being attacked. Distance had drained all
color from the flares and explosions and from here they
were just a steady flickering gray pinpoint.

"He'll never catch him now," said August in a long-
suffering voice. "Order: Orbit beacon at 6,000 meters."

He switched Beer off and connected himself to the red
Würzburg operator. "Give me another *Tommi.*"

"Very good, sir. There are still plenty coming."

Willi Reinecke had long since taken off his jacket and
tie and now he stretched his arms in great circling movements that relieved the aches in his limbs. With his battered face, shaggy hair and huge shoulders he looked like
a clown acting up for a circus audience. But no one
laughed.

"Is everything all right, Willi?"

Willi nodded, but August knew that all was not well.
"There's something wrong?" Anxiously August looked
back at the table and across at the altitude charts. Had he
made a fool of himself in front of them all? Had he put
that last one in at the wrong altitude and then blamed him
for failing to contact? He could see nothing wrong.

"Don't act up, Reinecke," said August coldly. He knew
that something was wrong, but he would not be made a
fool of by a subordinate. Not even by his second in
command. Unterfeldwebel Tschol, the senior messenger—
a white-haired old man from Innsbruck—was also looking at August in a way that was quite unlike his usual
demeanor.

Willi tried to pull his fingers off his hands and made
loud clicks with their joints. "It's the target," said Willi
finally.

"The target . . . ?"

"They marked it precisely as far as we know, although
some markers went down over Duisburg. The mist of the
Ruhr would make a difference. Perhaps there's a reason,
but could there really be?"

"What target?"

"The *Tommis* are carrying out a precision bombing attack upon Altgarten, sir." Now he'd said it.

"That's impossible."

"An error ... winds wrong ... a marker aircraft destroyed ... equipment damaged."

"Altgarten? The whole stream?"

"I'm afraid so, Herr Oberleutnant."

August tried to visualize the scene there and for a minute he did not speak. "Take over the table, Reinecke."

"Sir."

"Tschol, tell the telephone switchboard to connect my office phone to this number."

Tschol took the scrap of paper but stood for a long time before acting upon the instruction. They both knew that he was giving August plenty of time to change his mind about the call. Such a thing was strictly forbidden.

"In your office?" said the messenger finally.

"Yes," said August, "and they must try the other numbers if there's no answer from the first one."

"It's a court-martial offense," said Gefreiter Orth, the telephone operator, when he was told to connect the C.O. to a private phone number in Altgarten. His cunning little eyes glinted as he watched Tschol's reaction.

"It had better not be," said Unterfeldwebel Tschol.

"I'll fiddle it somehow," said the operator. "I wouldn't drop the old man into the dirt."

"You'd better not," said Tschol. "If we lost him we might get that old bastard from my last station. You'd be sitting there in best uniform, pressed and clean with a cropped head, just in case some high-ranking snooper came to call."

The telephonist, dressed in undershirt, shorts and sandals, rubbed his stubbly chin and shuddered at the thought. He looked round at his little sanctum. Pasted upon the wall above the P.B.X. there were a dozen nudes, a pair of baby's shoes, a crucifix and a warning notice: *"Feind hört mit!"* With a caricature of a big-eared Winston Churchill.

Orth was not only the most unsoldierlike man at Ermine, he was its most notorious black marketeer. It was a well-known fact that when Orth hung the enemy-listening sign on the door it meant that the police were tapping the phones for security purposes.

"Rotterdam? This is Luftwaffe Signals, Ermine. I want

a top priority connection to Altgarten, Rheinprovinz.
It's by order of General Christiansen and should not be
recorded in the log. If you want details ask Stabsfeldwebel
Braun for a written authority. Yes. I'll wait, but only for a
moment."

The white-haired Tschol bit his lip anxiously. "Is he
asking this fellow Braun?"

Orth winked. "Braun's one of our people for eggs," he
explained.

When the phone rang in the cellar Anna-Luisa was half
asleep, for the ventilation fans had stopped and the shelter
had grown warm and airless.

"Krefeld exchange here. Will you take an official call
routed via Luftwaffe Signals, Rotterdam?"

Before she could answer and even amid the crackling of
the damaged phone lines she recognizd August's voice.
"Anna-Luisa. Are you all right?"

"Perfectly all right, Herr Oberleutnant," said Anna-
Luisa. She was by now wide awake and guessed that
August was running a great risk by calling her. "I . . . that
is, Hans and myself are in the shelter of Herr Voss. Work
is going on as usual," she added to make it sound more
official.

"Work?" said August. "What are you talking about?"

She had been about to say, The air raid is going on, but
we are safe, but she remembered that it was a punishable
offense to reveal that a place had been under air attack
until three days afterward. She knew too that security
officials might be monitoring the call.

"All is in order," she said. "Everything exactly as I
promised you this afternoon."

"It will be as we decided," agreed August, cautious for
the same reasons.

The noise of Sweet's airplane coming across the town at
rooftop height was loud enough for Anna-Luisa to hear it
even in the depths of Voss's cellar. There was a great roar
as it struck the ground. It fractured into pieces of metal,
each one the size and weight of a motorcar, and the pieces
bounced across the fields, shaking the ground at each
impact.

"I can't hear you, Herr Oberleutnant. There's a
scratching noise and your voice is so faint."

"It will be as we planned it would."

"Will what?"

"Nothing," said August.

"What did you say after 'planned'? You said, 'It will be as we planned . . .' then what did you say?"

"I love you," said August desperately and rang off. "Thank God," he said quietly to himself and he returned to the Seeburg table.

"We have another," said Willi.

August took the microphone and spoke to Beer. "*Katze Eight*. Order: Steer 270 for parallel head-on interception. Question: Height."

"Announcing: Height, 4,500 meters," said Beer.

August turned to Willi. "When will the *Tommi* start to lose height, Willi?"

"Any minute," said Willi. "This one won't wait for the coast; I feel it."

"The colored-light stuff is Gilze-Rijn airfield. Breda beyond it. Fifty miles to the Dutch coast . . . With this wind, say sixteen minutes."

"I'm going to start losing height," said Lambert. "We'll put on a bit of speed if we put our nose down."

Kosher leaned forward and arranged Flanagan, the cross-eyed doll, more comfortably against the windshield. "Can't have Flan falling over," he said.

Lambert had been given the doll before his very first operational trip and it had traveled with him on every sortie. All of the crew firmly believed that to fly without Flanagan would lessen their chances of survival and Lambert had put him under lock and key between trips ever since a gunner from A Flight had borrowed him without asking permission. Lambert noticed that all of the crew would touch the battered doll at some time or other during the trip, although Cohen and Jimmy Grimm would find some rational excuse for doing so rather than admit to being superstitious. Jimmy's wife had darned Flan's foot last month and was making him blue velvet trousers.

Kosher returned to his navigation table and Lambert nosed down gently toward the cloud bank.

Willi Reinecke spit loudly upon his hands. August sincerely wished he would not do that—or at least not so loudly—but Reinecke's father had also done so for luck before starting any job, and in medieval times it had been a necessary defense against the devil. What chance did August stand of preventing Reinecke from doing it? Anyway, they could do with some luck, from any source available. Willi pressed the soft tip of his wax pencil upon the light blip to begin the trace. For the second time that night, *Creaking Door* was to begin a journey across Ermine's plotting table.

In the shelter a spellbound Anna-Luisa replaced the phone. Softly she sang her favorite song of the moment. It contained a promise of magic. And love, she knew, was magic.

"I know that sometime there will be a miracle.
And then a thousand fairy tales will come true.
I know that no love so big and wonderful can pass
    quickly.
We both have the same star
And your fate is also mine;
You are far away and yet so near
Because our souls are one;
And that is why there will be a miracle sometime
And I know that we'll see each other again."

# ❧ 33 ❧

GERD BÖLL was an expert in the strange new craft of bombed buildings. He knew that they could be divided into three main types. There were the ones that disintegrated into rubble and formed a pyramid of impenetrable debris. Then there were buildings that collapsed only at one side, so that all the floors on that side fell to the ground. The hospital had done that. Then there was this sort of ruin: the most difficult and treacherous of all. The floors had collapsed in the center of the building so that they now formed several V shapes, jammed one upon the other and waiting for an excuse to settle lower upon a careless rescuer.

Gerd knew some of the ways of debris. He knew that a flimsy chair could support several tons of brickwork or lock with another piece of furniture to produce a miraculous cavern in the very center of the wreckage. He knew that gas could collect in airless pockets and be dense enough to ignite a spark or overpower a man who put his head there. He knew the dangers of dripping water and he knew that a panicky person needed twice the diameter of a careful, calm one and because of that some rescue crews had been unable to return along their own tunnels. He knew the added strength of curving or crooked tunneling. In short, he was an expert.

"No smoking," he told a soldier.

There was no one way to tunnel into the heap of debris which covered Voss's cellar. Gerd Böll surveyed the whole heap of it. He peered at the piles of bricks and bits of wood. He lifted doors and mattresses to study the shape of the pile and to decide where the lines of thrust were. The top of the pile was twenty feet above street level and flattened abruptly into a plateau that had a slight bowl

of subsidence. Normally he would have begun to dig as
close to the ground as possible, but here at the top an old
sofa and kitchen table seemed to form the entrance to a
natural cavern through the rubbish. He tested it with his
foot and when only a toy dog and some shattered plaster
moved he decided that it was firm enough to burrow into.

He was able to get his whole body inside the wreckage
by moving only a few bits of flooring and breaking a chair
leg and passing it back to the men behind him.

"Herr Böll is on his way," he heard a soldier say. He
imagined that Anna-Luisa would be taking it very calmly.
She was a remarkably placid girl, Gerd thought, a schem-
er or a saint. No, saint certainly wasn't the word. "Often
debris provides a natural course for the tunneler and if
possible he is well advised to use it." Even though he was
now crawling at a more shallow angle, he continued to
move along the line of least resistance. He was deep inside
the pile of debris when he stopped for a moment to listen
to it. There were a few creaks and cracks and the shuffle
of powdered plaster, but no danger signals. When he was
a child he had had slight claustrophobia. The doctor had
told his parents to leave his bedroom door open. "He'll
grow out of it." Gerd had overcome his fears and was
proud of having done so.

"Saw," he whispered. Cocking his head back over his
shoulder, he took the handle of it and working with his
elbows against his chest and with the blade moving only
three or four inches, he was able to saw through the
bookcase in ten minutes. Beyond it there were books and
these he could only deal with one by one. Heine, Schiller,
*The Treasure of Silver Lake* by Karl May, *Love's La-
bour's Lost, Home Medicine, One Man's Journey Through
German West Africa, Memoirs of an Infantry General,
Hay-box Cooking* were all passed back to the TENO who
was at his heels, and each permitted Gerd to crawl forward
another inch. A pile of gramophone records cracked loudly under his elbow and a piece of fireplace cut his leg.

"Silence," said Gerd, and the word was repeated back
to the men at the entrance to the tunnel and then a
whistle was sounded to tell passers-by to listen for the
cries of the buried. But Gerd had been mistaken.

Anna Luisa was not crying; she was sitting in an armchair with little Hansl held close to her, rocking him gently
and smoothing his hair. He was asleep now, for something
of the girl's calm had reassured him. Since she had spoken
with August she had played the music box a dozen times,

examined the Meissen and the silver and walked round the
storehouse until she had seen it all. Now, with the oil lamp
flame turned very low—for she knew it would not get
light here in the morning—she waited patiently to be
rescued.

Gerd Böll made excellent progress, taking under an
hour to reach ground level. Progress slowed as he went
on, for Gerd preferred to jam a piece of wood or brick
tightly against the tunnel's roof to hold the wrecked house
intact. When he came back he would remove his pit props
one by one. However, this made passing debris back
difficult and whenever he could he packed it flat instead.
There was still enough room for him to progress through
the wreckage by removing only a minimum of obstruc-
tions. It was the easiest tunnel he had ever made, almost
as if someone else had made it for him.

Like an archaeologist Gerd recognized the compressed
layers that had once been stories: through bathroom tiles
into stair carpet and on through pieces of kitchen sink. The
kitchen floor was stone and Gerd anticipated a long hard
dig there, but it was simple enough. The flagstones had
shattered and there was a wide pit in the soft earth. Gerd
moved through the hole carefully but still he scraped his
shins on the broken stone. He was at an angle of forty-five
degrees now with his head downward and it was an effort
to prevent his legs from sliding upon him while his hands
were occupied with the blockages in front of him. Twice
he did slide forward and had to use all his strength to
stretch his legs out behind him to get purchase on the
bricks and timber.

He was almost into the cellar when he reached the end
of his easy tunneling. In front of him there was a green
metal barrier. It was two and a half feet across and circular in shape. It fitted close against the house debris, as the
circular door of a safe fits into a wall. Gerd stroked the
metal door and wondered what sort of household equipment it could possibly be. A water tank perhaps, but had
ever a water tank been as sturdily made as this? Thick
steel fixed together with massive bolts that could . . . A
bomb, my God!

Gerd decided that is was the end of a medium capacity
bomb. A six-foot steel canister that had been dropped set
for long delay with a celluloid heart full of acid eating its
way through to detonate the amatol.

It had dropped upon the wreckage and torn a passage
through the rubble, which was why Gerd had found the

natural path so easy to move along. He followed the
bomb. Long delay, but how long: one minute, two minutes,
twenty-four hours? Gerd went hot and cold and could
hear his heart beating like a drum. A 1,000-pound cookie
would obliterate half the street, and he was cuddling it.
He felt the bomb and fancied that it was hot, although he
knew it was probably the temperature of his nervous hands
that deceived him. He thought he could detect the sharp
odor of British paint and varnish that he'd smelled on other
R.A.F. bombs.

From now on he was tunneling in earnest. He worked
along the side of the metal, using strength of the canister
to support one side of his tunnel and building bits of
broken stone and wood from it when necessary. It seemed
as though his trip past the cookie would never end. He
moved past the smooth steel shape and was six feet lower at
the far end of it. Suddenly a piece of bedstead gave way
under his elbow, the cellar wall buckled and collapsed,
and he found himself sliding forward into space. He fell
because, with remarkable self-discipline, he refrained from
grasping at the bomb to steady himself. He landed heavily.

"Herr Böll," said Anna-Luisa, opening her eyes to find
the agile little man crouching on the wet floor, having
appeared with the suddenness of a Demon King in a
pantomime. He was covered with brick dust and rubbing a
sore elbow.

"That's a bomb," he said, awkwardly pointing at the
dark smooth shape that was only just visible through the
gap in the cellar ceiling.

"It looks like a water tank," said Anna-Luisa. She came
closer to stare at the metal shape.

"No, I think it's a bomb," said Gerd Böll, but now he
had an uneasy suspicion that she was right. He smiled
awkwardly at her and then asked. "Did you get the ring?"

"Yes," she said, "It's in my handbag. Do you want to see
it?"

"I think we'd better try and get you out," he said.

"I love Herr Bach." She took the oil lamp and turned
the wick on full and Gerd shone his torch too.

"It's thicker than any water tank I've ever seen."

"Herr Bach's hot water tank in the apartment in Krefeld was just like that."

"Have you got everything?"

"There are some wonderful treasures here, Herr Böll.
Did you know that Herr Voss had such wonderful things?"

Gerd switched off his torch. There were lots of things he

hadn't known before, he thought; like young Anna-Luisa having false teeth. Perhaps she'd forgotten that she hadn't put them in. He tried to think of some way of reminding her without causing embarrassment. "Voss is a wealthy man," he said.

"I like him," said Anna-Luisa. "We might be dead now if he hadn't made us take shelter."

"I'll help you climb up the tunnel," said Gerd, shifting an armchair upon which she could climb. "Leave the child. It will be easier for me to bring him; I've done it before."

"I'm glad it was you who came, Herr Böll."

"Why?"

"I always had the feeling that you disliked me."

"I don't dislike you," said Gerd, blushing. "About the marriage I'm not so sure, but I don't dislike you."

"But I would make Herr Bach a good wife, Herr Böll. I promise you, I promise you." the intensity of the girl's words and the simplicity of her emotions showed Gerd a side of her he never knew existed. He patted her arm awkwardly and feared she would weep. He wanted to tell her about the letter he'd written. So that she would not see his face he picked up the child.

"I promise," said Anna-Luisa again, and suddenly Gerd was happy for the two of them. He knew that his letter would have no effect upon two people really in love. It was August who'd been right. What did it matter what the girl had done or had been? The chances of happiness were too rare and too fleeting to be put under a microscope. He himself had been a rake in his young days and yet that had not prevented him from becoming a loyal and loving husband. Why should it not be true of this girl?

A. C. McDonald, R.A.F. armorer, whose father now sat in a Dundee kitchen with three cups of untouched cold tea at his elbow and the telegram still in his hand, had done his last day's work well. He had fitted the type 47 pistol that morning and the celluloid was of one of the thinnest types used. As the bomb had left Lambert's bomb bay a linen cord, still attached to the plane, had dragged the safety device from the pistol and rotated a pulley which screwed down a bolt upon a tiny bottle of acid. Now the acid had eaten through the celluloid until the spring-loaded striking pin had nothing left to restrain it. The pin struck the detonator and six hundred pounds of explosive destroyed the cellar and was heard across the whole town of Altgaren.

Two houses were totally destroyed and four severely damaged. Five people were injured, since by the time it exploded they had heard the All Clear and come back to their houses. Other delay bombs had been roped off but no one knew of this one. Seven TENO men, three policemen and Storp, the old Blockwart from number 29, who was still digging down toward his wife, were blown to pieces, and a wristwatch belonging to one of the TENOs was found four streets away. No recognizable part or possession or garment of Gerd Böll, Anna-Luisa or Hansl was ever found, although even today splinters of Meisson and shapeless blobs of silver turn up in the gardens there.

One of the difficulties that the rescue workers faced was in the removal of dead and injured. Many bodies were glued to the road surface by the heat and were impossible to move without special equipment. The body of the Burgomaster's wife, for instance, held up traffic on Nehringstrasse for two hours.

Near the cinema a rescue team of TENO men were burrowing deep into a pile of debris. A whistle blew. "Quiet, everyone." There was still a lot of noise but every head cocked toward the rubble, listening for a call or groan.

"Stretcher party," shouted an N.C.O.

"Wonderful," said a policeman. "There are thirty-eight people buried under that lot."

"Morphia," shouted the N.C.O., "quickly." The first light of dawn revealed deep craters in the streets and pavements littered with furniture salvaged from nearby houses.

On a piece of brickwork among the remains of Nehringstrasse 39 there was a chalked message: "Kurt I am with Frau Weber love Kate." Soon there were hundreds of such messages as the people of the town tried to reform themselves into groups: "News of Herr Stroop, please"; "Otto is dead"; "Peter is on leave"; "Mother stay here" were written alongside the bolder notes for rescue men: "Nine dead in rear part of cellar"; "Two dead first floor back room"; "Danger gas sump"; "Quicklime Danger."

# ♦ 34 ♦

THE radar Plotting Room was quiet enough to hear the electric clock jump each second.

"This fellow's a dud," said Willi Reinecke.

"Keep the other aircraft up close and if this one makes a mess of this interception we'll not give him a second chance."

On the Seeburg table the two men watched the dots crawling toward the coast. Both August Bach and his N.C.O. had removed their jackets, but in the heat of the Plotting Room their shirts showed patches of perspiration as the night wore on. It wasn't pleasant to see the destruction of a town happen before your very eyes, even if it was only represented by electronic dots. Willi picked up the glass of tea that had gone tepid. He drank without noticing that he did so. All the time the wax pencil in his left hand traced the moving dots across the table.

"He'll mess it up," said Willi Reinecke.

It was all right for the others, thought Leutnant Beer; they all regarded flying as a mystical experience. For some of them there was nothing in life more important than becoming expert at controlling these uncertain flying machines. Beer, a racing car driver, had gone to his medical examination hoping to become a transport official or an administrative officer. The doctors had classed him fit for air crew. The aptitude and intelligence tests showed suitable ratings and so he had found himself posted to the A/B School for pilot training. It was typical of the arrogance he'd met in the Luftwaffe that they all assumed he'd be grateful for the chance to fly.

Carefully he followed every instruction given by the controller at Ermine but he could tell the man was irritable.

Prussian arrogance! Beer was from Regensburg. His father and his family as far back as the Holy Roman Empire were Bavarian. To them all the so-called Germans outside the frontiers were Prussian. Bavarians were political animals, like the Austrians, and like the Austrians the world had labeled them *gemütliche* peasants and simple-minded clowns. Beer resented that.

Over his earphones came the voice of August Bach. "Order: Hold it."

"Announcement: Impossible," said Beer.

"Give it some flap, man," said August, abandoning procedure. "You won't stall."

Nor will you, thought Beer, in your cozy control hut, but he throttled back and put down more flap, although now he felt he must watch the airspeed needle very carefully.

Beer's radar man made contact. "He's ahead of us and slightly below." Beer eased the antlers forward a fraction.

"Kettledrums, kettledrums," said Beer.

"The man's a genius," said Willi. He put down his pencil.

"No, sir," called Beer's radar man desperately. "Much too much. I'll lose him off the top of the screen in a moment."

The observer had his binoculars to his eyes. "There he is."

Beer cupped his hand against the Perspex to block off the reflections of the instrument panel lights, but his movement tilted the control column and they banked. He sat well back in his seat and brought the controls to normal. "Still too far to port," said the radar man. "He's very close, you should see him."

"I can still see him," said the observer.

"Port and high?" asked the radar man.

"Yes."

Beer still couldn't see it, but he cocked the guns anyway. The compressed air gave a hiss of anticipation.

"Too fast again," said the observer.

"Yes," agreed the radar operator from the back seat.

Damn them, they showed no respect for his rank. They spoke together as if he were superfluous. He put the nose up a trifle and watched the airspeed needle dip, but now the variometer was edging up to show that they were climbing. This business of matching speed with the target was not only the most difficult but also the most dangerous.

"He's turning left."

"He must have seen us."

"No, just correcting course."

"Stop talking so much," snapped Beer. "I'm in command."

The observer looked at Beer with cold disdain. The N.C.O.s called him the cyclist because in the physical manner of a cyclist he trod upon his subordinates while nodding deferentially to his superiors. He wondered if Beer knew of his nickname and glanced at him again, but Beer didn't notice. He was staring ahead trying to see the *Tommi*.

Beer stared into the windshield but could see only a pink sweaty face staring back at him. He could smell stale smoke in his nostrils. Damn that fire-fighting bastard too.

At first he could see only the reflection of the instruments. Then two flickers of light detached themselves and he knew that he was looking at the exhausts of an R.A.F. Lancaster.

"We're right on top of him," said Beer, staring down at the airspeed needle, which was so close to stalling point. Perhaps he should increase speed. Christ, the slipstream threw the Junkers aside and almost wrenched the controls away from him. Quickly Beer recovered control.

"We must get closer than this," said the observer with a calm insolence. Beer reached for the throttles but changed his mind. He did not increase speed. He knew what a midair collision would mean. A giant like that would chop them into fragments and not even feel the bump. "Much closer," said the observer. There was a note of admonition in his voice.

Damned Prussian! Beer was the captain of this aircraft. Even if the target did not reach the edges of his gunsight, it was plumb in the center. This was close enough; the Lancaster seemed gigantic and very near. "Horrido," he called and pressed the gun button. He was yawing slightly, so the target slid to one side of the gunsight. He corrected with a touch of rudder. Not too much, he warned himself. Watch your airspeed.

The Ju88 was a fine airplane—a gentleman's machine— one that would fly hands off and respond gently and positively to the pilot. Yet it would not turn without plenty of rudder. Beer did not give enough and, as he tried to follow the Lancaster's turn, the Junkers slid sideways and Beer recovered only by means of a sudden burst of power that put his nose up.

Flash Gordon saw him because he was coming in high

enough to be on the skyline. He saw the whole shape of
Beer's Junkers pass across a piece of moonlit cloud. He had
told Lambert and now the whole crew waited while these
two pilots matched skills—and luck.

"He's a real expert," said Flash. "You can tell by the
way he's waiting out there."

"Scared shitless," said Binty, who was also watching
him, but his voice lacked conviction.

"Keep off the air," said Lambert. "Flash, give me his
ranges."

"One thousand five hundred yards. Beginning to close
now." His voice changed to a more urgent note. "Twelve
hundred." For an instant both gunners saw the Junkers as
the moonlight struck the propellers and made them shine
like a pair of spectacles in candlelight.

"Closing fast now," Then, from between the glassy disks,
there came white blobs that stretched and ran like spilt
mercury. "He's firing," said Flash. "Corkscrew port," said
Binty. Their voices middled together on the intercom.

Lambert didn't corkscrew. He kicked the rudder bar
and pulled both starboard throttles fully back. The Lancaster twisted abruptly to the right and jerked almost to a
stop. Lambert prayed but also fearfully waited for the
impact. Beer's Junkers came over them still firing, with
only twenty feet between the tips of its propeller blades
and the top of the Lancaster's rudders. The roar of it made
the Lancaster's metal body sing with the vibration. Afterward there was a kick of prop wash.

"See him go, Skip," said Binty gleefully from the top
turret. Lambert was too busy to answer.

Battersby was not looking out of the window. He had
watched Lambert's hands. It was the epitome of all he
had been taught never to do. In theory *Creaking Door*
should now have its tail ripped off. Battersby's hand
reached out to the throttles as soon as Lambert's left
them. Lambert nodded and with relief Battersby put the
starboard engines back to cruising power. The Lancaster
was sliding sideways like a sycamore seed. The compass
went spinning as the nose moved right round the horizon
and passed their original heading, the nose was inching
upward. The airspeed needle dropped toward stalling
speed and Battersby could see that the controls were
mushy. Battersby watched the needles as Lambert pushed
the stick well forward to put the nose down. The needle
hovered at 160 m.p.h., the airplane pulsating as it lost its

airworthiness. Grudgingly the nose dropped and the needle started a return journey.

Lambert spared a hand for his microphone. "Rear gunner, is the tail assemby O.K.?"

"It didn't half bend, Skip."

"O.K. now?"

"Looks O.K."

"Happy, engineer?"

"Yes, Skipper, but at the H.C.U. they told us never to do that or the tail would come off."

"Not unless you give her too much rudder. Remember that."

"I will, Skipper," said Battersy.

"Any signs of the night fighter, anyone?"

"We've lost him, I think," said Digby. "Nice work, skipper."

"Bloody marvelous," said Binty. "You should have seen the bastard go. He was a thousand yards off to port and still firing." Beer was still firing long after the target had almost magically stopped in midair and sped off under his starboard wing. Now there was just the sound of the motors and the airstream. Beer's clothes squelched with sweat. They had missed a midair collision by only a few feet.

"I think we hit him," said Beer.

"No, Herr Leutnant."

"I saw the cannon shells hitting him." There was no reply. Beer wanted a victory. He said, "There were flashes, you saw them."

"Your ammunition destroying itself at 800 meters. I saw them."

Son of a stand-up, sawdust-on-the-floor *Wurstlerei* owner in a sleazy part of Nuremberg. How could you shoot down a real flier? The observer had been washed out of A/B School with flying better than Beer's best attempts. He found it difficult to hide his contempt for this Bavarian peasant in officer's uniform.

So did Willi Reinecke. "Messed it up," he said, "the stupid schlemiel." The two blips had merged and when they separated again it was hard to know which was which.

"The *Tommi* is still going northwest," said August. "He's thirty kilometers from the main stream now."

"He's making sure that the night fighter doesn't get a visual. Shall I call him?"

"Leave him," said August. "Call the other fellow in."

"The *Tommi*'s coming a long way north of the stream, sir."

"Shaken up a bit."

"Faulty compass?"

"Could be."

"He must be here, almost overhead."

"He'll turn."

"Yes, there he goes."

"Bring in *Katze One*, Willi."

Victor von Löwenherz looked at his wristwatch. He didn't trust the cockpit clock; the ground crews were not careful enough with them. He switched over to his main fuel tank and set the mixture to weak. He might need every last drop of fuel, for the *Tommis* entering his sector now would take another hour to return through it on the return journey. The last few bombers would be the most vulnerable ones. It was a simple matter of natural selection: the best pilots got promotion and the best aircraft. The best pilots would get the best navigators and would lead the attack. The least skilled pilots lagged behind, missed landfalls, lost their way, muddled their radio signals and had equipment faults that their careless preflight checks had not revealed. Sometimes such planes never found the target. Long after the Main Force had gone home they would be wandering alone over some remote heavily defended area presenting a keen Würzburg operator and controller with their only target of the night. If they did get to the target they arrived last when the defenses were fully alert and the night fighters airborne with night vision adjusted. These crews got the planes that were the slowest and the ones that could not climb. They were vulnerable targets and Löwenherz wanted to be quite sure that he was in the air when they arrived in this sector.

For Löwenherz was still in his assigned sector right over the beacon. Other pilots, like Himmel and even Redenbacher, had disobeyed the standing orders and followed the bomber stream along its route to the target. Löwenherz had not done that. He had patrolled his sector and obeyed implicitly the orders of his controller, August Bach. Now Bach called him and told him that he had a four-motor *Tommi*.

"Announcement: A big car. Order: Steer 300 degrees."

"That's clear," said Löwenherz. He increased his speed to overtake the *Tommi* before he was out of the radar range of his sector.

On the antiaircraft cruiser *Held* "Admiral" Pawlak and

his K3 had had an eventful night of the sort that Pawlak
had predicted. Now he reminded his friends of his prediction for the eighth time that evening. From the moon-
rimmed cumulus to the southeast came the sound of a
plane. Then other planes.

"From the southeast," said Pawlak. "Why from the
south?"

"Night fighter."

"Looks like it."

"He's firing. He's got him."

"Got him?" scorned Pawlak. "Lost him, you mean." He
danced a little mime in which he threw a shell upon the
loading tray, swung the rammer, spun the elevation
wheel and the traverse and fired the gun. Klaus watched
him dolefully.

The alarm buzzer made them rush back into their
turret. Pawlak banged his elbow on the balancing spring
cover. Klaus smiled to himself.

In the fifty-five minutes that it had taken Lambert to fly
from the Geman convoy one hundred miles to the target
and back again, the convoy had sailed only nine nautical
miles along the coast—although the *Held* had done a little
more than that, for it was now a mile ahead of the convoy
instead of at its very rear.

Lambert's evasion movements had brought him well
north of the Flight Plan. Not even the edge of the bomber
stream passed over Scheveningen. So the only blip on the
*Held*'s Würzburg was *Creaking Door*, until Löwenherz
came creeping up behind them.

"Fire!" It was radar-controlled firing and twelve of the
guns were 10.5s like the one that Pawlak manned. The
explosions made a straight-line pattern of stars in the air.
The radar computer purred smoothly as it corrected the
sighting so that the next salvo would compensate for the
speed of the aircraft. The pointer moved and the gunners
followed it. The guns fired in salvos, so it was no advantage
that Pawlak loaded it almost twice the speed of all the
others. He waited. Pawlak only did it to demonstrate to
his friend Klaus Munte the way he wanted the loading done
in the future.

That no better rate of fire was achieved by Pawlak's
haste made the accident especially tragic. There was little
for the naval surgeon to do. "That damned gun breech has
made as neat a job of amputation as I ever saw." He
clipped the veins and sewed up the wrist as best he could
and let Pawlak sink into a deep, morphia-induced sleep.

Klaus Munte would not open the breech. The Leutnant in charge was about to insist that Munte do it but finally relented and did it himself. When they did open it the unused shell was difficult to remove. It was glued into the mechanism by an unrecognizable substance like raspberry jam.

Radar-controlled flak always bursts in patterns, one burst for each gun in the battery. Some R.A.F. crews remained calm enough to make notes of the flashes for the Intelligence Officer. This salvo was well spaced on a southeasterly axis. The next one was even better and the third was the most accurate of all.

Whether using radar or visual sighting, the aiming of an antiaircraft gun is a complex skill. Both Lambert and Löwenherz were travelling at 240 m.p.h., which required the shells to be aimed at a spot nearly one and a half miles ahead of them. Before each shot the fuse had to be set accurately and even if the target's course remained constant the range kept changing with the angle of the gun.

The rearmost shell of this salvo exploded 71 feet from Löwenherz's port motor. The theoretical lethal radius of an exploding 10.5-cm. shell was fifty feet. This one fragmented into 4,573 pieces of which 12 weighed over one ounce, 1,525 weighed between one ounce and a fiftieth of an ounce and 3,036 were fragments of less than a fiftieth of an ounce.

Twenty-eight fragments hit Löwenherz's Junkers. Four pieces penetrated the port motor and others went into the wing and fuselage. The antlers were wrenched out of his hands as the ailerons were torn and buffeted by the shock wave. The port motor's oil pressure and boost dropped, then the oil temperature shot out of its marked place and swept clockwise. The motor was losing oil rapidly. Mrosek could see it escaping into the air, looking not dark and turbid, but white and sugary.

Löwenherz put the nose down and closed the fuel cock. Then he gave the port motor a burst of throttle to use up the last of the fuel and thus lessen the fire risk. Feather the prop, ignition off, extinguisher on. He'd done the whole thing while subconsciously remembering the positions of neighboring airfields. None was very near. Valkenburg, the nearest, was right under the stream; he didn't fancy that. In the moonlight ahead he saw the complex pattern of the islands and estuaries of Zeeland, where outfalls of the great rivers of Europe fought a meandering battle with the low flat lands of Holland.

He recognized this coast. He'd done many forced landings here—in nightmares just before he awoke. Dump the fuel. He pulled the top off the emergency box beside his seat. The fuel came out of his tail like a fine silvery feather fifty feet long, glistening in the cold moonlight. He closed the cooling gills on the failed motor and gave the good motor a trifle more power. Then he changed the trim to keep her nose high. It was exactly like the emergency instructions in the instruction manual, except that the author of that manual had never flown on one motor in a plane with radar aerials stuck into the nose like a toasting fork. He watched the "Turn and bank" indicator and saw that the Junkers was flying lopsided. It was sinking at five meters a second according to the variometer and he couldn't lessen the rate of descent. The altimeter crawled backward.

"Strap tight," said Löwenherz to his white-faced crew. The Ju88 was not an easy aircraft to force-land on one motor. They had all watched one burst into flame at the end of Kroondijk's main runway only seven weeks ago.

Löwenherz looked at the man beside him. Not a word was exchanged, but Löwenherz was convinced by the look.

"Bale out." Mrosek wrestled with the floor hatch but it had been damaged and would not open. He looked up at Löwenherz in desperation.

Löwenherz detached the rear part of the cockpit cover and it flew off with a terrible roar that left them in an icy gale that whined and hissed across the edges of the windshield. It spoiled the trim, so he touched the wheel to bring the nose down. Mrosek went first. Carefully he tucked his Zeiss binoculars inside his tunic. "Lost in actions"—he would not be asked to account for them. Agile as ever, he climbed out through the top like an acrobat. One of his boots swung dangerously near to Löwenherz's head, then he had wriggled clear. At first it seemed a perfect job, but a nasty thump told them that the slipstream had batted him back against the plane's tail. The slipstream threw him forward so that the binoculars crushed his rib cage and broke four ribs. As he tumbled head over heels, his wrist struck the leading edge of the port tail plane and the fin gave his head a glancing blow before he was sucked away in a slipstream of fuel spraying from the jettison pipe. Overcome by the fuel and the blow on his head, Mrosek fell

3,000 feet. Then night air blowing across his soaked clothing refrigerated him. Without fully regaining consciousness, he pulled the rip cord and floated down under his canopy safely into a potato field.

Sachs had always been a bit timid. Löwenherz had seen his papers and knew that the pilot selection and officer candidate boards had both failed him because of this. Löwenherz decided that he would need more than just an order. Especially to use the top escape exit.

"If you don't go immediately, I'm going to jump and leave the airplane to you." Sachs climbed out then. Armed with the sort of luck that life had always provided for this rich young radar man, he was carried well clear and made a perfect descent.

The first sharp pang that Löwenherz had felt at the moment of the explosion had by now become a dull wet ache. It was as though an uncomfortably hot barber's towel had been pressed against his belly and wrapped around his middle. Its cause was a broken fragment of a knurled brass pin from the flak shell's nose cone fuse. The pin had punched a tiny hole in the stressed metal skin of the aircraft's nose and split into three parts after hitting the gyro compass. This piece, weighing only one-sixtieth of an ounce, entered Löwenherz's belly. It passed through the abdominal wall and the peritoneal cavity, puncturing his ascending colon. It began to tumble as it lost speed, chewing its way through small arteries and a kidney before cracking open one of his lumbar vertebrae. There it nestled against his spinal cord, compressing it slowly.

It was not easy to hold the starboard wing down now that the motor had failed on that side and it was buffeting fiercely under his hands because of the damage to the metal wings and the tattered fabric of the ailerons themselves.

Löwenherz smiled grimly to himself. It was the very devil of a predicament. When he throttled back he began to lose height immediately. Yet with the good motor on full throttle to maintain height it carried him round in huge circles. No matter how much he tried to correct the turn with the ailerons it made little or no difference. The Ju88s were all like this, they needed a lot of rudder to turn them, and Löwenherz couldn't even feel his feet, let alone use them upon the rudder bar. He pressed a hand upon his left knee to use his lower leg as one might use a stick to prod at the rudder, but the pain on his spine was terrible. He continued to do it until the moment when he almost blacked out.

He called up the controller and told him briefly that he'd been hit and wounded and was heading due west over one of the great islands south of Rotterdam.

"Get out, *Katze One*," called August Bach urgently.

"Announcement: Impossible," said Löwenherz. "I've damaged my back."

"Order: Turn back."

"Losing height too fast. These damned aerials."

"Order: Keep the radio on," said August. "We've switched the emergency service into the circuit. They'll take a fix on you for the rescue boats. The Würzburg will hold you too."

"Thank you," said Löwenherz.

The life had drained from Löwenherz's lower limbs so that only the upper part of him was truly alive. His vision was affected too: the red and green lights on his panel and the bright blue moonlight became a neutral gray. The noise of the one good engine seemed quieter and he wondered if that was why it could not hold the heavy Junkers in the air. The gray airplane descended down to the gray ocean and the flash it made as it hit the waves was gray like the water into which it sank.

Sadly the Würzburg at Ermine followed the Junkers out over the ocean until the blip became a phosphorescent glow that died away. The tube was blank except for a rain of interference.

When the great red flash appeared far out across the dark water a sentry phoned the control room to tell them.

"He's gone," said Willi. "The sentry saw the explosion."

"It's always the best ones we lose."

"It was the Staffelkapitän," said Willi. "I know his voice."

"One of the best pilots we worked with."

"He was a count or a baron."

"Damned bad luck."

"That bloody flak ship."

"There was no way they could know, Willi."

"They're probably painting a ring round one of the guns."

"Probably."

Each of *Creaking Door*'s encounters with night fighters had lasted only a few seconds, but between those encounters had come the tension and tiring concentration of one hundred miles of crosscountry instrument flying. After he had evaded Beer by the sudden turn to starboard Lambert continued on, nervously examining every quarter of the sky, but soon it was clear that they had escaped from that attack.

Binty Jones said, "Skip, can Jimmy give me a break? I've got a touch of cramp."

"O.K. with you, Jimmy?" Lambert said.

"O.K., Skip."

"Quickly then."

Lambert felt the trim change as first the wireless operator went back to the upper turret and then Binty climbed down from his seat in the roof and moved farther back to the Elsan, just ahead of the tail. Jimmy Grimm, like most of the wireless operators, was a trained air gunner and he enjoyed the view that the turret afforded him. He touched the grips and the turret turned obediently, the machine guns tilting at the merest finger touch. One of the worst aspects of the wireless operator's job was the heated-air outlet that emerged near his seat. Even wearing the minimum of flying kit, Jimmy had become uncomfortably hot. He slipped one side of his helmet off and pressed his face against the ice-cold Perspex of the turret. It was like a long draft of cold beer.

"O.K., Jimmy?"

"O.K., Skip."

Lambert saw the flicker of the navigator's light as his curtain was pushed aside and guessed that Binty had come forward to the cockpit for a moment. Binty cherished a conviction that flying a bomber was little different from driving a motorcycle and he liked to watch Lambert's activities and tried to commit them to memory. He noticed that the altimeter was steadily turning as they lost height. It was the usual procedure to exchange height for speed from the time the enemy coast was crossed on the return journey.

"What about the photoflash, Binty? See if you can push it out, will you?"

"Can someone give me a hand, Skipper?"

"No," said Lambert.

"I'll give a hand, Skipper," offered Cohen.

"O.K.," said Lambert. "See what you can do."

The moonlight that revealed the bombers to the night fighters was also reassuring to an alert bomber crew. Löwenherz was still dancing through the puffy cumulus far behind them over Rotterdam and no one in *Creaking Door* was aware of his existence. Leutnant Beer had been assigned to a southern part of the Ermine sector. In

short, there was not an enemy in sight. Over the ocean one
would not expect an 8.8-cm. flak gun, but even if by some
magic one was there, *Creaking Door* was nearly three
thousand feet higher than the effective range of an
8.8-cm. flak gun.

Lambert was relating these facts to himself when a
10.5-cm. shell—with its superior range—burst near *Creaking Door*'s tailplane. It came from the tail; a strangled
thump. A giant's belch that rumbled along the metal
throat of stringers and formers. Then came the bad breath
of cordite and burning, speeding on the wave of displaced
air that pushed Lambert forward against the controls, shook
the extinguishers loose and sent Kosher's charts to fill the
cockpit with fluttering paper. There was a flash of light
too. That came from inside the fuselage. It made the screen
turn white and blinded Lambert, whose eyes were adjusted
to the dark night.

The control column came to meet Lambert's belly and
even with all his strength he could not prevent it from
coming. *Door*'s nose reared up like a frightened horse and
the sound of the motors changed to a new note of anxiety.

"Micky," said Lambert, "Micky," and Battersby rushed
to his assistance, for he knew that he was the one that was
needed. Binty Jones had been thrown to the floor by the
explosion. As he picked himself up he knew that *Door* had
been mortally hit. Then there was another great flash—
bigger than any flak shell—a great white soundless explosion right under *Door*'s belly.

"Take a look, Binty," said Lambert. "Back there."

Binty got to his feet while Battersby put his foot on the
pilot's seat supports and pressed against the column as
hard as he could. His face was beet red and the veins on
his forehead shiny with exertion.

The controls remained unyielding, although, with little
Battersby there to push, Lambert was able to hold them
still. Lambert checked the other controls: the rudder bar
was slopping from side to side and the trimmer wheels did
not respond. The elevators were unmovable and all the
time the aircraft's nose was trying to come up. Both of
them were using a lot of energy and Lambert doubted
whether they could fight the column forward for the
whole trip across the North Sea.

Binty pushed the navigator's curtain aside and was met
by a blinding green light. It was so unnatural that he
crossed himself and wondered if they had entered Hell as
a crew. The green light flickered and died. Suddenly it was

pitch dark and there was a stench of burning cordite and
rags. Binty Jones edged aft through the darkness. He
groped toward Kosher's seat but he was not there. He
continued climbing up over the main spar and past the
bunk. The interior of the plane was billowing with smoke.
Cautiously he stepped into it and walked as far as his
turret before he saw the hole in the fuselage. He knew
that the metal skin was thin and that a blow with a
pencil's end could drive a hole right through it, but that
did not lessen the shock of seeing a gap big enough to
drive a small car through.

Because the explosion had broken a section of metal
skin away from its rivets and bent it back upon itself, the
hole was rectangular. The metal rattled angrily in the
airstream like a monstrous letterbox flap. For a moment
there was less smoke and Binty saw through the hole.
There were tripods of gray searchlight beams somewhere
near Rotterdam to the east of them, but the Lancaster
was turning and the searchlights passed and the smoke
closed in again.

"Jesus!" said Binty. He expected a reply from Jimmy
Grimm in the turret but when he looked up he found that
only the upper half of Jimmy remained. The leather-
jacketed torso and masked head was staring over the gun
sights as though ready to open fire, but the lower part of
him was not there. There was just a boggy puddle of bone
splinters, blood and liquidized viscera dumped on the floor
and dripping from the flare stowage. Into it was pumping
oil from the fractured pipes that led to the rear turret. Binty flashed his torch away from the obscene sight and
steadied himself against the ice-cold metal skin of the
fuselage.

Lambert had no rudder to steer with. Experimentally he
held the control column and gently turned it sideways to
operate the ailerons without letting it back an inch. For
what seemed a long time *Door* didn't respond. The fabric
covering on the starboard aileron was so tattered that
most of the slipstream was whistling through the holes.
The port aileron was spoiling the lift on that wing but the
starboard one was not giving extra lift to starboard. *Door*
settled down like a fitfully sleeping dog and dropped fifty
feet with a cranium-pressing lurch that pinned everyone
to the floor. When she staggered across the sky Lambert
feared the tail had broken but slowly the starboard wing
came up. Inch by inch it came until it pointed the way to
England. Lambert knew that they had suffered severe

structural damage at the rear. He wondered how much warning they would get if the airstream got busy and tried to rip the back end off. Already the drag was such that he could feel the rear part of the aircraft sagging and bucketing. He reduced speed, throttling back to minimize the strain upon the airframe.

Binty plugged into the intercom. "Are you there, Flash?"

There was no reply. "It's Binty, boy. Are you there, kiddo?"

Binty moved gingerly nearer to the gaping holes. Through them he could even see a ragged moon glinting on the black ocean. The floor creaked and tilted under him and nervously he stepped back. There were only a dozen stringers, an ammunition runway and that piece of metal floor plate holding *Creaking Door*'s tail on. Binty's weight might be the last straw.

"Binty, what's happening there?"

"Jimmy's had it, Skip, and I can't get no answer from Flash."

"Can't you open his turret doors?"

"Can't get as far as that, Skip. She's full of smoke. There's half the bloody fuselage side gone. Her tail's hanging on by its teeth."

"Kosher?"

For the first time Binty thought of Kosher. He seemed to have disappeared. "Kosher, you all right?" said Lambert over the intercom. There was an answering noise.

"Where are you?" said Lambert. The intercom gave only a monosyllabic grunt. "You hurt?" Again a bubbling sound came over the wires. Mother, perhaps. They never said Father. Mutti? Yes, it could be Mutti.

Lambert had carried dead and injured before. In 1941 he'd brought a Whitley two hundred and fifty miles with everyone, except himself, dead or semiconscious. By now he knew the signs. The silent ones were either dead or unharmed. The screamers were slightly injured and scared, for no one who was mortally torn could spare the stamina for long loud scream. It was the soft groans that needed the tourniquets and morphine. Voices like Cohen's.

"Find Kosher, Bint."

"I've found him, Skip."

"Is he O.K.?"

"No," A silence. "You'll have to lose altitude, Skip. He needs oxygen."

"Connect his tube."

"Tube's O.K. He's got no oxygen mask on."

"Put it on."

"Can't, Skip, It's gone."

"What do you mean, gone?"

"Burned away, Skipper. I'm going to have to get the morphine from the box."

Binty went to the rear. This time he stepped lightly and leaned well toward the least damaged side. He tried not to look down into the clouds and sea below and tried to lose weight by willpower.

"How much of this tube of morphine do I put into him?"

"Give him half a tube into the arm. That's still a double dose."

"It's difficult, Skip. I can't tell which is arm. Will the leg be O.K.?"

"O.K., Binty. Digby, go back and give Binty a hand, will you?"

To say that Binty was not a close friend of Kosher Cohen would be an understatement. The two men had so little in common that the overtures of friendship that Kosher had made to the Welshman merely underlined the differences of class, education and interests. Binty had spent his childhood in a children's home and his youth at an R.A.F. school for apprentices. He had always been shouted at and punished frequently and his life had run according to timetables and rulebooks. Little that was worth having came Binty's way and when it did he grabbed for it without worrying who got the elbow.

Cohen had been educated at public school and university. Also formalistic, male-dominated societies, but their rituals had ill prepared him for conversation with men like Binty, who was truly knowledgeable only about crumpet and motorcycles. Cohen spoke like an officer, a fact that prevented Binty—and others—from being able to confide to him their inadequacies.

"Here, Cohen. Want a lift to London? Grrr!" Binty jangled a bunch of door keys. "Last time I dropped in on my London piece by surprise she was in the bath. Took me the whole weekend to get my uniform dry."

"Thanks, Binty, but some of the fellows from school are climbing this weekend. I said I'd go along."

Binty flashed the torch around the bare metal interior: racks of signal flares, a first aid box and the curve of the ammunition runways that sloped gently all the way to the rear turret. Ten feet ahead of him were the remains of his mid-upper turret, bent and bloody. There were no flames, but now and again there was the crackle of a bullet exploding with the heat.

"I say, what good luck running into you, Binty. Would you like to come down to my parents' place this weekend?"

"Not unless there'll be spare crumpet there."

Binty tried to pull Cohen forward to the crew bunk built over the main spar, but Cohen was glued to the flare chute by cooked flesh. Binty was frightened that he might pull Cohen apart, for now with the morphia in him he would feel no pain until it was too late.

When the flak shell exploded Kosher had been trying to dislodge the photoflash from the bent chute. He had recovered his balance quickly, grabbed a fire extinguisher and hurried back toward the fire. A parachute was smoldering. It filled the fuselage with the black fumes of burning cloth. Some .303 bullets overheated and popped, making clinks and whines as they ricocheted around the metal structure. Very pistol signals, cartridges and other pyrotechnics caught fire, filling the narrow corridor with blinding light. Bright greens and reds lit up inside the smoke of a wind-drift flare. Some of them burned through the metal skin and fell gently to the sea. Jimmy Grimm was past aid. Oh God! His torch was stabbing at the smoke and the lights exploding as Cohen looked back to the great multimillion candlepower photoflash that he had been trying to dislodge from the damaged chute. It was smoldering. There was no one to help him and no one to appeal to. There was only one way to eject it from the aircraft and that was down the flare chute. He pushed at it with the new energy of desperation and dislodged it just a fraction of a second before it exploded. That was the soundless white explosion that had puzzled Lambert.

Perhaps if Kosher had been wearing his heavy leather air crew gauntlets he would have been less burned but, like most navigators, he wore only his silk linings, having found it impossible to draw pencil lines and turn the circular slide rule while wearing thick gloves. And if only he had not looked down the flare chute to see what he was doing ...

Binty cuddled the boy closely. After he had put the quarter of a grain of morphia into him Kosher began to shake like a man in a fit, but then he became still again. Kosher's eyes remained open but went glassy like a toy teddy bear.

Throughout years of skilled womanizing Binty had never needed words of tenderness, but now he began searching his memory for them. He found none. His childhood had been without kindness or love, but never before had he realized his loss.

"It's just a flesh wound, kiddo," he said finally, but by then Kosher was sinking into unconsciousness. Binty had got an oxygen mask on him now. The burnt place in Kosher's chest bubbled with froth and the silk glove that held it disappeared under pink foam.

In the cockpit Battersby rephrased a question in his mind a dozen times before asking it. Finally he said, "Shall I follow the elevator controls back to the tail?"

"Good idea," said Lambert.

"I'm the lightest weight," said Battersby. "I might be able to get to the rear turret."

"See what you can do, Batters. Take your chute with you."

"Can you hold her alone?"

"Ease off your weight and we'll see."

Lambert found he could hold the control column forward, but only by jamming his leg against it and twisting his body in the seat.

"O.K."

Binty shone his torch up at Battersby, who stepped over the two men huddled together on the floor. In spite of an icy wind the smoke still hung inside the plane. Battersby looked down dispassionately when he got to the hole in the fuselage. He had never been afraid of heights and he studied the edges of the damage with a technical eye. Battersby found the rudder control rod badly bent and kicked at it, but his strength was not sufficient to change the bend or even to make another. He reached along the rod to where it entered the tail plane spar but it was undamaged as far as he could reach. He flashed his torch but could still not see the damage. He plugged in his intercom to the connection near the Elsan. "The rods are not too bad. Probably the elevators themselves, Skip."

"Well, there's nothing you can do about that, Batters. See if you can get as far as the rear turret to see if Flash's O.K."

Suddenly they all heard Flash Gordon's voice. "Rear gunner to captain. I'm all right."

"Where the hell have you been?" asked Lambert.

"Sorry, Skip. My plug came adrift. I've been calling you and wondering what was happening."

Battersby said, "Skipper, would you let Flash come forward. His weight so far aft ... " He left the rest of it to Lambert to imagine.

"Can you come up here, Flash?" Lambert said. "We're in a bit of a mess amidships, so watch your step and bring your chute with you. Battersby is somewhere back there; do as he tells you, O.K.?"

"O.K., Skip," said Flash. "I could tell there was something wrong. My turret would only work on manual and there was a terrible smell."

Flash came forward. He was stiffened by the coldness of his open-panel turret and impeded by his parachute. When he got as far as Binty and Cohen he sat down on the floor with them. It seemed warm there where the metal structure had smoldered.

The only true tiredness stems from the ball of the foot. First it makes the calves ache and the thigh muscles throb and moves along the spine to produce a pressure upon the cranium that almost forces the eyelids closed. That was the sort of tiredness Lambert knew now. He felt as if he had marched fifty miles in full equipment.

Yet with no navigator to help him and no wireless operator to obtain radio fixes he was trying to draw a triangle of velocities in his head. It was no use him remembering courses they had drawn up at the briefing, for those winds had proved to be hopelessly incorrect and were probably still changing. In any case he had brought the Lancaster down to 4,000 feet so that Kosher wouldn't lack oxygen and here the winds might be different again.

"Shall I see if I can work the wireless set for an Q.D.M.?" Digby offered.

"Stay up front. Help me get a pinpoint when we cross the coast."

He had wandered far off the track of the bomber stream during Beer's attack. The moon was bright now, but all it showed him was the sea beneath and irregular formations of cloud ahead. He knew that if he was to make a landfall he must stay below the cloud and when the first particles wetted and darkened the Perspex he put the nose down until he could see again. The ocean was close below them. Those cold spiteful waves looked so gentle from here. Parallel and unmoving, they were patches of white cross-hatching drawn by moonbeams through the clouds.

Lambert had resolved that in this situation he would ask the crew whether they wanted him to turn back over the enemy coast and bail out. But he did not ask them. So many times he had brought back dead and dying. Now once again he was doing it, while he himself was unscathed. Ruth said that he couldn't hold himself responsible for that, but she didn't understand. He steered the kite: a touch of the foot, a movement of the hand changed their position by half a mile. Anything that happened was his fault; there was no escaping it. No authority without responsibility. They did as he told them without a murmur of protest. Cohen had gone back to the flare chute. No one had asked to bail out, nor had they mentioned that had he reacted more quickly to the flak ship's guns they would not have been hit.

"Battersby, take an extinguisher and have a careful look round amidships. If you can find the Aldis lamp take a look at the engines through the wireless window."

"The dials are fine, Skipper. All of them are running beautifully by the look of it."

"Stay here, lad, I'm just being neurotic."

"O.K., Skipper," said Battersby.

Racked by the guilt of not being disabled, Binty held tight to Kosher and tried to make amends. In a low voice, stumbling sometimes over the polysyllables and coughing because of the smoke, he recited nut for nut and bolt for bolt every component of the four motorcycles he'd owned. Flash sat on the floor listening to the litany and trying not to look up at the upper turret. At the controls Lambert and Battersby were struggling with the cantankerous unpredictable crippled *Door*. In the front Digby was staring down at the sea trying to make it into land. Finally he succeeded.

"It's the English coast all right: Aldeburgh."

"Southwold; I can see the river."

"Yes, well, I'm just a visitor here myself, sport." Two searchlights lit and searched the sky, passing close to their wingtip.

"Skipper to crew. I can put down at the emergency field at Manston or try to find Warley."

There was no answer for nearly two minutes. Then Binty said, "Let's get Cohen back home."

"Home it is," said Lambert.

Masked by the effects of the morphine Cohen was slipping into a coma. Binty rocked him in his arms. "Nearly home, Kosher, old son." Then he begun to cut his burned flesh away from the flare chute.

Tommy Carter's ground crew and air crew were celebrating the pilot's twenty-first birthday by bumping him on the hard tarmac. His flying gear deadened the shock of the buffeting. After twenty-one bumps he got to his feet surprised and a little angry, although when he saw Roland advancing on him with a tray of glasses and beer he was suitably placated. Every one of the ground crew was holding a glass of beer before Tommy would take one. The sergeant electrician held up his glass and said, "Many happy returns, Tommy lad. And here's to you and your next posting, Tapper, old son" They all drank happily. They'd hardly begun the second drink when one of them started up the song that had become Tommy's anthem. It was a well-known R.A.F. ditty, sung to the sune of "In and Out the Window."

> "The captain's name was Carter,
>     He was a champion farter,
>     He could play everything
>     From 'God Save the King'
>     To Beethoven's Fourth Sonata."

They all joined in the chorus of:

> "Orbiting the beacon,
>     Orbiting the beacon,
>     Orbiting the beacon,
>     As we have done before."

They were so pleased with the harmony at the end of it that they repeated it all through again and there was more clinking of glasses.

"Here you are, Tom," said Ben Gallacher, toasting his captain. "You're the best bloody driver in the air force."

By the light of the vertical searchlight and the flashing beacon Tommy could see that they were happy and the dangers and difficulties of the night were temporarily forgotten.

Lambert and Digby both saw the vertical searchlight and told each other. For a moment their tiredness disappeared. Using only his ailerons Lambert had brought *Door* around all the way from the coast. Degree by degree he had prepared the heading so that from fifty miles away he was approaching the main runway. Nine and a half miles from Warley he began his landing.

Flash and Binty held Cohen tight. The funnel lights were coming up too fast but old *Door* was trying. She really was doing her best. Lambert controlled his height by means of the throttles, letting the airplane drop gently through the air as it lost forward speed. The elevators were still useless.

"I'll need all of your weight, Micky," Lambert told Battersby.

The flare path was floating gently up toward them. Battersby put the undercarriage down and to their mutual relief it slid into position and locked with no trouble.

"Give me 20 degrees of flap."

"Flaps down," said Battersby.

The approach was good. "Flash and Binty—O.K.?"

"O.K., Skipper."

"Hold on tight to the structure. If the tail breaks off it will only be the end bit. Don't slide out. Digby, come back here. Battersby, 60 degrees of flap, please."

He was no more then 400 feet above the trees and still dropping nicely. Warley spire came up and pierced the skyline as Lambert struggled with the control column. Now he needed those elevators. Just this last time, *Door*, my love! Battersby and Lambert strained upon the controls until they both feared that they might bend the metal. Neither of the men spoke. They were overshooting. Still the wheels hadn't touched. They were flying across the airfield at 100 m.p.h. with an altitude that could be measured in inches.

"I can't hold her," muttered Lambert. They were sinking almost imperceptibly. Continuing on this shallow slope would bring them into violent and final contact with the ground in the middle of Witch Fen or, even worse, the copse just beyond it. Desperate, Lambert decided to slam all the throttles forward into emergency boost. He even started to reach for them; then paused. He doubted if the fragile machine could stand it and he knew that his subsequent circuit would have to be halfway across East Anglia since he couldn't use the tail to steer.

The airspeed needle quivered and dropped to 90 m.p.h. Still there was no bump of wheels touching.

"This is it," said Lambert. He cut the throttles right back. At speeds above its stalling speed an airplane is a fairy princess caring nothing for the law of gravity. But, like Cinderella at midnight, a plane going even a fraction below its stalling speed changes suddenly into a collection of metal components that, exactly as a brick, bomb or pumpkin, will drop earthward as gravity demands.

*Door* did that. It fell upon the runway like a fist upon a counter, shaking every rivet. The tires screeched like half-slaughtered hogs and repeated the scream as the bounding plane reapplied their hot rubber to the hard ground. Lambert had every last inch of flap down now, but they were still racing at sixty miles an hour toward the line of trees that marked the far end of the runway.

"She's swinging," shouted Battersby, but already Lambert was trying to correct it.

Two trees came up through the pale skyline, stabbing their fingers into the air in a rude gesture at having been singled out for doom at the hands of a runaway bombing plane.

Then the world went mad. Battersby knew that it wasn't possible that they could sink into the runway, and yet he knew beyond doubt that it was happening. Lower and lower. There was a very loud bang that shook the whole airplane. There were flashes on every side and a shower of yellow sparks filled the cabin windows. The skyline detached itself from the airfield and danced first round to the port windows and then more determinedly to starboard. This time it kept going and there were hangars in front of them. Then the lighted windows of the control tower, and then those damned trees came round again. The noise was tremendous. Metal was ripping itself to pieces in a frantic rhythm that matched the dance of the trees until, as the horizon lost its energy, the tumult slowed and stilled and there was a silence such as they had never known before. Digby for a moment thought he was dead. Then he heard the gurgling sounds of petrol flowing from broken tanks and the creaks and cracks of the bent metal settling down. There was a smell of scorching and 100-octane fuel and with it the similar sweet perfumes of human juices and fresh blood

They were all speechless and still. Even had the wreckage been on fire it is doubtful that they would have moved. Nowadays airplane accident investigators call it "negative panic"; then they called it being stunned.

"Sorry, lads," said Lambert. "Had to bring the undercart up. Out as quickly as you can, there's a fire hazard. Got Kosher there, Binty?"

"Yes, Skip. We'll see to him."

"Flash?"

" 'kay, Skip. Have you got Flanagan?"

Lambert reached for the cross-eyed rag doll. "Yes, Flanagan's O.K.," he said. Lately he'd begun to hate that doll but never more than now. He stuffed it into his tunic.

"Dig?"

"Ready to go."

"Unplug, get clear. Side door's best. Take it easy."

Only then did the crew recover their senses enough to unplug their microphone leads, release their parachute harnesses and make for the exits. Lambert gave Battersby a blow on the arm to tell him to hurry and he patted the airplane an affectionate farewell. For a moment he sat looking at his airplane. He felt an irrational sadness at saying good-bye to the wreck.

There was a lot of noise now: bells and shouts and ambulances and fire engines. Flash and Binty carried Cohen about a hundred yards before they sank down with him onto the cold ground and looked back toward *Door*, bent and broken and well off the runway. One wingtip had snapped and was silhouetted. Pieces of tail were scattered everywhere. Digby came racing past soon after they had stopped. He saw them and dropped down beside them, puffing and panting with exertion. "Lord bless you, Mother Earth," he said. The smell of the dew-wet grass almost overcame the smell of Cohen.

There was still no sign of Battersby. He was in the shadow of the wrecked bomber, standing by the exit waiting for Lambert to emerge. He could hear him moving around. Soon Lambert appeared in the doorway carrying something. Battersby moved to assist him, but then found he couldn't.

"You'll be all right, Jimmy," Lambert was saying to the wet bundle.


One after another the Lancasters came in on the main runway that took them over the village roofs. Old Sam Thatcher gave up the attempt to sleep and switched on the light by his bed and looked at the clock. "That damned wind. I knew she'd move round. I said so to young Cynthia."

"Go to sleep," mumbled Mrs. Thatcher.

He switched out the light but did not go back to sleep. Finally he got up and made himself tea.

In the Briefing Room there was a shot of rum for every returning crewman and a short dark WAAF with carefully applied makeup handed out cups of sweet milky tea. Two airmen were removing the shutters from the windows.

There was a trace of watery pink coloring the eastern sky. The debriefing officers were sitting behind folding tables writing furiously as the crews grouped round them trying to recreate the raid. It was not possible; their descriptions lapsed into jargon and cliché. Their voices were shrill, and their grimy faces bore the red "scars" of oxygen masks; like painted smiles on dirty clowns. The sudden realization that they had survived was far more intoxicating than one measure of Air Ministry rum.

"I got a real good burst in at him; definitely a Messerschmitt, wasn't it, Cliff?"

"I didn't see him, Dave."

"You stupid sod."

"And this is your twentieth trip, Captain?"

"Right on the target, but I couldn't tell what color the smoke was."

"Krefeld as a city no longer exists."

"If you don't believe me, look at my photo."

"It sounds like a good show."

"A piece of bloody cake."

For the bombs that missed Altgarten fell upon open land and did not burn, and so from the air the destruction of the little town appeared to be a highly concentrated and remarkably accurate attack upon the sprawling city of Krefeld.

Longfellow was pleased. "It will be something to tell your children about," he told Lambert, but Lambert had already resolved never to tell anyone.

The crew drifted away to their breakfast, still talking noisily. Lambert did not leave the room when the debriefing had finished; he waited. He always waited, but this time he waited in vain. He saw no sign of Murphy or any of Sweet's crew.

Out on the cold airfield half a dozen ground crew stood around on S for Sugar's tarmac pan. They'd heard distant singing from Carter's crew, but that had made them even quieter. They were wrapped in woolen helmets and long scarves. Their hands were thrust deep into their overcoat pockets and were removed only to light and relight cigarettes. The ground beneath their feet was dotted with white trampled butts. The men did not speak to each other except to ask the time. The sergeant fitter had done his basic training with Murphy. Finally he said, "Go and get some breakfast, lads." The distant screech of the London train came clearly across the dark fenland. They walked slowly back across the airfield, staring at the ground and hoping they wouldn't see anyone they knew.

At Kroonsdijk Christian Himmel was the last of the Staffel to land. The dud engine gave trouble during taxiing but Himmel expected that. He came past the old wreck quite fast and then Kugel brought him into position with hand signals. He hit the port toe brake so hard that his plane swung round abruptly on its pan. He brought the motors up to maximum revs. The motor banged as he tested the faulty magneto. He switched both engines off. The gyros ran down with a sweet musical hum and the cooling motors chimed prettily. Beyond Kugel there was a group of men. The Medical Officer was there and Christian could see Redenbacher too. A nervous Flying Control officer hurriedly switched off the runway lights.

"What's happening?" he asked Kugel as his feet touched the ground at the bottom of the ladder. Now that he had taken off his mask he was aware of the stink of the Junkers. Burnt oil, exhaust fumes, stale cordite and carbonized guns combined with the smell of his sweaty clothes. Kugel was looking at him in a curious way, perhaps because of this. Himmel stretched his limbs. It was a welcome relief after his cramped, closely fitting bucket seat.

On the far side of the airfield near the dijk there were flashing torches and motorcar headlights. He could tell from the movements of the torches that there was confusion and haste.

Kugel was bursting with news. "A fellow from Twente came in to refuel and left pieces of his undercarriage scattered along the runway. His flaps and brakes had failed. It caught fire. Two officers were trapped in it. Horst Knoll rescued them but he's badly burned on the hands. Funny, eh? him hating officers the way he does."

"Give me a cigarette, Kugel." The old man selected one and pushed it into Himmel's mouth. They walked away from the airplane before Kugel produced his matches. Although it was still quite dark the birds were singing noisily.

"It's been a bad night, Christian. The Staffelkapitän has been snatched and now they think the Leutnant Kokke has also gone. The other Staffein have lost four."

"You'll have to change that engine, Kugel. She cut on me tonight in the middle of an interception."

"It may not have been oiled plugs."

"It was oiled plugs," insisted Himmel, "and the valves are dud too. You heard it. Anyway, the Kommodore said it should be changed if it gave any more trouble." Kugel lit a match and Christian bent his head down to it.

"We'll put a new motor into her, Christian. By the way, Löwenherz's Knight's Cross came through on the tele-printer."

"It will be best. Löwenherz dead, are your sure?"

"The radar people at Ermine saw the explosion out at sea. A shell from a flak ship, they think. He would have got his Knight's Cross from Reichsmarschall Göring in person."

"And Kokke?"

"At first they thought it was his radio but he's not landed anywhere."

"Perhaps they'll turn up," said Christian. "Take good care of the dog or Löwenherz will be furious."

"The Kommodore's waiting for you," Kugel warned. "And that old civilian fellow."

"I was expecting them," said Christian. "In my locker there's a bottle of brandy and an American parachute canopy. You can have them."

"And the Medical Officer is there too," said Kugel.

"Yes, he would want to watch," said Christian. "He's a student of human nature."

Kugel looked over his shoulder to be sure the crew were out of earshot. "Hit me," said Kugel.

"What?"

"Hit me and run. Hit hard so it's convincing."

"You are a good friend, Kugel," said Christian. "Take good care of the dog." He walked toward the group of men waiting for him.

At Warley Fen Munro brought his Lancaster down as lightly as a feather. He kept the wind under his port wing and held off his damaged tire, tilting the controls gently so that it met the runway as gently as possible. So lightly did it touch that a gust of crosswind plucked the airplane back into the air and replaced it on a parallel run ten feet to starboard.

The lower a tire's pressure the lower is the speed at which it will come off its rim. In spite of Munro's skill the soft tire was punched flat by the hard tarmac rushing past at eighty miles an hour and then ripped into long rubber strips that scattered onto the runway, wriggling like hot black snakes as they curled into strange contortions and

went hard and brittle. Devoid of its tire, the wheel hub
struck a long gash of white sparks across the darkness
before digging into the tarmac, bending and tearing itself
into eight pieces that bowled along pealing like a set of
bells. But when the oleo leg touched the ground it was as
if the port wingtip had been grabbed by a giant and the
Lancaster twisted nearly off the runway before settling
lopsided onto the dew-wet grass almost undamaged. It was
only two hundred yards from the wreck of the *Door*.

"Ground flight to ground," said Munro, with formal
precision. An airplane died each time that order ended its
flight. The lights flickered off, the instruments ceased to
glow, the intercom ceased to talk and the generators and
gyros whined to a standstill.

"Ground flight to ground it is, sir," said the engineer,
turning the switch without any hurry. Munro released his
mask, unplugged, unstrapped, turned and thumped his
parachute harness release and reached for his peaked cap
and walking stick.

"Damn me, look at that, Jock." He waved the broken
end of his walking stick. A tiny fragment of shrapnel had
cut it in two. Munro shivered and decided he'd never
carry a lucky charm again. If before trying that dodgy
landing he had known it was broken he'd have been
convinced he was for the chop.

"Congratulations, Skipper," said Jock. "Good landing
and the end of a tour."

"Thanks, Jock."

The Briefing Room was littered with cigarette ends and
the air was heavy with stale smoke and the odor of Air
Ministry rum. When Munro's crew had been interrogated
the room was almost empty. A large notice on the wall
said, "Crews: don't wait around to see your photos. Go to
bed." Before they used that sign the place used to be
packed with noisy air crew until the morning. The Intelligence Officer pulled his greatcoat tighter about him and
looked at the clock. Munro saw him looking at it and
shook his head sadly. The three missing planes did not
have enough fuel still to be airborne. Longfellow gathered
the sortie reports together and went out. The three men
who had been waiting for friends near the entrance also
left without a word to each other.

In the Sergeants' Mess they played the gramophone and
the mess waiter went around complaining about sergeants
who put their wet beer glasses on the billiard table. One

sergeant gunner punched a friend who had refused to corroborate his claim for a Ju88 shot down. A bomb aimer was sick in the bar after drinking whisky mixed with rum. One of the sergeant cooks who was due on breakfast duty next morning came down to the lounge in his pajamas and asked them to make less noise. He was greeted with foul abuse. Sergeant Binty Jones allowed his friend Flash Gordon to push his motorcycle out of the boilerhouse where he kept it. It started at a touch of the kick starter and Binty stuffed a toothbrush into his pocket and was off to his rendezvous with Rose in Peterborough. He bumped his bike across the unofficial footpath behind the mess to get to the main road by the shortest route. He hurried along it, straddling the bike and letting his toes tap the ground just to keep his balance and giving the powerful engine little twists of throttle. He was almost level with a man coming the other way before he recognized who it was.

"Some of you fellows ... " protested the Squadron Commander in amazement. "Where are you going?"

Binty was too surprised to lie. "Peterborough, sir."

"To see some woman. Is that it?"

"Yes, sir," said Binty, unable to keep the nervousness he felt out of his voice.

Impulsively Munro said, "Well, how about giving me a lift to Peterborough station? I might just be able to catch the main line train home." He touched his pocket and heard the crackle of his wife's letter.

"Certainly, sir," said Binty in obsequious relief at not being charged with breaking out of camp. He turned the motorbike round. "Jump on the back. I'll take you up to the Officers' Mess and wait for you."

"That's the spirit, Gordon."

"Jones, sir. Gordon's my oppo. I'm the mid-upper on *Creaking Door*; *O Orange* that is."

"That's the spirit, Sergeant Jones, Peterborough, and don't spare the horses!"

"No, sir. I won't, sir."

When Lambert left the Briefing Room he could hear the gramophone in the Sergeants' Mess and smell the fried bacon of the air crew breakfasts. Tommy Carter, Tapper Collins, and Jock Hamilton from Munro's crew almost dragged him to the mess to join them for a drink but he wouldn't go. He heard Digby say, "Fair's fair; Sam's got to see his missus." Tommy had a bottle of whisky that he

had put in his locker. It was already half gone. They
wished him good night and wandered away singing.

"Happy birthday, Tommy," Lambert shouted after
them. They were singing the famous soldier's song:

> "That's my brother Sylvestre,
>     He's got a row of forty medals on his chest.
>     It take all the Army and the Navy
>     To put the wind up Sylvestre."

The chorus was a tuneless chant sung as speedily as
possible.

> "Don't push, just shove, plenty of room for you and me,
> He's got an arm that's like a leg and his punch will sink a
>     battleship."

Digby ended long after the others and clinging to Tommy's waist he swung round to shout good-bye again to
Lambert. Lambert waved again. Digby shared a room
with Grimm and Cohen. Tonight he'd have the room to
himself; that's why he'd not be going to bed.

By the time Lambert reached the changing room it was
empty. He was opening his locker when Battersby
emerged from the crew toilets even paler then usual. He
wiped his mouth and said to Lambert, "Was I all right,
Skipper?"

Lambert winked at him. "Like a bloody veteran, Batters."

The boy smiled.

"I phoned the sick bay."

"I did too, Batters."

"I was going along there but they said it was no use;
they're doing all they can."

"Get some sleep, Batters; the worst is over."

The boy was full of unasked questions but he smiled
and turned toward the door. Lambert reached for his shoes
on the shelf and in them found the group photo. They were
all there, grinning like immortals. He tossed it into the back
of his locker and after it threw Flanagan. He pulled off his
boots and flying suit and went to have a wash but changed
his mind. Someone had been sick in the W.C., there was a
bulb missing and the only towel had been stolen.

He unlocked his bicycle and pumped up the rear tire.
He had to push the bike through the gap in the wire
because the constant battle between the breakers and the

repairers was going a little in the latter's favor. After that it was only ten minutes' cycle ride to the village.

The sky was dribbling with the first streaks of a new day and the air was cold enough to condense his breath. Lambert liked these rides. The countryside was still and aromatic and there were rustles of animal life in the hedgerows. For Lambert it was the moment to congratulate himself upon surviving another trip. He propped his bicycle against the hedge and opened the front door as quietly as possible.

Ruth was awake when he opened the bedroom door. She was always awake when he returned. He imagined she never slept while he flew, although he never asked her about it. He undressed slowly without the light. The moonlight that had shone so brightly over the Dutch coast was diffused by the thin cloud and dusted the bedroom with just a trace of blue gloom.

"All right, darling?"

Lambert didn't answer, and that she knew was bad. The only other times that he'd been silent was when they'd been shot up and lost crew. When he got into bed he lay full length with his feet together like a block of wood. Or like a corpse, thought Ruth, and erased that thought. His skin was hard and cold and his breathing was almost inaudible. She put her head against his shoulder. He didn't either respond or move away. He'd come back, there was that for which to be thankful. It wasn't only cowards who died a thousand times, it was wives and mothers and sweethearts. Fathers too, perhaps.

"Cohen and Grimm," said Lambert; he didn't mention Micky.

She said nothing.

"I promised his father," said Lambert.

"He made you promise," said Ruth.

"I promised."

She wanted to tell him about the Group Captain but she couldn't add another worry.

"It's Tommy Carter's twenty-first birthday. They wanted me to go for a drink."

"You should have gone."

"No." A motorcycle came through the village at high speed, changed down at the crossroads and then opened the throttle with a roar as it turned onto the main road. Lambert bent over his wife and kissed her. "I didn't wash," he apologized. She could smell the awful night.

"I sent Dad a fiver."

"You are a fool, Sam. He won't use it to pay his bills. He'll never be any different."

"I know."

"You can't be responsible for all the world, Sam. You mustn't try."

"I'll not go again. They can do what they like, Ruth. I'm flown out, finished, kaput."

She reached to her bedside table and found a sleeping tablet for him. He took it like a small child, not caring what it was or where it had come from.

"Perhaps you should play cricket on Saturday. We can go to London the following week."

"You're a good girl, Ruth." He put his arm round her and closed his eyes but he did not sleep.

That was about the time when they found the Burgomaster. They all said it was the most obvious place to look, but no one said that until after he'd been found. A Hitler Jugend messenger almost ran over him on the wrecked site of his own house. He had collected as many undamaged bricks as he could find and he was building them into walls. He had no mortar, of course, which is why they fell over when the boy's bicycle hit them. The Burgomaster was very upset and so the fourteen-year-old messenger helped him build his little hut again. It was almost an hour before the boy realized that the Burgomaster was trying to build the tiny hut around himself.

In Liebefrauplatz a team of TENO engineers led by Bodo Reuter were heaving at a block and tackle. The sound of the chains rattled around the ruins of the still warm church. With each pull the tail assembly of Sweet's Lancaster rose higher until it was strung up in the town center suspended from a buttress. It swayed a little in the winds that had so aided the great fires of the night, looking like a piece of some prehistoric animal, displayed thus to assuage the anger of the gods. Smoke drifted across the scene. On the rudders there were the red, white and blue markings of Britain and the white stenciled letters that were its identity. Some of the TENO men wanted to leave the body of Sweet's rear gunner in the smashed rear turret, but Bodo Reuter forbade it. Even before the cables were secured citizens had begun to gather to exorcize the species that had plagued them.

"*Sieg Heil*," shouted one of them and the others also shouted. Sweet's wrecked airplane would stay there a week and then be melted down and within seven weeks fly again as a German airplane.

Luftwaffe Himmelbett Station Ermine was lucky with the mail. They were the first Luftwaffe unit along the coast on the mail route from Rotterdam. There were two letters for August Bach. One was from the jeweler in Altgarten. It was a receipt for the deposit and a bill for the engagement ring. As the jeweler said, an engagement ring is the riskiest item that a man can offer on credit. The other letter was from August's son. With characteristic confidence it was datelined "near Leningrad."

Pappi

Haven't got more than a moment. We were in the line until only four hours ago. Last night I was on patrol trying to get prisoners for questioning. Both died of wounds and tonight the company that relieved us will have to have another try. We are pretty sure that Ivan is all ready to attack us. When he does I shall get my promotion or a wooden overcoat. Either way it doesn't matter much, as long as as I don't get wounded.

Answers to questions: No. What we get to eat is entirely adequate. Eat your own rations. Yes, we shall be getting leave sometime during the next two months. Yes, I am coming home. Do you think I'd miss another roll in bed with that juicy little housekeeper you've tucked away? I was telling the boys about her. As one of them said, "Trust the Luftwaffe to get itself some civilian rations and then pretend they are going hungry." He meant you, of course. And don't go all sanctimonious on me. See you sometime in August and knock before coming into the bedroom.

Yours cheerfully,
PETER

P.S. Answer to unasked question: I haven't forgotten and will pay you back very soon now.

August folded both letters and put them into his pocket. "Reinecke," he said, "after breakfast I'll sentence the men who lost the bicycles. We'll see to the cash afterward. Anyone sick?"

"Only me, sir," said Reinecke and grinned.

"No," said August, "there are two of us."

"You'll feel better after some coffee, real coffee."

"The herons?"

"They've gone."

At the guardroom at Warley Fen, Flight Sergeant Bishop was looking at his galleon in full sail. He couldn't decide whether to call it "Cadiz Ahoy" or "Gold from the New World." The phone rang. The operator spoke to Bishop, who was for tonight the sergeant of the guard.

"It's some police station with a message," she said. "I can't get any answer in Orderly Room or Operations."

"O.K.," said Flight Sergeant Bishop. "Let's have them."

"Warley Fen R.A.F.?"

"That's it."

"Cambridgeshire Constabulary here. Sergeant Ford speaking. We've got two of your people here. There's been an accident between a Norton motorcycle and a lorry. They were speeding, by the sound of it. Their names are . . ." There was a pause as he shuffled the document on his desk. "Munro, John: Wing Commander. And Jones, William Gareth: Sergeant. Know them?"

"I know the Wing Commander but almost everyone is a sergeant on this stations."

"Very well. I take it your military police people will phone us in the morning to make your own arrangements and there's the damaged motorcycle to be moved too."

"Wait a moment," said Bishop, grinning to himself as he thought of it. "You can't hold the Wing Commander in the cells until morning. Not for a traffic offense."

"Ah, I'm sorry. I should have explained. Dead. Killed instantly. They hit the lorry at ninety."

"O.K.," said the Sergeant. "I'll leave a note about it." He replaced the phone. "Cadiz Ahoy" he decided would be better.

In the three kitchens at Warley the cooks were still heavy with sleep as they sat drinking their first mugs of sweet hot milky tea before they began to prepare the earliest of the early breakfasts. Maisie Holroyd, the Catering Officer, had a cup of tea and a joke in all three messes in spite of having been on duty—supervising the air crew's flying rations—until the middle of the previous night. The sun was clinging precariously to the horizon and killing the stars with its stare. Lambert turned in his sleep, groaned, laughed and went silent without waking his wife. For she had not yet gone to sleep and now she watched him like a mother with a sick child.

In the medical section two doctors stood upright for the

first time in two and a half hours and let Sergeant Cohen die.

In Altgarten they had long since run out of death certificates and were using pages from children's exercise books with the rubber stamp of the Rathaus imprinted at the top. They had also run out of bandages, blood, splints, burn dressings, iodine and morphine.

There were explosions as the TENOs demolished houses and shops on Dorfstrasse. Voss's shop was one of many that had become a dangerous ruin. The metallic voice from a loudspeaker van moved slowly along that same road telling the homeless to report to Party H.Q. for information and assistance. It ordered next-of-kin to report missing persons to the new temporary police station—a house on Zieglerstrasse. The only way to get there was via Koller Meadow, for like many of Altgarten's streets it was partly roped off because of unexploded bombs.

Not far from Altgarten, Billy Pace was the only survivor from Sweet's aircraft. His landing, however, had not been a lucky one. He had seen the dark shapes of the fir trees only a moment or so before hitting them. A branch struck his leg and then he was assailed by the sharp edges of more branches before he was jerked to a sudden stop by his canopy catching the treetoop. There was a tearing sound and he sank a few feet but then swung without descending more. It was pitch dark in the forest and he tried to get a grip on a branch, but they were all flimsy and springy and would not bear his weight. He tried to peer into the gloom but could see nothing. He found matches in his pocket and struck one, but that only illuminated the branches close to him and seemed to make his surroundings even darker. He dropped a burning match but it went out before he could see beyond his dangling stockinged toes, for he had lost both flying boots. Suspended in the tight harness he was so uncomfortable that he was tempted to hit the quick release and chance it, but caution prevailed. Especially when he heard the cry of wolves nearby. He dangled there for three hours with his imagination working overtime until the sun came over the horizon and inch by inch lit up the dark forest. It was then that he saw that the earth was only eighteen inches below his toes. He let himself drop to the ground but was still nervous of the wolves until a forester came past and explained that they were caged dogs. Pace had dropped into the small wood behind the Wald Hotel and had heard the noise of guard dogs being rounded up by dog handlers. He walked along with the forester to his hut and managed to exchange a few words of German.

Behind the forestry hut Billy Pace saw a stiff brown doll-like figure. Its little arms were drawn tight across its front like a boxer's high defense and its burnt mouth was stretched back in a demoniacal grin that exposed large even white teeth. Pace recognized the charred stubble of a moustache. It was young Speke, who had left *S Sweet* without permission. He had landed in a patch of blazing forest.

The forester let Pace look at it for a moment or two. *"Kamerad?"*

*"Ja, Kamerad,"* said Billy Pace and he went into the hut feeling hot and faint and slightly sick.

The old man gave him a cup of bitter brown liquid that he claimed was coffee and then he used the fire-warning phone to send for an escort. Billy still had a chocolate bar left from his flying ration. The old man ate it with relish. As the old forester explained, he would be safer with soldiers than walking through the bombed town without protection. He showed the forester a photo of his mother. Pace wondered how long it would take for his mother to hear that he was a prisoner and not killed in action.

For Fleming and his crew no comrades grieved. Their only friends had been each other, and none came back. Their stay at Warley had not lasted long enough to form friendships with the experienced crews and who could blame the men who came back for preferring that their friends survived rather than seven strangers.

In the Officers' Mess at Warley the Education Officer was collecting together the personal effects of P.O. Fleming. He'd been made Effects Officer only a week before. He made certain that there were no pornographic photos and read the letters carefully to be sure that they could cause no distress to parents or wives. It was a solemn job. He looked at his list; the next one was Flight Lieutenant Sweet.

When the last of the bombers landed the work of Warley Fen's Photographic Section began. Each of the bombers' F24 cameras was unloaded and the five-inch-wide lengths of extra-high-speed film were threaded onto spools and processed. It was all done at high speed. The developer was at 75 degrees F. and they had only a three minute fix and wash before going into a meth.-and-water bath for rapid drying. The flight sergeant then took the wet film and ran it across the front of a light box to check the exposure and development. He noticed nothing unusual, nor did anyone else until the films were being hung in the hot air of the drying cabinet by a WAAF corporal.

She went out into the trimming room and for a moment looked across the airfield. Several of the buildings were lit up, their windows making bright yellow patches, disembodied in the blue morning light. The paths and grass were shiny wet with dew and the beacon still flashed a Morse identity that lit everything like a lightning stroke. The girl found a shiny photograph that had been taken during a previous attack upon Krefeld and studied it carefully before looking at the negatives again. She told an L.A.C. before telling the Flight Sergeant. She didn't want to make a fool of herself.

"Flight Sergeant Booth here, sir, Photo Section. The attack hasn't hit Krefeld, sir, I've just been studying the negs. Street patterns are nothing like it. I don't know, sir. It doesn't look like anywhere. It doesn't look like anywhere."

*Gericht der Wehrmachtkommandantur*
*Berlin*                                 *Berlin NW* 40 den 23.8.43
L/W KS/78 ui                 *Lehrterstr.* 58

To the Supervisory Board of the Penitentiary in Brandenburg-Görden

On Monday, September 13, 1943, at 1 P.M., the death sentence against former Unteroffizier Christian Himmel, born September 12th, 1922, in Ottobeuren, Bayern, religion Catholic, will be executed with the guillotine in your prison.

Executioner Rötger is charged with carrying out the sentence. The sentence is to be notified there on the same day at 11:00.

Charged with the supervision of the execution is Ober-leutnant Dr. Henze, who will be attended by Feldjustizin-spektor Keyser.

The sentenced is in the remand prison of the Wehrmacht in Berlin-Tegel, Seidelstrasse 39.

The Polizeipräsidium Berlin as conveying authority is requested to send the sentenced to Brandenburg on the morning of September 13, 1943. Acceptance is requested.

The local prison doctor is requested to be made available for the execution.

      by direction
        (signed)                       JOST
                                Oberkriegsgerichtsrat

                               *Administration Officer*
*August 23, 1943*             *R.A.F. Station Warley Fen*
      ACH/GD LAMBERT, Samuel Charles

The above-named has been found unsuitable for any further duties in air crew capacity and his reduction from N.C.O. rank has therefore been ratified by Air Ministry. With effect from this date he will report to the Station Warrant Officer for work assignments with cleaning, sanitation and refuse disposal working parties.

While these duties are not intended as a punishment, no privileges will be granted to A.C. Lambert until further notice. This to include passes or permission to sleep off the station.

To Station Warrant Officer
R.A.F. Warley Fen

# EPILOGUE

SOME forgot the events of that night in 1943. Others could never forget and many did not live to remember. Löwenherz, Fleming and Sweet and the crews that flew with them were not the only ones to die. The Luftwaffe lost eight night fighters: three Ju88s, four Me110s and a Dornier 217 as well as three others that landed so heavily as to be written off strength. Ten Luftwaffe air crew died and two more were hurt so badly that they never again flew in combat.

The R.A.F.'s losses were forty-four bombers, of which thirty-one fell to German night fighters. Three hundred and one crewmen were lost: of these sixty-eight survived to become P.O.W.s. Nine of this latter group were seriously injured. Of the R.A.F. aircraft destroyed thirty had already bombed. Five aircraft jettisoned their bombs in the sea or in open country. One bomb load accidentally fell upon a Dutch village and caused eight deaths and three injured. Of the R.A.F. aircraft destroyed, nine were lost to flak and one was lost when an R.A.F. night fighter misidentified it and shot it down as it crossed the English coast forty miles south of the Flight Plan.

Three bombers made fatal navigation errors. One descended through cloud and crashed into a mountain near Stavanger in Norway. Another ran out of fuel 160 miles east of the Orkney Islands. One crashed in the south of France after being shot up. All of the crews perished.

P.O. Munro (John Munro's brother), a Stirling pilot, survived the raid and completed his tour of operations. He now runs his brother's estates, having married Sarah, his sister-in-law, and brought up the child and sent him to university, where he studied law. Tommy Carter and his crew were killed four operations after this one.

Lambert never flew again. Ruth was posted away, became pregnant, left the WAAF and stayed near her husband for the rest of the war. After the war Lambert went to work as a draftsman in an aircraft factory. In 1954 he patented a supercharger modification and went into business manufacturing it. He is happy and moderately wealthy, although like many bomber pilots he has a history of spinal pains and disorders. They have a daughter and two sons.

Battersby, Flash Gordon and Digby were reassigned to a new pilot. They completed their tour, were posted to Training Command and then returned to do four trips of a second tour before the war ended. On the last operation they were badly shot up and Flash Gordon lost his left arm. Many Lancaster turrets were modified to have a clear-view panel. The Group Captain persuaded Air Ministry to officially name this the Sweet Panel.

Battersby married the WAAF driver that he met that night. After the war he went to London University just as his father had planned and, somewhat to his father's surprise, chose to study English medieval history. He has written a book on medieval fortification and is at present a visiting professor at a large American university.

Digby returned to Australia. He has the Australian agency for a British light plane manufacturer and travels round the country selling them to farmers on the assurance that if he could learn to fly them anyone could. Sometimes the customers ask him if he was in the air force during the war but Digby stoutly maintains that he was too young to be in the war. Now completely bald, he wears a toupee.

Jammy Giles left the R.A.F. in 1949. He was drinking a lot by then and couldn't get used to the fact that postwar Officers' Mess parties had become rather more staid than he liked. His mother died and left him a little cash with which he started to buy a pub near Stratford-upon-Avon. In the first year it made money but that led Jammy into a false confidence, for really he is not a good businessman. Careless bookkeeping and generosity with credit made him bankrupt in 1954. However, after working as a waiter for two years he had another go at running his own place. While at his lowest point economically and psychologically he had met and married a beautiful girl named Bessie. Together they started a lorry driver's café on the A1 only about thirty miles from Warley. Jammy admits that it owes its success to Bessie, who works twice as hard as he does. She handles all the buying and hiring and firing and, as Jammy says "more drivers eat here to see her than to see me." However, sometimes squadron people visit them to recall old times. There are dark fly-blown pictures on the wall of Jammy standing under Lancaster bombers and one of him receiving his D.F.C. from the King. Only two years ago Peterson called in and they were laughing about the time he did a bombing run seated on the Elsan. Peterson lives in Montreal and is a vice-president of a small company that makes camping equipment.

In 1948 Cohen's parents both died within three months of each other. Nora Ashton still lives with her mother in the house down the lane. It puzzles some people that she never married, for they guess, rightly, that she had many proposals.

The Group Captain died in 1946 in a car accident in Germany while he was still in the R.A.F. Willi Reinecke also got a job with the R.A.F. in Germany after the war, although he had to falsify his age to do it. He worked in Air Traffic Control for nearly five years before retiring to live in the Ruhr. His son now works for Lufthansa, also in Air Traffic.

Fischer got another medal soon after D Day. He was awarded the oak leaves after rounding up a group of stragglers including cooks and clerks and, using Panzer-fäuste, repulsing an attack by British tanks outside Caen. He was killed after being cut off from his division in the fighting near Essen. He established a strong point with one hundred fifty men and refused all demands to surrender. Artillery fire destroyed them. He still had the three-hundred-year-old Kuba carpet with him. It was found in the ruins by an R.A.S.C. driver and ended its days as a floor covering in his lorry.

Frau Voss survived the war. Using the few works of art that her husband had—with typical foresight—stored in his son-in-law's house, she was able to live comfortably in Portugal until she died in 1959.

Bodo Reuter also survived the war. He worked on a freight boat for a year and then met a man in Athens who gave him a job crewing a luxury yacht for a Greek millionaire. For the first time in his life he began to drink to the point where it interfered with his work. He was dismissed and went to work on various ships but it was on a Panamanian oil tanker that he continued for the longest period, working as a cook. On Christmas Day, 1952, two policemen found a derelict old man on a park bench in Le

Havre. He'd sold his seaman's papers to buy wine so they were unable to identify him. They filled in his death certificate by guesswork. Shrewdly they guessed he was German, but, as one of the flics said, he looked more like a poet than a beggar. They compromised and wrote schoolteacher.

August Bach's S.S. son, Peter, within nine days of writing his letter, won one of the army's most coveted awards, a badge for the single-handed destruction of a tank. Three days after that he was promoted and four days later—on rest behind the lines—he died of shotgun wounds inflicted by a partisan.

August Bach is now a very old man with pure white hair and wrinkled skin. He went to Brazil after the war, married a local girl and had two sons and a daughter. The first job he got was with a small company that builds power boats for fishing enthusiasts, mostly from the U.S.A. After four years the owner gave Bach a small share of the business and a few months after that made him a full partner and retired. Bach was an old man already but by bringing his son and son-in-law into the business he has expanded its trade every year. Bach's younger son, Hans, returned to Germany. Having already flown light planes in Brazil, he got a job with Lufthansa and was trained as a pilot. He now has done nearly three thousand hours on jets. August Bach and his wife spend most of their days in their small cottage on the beach. In some ways it is not unlike the hut he had at Ermine and he still photographs birds and sometimes dissects them.

At Ermine itself there is virtually no trace of the radar station, although the concrete gun emplacements are still there. Dutch birdwatchers go there on Sundays in the summer but there are no herons there now. The nearby drainage workings have disturbed them.

The surviving Scheske twin served a six months' prison sentence for shooting the dogs but did not see combat until the closing weeks of the war. He was captured by the Red Army and served eleven years in a labor camp in the extreme north. He was a sick man when he was released and was permitted to go to West Germany, where he had relatives. He is unmarried and works as a storekeeper in a plastics factory near Hamburg. He only got that job because the manager was also in the Waffen S.S. and felt sorry for him.

Hans Furth was taken prisoner by the British in 1945

and continued to work as a doctor in the camp and later
for Allied Military Government. He ran as a candidate in
the local elections but did not win. However, one of the
people who worked for him on the election campaign was
the Munich manager of an American public relations
company. Furth was offered a job in the Chicago office.
He worked for them for eight years and then left to start
his own P.R. company in New York. Nowadays he works
there only two days a week and is able to afford long
holidays in Florida and a trip to Europe once a year.
Originally, most of his clients were German manufacturers
moving into the U.S. market but now those are in the
minority. Furth has become so American in his clothes and
speech that very few of his clients guess that he is not a
native. For this reason he employs only American-born
staff with the exception of an English secretary, an English
receptionist and an English telephone operator, "for the
image."

Dr. Starkhof, the Abwehr man, was arrested after the
attempt to assassinate Hitler on July 20, 1944. He conclu-
sively proved his innocence and so escaped the death
sentence. He was, however, sent to a concentration camp
and although he was still alive when the American troops
reached it he died only three months afterward.

The Burgomaster went into a mental home and died
before the war ended. The young Meyers who got married
with Andi Niels's aid immigrated to Israel and now work
on a fruit farm near Jerusalem. Redenbacher became an
Oberst at O.K.L. and was killed flying as a passenger in a
Ju52 in January 1945. Old Krugelheim was killed when a
low-flying U.S.A.A.F. Mustang shot up the Kroonsdijk
airfield in late 1944. The airfield itself still exists, although
it is only half its former area. There are only light planes
flying from it today, although there is a two-motor airplane that for only fifteen guilders takes sightseers for a
quick circuit of the IJsselmeer workings. Those same
workings drained a vast area of sea and found the remains
of Kokke's Ju88 last year. Although it was intended for a
museum it broke up when being moved.

Warley Fen's runways are still in position although
they cannot be seen for growing crops. If you go there
today you will also find some of the other buildings. The
Sick Quarters where Cohen died have become sheep pens
and the remains of the Sergeants' Mess where the gramophone was once so loud now echo to the grunt of many

pigs. Only the control tower is in anything like its original condition, although if you ascend the iron staircase be careful. You might end up writing a book about it.

# ACKNOWLEDGMENTS

WHEN finishing a book it is tempting to look back and try to remember the moment of its birth. Certainly this one goes back to an afternoon in 1944 when my boyhood friend Colin Smith—a flight engineer freshly returned from his first bombing raid—told me that during his briefing the crews had cheered when they heard that the more vulnerable Stirling bombers would be accompanying them.

Since then many people have generously given their time to help me make this story as accurate as possible. However, it remains a story and wherever research and storytelling have clashed I have favored the story.

Flight Lieutenant Alfred Price started my research off on a sound basis and his fine book about radar—*Instruments of Darkness*—has been of enormous help. That remarkable pathfinder veteran Hamish Mahaddie, D.S.O., D.F.C., A.F.C. and bar, Czech M.C., C.Eng., A.F.R.Ae.S., was an endless source of information about every aspect of the R.A.F. Vivian Bellamy, while flying me to Cologne in a Heinkel III was able to make me at last understand the relationship between boost, throttle and pitch.

I am grateful to Mr. John Shewring for details of his experiences as a bomb aimer and the loan of maps, *Tee Ems* and personal photographs. Another bomb aimer—Miles Tripp—author of *The Eighth Passenger* and *Faith Is a Windsock*, completed what is perhaps the unequaled total of forty trips on one tour. He gave me access to his own collection of technical clippings, maps and official publications as well as giving up his time to answering my questions.

My old friend Derek Coyte, publicity chief for the film

446          ACKNOWLEDGMENTS

*The Battle of Britain*, not only arranged my trip in the
Heinkel but also arranged a meeting with Gunter "Fips"
Radusch. Herr Radusch, a Knight's Cross winner with
sixty-three night fighter victories, was the earliest pioneer
of German night fighter experiments. On this same trip
Derek Coyte also arranged meetings with Hans Brustellin
and Adolf Galland, to both of whom I record my thanks.

Herr von Lossberg, Knight's Cross holder and Luftwaffe
staff officer, invented "Wilde Sau" tactics for night fighters
and was an operational pilot as well as a technical expert
who flew almost every type of German aircraft used
during the Second World War. Herr von Lossberg not only
talked with me at great length but also went to the trouble
of drawing a map of the radar scheme for 1943.

Karl Otto Hoffman, serving officer and author of a
three-volume history of German radar from 1933 to
1945, gave me a great deal of his time and his book has
been an important reference. Hajo Herrman, another
Knight's Cross winner, also described for me his experiences as a night fighter pilot.

For permission to visit Deelen airfield and see the
buildings that had been constructed for the Luftwaffe I
must thank Jonkheer de Ranitz. The Commanding
Officer, Colonel H. J. Doorenbos of the Netherlands
Air Force, was most hospitable, as were his staff: Major
M. C. Breemans, Lieutenant Lamers and Sergeant Major
Bolderman. For access to technical information, photos
and maps I must thank the engineer at Deelen, Mijnheer
Tieleman.

Dr. H. ten Kate of the Koninklijk Nederlands Meteoro-
logisch Instituut provided me with details of winds and
seas for the period of June 1943 and Mr. Van Dee, who
was at the Noordwijk lighthouse, answered various questions about the district at that time.

Many residents in the small towns to the northwest of
Krefeld helped me put together my fictional one: in particular, Johannes Hoeren of Gefrath, who also let me have
personal contemporary documents. Also Frau Overröder,
who, together with her husband, ran the Park Hotel—
now, alas, gone—not only sorted out for me the complex-
ities of the wartime nursing services but was able to find
her wartime uniform, now doing service as a kitchen overall.

My friend Fritz Sommer of Essen allowed me to go
through his collection of documents and made available to

me letters he had written while he was a serving Abwehr officer.

Don Elms and Mike Wooller helped me to find Anglo-American and German popular songs respectively. The latter also arranged a screening of his superb *Cities under Siege* documentary films. I must also thank Dr. V. G. Radclyffe and A. Flowers for their kindness in helping me with some of the medical details.

The Imperial War Museum were wonderful—as always—and in particular Mr. J. E. Sutters, the Film Librarian, found me German instruction films ranging from civil defense to Ju88 servicing.

In researching this story I have read more than two hundred books and I am much obliged to Pat Quorn of Hersants Bookshop for his remarkable memory and energetic help. For locating reference books that were no longer in print or of a special kind I am greatly indebted to the I.W.M. Library, the Westminster Reference Library and the *Daily Telegraph* Reference Department, as well as to the kindness of Miss Howlett at William Kimber Ltd. A very special thanks must also go to Mr. Jackets at the Air Ministry Historical Department and to *Flight* and the *Aeroplane*.

Advice about German shares and commerce came from Anton Felton. Other advice came from Ray Hawkey.

I am grateful to everyone at Jonathan Cape Ltd for their help and encouragement. Particularly to Tom Maschler, who read the first rough draft. For their efforts in connection with this book I am also obliged to Tony Colwell and Jean Mossop, and for their careful work on the typescript thanks to Robina Masters and James Atkins.

When I drew a plan of the fictional town of Altgarten Mr. F. N. B. Patterson, B.Sc., A.M.I.C.E., M.I.Mun.E., M.I.H.E, Borough Surveyor, Engineer and Planning Officer of Brighton, gave generously of his time to point out the basic working of town gas, sewage, water and electricity. As well as this he was most kind about explaining things to me by letter, often including the most lucid drawings.

Mr. Jacques Maisonrouge of I.B.M. must be thanked for his authoritative aid. This is perhaps the first book to be entirely recorded on magnetic tape for the I.B.M.72IV. This has enabled me to redraft many chapters over twenty times, and by means of memory coding to select certain technical passages at only a moment's notice. Ellenor Handley has operated this machine and given her expert and detailed attention to the MS at all stages as well as providing a cross-reference system that, together with color coding and reference cards, has enabled me to find my way around this very long book.

Last, and by no means least, Ysabele de Ranitz has patiently translated endless conversations, technical reports and books from both German and Dutch. Working from ancient recordings she has also provided the translations of German wartime popular songs.